ranslation Copyright © 1977 by Random House, Inc.

reserved under International and Pan-American Copy-
ventions. Published in the United States by Ballantine
division of Random House, Inc., New York, and simul-
in Canada by Ballantine Books of Canada, Ltd.,
Canada. Originally published in France in two volumes
re et la Florentine and Victoire et la Fille de Barbe
Presses de la Cité, Paris. Copyright © 1974 by Presses
.

d from the French by Peter Graham and Jennifer

f Congress Catalog Card Number: 77-6194

45-25397-3

on published by arrangement with Presses de la Cité

ured in the United States of America

antine Books Edition: December 1977

A PAIR OF STEELY HANDS PINNED HER TO THE BED BEFORE SHE COULD EVEN MOVE . . .

She heard the hated voice rasping in her ear.

"Ha, so we meet again, you filthy little heretic! Thought you could get away from God's servant, did you!"

"You let go of me!" screamed Victoire, clawing at the monk's neck and face.

"You don't think I'm going to miss an opportunity like this do you? You pretty young thing . . ."

The monk ripped open the girl's bodice. . . . Victoire was so paralyzed she couldn't move.

"Why you even seem to enjoy it, you little slut! Well, enjoy your pleasure while you can, because afterward I'm going to cut your throat! All heretics must die! You'll burn in hell for eternity!"

SEETHING EMOTIONS, SAVAGE LUSTS, AND A DEEP UNDYING LOVE IN A WORLD DIVIDED

The

Priceles

Passior

Angela Lan

Englis

All rig
right C
Books,
taneou
Toront
as *Vic*
Bleue b
de la C

Transla
Malkin

Library

ISBN 0

This edi

Manufa

First Ba

BALLANTINE BOOKS •

Part I

Chapter I

The balminess of the warm May day in 1572 was a bizarre contrast to the stark, macabre gallows standing at the crossroads. Two corpses, hands bound behind their backs, swung gently with the mild spring breeze while several crows circled expectantly overhead.

The sight horrified, but also fascinated, Victoire de Montmaur, a seventeen-year-old en route to Paris to attend the royal wedding of Henri de Navarre to Princess Marguerite de France. The beautiful blonde-haired girl was leaving her native province of Béarn in the southwest of the kingdom for the very first time. Accompanying her in the carriage were her mother, the Comtesse de Montmaur, her uncle Anselme, her cousin Gilone de Glymes, their sturdy country maidservant Héloïse, and her dog Triboulet.

"Those poor souls," exclaimed Victoire compassionately.

"Murderers, no doubt," said her mother.

"I don't think so," countered Anselme. "Look, they've got placards hanging around their necks."

"Stop!" he shouted to the driver. Anselme climbed from the coach and walked over to read the inscriptions. When he got back into the carriage his face was pale and tense.

"Uncle, what do they say?"

"They died because of their faith. Heretics. Protestants—like us."

The Comtesse gasped. Would she never escape from reminders of the terrible religious strife that had divided France for the last thirty years and had taken her husband Emeric's life? Anselme's older brother had been one of five hundred Huguenot noblemen who had joined a conspiracy to kidnap the King of France in 1560. It had been a desperate attempt to stop the ruthless persecution of Protestants by François II, acting under the influence of his mother, Catherine de Medici, and the powerful Catholic Guise family. The conspirators were surprised by the King's men, and the Duc de Guise, appointed Lieutenant-General of the Realm by the King, ordered the arrest of the rebellious Huguenots that had resulted in a bloodbath of hanging, drowning, and beheading.

Anselme de Montmaur sat deep in thought as the coach bumped and swayed along. A gentle, kindly man, he was a master glass blower by profession who occasionally dabbled in astronomy.

"A bad omen," he murmured so low only Victoire caught his words and immediately her face became pensive.

She was tall, with thick ash-blonde hair and large, luminous gray eyes. Neither pert nor shy, she was candid and direct. It was difficult to visualize her part in the ceremonies for Henri's sumptuous wedding, but at last she would see Paris, a city so often described to her by Anselme as both dangerous and beguiling.

Up to now, Victoire had lived quietly with her mother and uncle. She had been only five when her father was killed.

Her mother had made her swear that if worst came to worst, she must be prepared to die for the sake of her religion. Marie de Montmaur was obsessed with the idea of vengeance. Throughout Victoire's childhood and adolescence she emphasized one idea to her daughter: Catholics were to be hated and distrusted. Always.

This rather austere upbringing left its mark on Victoire, tending to make her more serious than most girls her age. Although she accepted her mother's dictates, she was very ignorant about the political implications of the religious antagonism.

When Uncle Anselme came to live with his sister-in-law and niece, he tried to fill the gap left by Emeric's sudden death. He taught Victoire history and geography. His tales of the time he had spent roaming all over Europe made her yearn to travel, although she wondered if she would ever do so after this trip to Paris.

On clear nights Anselme took her up to his observatory at the top of one of the castle towers. There he would explain the stars to her, or recite poetry, which, clumsily at first, she would try to imitate.

The education that Victoire received from her uncle was rather unusual, and her mother deplored her knowing nothing about weaving tapestries, flower arrangement, or how to play a musical instrument.

Gilone de Glymes' thick black hair made a striking contrast to that of her blonde cousin. Although small, Gilone had a superb figure. She always found time to linger in front of a faded looking glass in the Montmaur Castle to admire her amethyst-colored eyes and her full, naturally dark pink lips.

Her childhood had been very different from Victoire's, and she had lost her parents at an early age. Her mother died giving birth to a stillborn child, and her father was killed in battle shortly afterward. An aunt, pitying the orphaned Gilone, took her in. Then, when Gilone was five, she put her in a small convent and paid for her education. When her aunt died, Gilone, by now fifteen, went to live with a distant cousin of her mother's, Marie de Montmaur, who was happy for her daughter to have a companion the same age.

Barely three hours' drive from the capital they saw the coaches from the Queen of Navarre's suite changing horses. They reined in to join the others.

A young man of about twenty bowed gracefully as the girls looked curiously out the window. In his pink velvet doublet and snugly fitting purple tights, Philippe de Lévis cut a fine figure.

"Oh, isn't he handsome?" Gilone whispered to Victoire, perhaps even more impressed by the young man's elegant clothes than with his regular features.

"He's all right, I suppose," replied Victoire with indifference. She was more interested in catching a glimpse of Jeanne de Navarre, whom she had not seen in a long time, than in flirting with a stranger.

"I wish we weren't wearing our traveling clothes," complained Gilone. She looked down petulantly at her coarse cotton skirt, which was a drab gray and stained.

Victoire shook her silky hair, mildly annoyed as she often was by Gilone's interest in frivolities. "What difference does it make?"

Marie de Montmaur had insisted on the girls dressing very simply and practically for the long, dusty trip. What little finery they had the Comtesse wanted kept fresh for their presentation at Court.

"Is this your first visit to Paris?" Philippe de Lévis asked the two girls. They admitted it was. "This is my third," he announced with a faint touch of smugness in his voice.

"But *not* for any occasion like this," retorted Gilone, indignant at being taken for a country girl.

"True . . . They say the celebrations are going to be splendid," the young man went on. "There'll be fireworks!"

"Oh, I've never seen fireworks. Are they beautiful?" asked Victoire naively.

"Are they! They turn night into day with starbursts of every color imaginable."

"Have *you* ever seen fireworks?" asked Gilone.

Philippe admitted he had not. He had only heard how wonderful they could be. Gilone, gratified she had bested him, let her full lips turn up charmingly at the corners.

Drawing his eyes away from the two stunning girls, Philippe asked Anselme, "Do you still make those admirable iridescent glasses I've heard so much about?"

"I don't know whether they could be called admirable," replied Anselme modestly. "Queen Catherine asked me to make a set of twenty-five dozen glasses for the Louvre Palace. It has taken me many months to finish them, and now I'm bringing the set to her. I hope it will still be complete by the time these rough roads have done their job."

As the two men chatted, Marie de Montmaur devoted her attention to young Philippe. The Comtesse was counting on this trip to find suitable husbands for Victoire and Gilone. The Montmaurs were an old, noble, but impoverished family. Their castle was falling into ruins and they lived off the rents from farmers working the land, which made for a meager income. Philippe looked suitable enough. He clearly came from a good family, was well-connected, witty, and most presentable. But his current wealth and future prospects were unknown. The Comtesse decided to take it up with Anselme, who despite his unworldly airs was very knowledgeable about such matters.

The postilion came to tell them the horses were ready.

"I'm sure we shall be meeting again in Paris," Philippe said, bowing low in departure to the party as a whole, but looking speculatively at the girls.

"Oh, Victoire, did you see how he looked at me? I'm certain I'll see him again!" Gilone exclaimed when Philippe had gone.

"Then you really like him?"

Gilone sighed. "Oh, he'll do for the time being . . . Anyway, he is handsome, don't you think?"

"I can't say I looked at him that closely—unlike you," said Victoire, grinning.

Actually, she had found the young man rather conceited and something of a fop.

"Did you see his cuffs? They were of the finest Calais lace. I'd give anything to have a ruff made of that," said Gilone with determination.

The Montmaur coach jolted forward and took its place in the Navarre suite. Henri, mounted on a superb black charger, spotted them and came trotting briskly over to pay his respects to the Comtesse.

"*Morbleu!* It's my little childhood playmate Victoire. Why, you've grown into a real beauty, Mademoiselle."

"Henri!" protested the Comtesse. She tried to be stern, but found his good nature irresistible.

The young man threw back his head and roared with laughter. His brilliant smile, compact build, and sparkling lively eyes deeply set under bushy brows somehow made people forget his shortness and untidy, worn garb.

Gilone was disappointed—could this be the bridegroom for whom such a grand wedding was planned?

"My mother requests me to convey her compliments to you, and to wish you a pleasant journey to Paris," Henri de Navarre went on.

Victoire looked at the young man, trying to remember what he had been like when they used to play together as children. He still rolls his Rs like a true Gascon, she thought, though it did give him a certain charm. She looked him in the eyes and smiled, revealing her straight white teeth.

"Would you be so kind as to tell her that we shall present ourselves tomorrow," said Marie de Montmaur, "as Victoire will have the honor of waiting on her at Court as one of her maids of honor."

Henri gave Victoire a warm smile. "So, I shall have the pleasure of meeting you again."

Gilone and Victoire stared wide-eyed in amazement as they approached the Porte Saint-Germain, one of the main gates to Paris. They had never imagined a city could be so big, and were astonished that the Court should be surrounded by so much filth.

"Ladies' skirts must get terribly dirty when they walk in the streets," Victoire observed.

"They hardly walk at all, my dear," her mother said, smiling. "Either they have a carriage or they take a sedan-chair." It would take some getting used to for Victoire, who liked running through the fields free as air.

Eventually they found the Pont Saint-Michel, blocked by several coaches all trying to cross at the same time. The confusion increased as the drivers leaped down and tried to outshout each other with insults.

At last they managed to get across the bridge, and Marie de Montmaur pointed to a somber, rather forbidding building in the distance. "We'll be staying there since Victoire is privileged to serve the Queen of Navarre."

Suddenly the procession was brought to a halt. Victoire leaned out of the window and saw that a large angry crowd was gathering around the coaches and their outriders, having recognized from their sober garb that the people inside were Huguenots.

"Protestants!" yelled a fat man, perched on a cart laden with barrels.

"Go back to where you came from!" shouted someone else.

A growing crescendo of hatred was mounting from the mob.

"Why are they insulting us?" asked Victoire, per-

plexed. She had never seen such hostility before—
only the idyllic solitude of their remote family estate.

The Comtesse de Montmaur sighed. The scene was
only too familiar to her. The Parisian Catholics were
not about to let the War of Religion be a thing of the
past and live peacefully with the Protestants.

A wiry, badly shaven monk in a ragged robe clambered onto a handy platform and began to heave further abuse on the Huguenots, brandishing a crucifix
in the air.

"It is the duty of true Catholics," he raged, "to kill
every last Protestant. As long as there is one heretic
left on French soil, there can be no salvation for any
of us!"

"He's mad!" exclaimed Victoire. "Are all monks
like him?"

Anselme tried to calm the women. "Fortunately not
all of them are as intolerant or fanatical as that one."

Victoire could not take her eyes off the man. His
face was contorted with hatred, his full fleshy lips
contrasting with the asceticism of the rest of his appearance. He struck fear in the depths of her soul as
he fiercely continued his attack.

As they passed the monk he looked directly at Victoire and smiled with a thinly disguised leer. Chills
ran down her spine, lessening only when she thought
of the Louvre's safety.

"These heretics must be exterminated. They must
burn at the stake or hang from the gallows in every
village of France. Hear my words, all of you! The
gates of Heaven shall never open to those who do not
actively struggle for us! There can be no salvation for
those who hang back!"

Around the coach, the outriders reacted first with
gibes and insults, then by drawing their swords.

"Are they going to fight?" asked Victoire with more
interest than alarm.

"I don't think so," replied Anselme. "The crowd is

beginning to thin out. People are not too anxious to take a beating."

Very slowly, the carriages began to edge forward again through the narrow, uneven cobblestoned streets.

Anselme pointed out the Hôtel de Guise to the girls, who were still in the grip of the recent excitement. "That's the bastion of Catholic power in Paris."

"Those murderers," mumured Marie de Montmaur, who had sworn eternal hatred against the people who had executed her husband. "Girls, you must never in any way get involved with those people."

"Don't worry, Mother. I have no desire to do so."

Gilone remained silent.

A dozen young men and women, watching the coaches go past from the Hôtel balcony, began to jeer at the shabbiness of the Queen of Navarre's suite.

"Look how they're dressed!" one of them cried. "They look like beggars."

Victoire looked up. Nonchalantly leaning against the wrought-iron balcony was a young man of about twenty-five, with jet-black hair. His sarcastic expression was accentuated by a long, aquiline nose. Compared with his satin doublet of silver-flecked, dark-blue brocade, the clothes worn by Henri de Navarre and Philippe de Lévis seemed plain.

Some ladies shared the nobleman's amusement over the Huguenots, who seemed like such country bumpkins.

"What lovely dresses!" exclaimed Gilone, craning her neck so as not to miss a single detail. "Victoire, look at the jewelry!"

"You'll see much more beautiful things at Court," said Anselme with a smile.

"How lucky they are," Gilone murmured as she tried to imagine how such pearl pendants and gold-braided belts would look on *her*.

Victoire, on the other hand, could not forget the sight of the monk so determined to kill everyone of her faith. She wondered how a *holy* man could feel such hatred, and express it with such unreasoning vehemence. His face was fixed in her memory, and she knew she could never forget it.

It was dark when they finally entered the gates of the Louvre. The forty or so carriages deposited their passengers in the courtyard, which soon became as busy and confused as it had been during the day.

One of Jeanne de Navarre's ladies-in-waiting, the Comtesse d'Amaucourt, a small, dried-up woman dressed in a dark gown, led the Montmaur family through a labyrinth of corridors and staircases to the rooms assigned them. Victoire was surprised at the throngs of people they passed in the galleries and salons.

"Do all these people live here?" she asked her guide.

"Many people frequent the Louvre—too many," was all the Comtesse had to say by way of an answer. "Ah, we're almost there now."

They climbed one more flight of stairs and, following the valet who was carrying a torch, entered a corridor under the sloping roof with three small rooms giving onto it. Each chamber had a large fireplace and sparse furnishings made of dark wood.

The simple lodgings would have to do for the five of them, including Triboulet.

The lady-in-waiting was just leaving when Marie de Montmaur asked her, "Would you be so kind as to inform Her Majesty that we shall come and pay our respects to her tomorrow morning?"

"I shall not fail to do so," answered the Comtesse d'Amaucourt with a bitter little smile.

The girls ignored her expression, free at last to eagerly inspect their new quarters. It did not take them long: their room was tiny, with a high narrow window that let in light but permitted no view, beds, chairs, and a table. They had to admit with regret that their garret hardly lived up to their expectations of what life at the King's palace was going to be like.

"We were better off at Montmaur," sighed Victoire as she flopped onto the bed.

"Yes, but we are at Court," said Gilone.

Chapter II

Victoire set off to wait on the Queen of Navarre early in the afternoon. As she sought her way through the labyrinthine palace, she reflected about the simplicity of the countryside. She did not feel she was going to like the Louvre much. Already she felt homesick for her quiet life at Montmaur—for riding across the fragrant, freshly mown fields or deep into the autumn woods where she could hear the soft rustle of wildlife, sometimes glimpsing a red deer, a roebuck, or a boar.

She passed two gentlemen chatting in the recess of a window. One she recognized as the dark-haired young nobleman with the aquiline nose who had jeered at their coaches from the balcony of the Hôtel de Guise.

"My dear Guillaume," he was saying to the other man, also dark, young, and very handsome, "once again I'm going to have to make demands on your generosity. Could you lend me a few *écus?* I lost last night at cards."

"What, again?" the young man said in some heat. "Why, only the day before yesterday . . ."

"I can't help it," the first man said without a trace of embarrassment. "I'm just out of luck."

Victoire was a little disconcerted on overhearing such a conversation and hurried on her way. Even so, she had time to get a good glimpse of the strong face of the man addressed as Guillaume; his face radiated sincerity despite his annoyance, and suddenly the idea of being at the Louvre seemed much less gloomy than it had before.

In no time she had reached the small antechamber, where she found the Comtesse d'Amaucourt. In a few moments she would be seeing her godmother for the first time in several years. Perhaps she would no longer be the kind woman Victoire remembered, and truly be as puritanical as her reputation suggested.

The Queen's conversion to Protestantism twelve years before had not made her any less strait-laced, on the contrary. She made no secret of the fact that she was shocked by the debauchery and high living at Court. The way the courtiers flaunted their jewels, the very pomp and circumstance were highly offensive to her at a time when the people of France were in dire need. Such moral considerations were, however, of no concern at all to the royal Catholic family.

The Queen of Navarre had taken a long, hard, and far from charitable look at her future daughter-in-law. She had been forced to admit that she was indeed beautiful and would certainly appeal to a ladies' man like Henri. Yet she found her lacking in simplicity. Her heavily made-up face and exaggeratedly slim waist struck her as artifices to which no decent woman should resort. And her unbridled passion for expensive clothes and jewelry was surely to be deplored. The stern Protestant queen also feared Marguerite might lead her son astray and compromise his chances for eternal salvation.

Yet she let herself hope, perhaps unrealistically, that one day Marguerite would embrace the Protestant faith. In any case, the marriage meant there would now be peace in the land, and tolerance for those of her faith.

"The Queen has asked you, Mademoiselle Montmaur, to read to her."

Pleased at being chosen, Victoire followed the Comtesse into the next room, where Jeanne de Navarre was writing. She was wearing a robe of Parma velvet, open at the chest and drawn in at the waist by a braided cord, showing under it her satin gown with its high pleated collar.

The Queen looked at Victoire benevolently.

"I am happy to see you again, my child, and hope that you will like it here. Familiar as I am with your mother's high moral standards, I know that she has brought you up according to the precepts of our holy faith, and that your behavior will at all times be beyond reproach. I know you will not be a chatterbox whose only interests are gossip and clothes.

"You will read some psalms to me now and later will accompany me to the Queen Mother's supper."

"I shall do my best to give you satisfaction, Your Majesty."

Victoire blushed with delight at being so honored, and then wondered with apprehension if her clothes would be appropriate.

Victoire was so excited at the idea of seeing the King and the Queen Mother, and of being presented at Court, that she lost her way back to her room. She did not venture to ask for directions from a group of elegant and beautiful young women who were teasing an oafish gentleman who guffawed at their jokes. Still trying to orient herself, Victoire found herself at the end of a dimly lit, deserted gallery. She stopped, to turn back to where she had come from, when she caught the muffled sound of a conversation on the other side of a heavy curtain.

"No amount of punishment will ever suit the crimes of that accursed brood of scoundrels," said a savage voice, trembling with rage.

Before she realized what she was doing, she moved closer in order to make out every word.

"Of course, Father," a woman's voice answered. "You know how devoted I am to our cause."

"You will have to prove it by your acts. In our troubled times, the service of God requires it."

"What can I do?"

"Every last Huguenot must be exterminated!"

Victoire flinched; she had heard this ranting voice somewhere before.

"I want you to keep a close watch on the Queen of Navarre's suite. Find out who its most suspect members are and report them to me."

"And then what, Father Izard?" asked the woman softly, with perhaps a touch of reluctance.

"Leave that to me."

Victoire barely had time to dart behind a pillar. The curtain was drawn aside and a man in a dark cassock emerged. She froze in terror, recognizing the fanatic who had harangued the crowd on the bridge the day before. With a shattering realization she knew he was far more dangerous than the hysterical man he had seemed yesterday.

"You look as if you'd seen a ghost!" cried Gilone as her cousin came in. "What happened? Did your godmother . . ."

Victoire shook her head, barely able to speak. "The monk," she eventually managed to bring out, "the monk who was on the bridge . . ."

Gilone gave her a questioning look. "I don't understand."

"Yes you do. Remember that dreadful man on the platform crying for Protestant blood?"

"Oh, yes," said Gilone absently; the incident had not made much of an impression on her.

"Well, he's here—in the Louvre! I've just seen him."

"Are you sure?" she asked incredulously. "How could such a filthily dressed creature be let into the Court? It's unthinkable!"

"Obviously he must have some influence. He was telling a woman to keep a close watch on the Queen of Navarre's suite."

"What could he do to us?" asked Gilone, who couldn't understand why her cousin was getting herself into such a state.

"I don't know, but I'm worried . . ." murmured Victoire, her large gray eyes reflecting deadly fear.

Victoire was too frightened to tell her mother about the conversation she had overheard, so when the Comtesse returned with Anselme she told her only about the honor of being Jeanne de Navarre's reader.

"If you continue to stay in your godmother's good graces, maybe she'll arrange a marriage for you."

The idea of finding a husband seemed incredible when there was a fanatic loose in the palace halls. How could she think about *having* to marry somebody; it was so thoroughly disagreeable to Victoire. Yet she knew she would have to resign herself to the fact, like all young women of her position. It might be different, however, if the man chosen to be her husband would be someone who looked like the man Guillaume whom she had seen earlier. She was finding it very difficult not to think about him, although the chances of ever meeting him were slim.

A little later, the cousins heard furious barking and hurried out into the corridor. Triboulet had torn a ribbon from the dress of a young woman and was preventing her from getting it back by snarling ferociously.

"Triboulet! Come here immediately!" ordered Victoire. "Please do forgive him."

Meanwhile, Gilone succeeded in getting hold of the ribbon and was pulling it while Triboulet was tugging in the other direction. Although unevenly matched, neither won: the satin tore in half. Victoire was horror-stricken.

"Oh, your ribbon . . . I'm so sorry, I'll give you another."

The young woman burst out laughing. "Don't worry, I've got plenty of others. You must have just arrived. I haven't seen you around the Louvre before."

Victoire and Gilone introduced themselves, and the young woman, Mademoiselle de Chabrière, invited them to her room a little farther down the corridor. She handed them a silver comfit dish.

"Help yourselves. They're bergamot-flavored sweets from Italy. The Queen Mother gave them to me."

Gilone and Victoire were impressed. Who could this young lady be to be in favor with Catherine de Medici, who, following the death of her first-born, François II in 1560, had become regent during the minority of her second son, Charles IX.

"I'm one of her maids of honor," Mademoiselle de Chabrière explained. "And who are you serving?"

"The Queen of Navarre," replied Victoire.

Mademoiselle de Chabrière winced. "That can't be much fun. They say she's stern and stingy . . ."

"She has shown great kindness toward me," Victoire defended her godmother. "This evening I am to accompany her to the King's supper."

"Then I'll see you there."

She went over to a cupboard. "That reminds me, I must decide what to wear. I'd like your advice. Should I wear this blue dress with silver embroidery or the green one with lace trimmings? Or perhaps the rose-wood velvet?"

Gilone moved closer. She realized immediately that neither she nor Victoire had a wardrobe as lavish. Mademoiselle de Chabrière looked on with amusement as Gilone ran her fingers over each fabric—silk, taffeta, velvet.

At nineteen, Alix de Chabrière was already experienced in Court life, and more especially in its intrigues, for she belonged to Catherine's famous Flying Squadron. These young ladies, who were selected for their exceptional beauty and intelligence, provided the Queen with information of every kind and were given their nickname for the way they constantly flew about the corridors of the palace. She used them to recompense her friends and to discover the secrets of her enemies. Any gentleman singled out for attention by such a young lady immediately gained a certain cachet in society.

Alix de Chabrière smiled at Gilone's enthusiasm. "Would you like to try one on?"

"Oh, yes!"

Once again Victoire felt annoyed by her cousin's frivolity. Nevertheless, reclining on the bed, she stayed to watch her metamorphosis.

Gilone undressed quickly. Mademoiselle de Chabrière cast an expert and appreciative eye over her slim body and finely tapered legs.

"You have a very fine figure, my dear. Turn around so I can get a good look at you. There's no doubt about it, you'll do very well."

"Do you really think so?" asked Gilone ingenuously.

"Which dress would you like to try on?"

"Maybe the red one," said Gilone hesitantly.

"How right you are. The color suits brunettes, and will set off your complexion. And the cut will show off your lovely bosom."

Her flattering words made Gilone glow with pleasure. If such an elegant woman found her attractive, surely Philippe de Lévis would share her opinion.

"Of colurse you'll need some jewelry as a final touch."

Alix dipped into her jewel case and took out some pearls, which she clasped around Gilone's neck.

"What a superb necklace!" exclaimed Gilone, admiring herself in a mirror. "Is it yours?"

"It was a gift from a gentleman in return for services rendered," said Alix with a little laugh.

Gilone suddenly noticed her cousin was not saying anything. "Victoire, how do I look?"

"Very beautiful," said Victoire without much enthusiasm.

"Wouldn't you like to try on a dress, too? I'm sure our friend wouldn't mind."

"Of course not. Here, what about this green velvet? It'll suit you perfectly, setting off the highlights in your hair."

"No, thank you," replied Victoire a little more curtly than she had intended.

Gilone continued to pose in front of the mirror, imagining Philippe's bright eyes gazing at her.

The Queen of Navarre and her suite, all somberly dressed, moved forward through a series of shabby rooms and along interminable straight galleries, until they reached the brightly lit salons of the Court itself.

Victoire was dazzled by what she saw—gilded paneling, vast frescoes devoted to mythological subjects, and paintings by the great masters which the Queen had brought from Italy. Feeling she was in a dream, Victoire, head erect and shining, followed her godmother as she walked toward the King of France.

Charles IX was twenty-two years old. In his attitude toward his mother there was a mixture of fear and resentment at the fact that she patently preferred his younger brother, Henri, Duc d'Anjou.

This sickly young man had married a shy and meek girl, Elisabeth of Austria, two years before. But he had not abandoned his Protestant mistress.

Victoire gave a long, low curtsy when Jeanne de Navarre presented her to the King. Feeling his sharp, wild eyes examining her, she began to feel uncomfortable.

This feeling became even stronger when the King remarked with a sarcastic laugh, "Your presence would be more welcome if you wore something that better accented your lovely figure."

Victoire looked in bewilderment to Catherine de Medici, who was seated next to her son. She whispered something in the King's ear and his expression grew sullen. Catherine nodded to the girl to withdraw.

Victoire knew no one except Henri de Navarre, who gave her a friendly pinch on the cheek.

"Ah, my pretty one, I knew we'd meet again," he said exuberantly.

He smelled of garlic and had obviously been drinking, perhaps to help him to get through a rather unpleasant evening. His bride-to-be looked none too pleased with him. He cut a sorry figure compared with her own brothers, one of whom was wearing a gold brocade doublet, and the other, amaranthine velvet.

Mademoiselle de Chabrière, whose ample dress was supported by a farthingdale and had a breathtakingly low neckline, came up to Victoire.

"Well, what are your first impressions?" she asked patronizingly.

"I have never seen such beautiful things before, nor so much jewelry," Victoire admitted truthfully.

"I'm glad to see you are enjoying yourself. It seems you have an admirer already," said Alix with a snide little laugh. "He asked me if I would introduce him to you." With a quick gesture of her hand she beckoned to a skinny young man standing in the corner.

"Mademoiselle de Montmaur, may I have the honor of presenting Monsieur de Mèrande to you?" Whereupon Alix made a hasty retreat and faded into the crowd.

"Mademoiselle, I am delighted to make your acquaintance," he said.

Victoire was furious at Alix's action, for he had thin dry lips, a sallow complexion, and a fawning manner. At a loss for what to do, she began to ask him a few discreet questions about himself and his family.

He answered in a slightly nasal voice, occasionally glancing at Victoire with a lustful glint in his round eyes. He had bushy eyebrows that almost met above his nose—a sign of fierce jealousy, as Héloïse had explained many times.

Victoire quickly became bored with what he was saying and ceased to pay much attention to him.

Monsieur de Mèrande tried to impose his company on her, but she made sure that he soon fell far behind her when the rest of the assembly proceeded to the dining room.

Accustomed to the frugal fare at Montmaur, Victoire was overwhelmed by the sumptuous display of food lying before her on the long banqueting tables, each dish cooked and arranged with a skill and a taste that owed much to Catherine's Italian origins. The Queen, like all the ladies and gentlemen present, obviously had a very hearty appetite. Victoire found herself faced with unfamiliar dishes that she wanted, but did not dare, to try.

"Help yourself," said a baron who was sitting next to her. "They are artichokes. The Queen is mad about them. They say," he added, leaning toward the young lady, "that they have certain special properties, if you see what I mean." He gave what he thought was a subtle smile.

Then more familiar dishes were brought in: quail, starlings, thrushes, and ortolans. Victoire's neighbor had soon eaten a dozen of the tiny ortolans, crunching their heads noisily between his teeth.

The middle of the table was laden with superb set pieces—peacocks with all their feathers, kids, and suckling pigs. Most extraordinary of all were the desserts, masterpieces of sugar and frangipane concocted by the Florentine cooks the Queen brought with her when she came to France for her marriage.

Suddenly Victoire noticed, sitting some distance away, the young man who had made such a strong impression on her in the gallery. He was being very attentive to the lady sitting next to him. Judging by the way she was laughing, his conversation must have been most entertaining.

Victoire turned to the baron. "Can you tell me, sir, the name of the gentleman sitting next to the lady in green with the emerald earrings?"

"Of course I can. It is Guillaume de Louvencourt, a noted swordsman. Why do you ask?"

Victoire could feel herself blushing to the roots of her dusky blonde hair.

"He looks like someone I know, but I must have been mistaken."

By the time the cockscombs, the poultry quenelles, and the calf's liver had come and gone, Victoire felt her appetite shrinking rapidly. She had drunk some of the Burgundy that had been generously poured in vermeil goblets. When the meal was over and she found herself caught up in the bustling crowd of courtiers, she felt slightly dizzy. All of a sudden she caught her breath. Surely that was the voice of the lady who had been talking to horrible Father Izard behind the curtain?

She spun around, but there were several young women behind her and they had gone off in different directions before she could put a face to the voice.

Gilone opened her eyes long after everyone had left the room and continued to lie in bed thinking of her future.

If she just had clothes and jewelry like Mademoiselle de Chabrière, she'd get a suitor in no time, she thought. But not just any suitor would do. No. He'd have to be very rich and powerful. No eking out a miserable existence like her Aunt Marie, stuck in a crumbling old castle. Gilone wanted to partake in this glamorous Court life, let these gentlemen of the Court cast their lustful eyes on her pretty body. Now, if she could get Philippe de Lévis to take an interest in her, maybe she could use him to . . . Gilone said to herself, I'll meet him again, no matter what. She didn't care about serving that dull old stick of a puritanical Queen of Navarre. That was all right for her prude of a cousin, Victoire, but not for her.

Alix had shown herself to be most obliging. Maybe she could help her. Gilone got into her best clothes, then went and knocked on Alix's door.

"May I come in?" asked Gilone.

"Why, of course, my dear. Come talk to me while the maid is doing my hair. It's such a bore. It'll be delightful having you here."

The bed was still unmade and the room in some disorder. There was a trace of verbena in the air—a perfume much used by the gentlemen of the Court.

"I saw your cousin at supper yesterday evening. A charming girl, though a touch naive perhaps."

"It's the first time she has set foot outside her province," said Gilone contemptuously, as though the opposite were true of herself.

Gilone hesitated for a long while before taking the bull by the horns. After all, she had only known Mademoiselle de Chabrière since the previous day.

"I was wondering whether you could do me a service."

The maid finished her duties and was told to leave.

"I met a young man, called Philippe de Lévis . . ."

"And you're interested in him."

Gilone smiled, revealing a delicate row of teeth. "I know he's at Court. How can I meet him again?"

Mademoiselle de Chabrière carefully chose a rouge from her dressing table that would brighten up her rather pale complexion that morning. "I could probably help you."

"Oh, thank you so much!" exclaimed Gilone. "I should be grateful to you all my life."

"That would be asking too much of you," replied the maid of honor with a gently mocking laugh.

Anselme gathered the family together to tell them about his audience with Catherine and about her reception of the glasses he had made for her. "She did me the honor of calling them 'exquisite craftsmanship.' Then she invited all of us to join her for a small informal supper in her chambers."

"Oh, Uncle, that's wonderful, but I don't know if I want to go. She intimidates me so."

"Don't worry about it, my dear. Naturally she has to inspire fear and respect. What with all those pugnacious, self-seeking young lords, her task is not easy." He sighed with understanding and was happy he did not have to bear such responsibilities.

Gilone was ecstatic. This would be a big opportunity, and with Alix's help she would be able to make a good impression.

Her aunt, however, reacted far less enthusiastically. "You're dragging us into a den of perdition."

Anselme smiled and said, "You're exaggerating. I'm not taking you into a place of ill repute. We are to visit one of the most enlightened sovereigns of our time."

The Comtesse's face clouded and she turned to the girls. "Please leave the two of us alone for a moment. I have something to discuss in private." She smiled at their concerned expressions. "I will tell you about it when the time is appropriate."

Gilone and Victoire obediently left and returned to their own room.

"I'm worried for Victoire and Gilone. Those Catholics are a worthless lot—arrogant, debauched gentlemen painted like women and usually deep in debt from gambling. What if the girls should lapse from the faith? I've done my best to teach them to observe the precepts of our religion, and I of all people would be to blame."

Anselme tried to reassure his sister-in-law. "You're painting an extremely black picture of the Queen's entourage, aren't you? I think the girls are very sensible. They won't become infatuated with the first glib talker they meet."

"Then there are all those libertine young women who are around the Queen—the Flying Squadron. They're a disgraceful example!"

"Come now, there's no question of your daughter or your niece being enrolled. Be reasonable, Marie. You came to Paris to find them husbands. Where are the most eligible young men to be found? At Court. Certainly not at Montmaur."

"That is precisely what I want to talk to you about. The Queen of Navarre has a plan in mind."

Anselme settled into his chair and prepared to listen.

"Here, why don't you have some of this malmsey wine that you enjoy so much?" She poured him a glass and her eyes began to shine with enjoyment. "I believe that the Queen has had the kindness to take a real interest in the future of her goddaughter. She mentioned a gentleman to me who would make an excellent match for her."

Anselme pricked up his ears. Jeanne de Navarre's noted strictness and avarice were not characteristics that predisposed him in her favor, though he did admit that it was thanks to her that they were all at Court.

"Louis de Mèrande is a cousin of Monsieur de Châtillon."

"And what does the young man do?"

The Comtesse de Montmaur seemed a trifle embarrassed. "As he was the youngest son, his family had intended him for the cloth. He had even taken the minor orders and been promised the benefice of the Abbey of Pontavenet. But when his elder brother was killed in battle he chose the profession of arms, and at the request of the Admiral, the King promised him a regiment."

"A man of promise, one might say, then. Is he a Catholic?"

"He is a convert to our faith. You don't imagine I would let Victoire marry one of those dreadful Catholics, do you?" exclaimed the Comtesse.

"That makes him a very recent convert, it seems to me."

"The Queen guarantees Monsieur de Mèrande's sincerity and morals."

"As he has no title, is he at least wealthy?" asked Anselme, who felt that his niece deserved a more brilliant match.

"He has great expectations."

Anselme pondered a moment. "If I were you I wouldn't mention it to Victoire yet."

Chapter III

"*I* haven't seen you in that dress before, Gilone," said the Comtesse de Montmaur as she looked over her daughter and her niece before they left for supper with Queen Catherine.

Gilone blushed a little and lied. "Since I stained my satin dress, our neighbor Mademoiselle de Chabrière was kind enough to lend me this one for the evening."

"Well, all right. I suppose there is nothing else you could do considering the occasion, but I wish you would be very careful about any favors coming from Catherine's suite." She dreaded what might be asked in return and felt that Gilone's periwinkle-blue brocade, embroidered with pearls, was much too sophisticated for a seventeen-year-old girl. "And where, pray, did you get those pearls round your neck?"

"They belong to Mademoiselle de Chabrière also."

"Oh, Gilone, do be careful! What will you do if you lose them or if they are stolen?"

Gilone did not answer. She knew her aunt was offended by the sight of such finery, but was not sensitive to the true concern the Comtesse felt.

Anselme appeared, wearing a filemot doublet and chamois breeches.

"How fine you look, Uncle!" exclaimed Victoire, who was used to seeing him dressed in old clothes, blowing glass in his workshop or taking Triboulet for a run through the fields.

"It's in your honor. Girls, now I must warn you to be careful what you say, especially on the subject of religion. There are no secrets at Court. Everything anyone says is always repeated."

Suddenly Victoire felt the need to tell Uncle Anselme about Father Izard. But it was not the right time or place: they were walking along a corridor where footmen were lighting torches, often passing merry groups of people coming in the other direction.

Gilone was walking behind her aunt, and Victoire, who was with her, noticed Jacotte, a young servant girl assigned to helping both the Montmaur women and Alix, slyly slipping a note into her cousin's hand.

"Who is it from?" whispered Victoire, intrigued.

Gilone motioned to keep silent, and passed her the message once she had read it herself: "You will be expected at midnight tonight, in the recess of the third window on the right in the gallery of columns." To Gilone's delight, Alix had proved herself to be a remarkably quick and efficient go-between.

There were only about forty people in the small salon covered with scarlet damask tapestries. The Queen was receiving her guests and accompanied by her favorite son, the Duc d'Anjou.

His large, dark, and appealing eyes lacked that cruel, slightly mad glint that could be perceived in the King's. His gentle, almost frail, appearance, allied to the fact that he wore as much jewelry as most women, was surprising in a man who loved duels and other warlike pursuits. Maybe it was his sickly temperament that had given him a taste for heady perfumes and silky materials—all things he adored as much as his sister did.

She was not present herself, and neither was her future husband.

When Anselme presented Gilone, it seemed to Victoire that the Queen's gaze lingered overly long on her cousin's bare shoulders. Suddenly her thoughts were distracted when Guillaume de Louvencourt entered with the arrogant gambler.

"Who is that?" she asked Alix, who was standing next to her. She could barely conceal her excitement.

"Gontran de Louvencourt."

So they were brothers. How strange to be attracted by one of them, yet be repulsed by the other.

Gilone was creating a sensation in Alix's dress. Everyone wanted to know who the dazzling young beauty could be.

"Come," said Alix, taking her by the arm. "I'm going to introduce you to some gentlemen who will certainly seek to woo you."

"Thank you," whispered Gilone, and then eagerly copied Alix's flirtatious manners.

Quite to her surprise, Victoire felt annoyed that her cousin was monopolizing the attention of the male guests. Even the King's brother approached her. A wave of anger swept over her, however, when Guillaume de Louvencourt sat down next to Gilone at the dinner table.

Victoire maneuvered herself so that she sat directly across from him. In spite of the hubbub, the table was narrow enough for her to hope that if she listened attentively she might be able to pick up a few snatches of conversation. While doing her best to show a polite interest in her neighbor's conversation, she gazed in admiration at Guillaume's athletic physique and his forthright, determined expression, tempered by a mischievous gleam in his blue eyes. She was lost in a puzzle of how to attract his attention.

Admiral Gaspard de Coligny, with whom the Queen had a long private talk after the meal, was a tall, imposing man with a gray beard. As the leader of the Huguenots, Protestants swore undying loyalty to him, yet his blunt uncompromising speeches had also earned him many enemies. Until 1562 he was thought an honorable, disinterested man. Although a devout Calvinist, he was nevertheless loyal to the crown. Unlike the Guise family, he did not turn his religion to political ends, and the Queen trusted him enough to bring him into her government.

However, during the civil war in 1562, the Admiral was forced to choose between his country and his faith. As governor of the city of Le Havre, he did not hesitate to open its gates to the English and provide them with a fortress in his own country.

A decade had elapsed since then, and there had been a reconciliation the previous year. Charles IX, who was looking for support to counter his mother's oppressive influence, spoke of the Admiral as "his father." And Catherine, who had tried to have him assassinated, now treated him as her confidant.

She had just learned from her spies that the Spanish ambassador was being rather more active than his diplomatic role required. He was trying to establish contacts with the Guise family and their followers with a view to organizing a rebellion and paving the way for an invasion of France. The man behind the plan was, of course, his master, Philip II, King of Spain— Catherine's former-son-in-law!

"I've known for a long time," said the Admiral, who had always suspected and hated the Spanish, "that the Guisards would turn to Madrid for help."

"They have even received large sums of money to foment sedition."

"Philip II would like to see the Inquisition set up in France."

The Queen shuddered. The relentless, unfeeling cruelty with which her former son-in-law was hounding the heretics struck her as an absurd and dangerous policy for a country that was trying to reconcile factions and maintain a delicate balance between them.

"If ever the Guisards formed an alliance with the Spanish . . ." Her voice trailed off in mid-sentence.

If that happened, de Coligny knew all Huguenots would be ruthlessly crushed by what would become the strongest party in the land. He had to find a quick answer.

"Hardly any power would remain in your hands," he said.

The Queen-Regent, a strong, intelligent woman, smiled. "I know."

Following her private conversation with de Coligny, the Queen beckoned to Alix.

"I notice that Mademoiselle de Glymes seems to be one of your friends."

"I met her yesterday, Your Majesty. She was given the room next to mine."

"She was wearing one of your dresses," said the Queen, who did not miss a thing.

"I was doing her a favor."

"So she likes fine clothes, does she?"

"Indeed she does, Your Majesty."

The Queen remained pensive a moment. "Perhaps it might not be such a bad idea to enlist the services of such a provocatively attractive little Protestant. Do your best to gain her confidence and her friendship. Make her a gift of one of your dresses. I shall see that it is replaced."

"As you say, Your Majesty."

When the sovereign had retired, Marie de Montmaur and Anselme, exhausted by their unusually lively evening, left the noise of the red salon and began to make their way back to their rooms along the never-ending, dimly lit corridors.

The Comtesse had been reluctant to leave the girls in the company of gentlemen and maids of honor whose flamboyance and dissipation she considered not only unpleasant, but disturbing. Yet, since they were playing cards with the Duc d'Anjou, it was impossible to interrupt the game.

It did in fact come to an end shortly afterward, and the guests retired.

"About time, too," Gilone whispered to Victoire. "Had it gone on any longer, I would have missed my *rendezvous*."

"You mean you're really going to keep it?"

Gilone looked at her with amazement. "Of course I am. I do want to see him. Anyway, he might be useful to me."

Victoire fell silent. She refrained from saying how unseemly she found such a midnight rendezvous with a virtual stranger in a deserted gallery of the Louvre. Particularly when Gilone's low neckline exposed much of her full breasts. It had already attracted the attention of virtually every man at the supper, including Guillaume de Louvencourt, who had not given Victoire a single glance the whole evening.

Gilone rushed off to meet Philippe de Lévis, who, she hoped, was waiting for her impatiently.

Victoire returned alone and dejectedly to her attic room. Only Triboulet was there to greet her. Soon he cheered her up by jumping onto the bed beside her and licking her pert nose affectionately.

Unlike the previous day, when she had been so bewildered and paralyzed by her first contact with the Court, Victoire had had time on this occasion to observe the guests, who were less numerous. She quickly realized how much the two factions hated each other, even though their surface relations were cordial and sometimes openly jovial. The Queen tried to strike a balance between them, so that she could not be accused of favoring one side to the detriment of the other. But whichever group they belonged to, all the courtiers seemed to be striving equally to get on the right side of the Queen—and of the Admiral, who was so patently in high favor at the moment.

On one or two occasions, Victoire had felt people looking at her with hostility. It was easy to guess her religion from the plainness of her clothes, which contrasted so strongly with the dazzling finery of the other women. With a touch of envy, she had looked admiringly at dresses that she would never possess. Gilone had been resourceful enough to borrow one. But Victoire was deeply reluctant to be in any kind of debt to Mademoiselle de Chabrière, even though she had shown herself to be extremely considerate, telling Victoire the names of people she did not know and introducing her to the other maids of honor. Although they all made friendly conversation, Victoire felt an outsider among them. She had noticed that one maid of honor seemed to be a close friend of Gontran de Louvencourt, so Victoire had gone and sat next to her in the hope of finding out something about Guillaume.

"Gontran de Louvencourt is one of the keenest supporters of the Duc de Guise and is thought to be seeking office with him." The maid of honor lowered her voice. "He has a very bad reputation. His gambling losses have left him deep in debt. So he constantly has to devise new ways of finding money."

"How?" asked Victoire, who was too honest to imagine what that could involve.

"He has a mistress who is a very wealthy widow ten years his senior. She is so infatuated with him that she gives him whatever he wants."

"What about his brother?" Victoire inquired, hoping fervently that Guillaume would not turn out to be equally despicable.

"He's just come from Lorraine, where they both grew up. So far he seems to have remained unattached. Unlike Gontran, he isn't very political. But they say he believes his mother died unjustly and he is seeking to avenge her death."

Victoire breathed a sigh of relief. As the maid of honor clearly loved to relay scandals, she would hardly have spared Guillaume had there been any fault with him.

Uncle Anselme and Victoire were sitting in a carriage that was taking them to his old friend, the magician and astrologer, Cassitère.

"Uncle Anselme, I must tell you something." The girl described the conversation she had overheard between Father Izard and an anonymous woman. That very morning she had again seen the monk, talking to a bitter enemy of the Protestants, the Duchesse de Guise.

"The man scares me terribly," said Victoire with a shudder, "and I've the feeling he lives in the Louvre."

"It's not impossible," said Anselme pensively. "It's impossible to know everyone living in such a vast palace." He was more worried than he wanted to let on. Victoire needed to be reassured, yet at the same time he wanted to make sure she kept alert. He was very aware of to what fanatical lengths human beings could go when incited by a holy cause.

"He didn't see you, did he?"

"I don't think so. I hid behind a pillar in time."

"Try to keep out of his sight, and we'll ask Cassitère's advice. He may know what to do."

Anselme had made the acquaintance of the magician in Padua while on a long stay there. The Florentines had taught Cassitère how to concoct philters to cure certain illnesses, and he was also skilled in predicting the future.

Cassitère lived in a tall, narrow house at the end of a dark alley.

When they arrived, they were shown into a huge, thickly carpeted room which smelled of friar's balsam. There were rows and rows of shelves cluttered with bottles containing liquids of various colors, alembics, countless jars of ointments and pomades, and some herbs were drying on a table. The bookcase contained large manuscripts in Italian, Greek, and Hebrew. On the wall there was a big copper dial engraved with the signs of the zodiac and of the planets, as well as other signs Victoire did not recognize.

Suddenly Cassitère was standing there, dressed in black and wearing a fur-trimmed cap. He smiled at Anselme, and the two men embraced, delighted to meet again after so many years.

"This is my niece Victoire," said the Comte de Montmaur. "She was unfortunate enough to lose her father, and has become almost a daughter to me."

The seer gazed at her, and within a few seconds she could feel a warm, agreeable sensation run through her body.

"She is well built," said Cassitère. "Safe from illnesses . . . but not from shocks or accidents."

Anselme looked worried. "Can you tell us more?"

The seer thought for a moment. "Yes," he said, "the day is favorable. Come."

He drew aside a curtain, which concealed a staircase, and they walked up two flights.

Victoire could feel her heart beating. What was she going to be told? She was not at all sure that her mother would have approved of their visit, which Anselme had asked her to keep secret.

They entered a small, windowless room. Its only furniture was a cupboard and a small round oak table. Cassitère told Victoire to sit on his left and Anselme opposite him. He took a parchment out of the cupboard and began to unroll it. Victoire craned her neck: all she could see was a diagram covered with figures and signs.

"What is your date of birth?"

"The 6th of August, 1555."

"The sign of Leo and the year of Jupiter," he murmured, immersing himself in an interminable series of calculations.

"There we are," he said at last. "Now we can begin."

He pulled a cord, and soon a servant appeared carrying a steaming pan and a small black box from which Cassitère took a phial containing red liquid. He poured a few drops of it into the water, which immediately began to seethe. A wisp of bluish vapor rose into the air and was inhaled deeply by the magician three times.

"What do you want to know?" he asked in a completely different voice, as though from very far away.

"Victoire's destiny," said Anselme, trying to conceal the quiver in his voice. More than fifteen years before, Cassitère had predicted that his brother would die a violent death.

"I see much blood and turmoil in Paris and the Louvre . . . an evil force in the disguise of good . . . travel . . . more death—everywhere." The seer's head dropped with exhaustion. "I cannot tell you any more for the moment."

Anselme wiped the sweat from his forehead and began to regret ever having brought his niece to see Cassitère.

Trembling, Victoire followed the two men downstairs again.

When they reached the street floor, Cassitère offered his visitors an exquisite liqueur flavored with hazelnuts. Seeing that Victoire had still not recovered from the shock of hearing his strange predictions, the magician regarded her seriously.

"I can only tell you one more thing. Beware of treachery."

Cassitère's strong personality had made a deep impression on her, and she did not doubt for a moment that his predictions would come true.

As they drove back to the Louvre via the Rue Saint-Martin, Anselme and Victoire remained silent at first as they tried to put their thoughts in order and recover from the shock created by Cassitère's strange prophecies.

"There is no point in worrying your mother with all this," said Anselme at last. He realized his sister-in-law's health was not good and that in all likelihood Victoire might soon be an orphan. And what about himself? Would he survive to protect her? He had not ventured to ask the magician.

Victoire looked at him and was alarmed by his somber expression.

"Don't worry, Uncle," she reached over to pat his hand gently. "I won't say anything, not even to Gilone. What's going to happen to her?"

"I've no idea . . ."

To tell the truth, Anselme had never felt an overwhelming affection for his niece who had happened to land in the same household as himself. Besides, she could never tell Cassiopeia from Alpha of Centaur— he had never imagined that such a degree of stupidity could exist.

"You were right to tell me about Father Izard. He is probably the man you'll have to be on your guard against." The Comte de Montmaur was wary of clergymen and vowed to keep a sharp eye on all of them.

"Surely we must try to do something to avert all the bloodshed!" she suddenly exclaimed.

Anselme shrugged resignedly. "You can't change the course of fate."

Such a passive attitude toward events ran against the grain of Victoire's enterprising nature. She felt that she should put up as great a struggle as possible. But what was she fighting? She would have to get as much information as possible and planned an effort to learn every secret of the Louvre, or at least as many as she could.

They crossed the Seine by the Pont des Meuniers and the Pont Saint-Michel, the same route they had taken into Paris. When they reached the Pré aux Clercs, their carriage was brought to an abrupt halt by a crowd gathered to watch a duel. Although very frequent, such occasions could be counted on to always draw large numbers of onlookers.

To her consternation, Victoire recognized one of the duelers: Guillaume de Louvencourt. She leaned out of the window to get a better look, her lovely face drawn with tension.

"This duel seems to be of enormous interest to you, my niece . . ."

"I know one of them." Victorie blushed. "I wonder who the other can be?"

"If you truly want to know," said Anselme with a mischievous twinkle in his eye, "I'll send our driver Léon to find out."

"Oh, yes, please, I beg you."

As the coachman went off to find out who the other duelist was, Victoire noticed a giant of a man help Guillaume off with his doublet and hand him his sword. He was a strange figure, with swarthy features and slanting eyes.

Léon came back. "The two gentlemen are Monsieur the Comte de Louvencourt, who is the offended party and has chosen to fight with rapiers, and Monsieur the Comte d'Etivey."

"Why are they fighting?" cried Victoire.

Monsieur d'Etivey looked a formidable opponent; he was taller and more broad-shouldered than Guillaume.

"That I don't know, Mademoiselle. Perhaps I could ask Monsieur de Louvencourt's valet, Boris. We fed the horses together yesterday evening and, you know how it is, we struck up a friendship."

"Well, try and find out, my good man," said Anselme, who did not want Victoire to be seen displaying too much interest in the matter.

The duel began. After a few moments of terrible

anxiety, Victoire realized Guillaume was the quicker, more expert swordsman and that he was extremely skilled at parrying his opponent's thrusts.

Suddenly Guillaume's shirt turned crimson. Her usually rosy complexion turned stark white and she clutched the carriage door.

"Control yourself, Victoire, it's only a scratch. Look, they're still fighting."

The color returned to her cheeks.

"How emotional you are," Anselme added. "You must learn to hide your feelings better—particularly at Court."

After a few moments, during which neither adversary gained the upper hand, it was Guillaume's turn to score a hit. Monsieur d'Etivey crumpled to the ground. His seconds, seeing that he was unable to rise, rushed forward to help him.

"He's not dead," murmured the crowd in disappointment before breaking up.

Léon took his seat again and drove the horses off.

Chapter IV

*V*ictoire rose early the next morning, as the Queen of Navarre wished to be read some edifying pages before confronting a day's activity. Such sessions were draining the girl because she curiously felt she had to be forever on her guard in the Queen's chambers.

She was about to leave her room when Gilone yawned.

"I didn't hear you come in last night," said Victoire. "What an evening . . ."

"Tell me about it," said Victoire, anxious to hear what her cousin had been up to.

"Philippe was most friendly. We had a long, long talk."

"What, while you were standing in the window recess where anyone could have seen you?"

"Of course not," replied Gilone, dismayed that Victoire thought she had no discretion. She lifted her chin smugly. "He took me to supper with the Duc de Cavalade, who made me very welcome and invited me to return whenever I wished."

"What's he like?" asked Victoire, her eyes wide with amazement.

"He's very handsome; tall, with silvery hair. He must be about fifty. His rooms are decorated with exquisite taste, his fare is lavish, and he has a bedspread made from the skin of a polar bear. How soft it was!"

"You mean he took you into his bedroom?"

"Just to show it to me. Anyway, Philippe was with us."

"And then?" Victoire demanded suspiciously.

"Philippe escorted me home . . . and kissed me."

"In the corridor?"

"Yes."

"But anyone might have seen you! What if my mother or Uncle Anselme had come out?"

"It was dark. I'm seeing him again this evening." Gilone was smiling like a cat who had just finished a jug of cream.

Victoire looked absorbed as she walked down to the Queen of Navarre's chambers. She was surprised by the boldness of Gilone's behavior, and a little envious that she had seduced a young man. Her gray eyes clouded as she fantasized what it would be like to be held in Guillaume's muscular arms and to feel his lips on hers.

Gilone's conduct, however, seemed lacking in self-respect—running after Philippe. She had changed so much in the short time since she had come to Paris that Victoire could scarcely recognize the girl she used to play with at Montmaur. Victoire felt unable to offer herself to a man in that way and wondered if she ever would; under what circumstances.

Without realizing it she had come abreast of a group of gentlemen who had spotted her going toward the Queen of Navarre's quarters, and who started gibing her.

"She's going to see the Queen of Navarre! She's a Huguenot!"

"Mademoiselle has just arrived from the provinces, I see."

"Look at the little frump!"

One of her assailants she recognized as Gontran de Louvencourt. Although a little abashed and frightened at first by such a sudden, unexpected attack, she soon recovered her self-possession.

"And you, sir," she said, addressing herself to Monsieur de Louvencourt, her eyes flashing and setting her jaw determinedly, "you hail from the province of Lorraine, I believe. I never knew it was an area noted for its sophistication."

Several of the young men began to laugh.

"That Protestant girl's got spirit!"

Victoire froze. "I am not 'that Protestant girl.' I am Mademoiselle de Montmaur."

"Well, Mademoiselle," said Gontran, smarting from the reminder of his origins, "can you tell us why you look so dowdy?"

"Has it ever occurred to you that I prefer to dress

simply, rather than be disguised as woman, like you?"

Victoire did not quite know how that remark escaped her lips, but she did think that Gontran, with his lace, his ribbons, and his necklaces, cut a preposterous figure.

"Well said, Mademoiselle! That'll teach you, my brother, to pick on a girl who knows how to defend herself."

With delight, Victoire realized that Guillaume, whom she had not noticed, was coming to her aid. Looking at him gratefully, she found him even more attractive than she had the day before, with his slightly disheveled, glossy black hair and very bright sapphire eyes.

"And which province are you from?" Guillaume asked with warmth and courtesy. He looked at her in a way that made Victoire sure he did not think her a mere country wench.

"I'm from Béarn, sir," she began, but then decided it would be best if she made her leave from this group before they had an opportunity to begin insulting her again.

"I shall acompany you, if you don't mind," said Guillaume suddenly. "I wouldn't want you to have any more nasty experiences."

Victoire accepted, but could not prevent herself from blushing at his interest. What a pity it was that Guillaume was a Catholic! Mother would certainly not approve of him.

"You're a spirited girl," said Guillaume, once they were alone. "I like people who refuse to take the easy way out."

Victoire looked at him, her gray eyes wide with surprise, unable to prevent her sensuous pink lips from parting slightly.

"I wasn't going to stand there and allow myself to be insulted by those . . ."

"Ruffians. It's the right word."

"I'm sorry that it was your brother," she added a bit remorsefully.

Guillaume shrugged and gave a sigh of contempt. "Oh, him . . ."

Apparently the two brothers were on far from good terms.

Forcing her shyness down, Victoire said, "I saw you, sir, fighting a duel with Monsieur d'Etivey."

Guillaume's strong, even teeth sparkled and Victoire found it very difficult not to stare.

"He's in a sorry state this morning. It'll be quite some time before he can go hunting again."

"I was so afraid for you," she could not help blurting out.

He looked at her inquiringly. "And why, pray?"

She bit her lips as she realized she had gone too far. "You didn't seem to be equally matched . . . May I ask you why you had taken offense?"

It was an indiscreet question, but Victoire's interest had gotten the better of her.

Guillaume's bright eyes became steely, and his upper lip curled in anger. "Adrien d'Etivey is an enemy of my family." Then he added with a murmur, speaking to himself rather than to Victoire, "I was a fool not to take advantage of the occasion to get rid of him once and for all . . ."

A small gasp of horror escaped from Victoire, shocked at the intensity of his tone.

Collecting himself, Guillaume said, "Forgive me, I forgot myself for a moment. Let us not talk about him anymore. I must admit that I had an ulterior motive for coming to your aid a moment ago. I was taken by your beauty last evening and had to seize this opportunity to speak with you."

Victoire was completely astonished and her complexion grew quite red. He had made no acknowledgment of her at supper.

"I very much wanted to make your acquaintance, but people kept distracting me."

By this time they had approached the entrance of Jeanne de Navarre's chambers. Victoire hesitated. "I regret that I must say good-by. I am the Queen's reader and am late already." She wanted desperately to continue walking with and looking at him.

Guillaume pointed one brown boot before him and made a low sweep with his arm across it. "I shall look forward wtih great anticipation to seeing you again sometime soon." He flashed an engaging smile toward her and then turned to stride down the hall, leaving Victoire with burning cheeks and an unnamed sensasation coursing through her.

When Victoire arrived in her godmother's chambers, she found her confined to bed. Henri de Navarre and a number of ladies were standing chatting by her bedside, while the Comtesse d'Amaucourt gave her the medicine that had been prescribed by Catherine de Medici's own, extremely skilled physician who concocted a potion that was to be taken a spoonful every hour. The stomach pains from which she was suffering were *bound* to disappear. For the time being, however, the remedy was having no effect—much to the obvious annoyance of Jeanne de Navarre.

"You are here at last, Mademoiselle! Come and read me a few pages from the psalms. They will relieve the pain much better than all those potions."

For nearly forty-five minutes the young girl applied herself to the task as best she could, though she was aware that the attendance was gradually sinking into a state of bored somnolence.

"That will be enough," the sick woman said, much to the relief of everyone present. "I shall rest now."

The Queen's visitors took their leave, and Victoire helped tidy up the room with Madame d'Amaucourt, who appeared increasingly annoyed at the way the girl was finding favor. Then, wearied by the long day, Victoire made her way back to her room.

She was walking across a salon dimly lit by a single candle whose unsteady flame made the shadows dance on the wall, when she suddenly heard a giggle, followed by some faint moans. She could make out two bodies in a close embrace on a couch. The woman's sighs of pleasure became more intense, and Victoire could hear the man's heavy, raucous breathing.

Fascinated, she stayed there not far from the couple, who, unaware of her presence, became more and more enraptured. Somehow she couldn't bring herself to go.

One part of her was deeply revolted and shocked at the idea that people could make such an exhibition of themselves for anyone to see. The strict principles her mother had inculcated in her were having their effect.

Yet there was something about the steady moaning of the woman—whom Victoire could hardly make out except for a mass of black hair that reminded her strongly of Gilone—that produced a strange, flustered feeling in her. Soon she was feeling herself throbbing, quivering.

She had never thought of the physical side of love before. Now the girl on the couch gave a cry of release, and as she rushed from the room, Victoire suddenly found herself imagining just such a scene between herself and Guillaume de Louvencourt.

Chapter V

In a daze Victoire began to rush back to her room
with such precipitation that once again she lost her
way.

She ended up in a very dark, narrow corridor. Triboulet appeared and trotted along beside her, sniffing
the air expectantly as though remembering the delightful smells of the lofts at Montmaur. Victoire
stopped in a quandary. Should she go on or retrace her
steps? She climbed a spiral staircase, which was hardly
ever used, to judge from the thick layer of dust on the
banisters. She opened a creaking door and found herself in the storerooms of the Louvre.

It was a fascinating sight: half-open old chests spilling over with clothes dating from François I's reign,
discarded furniture, paintings the Queen no longer
liked, and rusty suits of armor.

Victoire went over to a dormer window and looked
down with wonderment at the dark, seething, flowing
waters of the river Seine. The moon had just risen,
and a few lamps were twinkling here and there. A small
group of soldiers walked along the embankment, carrying torches that created a pool of bright light.

Triboulet had got into a chest and was energetically
tearing a satin doublet to pieces.

"Will you stop that now!"

Victoire realized, to her surprise, that she was talking in a whisper, which seemed rather silly in such a
deserted place.

Now that her eyes had become accustomed to the darkness, she could make out an almost imperceptible ray of light coming through the floor in the middle of the room. She bent down and saw from the bright square-shaped crack that there was a trapdoor. Putting her ear close to the floor, Victoire could just hear the muffled sound of distant conversation. How could she open the trapdoor? There must be a ring somewhere. She ran her hand slowly over the whole surface of the panel, stifling a cry as a splinter went into her thumb. In the end she found a metal ring. Victoire was surprised by the weight of the trapdoor and had to use all her strength in order to raise it. Very soon she lowered it again silently and looked around for something to wedge it open with.

As soon as she had done so, she lay down on her stomach, oblivious to the fact that she was spoiling her dress, and heard a very distinct, authoritarian voice.

"You know full well that we must put an end to this somehow or other. They are gaining influence every day."

"They will all be in the capital at the same time for the Princess's wedding," answered another voice that was oddly reminiscent of that of the woman with Father Izard.

Victoire was not content just to listen. She wanted to see. With a strenuous effort she managed to raise the plank she was using as a wedge so that it stood on its edge. The gap was now about six inches wide, and enabled her to see down into a sumptuous room, hung with tapestries, in which two women, one seated, the other striding up and down, were conversing.

"The most important person we must get rid of is Admiral de Coligny."

How was it that Victoire had failed to recognize that Florentine accent straightaway?

"He is becoming too important. I cannot really trust him in spite of his assurances. He has already proved

himself a traitor. I have always promised myself that I will have my revenge, and I have waited a
long time. Now the moment has come."

Horrified at what they were saying, Victoire craned
her neck to get a glimpse of the extravagantly dressed
woman who was agreeing so emphatically with the
Queen.

"Seven years ago, in Bayonne," she continued mus-
ingly, halting in her stride, "the Duc d'Albe advised
me to take the leaders of the Reformed Church by
surprise and put them all to death."

"With an example like that, the survivors would
certainly end up by abandoning their faith."

Triboulet spotted a mouse and dashed after it, barking excitedly. The two women looked up suddenly, and
Victoire recognized the dowager Duchesse de Guise.

"We have an eavesdropper!" cried the Queen.
"Guards! Quick!"

Six men rushed in.

Orders came thick and fast.

"Go up to the garret. There is a spy. Bring him to
me. I want him alive."

Victoire's heart started beating fast at the thought of
the dangers that now lay ahead of her: the Queen
would not balk at putting her to death if she learned
that her most jealously guarded secrets had been found
out. The girl carefully lowered the trapdoor and looked
around desperately for a place to hide. She could already hear the footsteps of the guards running along
a gallery lower down—there must be twenty of them
at least. She imagined them seizing her brutally and
dragging her away. What was she to do? All the time
she had left was two minutes, if that. She slipped into
a chest, pulled the clothes over her, and closed the lid.
It was only just in time: the door burst open and men
carrying torches rushed in shouting:

"Out you come! We know you're in here."

They knocked over the furniture, emptied boxes, and wrecked the whole room.

Victoire was on the point of fainting. Somebody had opened the chest in which she was huddling more dead than alive and scarcely daring to breathe. A sword jabbed into the clothes, and she felt its cold blade slide against her leg.

"There's nothing in here."

Having finally caught his mouse, Triboulet gave a bark of triumph.

The guards surrounded the animal.

"It's only a dog!"

"Her Majesty must have heard it running about, and as she sees spies everywhere . . . !"

"We'll show it to her. Come here, Fido, we're taking you to see the Queen," said one of the guards with a guffaw.

Triboulet allowed himself to be carried away without any resistance. The man who had picked him up gave off a strong smell of roast lamb that was full of promise. Victoire waited a long while before daring to leave her hiding place. Triboulet had saved her. If it had not been for him, the soldiers would have gone on looking until they had found her.

She shuddered in retrospect, imagining what might now be her fate if she had been discovered: She would be brutally led before the Queen and the Duchesse de Guise. Then she would be flung in prison for the rest of her days. Or more likely, someone would come in the middle of the night to strangle her or sink a dagger into her heart.

The fearful thoughts running through her mind almost made her forget the terrible dangers in store for her fellow Protestants. So the Queen had decided to kill them all? Victoire found it difficult to understand how reasons of state could possibly justify such a massacre.

Gilone came in looking flushed. Her hair was in disarray, and she had obviously just readjusted her clothes.

"Well, I never. Aren't you asleep?"

"No," replied Victoire. "And where have *you* been?"

Gilone smiled quizzically. "Certainly not spending an evening alone. *I* try to have a bit of fun."

"It doesn't seem to me that you find that too difficult," said Victoire more curtly than she had intended.

Why was it that just when she felt such a strong need to confide in her cousin, Gilone had to irritate her so? But then she had no other girlfriend.

Gilone sat down on her cousin's bed and began to take off her stockings.

Suddenly Victoire found herself blurting out, "We're all going to be massacred."

"What are you talking about? Who do you mean by 'we'?"

"The Protestants at Court—de Coligny, the Queen of Navarre, and all the party leaders . . ."

Gilone looked at Victoire as though she were stark raving mad. "You must be out of your mind! How ever did you get that idea?"

Victoire told her about her adventure in the garret and about the conversation she had overheard.

"According to what you heard, the Queen will only kill Protestants of some importance. So there is no danger for insignificant people like us."

Victoire felt indignant at such selfishness. "Should we stand back and watch while all the others are slaughtered? At least we can warn them. Some of them can escape."

"If I were you," said Gilone, rising from the bed, "I wouldn't get involved. The affairs of state have nothing to do with us."

"But the fate of our fellow Protestants *is* our responsibility!" exclaimed Victoire, who felt outraged at such indifference.

"You know, it may be and probably is true that the Queen wants to get rid of the Protestants, or at least force them to become Catholics. But that's quite a different thing from exterminating them all."

"What about Amboise?" Victoire countered bitterly.

"That wasn't the same thing. There had been a plot. For the time being, nobody has a thought for anything but the Princess's wedding. You've seen for yourself that members of both the Guise and the leading Protestant families have been having a great time together. Don't forget, Amboise happened twelve years ago."

"That doesn't mean the persecution has stopped. It's rumored that the Admiral's brother died of poison a few months ago."

"If you believed every rumor?" said Gilone, shrugging her shoulders. "As soon as anyone has an attack of colic, there's talk of poison. But nobody bothers to find out whether the victim didn't wolf down a basketful of unripe plums."

She opened the wardrobe and could not resist showing off a new crimson satin dress with a decoration of pearls on the collar and cuffs.

"Look!"

"Another loan from Mademoiselle de Chabrière?"

"No. It's a gift. From the Queen."

"And why should she be giving you clothes?" asked Victoire with surprise.

"She wants me to go into her service."

Victoire gave a start. "You mean in the Flying Squadron?"

"I'll be a maid of honor. One of the other girls is getting married, and I shall take her place."

"Come now, Gilone, you can't be serious. You're not going into the service of the Catholics?"

"When it's the Queen who asks you . . ."

"You know as well as I do what sort of job you'll

be required to do. Surely you're not going to sell your-self for a few dresses? What a disgrace!"

"My dear Victoire," said Gilone, slipping into her fine cambray nightdress, "as I've already explained to you, I've no intention of mouldering away for the rest of my life at Montmaur."

'What about Philippe de Lévis?"

"He hasn't got a sou—he told me so himself. It's a pity, because I find him charming. He may just inherit something from a childless younger sister of his father. But God only knows when."

"I thought you were in love with him."

"If you really want to know, I've just come from his room. I can't say it was unpleasant."

Victoire remembered the couple on the couch. So Gilone had a lover . . .

"What if you have a baby?" she asked.

"We shall see. Meanwhile . . ."

When Victoire fell asleep, she had an unending se-ries of nightmares. One moment she saw Cassitère in a trance before his steaming pan and then one of Queen Catherine's men was chasing her through the garrets of the Louvre.

Early the next morning she woke up bathed in sweat, and heard the sound of gentle scratching at the door. It was Triboulet. When Victoire let him in, he jumped up at her, more eager than ever to be stroked and patted. His mistress promised him that his next meal would be a feast—that was the least he deserved.

In the next bed, where Gilone was sleeping peace-fully, all that could be seen was her mass of black hair. Victoire looked at her with a touch of contempt, then turned her attention to more serious subjects.

She devoted a great deal of thought to deciding on the best course of action. What she was most afraid of was that nobody would believe her revelations because she was so young.

Victoire went down at the usual time to read to the

Queen of Navarre, in whom she had decided to confide. The Queen would then determine what should be done.

As usual there were many people busying themselves in the Queen's chambers. After a moment's hesitation, Victoire made up her mind.

"May I take the liberty, Your Majesty, of requesting an immediate interview with you?"

Jeanne de Navarre, who was in the final stages of being dressed by the Comtesse d'Amaucourt, looked at her goddaughter with surprise.

"By all means, my child, do not be afraid to speak out."

"Your Majesty," said Victoire, blushing, "what I meant was . . . a completely private interview. It's a very serious matter."

The Queen assumed that the girl had done something silly and wanted to confess to her alone, so she gestured to all those present. "Leave me alone with Mademoiselle de Montmaur for a moment."

Suddenly Victoire was at a loss. She did not know how to begin her story in such a way as to make it believable. She was well aware that it might sound rather farfetched. "Your Majesty, you are in very great danger. And so is Admiral de Coligny."

Jeanne de Navarre listened without interruption, and much to her goddaughter's relief, believed what she said.

"I knew very well," she muttered angrily, "that she was laying a trap by luring me to the Louvre. I don't understand how I allowed myself to be taken in by her declarations of friendship. Mademoiselle, you have rendered an invaluable service to our cause. Thanks to you, many lives will be spared. It is true, isn't it, that I am the first person in whom you have confided?"

"Yes, Your Majesty," said Victoire, who did not dare admit that she had already told Gilone.

"I exempt you from your duties today. You shall

come tomorrow morning to repeat to the Admiral what you have told me. And we shall do what we can. Do not breathe a word of this to anyone."

Chapter VI

*V*ictoire felt an enormous sense of relief as she left the Queen's chambers. By imparting her secret to a responsible person, she no longer had to bear its terrible burden alone.

She met Guillaume de Louvencourt in the gallery, who was looking at her very attentively. That morning he was wearing a dark-blue velvet doublet with gold thread decorations and a matching cap with an ostrich feather. He seemed more attractive than ever.

They chatted for a while, and then suddenly he smiled at her and made a suggestion.

"Would you care to join me on a tour of the town? As you so aptly reminded my brother, we've only just arrived from the provinces, and I've hardly had time yet to visit the capital."

Victoire answered warmly, trying to temper her enthusiasm a bit so she wouldn't appear too giddy.

"Gladly, sir. I was wondering how to occupy my day."

She was about to follow Guillaume when his brother suddenly appeared, elaborately dressed in lace and ribbons.

"Fine company you keep!" remarked Gontran with heavy sarcasm.

"Precisely," replied Guillaume sharply. "Which is why we do not need yours. Come, Mademoiselle."

They crossed the courtyard. Fortunately, none of the many people there seemed likely to tell the Comtesse de Montmaur that her daughter was being escorted by a Catholic gentleman.

They got into the de Louvencourt's coach, and Boris sat next to the driver.

"I'm intrigued by your servant's face. Why is his skin so yellow?"

"Boris comes from Mongolia. My father took him in many years ago. He was wounded and starving, and had been abandoned by his fellow soldiers, mercenaries in the service of William of Orange. We took a liking to each other and since then, he has scarcely ever left me."

They crossed the bridge where Jeanne de Navarre's retinue had been held up by a crowd.

"I would like to see some of the stalls."

They got out of the coach and watched amusedly as the hawkers vaunted their wares. A tooth extractor was at work on the platform from which Father Izard had called down the wrath of heaven upon the Protestants. Victoire could not stop herself describing the scene to her companion and confiding her fears to him, even though he was Catholic.

Guillaume took her by the hand. "With me, you need have no fear."

His strong hand gripping hers produced such an intense feeling of happiness in Victoire that she was taken aback. Could she really be so fond of Guillaume? Why, she hardly knew him . . .

All of a sudden she sensed that somewhere in the milling crowd Father Izard's ruthless eyes were staring at her. She whipped around. "I'm sure he's here! I can feel it!"

They spent some time trying to get a glimpse of the monk's habit, but without success.

"You must have been imagining it, Victoire."

After a while she relaxed and they stopped near the Pont Saint-Michel to have lunch at the *Golden Pheasant*. As their prepossessing appearance betokened a well-lined purse, they were served hare pâté, spit-roasted ducklings, shoulder of lamb, and trout that had been caught the day before, washed down with claret straight from the barrel. At neighboring tables, merchants were putting away more simple dishes.

After a leisurely stroll, they crossed back over the Seine.

"Would you dare accompany me into the church of Saint-Germain-l'Auxerrois to see its famous altarpiece?"

Victoire hesitated. If her mother ever found out, she would never hear the end of it. "Yes," she relented.

On the parvis, there was an opulent litter escorted by several guards. Nearby beggars held out bowls beseeching good Christians to take pity on their sorry condition.

"Please give alms, milady, and the Lord will reward you."

Victoire dropped a small coin into an outstretched hand. No sooner had she done so than she was surrounded by a dozen one-eyed, one-armed persons who clung to her clothes. It was all Guillaume could do to drive them away.

"If you give one of them something," he said, "they all want their share. Be more careful next time. Anyway, most of them are not really cripples at all."

As Victoire entered a Catholic church for the first time in her life, she could feel a hollow in the pit of her stomach. The dingy interior was heavy with the smell of burning tallow and incense. She could just make out some statues and flickering candles. In a corner, an old woman was chanting a litany in a plaintive monotone. As they were trying to find the altarpiece, they passed a kneeling figure whose black cape did not completely conceal a highly ornate, lavender-colored satin dress. When she raised her head, they recognized Henri de Navarre's future wife sunk deep in prayer.

Guillaume escorted Victoire out of the dark church and back across the street in the bright sunshine and into the courtyard of the Louvre, where he took leave of her, promising they'd meet again that evening.

As she made her way back to the family quarters and mused over the time spent with Guillaume, she began to think that perhaps her mother was exaggerating about the evils of Catholicism. The cathedral really was not that much different than Protestant churches; more lavish certainly, but wasn't it the same god that they all worshipped? And Guillaume was most definitely the nicest, most charming man she had ever met despite his religion.

A masked ball had been planned following an early dinner, and the Comtesse de Montmaur had decided that for such an occasion she would be justified in giving her daughter a new dress. She did likewise for her niece and couldn't help hoping that it would stop her from borrowing other people's clothes.

Jacotte, who was assisting both Alix and the Montmaurs, was in continual demand, and had to run back and forth between the rooms.

"Quick, please sew this ribbon back on!"

"I've stained my dress, please help me clean it!"

The girls were almost ready when the Comtesse entered their chamber.

"Girls, you look lovely. I am so proud of you." She turned to Victoire and said affectionately, "Come here, dear. Let me fix your hair. I haven't done so in a long time."

Victoire sat down at the rude table and her mother began to brush her hair with firm but gentle strokes.

Victoire reached up, taking her mother's hand and caressing it against her cheek.

"There is some good news that I want to tell you about, my daughter. The Queen of Navarre has agreed to intercede in marriage arrangements for you. Apparently an eligible young man has asked for your hand—Monsieur de Mèrande."

Victoire was aghast. Her face paled and she turned her head suddenly, which made her lush blonde hair pull tightly under her mother's unsuspecting hands. "Monsieur de Mèrande!"

"Why, yes."

"Oh, Maman, he is so terribly dull and ugly. Must I?" She had been at Court for only a short time, and already she would have to say good-by to all the fun and meekly follow a nobleman back to his country estate, where life would be much the same as at Montmaur—not that she didn't love country life, but she wanted time to get to know this exciting new world before saying good-by to it for good.

Her good mood vanished instantly, and the ball she had been looking forward to so much suddenly seemed irksome. Why was her mother in such a hurry to find her a husband? She was only seventeen, and wanted to enjoy for a little longer the pleasures of the Louvre, with its receptions, parties, and attentive handsome men—especially Guillaume. She resolved to make her own match; she would never marry Monsieur de Mèrande.

"You are not behaving very well, Victoire."

"But, Maman, I have already met the gentleman and he is so boring."

"You must not be solely concerned with his personality or appearance. Monsieur de Mèrande is extremely well connected, he has perfect manners, and, most important, his morals are beyond reproach. His wife would be a happy woman."

"I doubt that. He doesn't appeal to me in the slightest," persisted Victoire.

"You will learn to know him better and to appreciate his qualities."

"I have absolutely no desire to do so," she replied. She was guilt-ridden at the thought of defying her mother and Jeanne de Navarre, but she was determined to resist with all the strength she could muster.

Marie de Montmaur was clearly annoyed with her daughter's outburst. "He is, however, your future husband!"

"Never!"

"Enough of this childish behavior. We will not discuss it for now. Your hair is finished."

Desolate, Victoire stood up and put on a black velvet mask. As if on cue, Gilone, who had remained quiet during the argument, put on a dark-ruby one.

"We shan't be able to recognize anyone," said Victoire morosely, fearing that she might accidentally bump into Monsieur de Mèrande.

"It'll be much more fun." Gilone smiled mysteriously, ignoring her cousin's feelings.

Hundreds of masked figures were already beginning to make their way toward the salons lit with a myriad of candelabras, flashing like sparkling jewels so that the air seemed to glitter. The two cousins paused for a moment in wonder at the magical sight, then disappeared into the crowd, one of them looking for Guillaume de Louvencourt, the other for Philippe de Lévis.

An orchestra began to play in one of the salons, and Victoire was soon caught up in a quadrille. It was impossible to guess whose dark eyes were peering from behind the dark-blue satin mask. She sensed a certain warmth in the man's look and hoped for a second that she had found Guillaume. But no, this gentleman was slightly taller.

"Who are you?" she asked him as he escorted her toward one of the several refreshment tables.

"Tonight everyone must remain a stranger," he answered with a twinkle in his eye. "I'll just tell you my first name: Renaud. Will you tell me yours in exchange?"

"Victoire."

A little later, her escort unobtrusively pointed to a beautiful young woman who was standing in a window recess and receiving the compliments of several noblemen.

"Do you know who she is?" he whispered.

"No."

"The Duc d'Anjou."

"It's not possible!" she exclaimed in amazement. "Disguised as a woman?"

Renaud smiled at her naivety. "Does that surprise you? The King's brother quite often dresses up like that, you know."

Two men walked past, and Victoire recognized them as the Louvencourt brothers. She waited until Renaud was looking the other way, then ran after Guillaume, whispering his name.

"Who can this little devil be who recognizes me?"

"The little devil who dared enter a Catholic church with you earlier today."

Guillaume roared with laughter, picked up a glass of champagne from the table, and handed it to her. It must have been the third or fourth she had drunk . . . and she was beginning to feel rather light-headed.

Several times she danced opposite Guillaume, doing her best to be as graceful and relaxed as the other women appeared. It was hard, though, to get every step just right as she had not had much occasion for practice at Montmaur. Guillaume pretended not to notice. Every time they came face to face in the dance he flashed her a radiant smile, and through the mask she could see his blue eyes peering intently into hers.

"I think there's much to be said for country girls," Guillaume said as they crossed on the floor.

"And country boys, too," retorted Victoire, emboldened by masked identity.

Guillaume threw back his head and laughed. "You *are* a girl of spirit." He took her hand in the dance. It was cool and strong, and his touch made Victoire feel for an instant that they were all alone together in the huge room. She missed a beat and blushed furiously. His hand tightened on hers. "After this dance," he began, when to Victoire's intense annoyance Gontran suddenly appeared among the dancers. He put a hand on his brother's shoulder and whispered at length to him. His manner seemed very urgent. The dancers changed partners, and Victoire could only watch, distressed, over her shoulder as Guillaume strode off with his brother out the room.

All the fun had suddenly been swept away. What she most wanted to do right now was to run away from all these merry dancers and cry in angry frustration. Oh, it was unfair. That hateful Gontran!

"Ah! At last I've found you again!"

It was Renaud, who wanted her to join a dance that was just beginning.

"Oh, leave me alone," she said. "I'm going to leave."

"But whatever for?" he asked, surprised. "The party's not over yet—far from it in fact."

"I don't feel like having any fun."

Renaud took Victoire's hand and led her out onto a deserted balcony.

"What's the matter?" he asked gently. "You're shivering. Are you cold?"

Unable to utter a word, Victoire shook her head. Such concern for her made her feel even more unhappy. A single unrestrained tear trickled from below the mask down her pink cheek.

"You're weeping!"

Victoire offered no resistance as he gently removed

her velvet mask and wiped away her tears with a fine cambray handkerchief.

"I've made a fool of myself," she said, trying to pull herself together. "Will you please forgive me, Renaud?"

His only answer was to draw her closer, gently stroking her soft hair. As she sank her face against his shoulder, Victoire began to ask herself why this stranger was showing such kindness toward her. Although she was still thinking of Guillaume, she had to admit that she felt happy in the arms of a man whose face she had never even seen.

"Are you feeling better now?"

"Yes," said Victoire more confidently. "How can I thank you?"

Renaud smiled, and brushed his lips against those of the young girl.

"We shall meet again," he promised.

The Comtesse d'Amaucourt gave Victoire a sour welcome.

"Well, Mademoiselle, we did not see much of you yesterday, did we?"

"Her Majesty exempted me from service."

"And may one know why?"

"I'd prefer not to say," replied Victoire, fully intending to maintain her godmother's confidence and wanting to protect the privacy of her day with Guillaume. She felt she must stand up to the lady-in-waiting who would not understand being in love with a Catholic.

The Comtesse almost choked with anger. "I shall tell the Queen how insolent you are!"

Followed by the lady-in-waiting who was going to denounce her bad behavior, Victoire entered the little room in which Admiral de Coligny was conversing with Jeanne de Navarre.

"You may leave, Madame," said the Queen without even looking at Madame d'Amaucourt. "Come here, my child. This is the Admiral. Now tell him what you overheard."

Although rather intimidated by her listener's stern features, Victoire repeated her story in all its details. She quickly realized that he did not attach too much credence to what she was saying.

"Come now, Your Majesty, such treachery is impossible. You know how much importance Catherine de Medici attaches to the marriage of your children; you know she sees it as a guarantee of good feeling between the two parties."

"Don't forget she burned you in effigy and tried to have you murdered."

"That's true . . . But since then we have become friends again," said the Admiral, who was determined to remain unruffled. Surely the maid of honor must have imagined this fanciful story. How could Catherine de Medici, who summoned him for advice almost every day, possibly be thinking of eliminating her confidant? And would the King, who displayed such friendship toward him and called him "Father," allow anything of the sort to happen?

"I still think it is urgent to warn our co-religionists. I shall answer for the truth of Mademoiselle de Montmaur's story."

"Naturally," said Coligny. "But isn't it a little premature to alert our comrades?"

The Queen of Navarre repressed a gesture of exasperation. She was greatly vexed by the Admiral's attitude. Were men completely incapable of smelling danger? If Catherine had decided to slaughter the Protestants, nothing in the world would stop her.

"So the massacre is supposed to take place during preparations for the wedding celebrations?" asked the Admiral skeptically.

"I don't know for the moment. The Queen did not

mention any date, did she?" she asked, turning to Victoire.

"No, Your Majesty." She was reluctant to tell of Cassitère's—a magician's—prediction.

"I say, you look cheerful this morning," said Gilone, yawning sarcastically.

Victoire did not answer and began to dress listlessly, helped that morning by Héloïse, who soon irritated her with ceaseless chattering. When Héloïse inadvertently pulled her hair, Victoire gave her a sound scolding— which was very unlike her. Immediately Victoire regretted what she had done. Just because she was in a bad mood, did that mean she should take it out on other people?

There was a state of enormous agitation in the great gallery. Servants were rushing about in panic, and people were conferring by every window. Victoire, stepping outside to discover the cause, approached a gentleman and asked, "What is happening?"

"The Queen of Navarre is dying!"

Chapter VII

*F*or several days Victoire did not know where to turn. To make matters worse, someone had told her that the Queen, the day before she died, had been presented a gift by Catherine de Medici, and the girl holding the present had heard her murmur, "Surely one doesn't send gifts to people one intends to murder?"

Victoire was convinced that the Queen had been poisoned, though ever since she had been treated with such skepticism by the Admiral, she dared not mention her suspicions to anyone.

She also wondered why the murder had been committed before the wedding, which would now have to be postponed. Perhaps Catherine had been slowly poisoning Jeanne de Navarre through her physician's medication, and then, when it was realized the plan was known, had been hastened before anything could be done. The thought that her revelations might have been indirectly responsible filled Victoire with grief. If that were so, then her life was in danger, too.

Victoire suspected the Comtesse d'Amaucourt. She had an unpleasant prying manner, always wanting to know everything, creeping furtively about like a cat, and tending to be where one least expected to find her. Could she be an agent of Catherine de Medici? The evidence, of course, was completely circumstantial.

Now that the Queen was dead, and since the Admiral was still doubtful, Victoire felt it was up to her to try and warn the Protestants. She was fully aware of the difficulty of the task that faced her. No one would believe her. She was just a girl from the provinces, and the death of her protectress had made her imagine all sorts of things. But what about Henri, her childhood friend?

One evening, she paid a visit to the King of Navarre's chambers. In the antechamber there were several gentlemen playing dice and drinking wine. They were slightly the worse for wear and tried to get Victoire to join them.

"Pray be seated, my beauty. You'll bring me luck," one of them said, grabbing her around the waist.

"No, come and sit over here," said another player. "If I win I'll buy you ribbons for your dress."

With warm smiles and clever answers she managed

to brush off their invitations and their jests. She walked through to the room where Henri de Navarre was sitting, dressed in black, and surrounded by a bevy of girls. The tables were laden with silver-woven baskets full of fruit gums, frangipane cakes, and other tidbits. Victoire wondered how she could carry on a conversation in such a merry and frivolous atmosphere, so out of place only one week after the funeral.

Henri gave her a hearty welcome and bade her sit next to him, offering sugared almonds.

Somehow she succeeded in whispering into his ear, "I must speak to you. And alone."

"It'll be a pleasure, my pretty Victoire."

She realized, as his eyes suddenly lit up and his hand began to caress her arm, that he had quite misunderstood. Was that all he thought of—running after other women instead of thinking of his bride-to-be? It was true that no one ever mentioned the Princess. She doubtless preferred more refined company than the ribald, rollicking country gentry that formed Henri's entourage.

A meal was brought in, and during the bustle of moving the tables and laying places for the guests, the King of Navarre whisked Victoire into an adjacent room.

"How beautiful you are, Mademoiselle," he said, trying to embrace her.

She pushed him away from her as nicely as she could, put off by the strong smell of alcohol and intent on her mission.

"I came to talk to you about something very serious, sir. Your mother was poisoned."

"How do you know?" exclaimed Henri, immediately forgetting his amorous intentions.

She told him of the overheard conversation and her suspicions.

"My God! If only I had been able to get back in time . . ."

His eyes welled with tears. The man pondered a long while, his face taking on a serious expression. For the time being, he had forgotten his fun-loving companions, whose muffled laughter could be heard through the heavy velvet curtains.

"Let's try to retrace the order of events," he said. "First you overhear a plot. Then you tell my mother about it. You repeat your story in front of the Admiral, who refuses to believe you, and who, because he feels he has the favor of Charles IX, doesn't bother to do anything to stop the massacre or get the Protestants to flee. Immediately afterward my mother is poisoned. So someone must have eavesdropped on you and passed the information on to Catherine de Medici. We can rule out the Admiral."

"That's true, it isn't likely it would have been him."

"Now, in my mother's entourage. . ." Henri went on. "There were many new people in her Court after she arrived in Paris. I don't even know half of them."

Victoire wondered whether to tell him that she suspected Comtesse d'Amaucourt.

"You spoke to no one else but my mother?" asked Henri.

To her horror, Victoire suddenly remembered a conversation she had had with Gilone. Surely it could not be her . . .

"No," she murmured, not willing to believe her cousin could do such a thing.

From that moment on there was a nagging doubt in Victoire's mind, even though she was extremely loath to suspect Gilone, her playfellow and confidante. And yet, however much she racked her brains, there were only two solutions to the problem: either a spy had overheard her conversation with the Queen of Navarre, or else Gilone had betrayed the cause of her co-religionists—possibly through Mademoiselle de Chabrière.

Victoire wondered whether Gilone had revealed the source of her information. It was by no means certain.

Victoire could not bring herself to believe that Gilone was capable of wanting her cousin to die. Nevertheless, it would not be very difficult for the Queen to trace the information back to its source if she really wanted to.

In any case, she would have to be more than ever on her guard. If only she had managed to find a more serious-natured protector at Court than Henri de Navarre and one a little more on his toes than Uncle Anselme, who was getting rather doddering.

As for her mother, the Comtesse de Montmaur had been forced, shortly after the Queen's death, to return urgently to her estate because of the death of the bailiff. However quickly she settled her affairs, she would not be back in Paris for a good fortnight.

Victoire had been invited to a small supper by the Admiral's son-in-law and hoped that someone there could help her. While the Catholics made no attempt to hide their delight at the Queen of Navarre's death, and hoped that it would lead to the calling-off of the projected marriage, the mourning Protestants were still in a shocked daze. Word had got round that the Queen had been poisoned, and the Protestants' mood was one of extreme anxiety. Only the Admiral seemed to have no fears.

When she opened the wardrobe to select something to wear, Victoire gave a cry of surprise: her cousin had two new dresses. Could they be the reward for her treachery?

Gilone was now often absent for entire days, coming back to her room at daybreak and continuing to sleep most of the daylight hours.

Victoire walked downstairs pensively. As she was crossing a dingy antechamber she could hear someone striding up quickly behind her. In a panic she stepped up her pace, then began to run, imagining that she was being pursued by the lascivious Father Izard. She lost one of her shoes, and a pair of strong arms gripped her from behind, preventing her from falling. She gave a shriek and struggled to get free. Victoire was just about to bite her aggressor on the hand when she recognized the voice of Guillaume de Louvencourt.

"Don't run away from me like that, Mademoiselle. I was coming to throw myself at your feet and beseech your forgiveness for having gone off the other night without saying farewell."

The color returned to Victoire's cheeks. "You gave me such a fright."

"Did I?" he asked, surprised. "But why?"

She now realized how silly she had been to get into such a panic. "I thought . . . I thought it was someone else."

"The monk?"

"Yes," she admitted. "I think he is evil. Ever since I first saw him I've been afraid. He looked at me in such a lecherous way."

"Well, I don't know if he could be called evil, but he does have a reputation for seeking out beautiful women. Don't worry, though, I'll see that no harm comes to you." Guillaume sat her down on a couch. "Now I'm going to find your shoe."

After a short interval he picked it up from where it had fallen. Then he took her slim ankle and slipped her satin shoe gently on. She could feel the warmth of his hand through her silk stocking.

He sat down next to her. "Say that you forgive me." He wrapped his arm around Victoire's bare shoulders. She shivered and halfheartedly tried to brush him off. Was she going to behave like Gilone?

Guillaume's face was so close to hers that she could feel his breath on her. She no longer had the energy or the desire to reject his ever more insistent embrace, or to escape the mouth that met hers. In spite of herself, she responded to his tender, passionate kiss. The sensation made her weak, and she would have loved to stay in his protecting arms all night, every night . . .

One evening, on her return from a particularly long and exhausting day's hunting at Fontainebleau, she heard some rapid footsteps and saw a brown robe disappear round the corner at the end of the corridor outside her room. Her heart missed a beat. Was she really sure she had just seen the monk? She just didn't know; it might have been a woman. But the hairs prickled at the back of her neck.

Entering her room, where Héloïse had lit a single candle, she found its flicker a little sinister. Although she intended to go to sleep soon, she lit two more candlesticks.

The sound of scratching on the door told her that Triboulet wanted to be with her. She let him in and he bounded up playfully barking, wanting a bit of frolic after being alone all day. She spied a platter of delicious-looking sweetmeats on the table. Supposing that her mother, due back that day, had brought them back to Paris with her, she picked one up and called to Triboulet.

He walked over with interest and sniffed at the cake, which Victoire crumbled into a saucer. Triboulet wolfed it down, wagging his tail.

Victoire was starting to undress when she heard a terrible howling coming from the corner. Triboulet was on his back, with his feet in the air, writhing in agony and whimpering pitifully. White foam spewed from his mouth onto his black fur. Suddenly his feet stiffened and he slumped over.

She stared at the empty saucer, rushed over to the remaining cakes, picked them up, and threw them out of the window. Although it was a warm summer night, she shivered as she looked for the last time at the tiny crumpled figure that had saved her life. She knew now that it was Father Izard whom she had seen.

Chapter VIII

On the morning of August 18, the capital was bathed in sunshine. As she drove to Notre Dame Cathedral in the Montmaurs' carriage, Victoire looked admiringly at the triumphal arches that had been built at each crossroads, the balconies hung with heavy tapestries, and the Parisians themselves donned in their finest clothes for the occasion.

The whole city had spent the previous night in revelry. The controversial nature of the marriage between the King's sister and a Huguenot was forgotten, and for a few hours old quarrels and dissensions faded into the background. But behind all the merriment and drinking and festivity there was the rumble of revolt. This was particularly true of the Court, where the atmosphere was extremely ominous: the Protestants, now certain of victory, were triumphantly lording it over the Catholics, who had failed to prevent the marriage.

The procession following the King and the Queen Mother on their way to the bishop's palace, where the Princess had spent the night, surpassed the wildest bounds of the imagination in its splendor. For once Catherine de Medici had decided not to wear mourning for her husband and was wearing her finest diamonds.

The King's brother was wearing a yellow satin coat decorated with silver and pearl embroidery, while the King himself was dressed up as the sun.

"Have you seen Marguerite?" asked Gilone.

Victoire leaned out of the window. "No. But here she comes, out of the bishop's palace. Her golden dress is covered by a cloak with a train!"

"How beautiful she is! She puts every other lady in the shade."

"She doesn't look very happy," said Victoire, who could not help thinking how she herself would look in a similar situation if her mother succeeded in her aims. She had met Monsieur de Mèrande four or five times again, and still could not bring herself to like him. Fortunately she had found support from her uncle, who, although never openly criticizing a marriage that was not at all to his taste—which would have been asking for trouble from his strong-willed sister-in-law —contrived to slip in an unflattering remark or two about the young man.

Quickly Victoire turned her thoughts from skinny Louis de Mèrande to the much more interesting spectacle that was about to take place. A special ceremony had had to be devised for this interdenominational marriage, for which no precedents existed. After much weighing of the pros and cons, it had been decided that Henri de Navarre would not enter Notre Dame and that the Duc d'Anjou would take his place during the service. It was rumored, indeed stated for a fact, that he had already done so on other occasions of a rather different nature.

Afterward, the nuptial blessing was given on a dais in front of the cathedral. The future Queen of Navarre, stony-faced, did not even deign to say "I will" as required by the ceremony, and the Cardinal presiding over the ceremony had to make do without it.

"From now on, we shall be at peace," said the Comtesse de Montmaur, who had returned on the night of Triboulet's death.

"Do you really think so?" asked Anselme skeptically. "Listen to the crowd. They're already muttering discontentedly."

The Gascons of Henri de Navarre were massed in front of the church and were jeering exultantly at the Catholics as they came out. Their reaction was immediate.

"You'll see, we'll force you to enter the church!" the Catholics shouted.

There were sharp exchanges of insults. The two sides jostled each other, and isolated brawls broke out.

"This is only the beginning," predicted Anselme.

"You are always exaggerating," said his sister-in-law. "It's just the blustering horseplay of people who have had too much to drink."

Anselme did not answer.

That evening there was a dinner, a ball, and a play. Victoire watched Gilone as she eagerly prepared herself and tried to make up her mind which of the many dresses she now possessed would be suitable for the occasion.

Victoire had never hinted to Gilone that she suspected a possible betrayal. But Gilone no longer played the role of a confidante, caught up as she was in a whirlwind of merrymaking, love affairs, and intrigue.

Victoire was now determined to find out the truth at all costs. In a week's time the marriage festivities would draw to a close. Her mother had warned her that she would have to go back to Montmaur if she refused to accept Monsieur de Mèrande, and remain there until she changed her mind.

Gilone would, of course, stay at Court. Her aunt had lost interest in the girl: she was a wanton, had gone over to the Catholics' side, and was bound to come to an unsavory end. Gilone, who had now found employment for herself, simply laughed off the Comtesse's rebukes.

Before they were separated Victoire wanted to clear the matter up, because she did not want to harbor a tarnished memory of the girl with whom she had shared all the joys and sorrows of adolescence. Taking advantage of the fact that Hèloïse had left the room to go and do the Comtesse's hair, she put the question straight to Gilone. "Do you remember my adventures in the storeroom, and the plot to massacre the Protestants?"

Gilone, who had been peering at herself in the looking glass and wondering whether she had put on enough rouge, was taken aback by the seriousness of her cousin's tone. She turned around. "Oh, yes . . . So you see now that nothing has happened. You must have imagined it all—unless, of course, it was a dream!"

"I'm quite positive about what I overheard. And the Queen of Navarre died very soon after. She was poisoned."

"That's what they say."

"Aren't you struck by the coincidence? The very day after I told you what I had discovered, a person you knew I was going to tell all about it suddenly died."

"I can't see what you're driving at," said Gilone casually.

"I think you can if you really try," said her cousin slowly.

"Come now, what are you accusing me of? Passing your secrets on to Catherine?"

"Precisely."

Gilone burst out laughing. "Poor Victoire! You're so naive. Do you think Her Majesty would have taken the trouble to receive an unknown little Protestant girl from the provinces and listen to her blatherings?"

"You're one of her maids of honor."

"I wasn't at the time. Anyway, Alix de Chabrière screamed with laughter when I told her what you suspected. What, the Queen was going to wipe out half the Court? And her son-in-law, too, perhaps? What nonsense!"

"Ah, so you told Mademoiselle de Chabrière . . ."

Gilone left and Victoire returned listlessly to the task of getting ready for the evening. Yet at dinner she would see Guillaume de Louvencourt. Every evening she put herself to sleep thinking of him; the memory of the moment when he took her into his arms and kissed her filled her with a strange languishing feeling —an expectancy that was both delightful and pointless. For what indeed could she expect? Within a week she would have lost him forever. She knew that she would never love anyone else.

There was a knock on the door.

"Are you ready, Victoire?"

"Yes, Uncle. Just give me a minute."

"How gorgeous you're looking this evening! You'll cause a sensation," he said, smiling.

"I've already worn this dress several times."

"The number of clothes you have is of no importance. Real elegance comes from knowing *how* to wear them."

The Comte de Montmaur had aged a great deal since arriving at the Louvre. The hurly-burly of life there—the atmosphere of insecurity, the constant late nights, the carousing—had worn him down, and all he wanted to do was to get back to the peace and quiet of his tower and his stars.

When he had been told that Triboulet had died, he had insisted on escorting his niece everywhere so as to be able to watch over her to the best of his ability.

"Uncle Anselme, I need your help. Couldn't you ask Cassitère to concoct a philter which would keep Monsieur de Mèrande away from me?"

"No, my child," he answered with a wistful smile. "Our friend doesn't make that sort of potion. But don't worry, soon you won't be forced to marry the man."

"Really?" exclaimed Victoire hopefully.

Anselme sighed; he was sure his sister-in-law's days were numbered. Although she liked to pretend otherwise, she was far from well.

The dinner was by far the most sumptuous Victoire had attended since her arrival at Court. The Florentine cooks, masters of their art, had worked all through the night and during the day, and the long tables glittered with vermeil dishes that reflected the light from heavy silver candlesticks decorated with garlands of flowers.

At the high table, destined for the bride, bridegroom, and royal family, the whiteness of the damask cloth was beautifully set off by the bluish color of Anselme de Montmaur's glasses.

"Your goblets are superb," said Victoire. "Everyone is wondering where they came from."

"They don't look at all bad," he admitted, flattered that the Queen had asked for them to be brought out for such a grand occasion.

Victoire was so engrossed by the spectacle that she did not notice that the man she was so eagerly awaiting had arrived. He suddenly stepped before her and bowed. Unable to stifle her joy, she cried, "Guillaume! Uncle Anselme, may I introduce the Comte de Louvencourt?"

"Didn't I see you at the Pré aux Clercs?"

"You have a good memory, sir. That was about two months ago. I wounded Adrien d'Etivey."

"Has he recovered?" asked Victoire.

"Yes, I'm afraid he has. You can see him over there, standing by the door with Henri de Guise."

She turned slightly and saw Monsieur d'Etivey gazing darkly at them like a wild animal on the lookout for its prey. His face bore an expression of such malevolence that she shuddered.

"It seems to me that he is vowing us eternal hatred," said Victoire with alarm in her voice.

Guillaume shrugged. "He's waiting to get his revenge. Next time I won't let him off so easily."

Victoire and Guillaume sat next to each other at dinner, paying little attention to their neighbors.

"When I come to think of it, I know nothing about you," said Victoire.

Guillaume smiled. "What do you want to know?"

"Everything!"

"Such curiosity! Well, I'll do my best to satisfy it. Perhaps I should begin with my parents. My father lost his wife when I was a child. The circumstances were rather strange. One evening my mother went boating on a lake near the castle, a habit with her every evening in summer: she claimed that the sight of the water soothed her. That night she disappeared. The boat was found, but there was no leak in it . . . A little later her body was found floating among some reeds, with a cord tied tightly around her neck."

"Oh, how awful!" cried Victoire.

"Did she have enemies?" Guillaume went on. "I really don't know. I was only a child at the time. But since then I have had my suspicions."

As though wishing to change the subject, Guillaume showed Victoire his left hand, which bore a ring engraved with a mythical animal—a goat with a fish's tail.

"What a strange beast."

"It's the sign of Capricorn," he explained. "My mother gave it to me on my fifth birthday, a few days before her death. It was as though she had a premonition and could not wait any longer before giving away the ring. My father scolded her for making such an expensive gift to such a young child who, on top of everything, kept on losing things."

"But you never lost it."

"No," said Guillaume pensively. "As she put it on my finger my mother told me that this animal would give me access to a hidden treasure. When I asked her to tell me more, she admitted that all she knew was that. It was a legend that was handed down by each generation of the family."

"What if it were true?" said Victoire, who was fascinated by the story. "Perhaps you will discover the treasure one day."

The dinner was followed by a fireworks display on the other side of the Seine. It promised to be magnificent.

While the final preparations were made for the display, many of the guests walked out into the Tuileries gardens to get some fresh air after what had been a long, hot, and tiring day.

Guillaume led Victoire to a deserted gallery. She was beginning to find Anselme's custodianship rather a nuisance, although animated by the best intentions, and was glad to be able to slip away when he was not looking.

As soon as Guillaume drew her close to him in the darkness she was oblivious to everything except the contact of his warm, gentle lips against hers and the strength of his arms as they clasped her waist. After a while, he held her at arm's length. Victoire could see his glowing eyes fill with almost uncontrollable desire, and she felt a strange stirring within her.

"I would like you to be mine," he said quietly.

Victoire knew she could not resist: she was ready to belong to him, forever if he wished.

"If only I could love you . . . " he added with a sigh.

Again he clasped her, this time as though in a fury. But she no longer responded fully to his embrace, for she was wondering what he had meant by his remark.

It was she who first heard the sound of footsteps and some whispering. Breaking away, she warned, "There are some people coming."

Two masked figures, who had been hiding up to then at the end of the gallery, began to approach them. Their prancing gait and laughter seemed threatening, though Victoire reasoned there should be nothing to fear.

They came up and stood motionless a few feet from

Guillaume and Victoire, who had backed against the wall. The inky darkness obscured the features of the men, despite their closeness. The men were somehow terrifying, and the atmosphere became unbearably tense. One suddenly drew a rapier while the second began to tear at Victoire's dress with a knife. Paralyzed with fear, Victoire hardly dared to struggle. The first thrust through Guillaume's doublet at the very spot where he had been wounded in his duel with Monsieur d'Etivey. His skin had hardly had time to heal, and the pain was intense. Guillaume reacted violently: he pushed Victoire behind him and drew his sword.

"Back or I'll kill you!" he snarled fiercely.

Surrounded, with their backs to the wall, Victoire began to scream as loudly as she could. She had no intention of letting herself be slaughtered. Perhaps somebody would hear her and come to their aid. The men stopped in their tracks, and with a flourish of his sword Guillaume stripped his attacker of the rapier and the other of his blade. Disarmed, and worried by Victoire's calls for help, they wavered a moment. Guillaume took this opportunity to sink his sword into his assailant's arm, drawing abundant blood. The man blurted out an obscene oath. With amazement Guillaume recognized the voice of the man he hated so much.

"So, Monsieur d'Etivey, it would seem you need to disguise yourself and have the help of a henchman before you try to kill me! I must congratulate you on your courage!"

Guillaume furiously tore the red mask from the second man's face. Once unmasked, Henri d'Anjou and his accomplice dashed away down the gallery.

"You'll pay for this!" he shouted.

Guillaume was put out for a moment, then he ran after them. This time he would kill Adrien d'Etivey, and damn the consequences.

Before he was able to catch up to them, they had

vanished behind a curtain; then a door slammed. Cheated of his quarry, Guillaume came back to Victoire, who, with trembling hands, was trying to rearrange her torn dress.

"I was so afraid!" she exclaimed. "How on earth could the King's brother get mixed up in such an affair? I was sure our last hour had come."

"It may well have been if you hadn't shouted for help," said Guillaume pensively.

"Monsieur d'Etivey is out to kill you."

"I'll kill him first."

Blood was spurting onto Guillaume's doublet.

"We shan't be able to attend the fireworks display dressed like this," remarked Victoire dejectedly. "And you must have your wound taken care of!"

They separated as Guillaume left to have his injury bound and Victoire returned to her room to change.

While Victoire was hurriedly changing her dress, she suddenly noticed that the door of her bedroom was ajar. Yet she was sure she had closed it.

In her haste to get back to Guillaume, she had lit only a single candle and could hardly see herself in the small looking glass. Only partially clothed, she had the unpleasant feeling that she was being watched. She wondered anxiously whether Adrien d'Etivey might not be lying in wait for her, hoping to get at Guillaume through her. He had looked at her with such hatred at the dinner.

She felt she had to make sure one way or the other.

Victoire was overcome with terror when she heard a faint sound. The memory of poor Triboulet made her cautious. She managed to recover some of her composure and began to think rapidly as she finished dressing. It would obviously be a mistake to rush out into the gallery without a weapon. Someone might be waiting for her. She looked round the bedroom for an object with which to defend herself. Her uncle's dagger was inaccessible in the next room, so she picked up a heavy silver candlestick instead.

Blowing out the candle, Victoire remained motionless for a minute or two and then walked silently over to the door. Very slowly, it began to open. Victoire flattened herself against the wall so as not to be seen, but was certain that the loud beating of her heart could be heard.

A leather-sandaled foot edged cautiously into the room. It was followed by a man wearing a dark robe tied about the waist with a white cord. Her nightmare had come true.

The monk silently walked toward the bed where he thought she was sleeping. Before flinging himself against the pillow, he hissed, "I'm going to possess you, you filthy little heretic, then I'll kill you. All the Protestants will die. But first I'll have you and make you scream with desire!"

Horror-stricken, Victoire dropped the candlestick with a clang onto the wooden floor. The monk sprang up. In a flash, Victoire ran out into the corridor, slamming the door behind her, and rushed downstairs to Guillaume, who, bandaged, was pacing up and down waiting for her.

"You're in a fine state! What's the matter?"

"Father Izard," Victoire managed to gasp, even though she was still paralyzed with fear. "He came into my room. He wanted to rape and kill me. Do you think we'll be safe here?"

"Of course, no one would dare try anything with such a crowd around," he reassured her. "Are you sure it was Izard?"

"Absolutely."

"Who could have sent him?"

"Maybe he was acting on his own."

The fireworks were beginning, and the couple ran outside. Massed on either side of the Seine, the huge crowd roared with excitement and amazement each time the sky lit up with a blaze of gold, azure, or ruby.

Caught up by the beauty and novelty of the extraordinary display, and comforted by Guillaume's strong hand clasping hers, Victoire began to calm down a little. She would never dare go back to her room alone.

A huge ball of fire then rose into the air and exploded into a thousand stars, which hovered a moment before falling into the Seine.

Victoire was jostled and lost contact with Guillaume. Two drunkards started fighting beside her. All of a sudden she felt a sharp instrument being pushed into her back. She turned with a cry of pain. All she could see were rows of faces looking up at the sky, which had just lit up with more fireworks.

"Guillaume!"

He thrust his way through a group of people who had boxed him in and cut him off from Victoire. He immediately saw that there was blood seeping through her flimsy gown and making a stain that spread with every second.

"You've been wounded!" he exclaimed, cursing his own carelessness.

"I think so," mumbled Victoire, who could feel the ground giving way under her feet as she lost consciousness.

Chapter IX

Sunlight was flooding the room when Victoire opened her eyes. Her mother, sitting next to the bed, quietly dropped her needlework and quickly leaned forward. "How do you feel?"

"My back hurts," Victoire groaned.

"Don't worry, my dear, it's not a deep cut."

"The monk . . ."

"Was it a monk who stabbed you?" asked the Comtesse with surprise.

"No. I don't think so. I can't remember."

"Rest now. The doctor will be back later."

Victoire tried to fall back to sleep, but in her half-awake state she kept having terrible visions of Father Izard dancing diabolically with the two disguised men.

Very far away, she could barely hear someone saying, "I'm entirely to blame. I should never have let her out of my sight for a moment."

"It's not your fault in the least. She must have been taken for someone else."

Anselme was not so sure. After all, there had been a previous attempt to murder his niece. But he decided against telling his sister-in-law what he suspected. Her nerves had already been sufficiently tried when, in the middle of the night, Monsieur de Louvencourt's man-servant had burst in and laid her unconscious, blood-covered daughter on the bed. Monsieur de Louvencourt had knelt down beside Victoire, trying to bring her to by splashing water on her face.

A little later, Victoire reawoke.

"I'm feeling better," she murmured, trying to sit up. She gave a little cry as she suddenly felt a sharp jab of pain.

"You mustn't move," said Héloïse, rushing to her side. "There now, lie down . . ."

"What a fright you gave me, my child," said Anselme, who had taken over the watch so that Madame de Montmaur could take a nap after an exhausting night.

"I'm hungry and thirsty."

The old man smiled. "Well, that means you're well on the way to recovery."

He helped her to sit up, propped her up with pillows, and brought her a plate of cold meat. His hands shook nervously. "Eat well, you must get your strength back." He dared not tell her that she had lost a lot of blood.

After her meal, Victoire wanted to tell her uncle exactly what had happened. "You don't know the whole story."

She then proceeded to describe the events of the previous evening in detail.

"I don't understand," pondered Anselme.

"The first attack was not intended for me. And when the second one failed, he had another try."

"Who? The same person that killed Triboulet?"

"I don't know for certain." She seemed to have three enemies now: the Queen Mother, Father Izard, and Monsieur d'Etivey. A formidable trio for a seventeen-year-old girl . . .

The next morning the doctor gave permission to get up and walk round the room. "Careful now, no abrupt movements," he told Victoire. "Your wound has not healed yet."

He changed the dressing and applied a herbal plaster. "Another ten days' rest, and you'll be able to ride again," he said encouragingly. "But not six hours at a time."

Guillaume came to visit her that afternoon. Boris had already been sent four times since the incident to find out how she was getting on. Victoire was puzzled by such obvious signs of interest: why, then, could he not love her?

The Comtesse hardly approved of the young Catholic, particularly because Victoire, who had given Monsieur de Mèrande such short shrift, was clearly attracted to him. But since Guillaume had saved her daughter's life, it was difficult to forbid him from seeing her.

Her brother-in-law, on the other hand, was absolutely delighted at the way things were turning out: if ever he were to die, Victoire would have someone to look after her.

"In two or three days," Victoire told Guillaume, "I'll be allowed to go outdoors. Will you come with me to the Tuileries?"

"Why, of course, I should be delighted to. By the way, I've brought you a present, if one can call it that. I thought it might come in useful. In any case, I'll feel better knowing you have it with you when I'm not around."

He handed her a small dagger with a finely engraved handle, in a blue leather sheath.

"It's beautiful," exclaimed Victoire. "I was wondering how I was going to get a weapon."

"You're going to have to learn how to use it. Boris, who is expert in such matters, will give you a few lessons once you're better. I hope it will never be necessary, but I don't want you to have any qualms about using it."

"Rest assured of that," said Victoire resolutely.

It hardly took any effort of imagination on her part at all to see herself plunging the sharp blade into Father

Izard's heart. "It's so awfully nice of you to show such concern for me."

By way of an answer, he took her hand in his and gently stroked her slender wrist. The mere touch of his fingers on her skin gave Victoire an almost uncontrollable urge to throw herself into his arms. Guillaume immediately sensed her feelings, and smiled down at her with affection and desire. "Soon," he said softly. "As soon as you're well."

Contrary to expectations, relations between Catholics and Protestants improved little following the royal marriage. The King himself was worried and had expressed his fears to the Admiral: might not the Huguenots, who were becoming increasingly sure of themselves, make trouble?

As a precaution, His Majesty called the archers of his own guard to Paris. News of their arrival spread quickly. This greatly alarmed the governor of Paris whose task it was to keep the peace. The governor preferred to leave the capital he was supposed to be guarding rather than be forced to make some impossible decisions. His departure left the city open to anarchy.

Even so, the wedding celebrations continued. The previous day, August 21, Victoire had bitterly regretted she was not yet strong enough to attend the tournament organized by the Duc d'Anjou on the theme of Turks and Amazons. She was looking forward to telling Guillaume all about it.

Victoire was thinking about him, and what promised to soon take place between them, when Anselme de Montmaur burst into her room without knocking on the door. His face was pale and drawn. He couldn't speak at first.

"Uncle! What's the matter?" she exclaimed, leaping out of bed and running over to him.

"It's started . . ." he mumbled.

Victoire immediately understood, and felt reassuringly for the dagger that she wore under her gown next to her thigh. "So soon?"

"The Admiral was wounded while he was walking along Rue des Poulies."

"Seriously?"

"If he hadn't bent down just as the shot was fired, his fate would have been sealed."

"Oh my God!"

"One bullet went into his elbow, and the other severed his right index finger. But he survived. Members of his retinue immediately rushed into the house where the shots came from. All they found was a musket by a window. The assassin had disappeared."

"It had been carefully planned, then."

"The Admiral was brought home covered with blood. A doctor is at his bedside."

"That's their second victim, after the Queen of Navarre. I wonder who's next on the list . . ."

"But he's not dead," Anselme pointed out. "The King's surgeon managed to remove the bullet."

"Have you seen him?"

"I've just come from there. As soon as I heard the news I went straight to see him."

"Who does he suspect?"

"The Guises."

When her uncle left, Victoire mulled over the recent events in her mind. This attempted murder was bound to be followed by reprisals from the Protestants, which in turn would spur the Catholics into action. Events would then proceed inexorably. But who had first triggered them off? Was it really the Guises, on their own initiative? Or had they simply been manipulated?

Victoire decided that she felt well enough to go and try to pick up some news in the great gallery. It was thronged with courtiers, who were excitedly discussing the event.

After mingling with several groups, she learned that

the Court had paid an elaborately ceremonial visit to the victim.

The King was furious, it was said, and had pledged in front of witnesses to avenge the outrage and to mete out punishment on its perpetrators. Coligny had apparently replied by saying that they would probably be quite easy to find.

A suggestion was made, with the King's consent, that the Admiral be moved to the Louvre for his own safety. But the doctors were opposed to the idea. The patient was, for the moment, in no condition to be moved. The houses near Rue de Béthizy, where Coligny lived, were nevertheless commandeered and handed over to Protestants.

Feelings were running high, and terrifying rumors were circulating. People were weighing the probabilities of a Protestant attack on the Guises—stones had already been thrown through windows of the Hôtel de Guise.

And passions moreover were inflamed by the sweltering August heat.

Chapter X

*G*uillaume looked deeply worried. His darkly handsome features were pale and drawn-looking as if he had not slept all night.

"Last night I was out drinking with some courtiers at an inn. The one subject of conversation was the attempt on the Admiral's life."

"It's only a question of time now," said Victoire.

"Yes, I fear so. Do you know what they were saying? That the killer was none other than the King's hired assassin."

"Or the Queen's."

"True. She used him once before to try and get rid of Coligny."

"He's not very efficient for a paid killer," said Victoire with a smile. "Or else the Admiral is very lucky."

Victoire and Guillaume fell silent a moment. Dusk crept over the Tuileries gardens, which Catherine de Medici had turned into a veritable Garden of Eden with roses, irises, mignonettes, and countless flowers from Italy. After the heat of the day, they gave off a delectable odor, perfuming the evening air.

"Twice on our way back to the Louvre," Guillaume went on, "we were attacked by gangs of ruffians. We only just gained the upper hand. Paris is so full of cutthroats you can no longer venture into its streets alone."

Victoire shuddered. "Paris frightens me. I've the feeling we're gradually being hemmed in by a host of dangers. If we're pushed one step further, we'll be over the precipice and lost forever . . . I always carry the dagger you gave me. This morning Boris taught me how to throw it into a door from nine feet away. He also showed me where to stab in a hand-to-hand struggle."

Victoire had found a friend in the Mongol. Although at first she had been frightened by him, she soon realized how utterly devoted he was to Guillaume and to his master's friends. Now that he had taken Victoire under his wing, she felt reassured whenever she saw Boris's large but graceful figure nearby.

It was her first outing since she had been stabbed. She no longer felt any pain, but the fresh air made her feel giddy.

Night had fallen and Guillaume had his arm about Victoire's waist.

"I expect all this walking has tired you. Let's rest a while," he suggested.

They sat down on the grass behind some shrubbery, away from prying eyes. The sound of laughter and animated conversation came from other people in the gardens. A man was singing in a gentle, melancholy voice and accompanying himself on the lute.

"Victoire . . ." Guillaume's sparkling blue eyes caressed her softly.

He lay down beside her. As she felt the delectable contact of his lips on her shoulders and in the hollow of her throat, Victoire was overcome by new sensations. Thrilling to the caresses of Guillaume's hands, which were now moving more purposefully over her body, she forgot where she was, and became quite oblivious to the people who were walking nearby. The nervousness she had felt as she realized that this time Guillaume was going to possess her gradually subsided. All that remained was a deep sensation of pleasure as his body weighed down on hers ever more insistently, as his eyes burned with uncontrollable desire, as his lips brushed her ears and he murmured, "You are so beautiful, Victoire. I could go on kissing such soft skin forever and ever."

Victoire's breast had slipped out of her bodice and was quickly cupped by a warm, strong, attentive hand. Guillaume had taken off his doublet and unbuttoned his shirt. Repeatedly he rubbed his darkly haired chest against her. How was it possible, wondered Victoire, to feel such a delicious, such an insidious pleasure that it spread through every fiber of her being? But she soon realized it was nothing compared to the ecstasy she felt as the young man slipped his hand under her gown and ran his fingers up her firm rounded thighs.

"Let me have you . . ."

It was both a request and an order. Quite unable to

resist the languishment that had overtaken her whole body, Victoire obeyed. She could hear Guillaume's breathing quicken; then, as he penetrated her, she stifled a cry of pain.

She felt one sharp pang, then let her body move to a rhythm imposed by Guillaume. As they reached a climax she felt as if she were dying in his arms.

As she lay in the grass with her head on Guillaume's chest, Victoire felt wonderfully happy and found herself taking a more indulgent view of Gilone's hedonist approach to life, though she still could not comprehend her promiscuity: Victoire could not imagine giving herself to anyone in the world but Guillaume.

Smoothly Guillaume's hand gently stroked her shoulder. She was more deeply moved by this sign of his affection. Héloïse, with her sound common sense and her experience of life, had taught Victoire more than the Comtesse de Montmaur's rigid principles. Many times she had told Victoire that once men got what they wanted they lost interest in their conquests. Perhaps Héloïse had just been unlucky . . .

Suddenly Victoire's feeling of perfect bliss was spoiled by the realization that he had not once told her he loved her. The other day, in the gallery, he had told her he could not. Yet *she* loved him with all her heart, though she had not dared be the first to confess it.

"Guillaume . . ."

He opened his eyes and smiled tenderly.

"You're wonderful, Victoire."

Again he covered her face with gentle little kisses. "You were made to be loved," he went on. "I'm so happy I was the first to teach you what love can be like."

Victoire remained thoughtful for a moment.

"Guillaume, do you love me?"

The moment she saw his face stiffen, she wished she had never asked. It might have been better to wait.

"No," he said sadly and gently. "And it would be dishonest of me to say I did. But I do feel a tremendous affection for you."

"It's not the same thing," Victoire murmured, tears filling her eyes.

"Let me try to explain, my darling Victoire. After all, you have a right to know. I don't want you to remain under any illusions."

They sat up, leaning against a tree trunk. A sparrow flitted past them and perched on a branch above their heads.

"When I was sixteen," Guillaume continued, "I fell in love with a girl of my age, Marie, in Lorraine. She was beautiful—dark auburn hair with copper glints, and a skin so white and so delicate she flushed at the slightest emotion. She was always laughing, though she could be serious, too, and would look at me with her large green eyes when I spoke to her. Marie . . . what a sweet, good, joyous person . . . I loved her to distraction, and she felt the same. For more than a year we lived just for one another, spending all our time in the woods and fields, gathering wild strawberries in summer, blackberries in autumn, and chestnuts in winter. Then one day she realized she was pregnant."

What if that happened to me, Victoire thought with shock for the first time.

"Of course I wanted to marry her, though we were too young. My father was not very pleased at the prospect of such a marriage, but he was too much of a gentleman to express his misgivings. When I confessed what I had done, he told me, 'We must make amends. I shall take Marie into my house as though she were my own daughter, since you love her. I loved your mother so much that life has lost all meaning for me since her death. I pray your happiness will last longer than mine.'"

"How lucky you are to have a father like that," said Victoire. She wondered whether her own father would have behaved like that if he had survived. Possibly. But she could not expect her mother to show such understanding. How furious she would be when she learned that her daughter had a lover, and a Catholic as well.

"Yes," said Guillaume with a sigh. "Unfortunately, Marie's father didn't see things the same way. As you know, we Louvencourts are far from wealthy; and such a marriage, although it would have been a most honorable one, did not seem to him to be advantageous enough for his only daughter—several wealthy suitors had already been attracted by her beauty and charm. Marie didn't dare tell him she was pregnant, and when a marriage had already been arranged with another man and the preparations were well under way, she poisoned herself wtih venomous mushrooms."

"The poor girl," said Victoire, who found herself moved by the fate of Marie, a girl her own age.

"So you see why it's impossible for me to love any girl," said Guillaume sadly. "I was responsible for Marie's death. How could I ever forget that?"

Strangely enough, Guillaume's story only made Victoire feel all the more strongly attached to him. She decided that somehow she would get him to forget his adolescent love affair and its tragic outcome. Although aware of how hard it might prove, she was certain she could contend with the memory of the dead woman and emerge the victor. All she needed was patience and time.

"Thank you for confiding in me," she said finally, gazing into his eyes.

He turned toward her and caressed her blonde hair, pulling out a few blades of grass.

"Usually, when I take a fancy to a girl, I seduce her, then drop her. I suppose that sounds cruel, but that's the way it's been. I have no feelings for her other than a fleeting moment of desire. It's different with you. I esteem your character and your spirit, and I think of you as a friend and not as a quarry, though I must say I do desire you most terribly . . . " he added with a smile.

For the moment, Victoire would have to be satisfied with that.

The sound of voices approaching made Victoire and Guillaume withdraw a little further into the thicket. With her hair disheveled and her clothes awry, it would be all too obvious how they had been spending the evening. And if ever the strollers belonged to the late Queen of Navarre's suite, it would quickly reach the Comtesse de Montmaur's ears that her daughter fancied an enemy of the Church.

The moon was so bright it was possible to see almost as clearly as during the daytime. The young couple could not help hearing what was being said a few feet away from them.

"It'll have to be tonight or never . . ."

"Are you sure, Madame, that all the necessary arrangements have been made?"

"Yes. I am sure you realize the biggest problem is getting the King's consent."

"Try to see who they are," whispered Victoire anxiously. Surely that Florentine accent was the Queen's?

Guillaume crept stealthily between the shrubs, making very certain not to give himself away. The conversation was between two women, who were sitting on a bench, a young man striding agitatedly up and down in front of them, and another man. He recognized the Duc d'Anjou, his mother, the Duchesse de Guise, and another man.

"He bungled the job," said the Duchesse de Guise. "The Admiral will be on his guard now, and a much more difficult man to get."

There was a sardonic, sinister chuckle.

"Don't worry. By dawn he'll be dead."

Victoire wondered desperately how they could warn

the intended victim. It was almost midnight. Would she even be able to get out of the Louvre?

"Guillaume," she whispered into his ear, "we can't let them get away with assassination."

He gestured to her to wait and hear the rest of their conversation. In any case, they could not move without revealing their presence.

"How will the Parisians react?"

"Yes, tell us what the mood was like in the capital earlier today."

"I went out in a closed carriage, with no coat of arms," said the Duc d'Anjou. "I drove along the Rue Saint-Honoré and imprudently put my head out of the window. I was recognized by some people in the street . . ."

"Then what?" Catherine de Medici asked eagerly.

" 'Jarnac,' 'Moncontour,' they yelled."

"Battle cries! Quiet! I hear someone."

Some hurried footsteps came to a halt. A breathless voice could be heard.

"Madame . . ."

"Monsieur! What news do you bring us?"

"Bad, Madame, very bad! The heretics are plotting to avenge the attack on Admiral de Coligny. They intend to kill . . ."

The messenger broke off, not daring to end his sentence.

"Who, pray?" asked the Queen quietly.

"Your Majesty . . . and even the King of Navarre."

"Well, now," said Catherine de Medici, who seemed curiously pleased at the news. "Doesn't that confirm our fears? What do you think?"

"Don't let's shilly-shally anymore!" exclaimed Henri d'Anjou, whose nerves were at breaking point. "They've all got to be killed!"

"That's what we've got to convince your brother."

"He won't hear of it!"

"If we succeed in bringing him over to our thinking," the Queen went on, "what should the signal be?"

"The bells of Saint-Germain-l'Auxerrois Church."

Once the conspirators had gone, Guillaume and Victoire kept still for some time before they dared move. Victoire was horror-stricken.

"So Cassitère's predictions are coming true . . ." she murmured with a tremble in her voice.

"Are you referring to the magician?" asked Guillaume. "He has a high reputation. What did he tell you?"

"Rivers of blood . . . In the Louvre and in Paris."

"In the Louvre?" exclaimed Guillaume. "Are you quite sure?"

She nodded. She could still hear his words issuing from a cloud of steam as though from another world.

Guillaume was deeply perplexed. How could a plot to massacre the Protestants, and in particular the Admiral, get the King's consent? How could the King agree to the murder of Protestants who were especially close to him? They were his partners at tennis, they hunted with him, they even accompanied him on those nightly outings when he, Charles IX, delighted in donning a mask and scaring the townsfolk.

"It's not sure yet," said Guillaume, who wanted to be reassuring. "You heard what they said. It all depends on the King."

"His mother will find the right arguments to prevail on him." In Victoire's eyes, Catherine de Medici had turned into a bloodthirsty and vengeful monster. How could the weak, irresolute, and fickle King stand up to someone with far greater authority?

"Why don't we go and see Cassitère?" suggested Guillaume. "He'll know if their plans are going to be put into action tonight. If so, he'll be in a better position than we to warn some of your co-religionists."

Suddenly Victoire realized that circumstances had turned her lover into an enemy. He belonged to the party that had murdered so many Huguenots, including her father. Ought she to trust him merely because of what had occurred between them? Her qualms sent a shiver running down her back, and she realized with a dreadful sinking feeling that they were doomed to be separated. It was her duty to try to save those of her own faith, and to reject the protection of a Catholic, even one whom she loved. Her mind was made up.

"Guillaume, we must part," she said, rising to her feet. "We belong to different faiths. It's not right that I should force you to share the fate of the Protestants."

Guillaume burst out laughing and took her into his arms. "Do you imagine I'd leave you all alone in the lion's den? Anyway, without me you wouldn't even be able to get past the palace gates."

She had to admit he was right.

"Let's not waste any time," he said, leading her through the gardens. "They haven't rung the bell yet, so the road should still be clear."

Masked and swathed in a dark cloak, Victoire climbed into the saddle behind Guillaume. The silent figure of Boris appeared out of the night.

"Where are you going at such a late hour, sir? It's no night to be abroad, especially with a young lady."

"We have to visit the magician Cassitère."

"I shall come with you," Boris decreed. "Wait a moment while I take a few precautions."

The Mongol's "precautions" consisted of a pistol and a long dagger with a triangular tip.

Guillaume gave the de Louvencourt name to the archers who were on duty, and the three of them were let through.

The air in the city was oppressive and stifling, as though a storm were about to break. The chimes of midnight rang out from the Hôtel de Guise; although a familiar sound to Victoire's ears, that evening they seemed sinister.

"Already," she said under her breath.

They could proceed only at walking pace through

the narrow streets, which were littered with barrels, bundles of wood, and rat-infested garbage. A dozen or so people were standing at a crossroads, watching a brawl and egging both sides on.

"It's not far now," said Victoire, who had been acting as a guide through the labyrinth of streets. "Turn right, and then left down a cul-de-sac."

The moon had disappeared behind a cloud, and it was pitch dark.

"This looks very much like a thieves' alley," said Boris. "Let me go first." He moved cautiously down between the houses, pistol in hand.

Guillaume had drawn his sword and was ready for anything. A whistle told them there was nothing to fear. Victoire dismounted and knocked several times on the seer's door before a peephole was opened a few inches.

"Who's there?"

She recognized the magician's servant. "It's Mademoiselle de Montmaur. I must see your master urgently."

The door opened a little to let her through.

"Who are they?" asked the servant suspiciously.

"Friends of mine."

Reluctantly the two men were let in and the heavy, iron-studded oak door closed behind them.

"You are safe here," whispered Guillaume.

She was, but what about her mother, Uncle Anselme, Gilone, and Héloïse? With a shock, she realized she had virtually forgotten about them.

Cassitère appeared, his worried face even paler than usual. "I know what you have come to ask me. The answer is yes. Take refuge here. No one will dare attack my house." He smiled. "They'd be afraid I might cast a spell on them."

"But what about my family?"

"Stay here," said Guillaume. "I'll go and fetch them with Boris. We'll bring them all back here."

"But my mother will never go with you," said Victoire. "I'm coming with you."

"I don't think it's wise, Victoire," said Guillaume hesitantly.

"It's the only way."

Chapter XI

Time was running short, and it would take almost another hour to get back to the Louvre. Every moment meant the de Montmaur family was in increasing danger. Victoire could only feel a terrible sense of guilt at having fled before making sure everyone close to her was safe.

With Boris leading the way, Guillaume and Victoire rode slowly, forced to check their speed because of the winding and crooked streets.

The air reeked from the heavy smell of decaying refuse, and stray pigs foraging through garbage further hindered their way.

A little farther on, a group of scrawny tomcats shattered the silence of the sultry night with piercing cries. They were caterwauling before a plump female in heat, each trying to get to her first.

Distracted, they did not hear the rasp of swords being drawn from scabbards. Before they realized what was happening, they were surrounded and forced to dismount by a dozen masked men.

"Take my purse," said Guillaume, "and let us continue on our way."

Sneering laughter greeted him.

Victoire peered at their attackers and saw from their clothing that they were too well dressed to be common thieves. "They look like gentleman," she whispered to Guillaume.

"Yes, I'm afraid they do."

"This will be a costly delay!"

"If ever we can get away . . ." murmured Guillaume, convinced they had been ambushed.

The three prisoners were led into a small house and through it into a walled garden with trees. They stumbled across the enclosure toward a huge building that loomed in front of them, barely visible in the darkness. Unceremoniously they were pushed through the door.

"Where are you taking us?" demanded Guillaume, not really expecting to get an answer.

"Keep going," said one of the men. "You'll see for yourself."

A spiral staircase led them to the second floor, where they were met by a man dressed completely in black standing in a sparsely furnished room.

"Well, Monsieur de Louvencourt, what do you think of my little caper, eh?"

Exultant at the prospect of being able to taunt his captives, Adrien d'Etivey looked at them pitilessly like a bird of prey.

"What do you want from me?" asked Guillaume contemptuously. "Ransom? Or do you intend to kill me along with Mademoiselle and my manservant?"

"Not immediately. I will wait a few hours," replied d'Etivey. "First, I want to savor your feeling of frustrated rage. I've had enough of your constant interference in my affairs. The Louvencourts—especially you—have given my family nothing but problems. Soon I'll put an end to you forever. It will be even sweeter to watch you agonize over your lovely companion's death. How considerate of you to provide me with this extra bonus."

Guillaume shrugged. "How typical of an Etivey! Just the sort of behavior one expects of someone from your family!"

Monsieur d'Etivey stiffened. "What do you mean?"

"Aren't you murderers from father to son?"

The other man could not help going pale. "I don't see . . ."

"Do you mean your father didn't strangle my mother before drowning her?"

Actually, Guillaume was not at all sure of what he was claiming. But all the evidence he had discovered in his attempt to find his mother's murderer pointed in the general direction of the Etiveys.

"Ah, so you found that out?" said Adrien d'Etivey, seemingly resigning himself to the fact.

Not for a second did Guillaume's enemy even attempt to deny the crime of which his father was being accused. Once again, Guillaume bitterly regretted he had not finished off d'Etivey at the Pré aux Clercs. But he had to seize this opportunity to find out at last the whole truth about the events that had darkened his childhood and adolescence.

"Would you be so kind, sir, to tell me why it was necessary to murder such a good, gentle woman?"

D'Etivey seemed reluctant to answer. "Madame de Louvencourt died because by chance she discovered a secret," he replied in the end.

"What was it?"

"Rest assured, I will gratify your curiosity . . . Just before I kill you!"

"Kill me if you like!" exclaimed Guillaume furiously. "But spare Mademoiselle de Montmaur and Boris."

"I have nothing against them," said their captor with an evil smile. "Unfortunately they had the ill fortune of being with you this evening and could be witnesses against me. No, they will, however, die with you. I trust the company of this charming young lady will help you to pass your last few remaining hours agreeably."

Guillaume clenched his fists with rage. He was totally at the mercy of someone determined to kill him, and he could not even save Victoire. She would die because of him. Her quiet, composed manner belied the terrible despair he could see in her tearless eyes—those wonderful translucent gray eyes that had shone with such passion earlier that evening in the Tuileries. He loved her despite himself.

After disarming Guillaume and Boris, d'Etivey and his henchmen started to withdraw. "Sleep well! We'll meet again soon," he said with a sarcastic smile. "Don't be so foolish as to try to escape. Every door is guarded."

The door closed and a key turned in the lock. Then, as an extra precaution, the bolt was drawn.

"We're in a fine fix," said Boris in a pained voice. "I told you it was unwise to go out this evening, sir."

Guillaume was so downcast he did not even react.

As for Victoire, her faith in Cassitère was shaken. "Why didn't he warn us?"

"He can't know everything. Anyway, the danger was lying in store for me, not you."

"Surely since I was with you it's the same thing? We've got to escape," she said resolutely. "And quickly. I must get to my family."

The two men turned and looked at her with cynicism.

"How do you think we can do it, Mademoiselle?" asked Boris, leaning out of the window. "We're on the second floor, nearly twenty-five feet from the ground."

"And apart from this locked door, which is probably under guard as well, there's no other way out of this room. Supposing we managed to knock the door down, it's still ten men against two."

"Three," Victoire chipped in. "*I* am still armed."

Abandoning modesty, she raised her skirt and triumphantly drew the dagger from the sheath tied round her thigh.

Guillaume recovered his spirits somewhat when he saw the weapon. "Well, at least we'll be able to fight for our lives."

Victoire, however, was not thinking of fighting, but of escaping and getting back to the Louvre. She too leaned out of the window. There seemed to be two shadowy figures walking in the garden. Somewhere in the distance a dog barked. Then silence fell again. It was a stillness made almost unbearable by the presence of the enemy, whose movements could vaguely be sensed, and whose conversation wafted up from the ground floor.

Their discussion gradually became heated, and the two guards, after a moment's hesitation, decided to leave their posts outside and join their companions.

"They must be drinking or gambling," suggested Boris.

"So much the better. It means they won't be bothering about us. Our escape route is across the roof," said Victoire with conviction. "Since it is the only way out, we will have to use it."

Guillaume could not help running over to the window, straddling the balcony, and hoisting himself up to get a look at the roof. Above their window there was a ledge about a foot wide that ran round the house. It led to the garden wall, some five or six yards away. He and Boris would be able to negotiate it . . . but not Victoire. Disappointedly he climbed back into the room.

"I think Boris and I could get as far as the wall . . ." he said falteringly.

"Then so could I," announced Victoire firmly.

"It's impossible."

"No, it isn't, not if I carry my shoes and take off my skirt." Refusing to listen to further arguments, she promptly began to undress in front of the two startled men. "My petticoat is short and won't hinder my movements."

"Well, I see that you're determined. Are you prepared to jump once we get to the wall?"

"If you can do it, I can, too. Now, let's go." Her voice was as strong as steel.

Guillaume looked at Boris incredulously.

"We've got nothing to lose by taking a look," said the Mongol finally.

His master helped him clamber up onto the ledge, and watched him anxiously as he moved slowly forward, seemingly oblivious to the drop below him. Boris edged along with surprising catlike ease.

He had no trouble in reaching the wall. Then he lay down on his stomach to look over into the next garden.

Guillaume realized from the delighted expression on Boris's face when he returned that the plan was possible, and turned to look at Victoire with a mixture of admiration and perplexity. They hurried out the window.

Guillaume was already on the roof and about to hoist Victoire up with the help of Boris, who was supporting her from below, when there was the sound of heavy footsteps on the stairs.

"They're coming," said Boris.

"Guillaume! Quick! Down!"

Fortunately the guard took his time, and Victoire was able to put her skirt and shoes back on.

The key turned in the lock and a guard peered in, holding a shaking candlestick, clearly drunk. "My orders are to come and see if you're all right," he said, without any trace of irony.

"We're still here," replied Monsieur de Louvencourt.

"So y' are, so y' are. Sorry t' bothe' y', " he said, slurring his words. "But I expec' I won't h've t' again."

He shut the door, swearing as the bolt refused to lock with only one try.

"It's high time we got out of here," said Victoire,

even though she felt apprehensive about the climb that awaited her.

With the help of the two men, Victoire easily got up on the ledge. She could not help glancing down at the ground, far below, which suddenly made her panic. How would she ever be able to move along such a narrow ledge? The escape route was her idea, though, and she would not let Guillaume know of her fear. Concentrating to control herself, she sensed the reassuring presence of Boris behind her. If she slipped and fell, he would never be able to catch her.

"Are you all right, Mademoiselle?" he whispered.

"Yes," she replied, trying to restrain the desire to choke.

The three inched forward without a sound. With her bare feet Victoire could feel the remainder of the heat of the day still stored in the slates on the roof. Boris carried the bundle containing her skirt, stockings, and shoes. Her cotton petticoat only came to her knees and did not hinder her movements.

Finally Guillaume reached the wall. He sat astride it and held out his hand to Victoire. There was a gap between the roof and the wall, nearly four feet lower down.

I'll never manage, moaned Victoire to herself.

But she *had* to: freedom was on the other side.

Sitting on the roof and letting her legs dangle, Victoire succeeded in reaching Guillaume's outstretched hands while Boris held her under the arms. Carefully she was lowered to the top of the wall. She gave a sigh of relief; there was only a short distance to go.

"Well done!" said Guillaume.

Boris quickly joined them.

Victoire could not help laughing when she imagined how her mother and her uncle would react if they could see her straddling a wall, in her petticoat, with bare feet, in the dead of night, with two men!

"Oh, God!" exclaimed Guillaume with dismay. "All is lost. This wall is higher than I anticipated!"

"I could jump down perhaps," suggested Boris.

"Yes, and break your leg. The only thing we can do is go back."

"Oh, no!" cried Victoire, who felt quite unable to repeat her climbing exploit. "We've got to find another way."

All three of them gazed gloomily down into the blackness that meant safety.

"I think I've an idea," said Guillaume suddenly. "I'll hang down from the top of the wall, then Boris can climb down my body and hang from my feet. From there he can drop to the ground, as the distance will have been shortened considerably. Next I'll get back onto the ledge, and by your grabbing onto my hands, Victoire, I can lower you to Boris quite easily. I'll go last, but both of you will be there to break my fall."

The idea was agreed to, and a few moments later Boris had indeed reached the ground quite easily.

"We're saved! D'Etivey had better watch out. There's nothing I'd like better than to disembowel him!" said Guillaume darkly.

They made their way toward the house, which was completely dark. After scouting around, Boris found a window ajar, through which they entered. They wandered through a few empty rooms and eventually found the front door. Boris drew back the heavy iron bar that kept it closed, and then they were free. Unfortunately they no longer had their horses.

Hardly had they begun walking down the street, trying to find their bearings, when they heard the bells of Saint-Germain-l'Auxerrois Church peal out.

Chapter XII

$\mathcal{T}$*he* dreaded signal sent a shiver down Victoire's spine. "We're going to be too late!" she exclaimed in despair.

"If we even manage to get as far as the Louvre . . . Look!"

The street, deserted only a few moments before, suddenly filled with shadow figures carrying torches. As though by magic groups of a dozen men gathered, marching off to an unknown destination.

"What are we to do?"

"We'll have to be careful not to attract attention," said Boris.

They set off, keeping close to the walls. It was the first time Victoire had had to cover any distance on foot in the capital, and she soon realized that picking her way through garbage, rubble, and debris inhabited by legions of rats was a far more harrowing experience than her spell on the rooftops. She stifled a cry of horror as she stumbled over the rotting corpse of a dog. Thereafter Guillaume or Boris would frequently give her a hand to help her over obstacles.

A small group of men in front of them stopped at a house whose door was marked with a white cross. One broke down the entrance and the others rushed in after him.

"Oh, my God!" whispered Victoire. "What are they going to do?"

Guillaume did not answer. He had little doubt about

the fate that awaited the unfortunate occupants of the house.

Soon the night was filled with pistol shots, screams, savage cries, and the moans of the dying.

"But they're killing them all . . ." murmured Victoire, numb with terror. "The white cross on the door is a sign, isn't it?"

Although it pained him, Guillaume had to agree. "They've probably used it to show the houses of the more important Protestants. Look, here's one . . . and there's another."

They reached Rue de Béthizy, where the Admiral lived.

"Surely it must be guarded, after what happened the other day."

Hearing a large group of men running in their direction, they backed out of sight into a doorway. Monsieur de Coligny's house was clearly indicated with a huge white cross. It was four o'clock in the morning, and dawn was about to break.

One of the men began to thump on the door with his fists. "Open in the King's name!"

Victoire and Guillaume recognized Henri de Guise with the others. "They're not going to be so mad as to open the door," she exclaimed indignantly.

But they were. A retainer, who had obeyed the orders from outside, immediately paid for his rashness with his life. He was stabbed to death and crumpled in a heap on the threshold.

The Duc de Guise's henchmen clambered over his body and ran amok inside the house, killing everyone in their path while he waited in the street. "At last you will be avenged, Father," said Henri de Guise with a cruel smile.

The commotion in the house reached its peak. Then suddenly a man was flung out of one of the windows: he was still alive despite numerous dagger wounds, and managed to catch hold of the balcony with one hand for a second before dropping with a thump at the Duc's feet.

"Is it really him?" asked a priest, whose sadistic expression betrayed the pleasure he was experiencing at all this carnage in the name of God.

He bent down, and with his sleeve wiped away the blood covering the man's face. "Upon my word, it is indeed him."

To round off his act of filial vengeance, the Duc kicked the Admiral de Coligny's inert head.

Almost sick with horror, Victoire was unable to take her eyes off the terrible scene that had just taken place before her in the space of a few minutes.

One of the Duc's henchmen tore the dead man's gold chain from his neck. Another beheaded him with one stroke of his sword, triumphantly holding up the head of the man that Charles IX used to call his father.

"Don't look," said Guillaume, drawing Victoire close to him.

She buried her head in his shoulder and began to sob uncontrollably. She could feel her lover shudder. "What are they doing now?"

"Dismembering him."

Victoire thought she would faint.

"Courage!" said Guillaume in an unrecognizable voice. "Think of your mother and your uncle. We're not very far from the Louvre now."

Once they had done their dirty work, the Duc's murderers disappeared down the street in search of more people to kill.

"We must get moving," said Guillaume quietly.

"What a massacre," said Boris. "I didn't know the French could be so brutal."

"They've gone mad," cried Guillaume somberly.

"It's not the first time," said Victoire. "Remember Amboise." The Admiral's murder reminded her all too vividly of how her father and other noblemen had died during the conspiracy.

"They certainly won't stop at the murder of Monsieur de Coligny," added Guillaume.

What could be happening in the Louvre, full of Protestants, since the ringing of the tocsin?

"It was the Queen who ordered her fellow countrymen to be massacred," said Victoire so bitterly she almost forgot her fear.

As they made their way back to the Louvre they encountered nightmare scenes of horror and destruction. They could hardly take a step without stumbling over some mutilated or disemboweled corpse. Sluggish streams of blood trickled down the streets and collected into large brownish pools. Wounded children wandered about, crying desperately for the parents they would never see again, or huddled against a still-warm body, waiting in vain for it to wake up.

Protestants that no one had bothered to finish off lay on the ground, groaning and calling for help, until they, too, at last fell silent. The slaughter was going on in every street. Men ran everywhere, knocking down doors, ramming their quarry with halberds, strangling them with their bare hands, or throwing them out of windows. The screams and death cries of their victims, men and women, rose mournfully into the balmy summer night—a night meant for love, not death.

Finally they reached the Seine, whose muddy waters bore corpses downstream.

"They're throwing them in from the Pont des Jeuneurs," said Guillaume.

The sight that awaited them in the courtyard and galleries of the Louvre made them recoil with horror. It was similar to what they had seen in the streets, except that this time they knew most of the stark and stiff faces, with their eyes wide open staring into space. Constables and Swiss mercenaries were scouring every gallery and every room in search of their victims, the Protestant nobles and their servants who had come to the Louvre to celebrate the marriage between a man of their own faith and the King's sister.

"I can't bear it! Look! There's Pardaillan . . ." groaned Victoire. "And Beauvais, the King of Navarre's tutor!"

Her stomach knotted with terrible anguish as she realized she might recognize her mother and Anselme at any moment among all those bloodstained, motionless corpses.

The first rays of dawn were appearing through the high windows of the gallery. They cast a funereal light over the piles of sprawling bodies. The killing had not yet ended. A band of Swiss mercenaries burst into the hall pursuing three Huguenots trying to escape. They bumped into Victoire. She fell to the ground, trying desperately to avoid the flailing swords and pikestaffs, and succeeded in crawling under a divan, where she remained motionless. The three fugitives fell, stabbed to death, as the mercenaries drunkenly ran off yelling like savages.

Victoire cautiously got to her feet and looked round for Guillaume and Boris. They were nowhere to be seen. She was terrified, not for herself but for Guillaume. What had become of her lover? Had the Swiss mercenaries taken him for a Huguenot and killed him? She bent down over a groaning body still moving slightly. No, thank God, it wasn't Guillaume.

She looked out of the window into the courtyard and shuddered as she tried to calculate the number of victims. On the far side of the courtyard stood the King, his crazed eyes feasting on the terrible massacre he had authorized.

Darting out of sight for fear of being seen, she caught sight of herself in a mirror, a disheveled creature in a torn dress stained with mud and blood.

She ran as fast as she could upstairs, leaping over bodies and splashing through pools of blood, numb to all the horror around her.

The door of her mother's bedroom was ajar. Overtaken by a terrible sense of foreboding, Victoire paused a moment in the corridor before she could bring herself to enter. She *knew* what she was about to see, but even so she could not prevent herself from screaming as she saw her mother lying on the bed drenched in blood. Her throat had been slit, and her open eyes still reflected terror.

Victoire collapsed beside the bed. Now she was an orphan, and the sight of her cruelly slaughtered mother would haunt her for the rest of her life. Uncle Anselme . . . She had to know at once. She could not bear not knowing what had happened to the man she loved like a father. Leaving her mother's body, she ran into the next room: empty. She sighed with relief. But immediately she began to worry again. What if Anselme were one of those crumpled corpses in some corner of the courtyard that had been turned into a charnel house? The thought made her so desperate that all she could do was fling herself on a bed and sob into the pillow. She did not know what had happened to Gilone or Héloïse either. Maybe they too were dead?

While she was sobbing, she did not hear the door open. A pair of steely hands pinned her to the bed before she could even move. She heard the hated voice rasping in her ear.

"Ha, so we meet again, you filthy little heretic! Thought you could get away from God's servant, did you!"

"Let go of me!" screamed Victoire, clawing at the monk's face and neck.

"You don't think I'm going to miss an opportunity like this, do you? You pretty young thing."

The monk ripped open the girl's bodice with one hand and greedily began licking and slobbering on her tender breasts. Victoire shivered and was so paralyzed with horror and disgust that she couldn't move.

"Why, you even seem to enjoy it, you little slut!

Well, enjoy your pleasure while you can, because afterward I'm going to cut your throat! All heretics must die! You will burn in hell for eternity!"

The hand sliding up her thigh suddenly made her recall the dagger. Pretending to respond to the caresses of the licentious monk, she succeeded in drawing the weapon from its sheath and plunging it into the back of her attacker.

She saw his eyes widen incredulously and felt his grip slacken. She continued to thrust the dagger in as hard as she could, again and again, until she felt the man become a lifeless weight on top of her.

Chapter XIII

*H*ours later Victoire regained consciousness, having fainted following her ordeal. She felt exhausted, ached all over, and could not understand why her limbs seemed so leaden. Where was Héloïse? Why hadn't she come, as usual, with a pitcher of water for her to wash in? She had completely lost her sense of time.

Then she realized she had been sleeping fully dressed, her bodice was ripped lengthwise to the waist, and her skirt was stained with blood and filth. Her memory came flooding back to her of that hellish night, which had begun so wonderfully in the Tuileries gardens. Could all that really have happened?

It was a few minutes before she could bring herself to look down between the two beds. But when she did, to her amazement she saw nothing there except a pool of dried blood. Father Izard's body had vanished! Had he been taken away while she was asleep? Or had he managed to leave unaided? She had shoved the dagger in up to the hilt, but perhaps she had missed his vital organs? Could it be that she had merely wounded the monster? But in that case he would have taken advantage of the fact she was unconscious and finished her off.

Victoire could find no answer to any of these questions. The first thing for her to do was to get up and try to find Guillaume and Anselme. She stripped off her clothes, gave her body a good wash with marjoram water, and put on a clean dress. She tried to do her hair, but accustomed as she was to being helped by Héloïse she proved very clumsy at the job and broke her tortoiseshell comb. Perhaps Jacotte was around.

Victoire went out into the corridor and called. Within moments the child appeared in tears.

"Oh, Mademoiselle! I've seen such terrible things!"

She comforted the girl, gave her a sweet, and asked her to do her hair.

Jacotte went to borrow a comb from Mademoiselle de Chabrière, who was not in her room, and got down to work.

"Does Mademoiselle know?" she asked, after some hesitation.

"What?"

"About Madame the Comtesse."

"Yes, I know," said Victoire, feeling tears welling in her eyes. "Do you know who killed her?"

"I saw three Swiss soldiers enter her room. They were led by a monk. They went straight to Madame the Comtesse's room, then to yours. Luckily you weren't there. The monk was furious."

Victoire bitterly regretted she had not stabbed him harder and deeper.

"And what about my uncle?"

"I don't know."

"And Mademoiselle Gilone? And Héloïse?"

"Héloïse was wounded in the arm when she tried to defend Madame the Comtesse. She took refuge with the Baron de Lévis' footman, who is her friend. As for Mademoiselle Gilone, I've not seen her since yesterday evening."

"Well, anyway, I'll try to find Héloïse, as you say she's still alive . . . What's the time?"

"Just seven o'clock, Mademoiselle."

Victoire soon realized that the killing was still going on in the Louvre, and that she would have to be extremely cautious to stay alive.

In the corridor she asked a bewildered servant, who stuttered nervously, where she could find the apartments of the Duc de Cavalade, with whom Philippe de Lévis was supposed to be staying. Suddenly de Lévis appeared out of nowhere, covered with blood, his doublet in shreds. He was running for his life, pursued by four constables.

Victoire flattened herself against the wall, then followed the soldiers, who were so eager to catch their victim they didn't notice her. The young man ran as fast as his wounds permitted and reached the Queen of Navarre's door in a state of total exhaustion.

"Navarre! Navarre!" he bellowed, banging on the door.

The door opened. Philippe de Lévis dashed into the bedroom followed by the constables, and, not far behind, by Victoire. He stumbled to the bed, where Madame Marguerite was resting. The Queen and the young man tumbled to the floor together screaming, as it seemed the soldiers were going to kill them both. Hidden behind a cabinet, Victoire was angry she could do nothing to help, having left her dagger in Father Izard's back. In any case, she could have done little against four bloodthirsty maniacs.

Help did come, just in time, when the captain of the

guards entered the room and calmed down the four soldiers.

"Gentlemen, you are attacking the Queen whom it is your task to protect."

The men suddenly came to their senses on hearing a voice they were accustomed to obey. They let go of the two blood-spattered bodies and withdrew.

"Are you wounded, Madame?" the captain asked anxiously, helping the Queen to her feet.

"I think my chemise has been stained with Monsieur de Lévis' blood," she said in a detached voice.

"I'll take him away."

"No, please don't! He came to seek refuge here. Leave him with me!"

The captain reluctantly agreed. Victoire realized she was an intruder in the royal chambers, and dared not show her face. Charles IX's sister called her maidservant, who had opened the door for Philippe.

"Help me dress this poor man's wounds."

He had been slashed on the elbow by a sword and stabbed with a halberd through the arm. The maidservant brought water to wash his wounds.

"Madame," he mumbled, close to delirium, "how can I thank you for helping me?"

"By staying here. If you leave you won't survive for long."

Once his arm was dressed with lint, Philippe de Lévis was hidden in a wardrobe and carefully closed the door.

"Madame," said the captain, "you are not at all safe in your chambers."

"I realize that, thank you very much," retorted Marguerite. "Your constables just tried to cut my throat in my own bedroom. Where's my husband? He left me at the crack of dawn."

"Do not worry, Madame, he is all right . . ."

"Why has that bell been ringing since four this morning?"

The captain looked embarrassed.

"The King gave the order for all Huguenots to be executed."

"All the Huguenots in the Louvre?" she cried with horror.

"All those in the capital, Madame. Permit me to take you to your sister, the Duchesse de Lorraine."

"She warned me yesterday evening," Marguerite said quietly, "and I refused to believe her."

She put a cloak over her chemise and followed the captain out of the room.

Now that she was alone, Victoire opened the door of the wardrobe where Philippe was hiding.

"What are you doing here?" he asked, doing his best to smile. "Are you also seeking refuge?"

Victoire explained what she was doing there, and Philippe told her where to find his valet and probably Héloïse, too.

"Tell him I'm still alive," he added.

"Thank God you're alive, Mademoiselle!" exclaimed Héloïse. "I'd lost all hope of ever seeing you again . . . after what happened to the poor Comtesse."

Héloïse began to weep, and was soon followed by Victoire, whose nerves finally gave way.

"Poor Héloïse," she said after a time. "Where did they hurt you?"

"On the arm and the thigh. The soldiers jabbed me with their pikestaffs and opened a six-inch gash in my leg. Madame the Comtesse was right when she said the Catholics were monsters. Especially that monk!"

"Did he kill my mother?" Victoire asked sharply.

"No, he ordered the others to do it. 'First that one,' he said, 'she's a dangerous heretic.' "

"What happened then?"

"I fainted. I just knew they were going to murder you, too."

"And what about my uncle?"

"The Queen's guards came to take him away shortly before."

Suddenly Victoire felt a wild glimmer of hope. What if Catherine de Medici had decided to protect him because she esteemed his artistic talents?

It was the middle of the morning and Victoire realized she was famished. Joseph, Philippe de Lévis' valet, brought her ham and cold veal. She felt pangs of guilt as she ate, when her mothe lay dead—brutally murdered—and the fate of her uncle was still in doubt.

"I put Héloïse in your hands," she said to Joseph, a good-looking fellow whose black mustache gave him a martial air, and who was obviously deeply in love with Héloïse. Confident that Héloïse was in good hands, Victoire went to search for Anselme. And Guillaume, too. How was it that he and Boris had disappeared so suddenly, almost before her very eyes?

As she walked through an antechamber Victoire saw two lifeless figures on the floor. The sight reminded her again of the horrors of the previous night and she began to realize how extraordinarily lucky she had been. It was a miracle to have escaped unscathed except for a few bruises from the monk, when so many of her fellow Protestants were lying dead. Their bodies lay in every room, the corridors, and even the staircases of the Louvre, which had been transformed into a vast charnel house by the decree of a madman. All these poor unfortunate innocent souls, to have been slain so cruelly.

Again she looked out of a window into the courtyard, and was seized with an insatiable hatred for the woman who had instigated the massacre. She was furious at her inability to avenge these deaths and noticed, to her dismay, that the thought of killing was no longer as repugnant to her as it used to be. Was she, too, turning into a bloodthirsty animal?

Victoire was turning over these ideas in her mind when she was grabbed brutally round the waist. Before she could scream, a mask was pressed over her face preventing her from either calling for help or seeing. Her hands and feet were tightly bound with rope; and she was swiftly carried out of the Louvre by two men, dumped unceremoniously into a carriage, and driven away.

Chapter XIV

*A*lthough she estimated she had probably been traveling less than an hour, Victoire found it very long. Quite soon she sensed the absence of any guard inside the coach, and in spite of her bonds she succeeded, after several attempts, to settle herself more comfortably on the thick velvet seat. If only she could pull off the mask covering her face . . . She struggled for several minutes to free one of her hands. But the rope around her wrists merely chafed the skin, and before long she angrily gave up.

Gradually her anger turned to despair: what good was it to have escaped so many dangers, to be stupidly captured right in the Louvre?

The carriage was traveling faster. It seemed they were approaching one of the gates of Paris. The air was getting fresher, the sickening smells less strong. Victoire began to find the heat tiring. Apart from the short time she had fainted, she had not slept. She was roused from an overwhelming sense of drowsiness by the clanging of an iron gate being shut behind her. By now she had lost all sense of time and distance.

The coach drove on for about another two hundred yards, then the door was opened and someone gently took hold of her.

"Unbind her," ordered a woman's curt voice.

Victoire's bonds were severed and she sighed with relief as she felt the blood circulating freely again. Her legs felt as though they were being pricked by hundreds of pins and needles, and her feet and hands were icy in spite of the heat.

A hand took hers.

"Come along, my child," said the voice. "The rest of you can go back."

"At your service, Abbess."

The nun led Victoire firmly along a passage and into a room where the door was closed behind them.

"Sit down."

Victoire had scarcely seated herself on a straw chair before she pulled off the blindfold. The sudden bright light was disorienting and caused her to ask, "Where am I?"

"In the Convent of the Visitation."

The Abbess was a tall, thin woman in her mid-thirties. Only her intense green eyes lit up an austere countenance, whose pale skin was devoid of the heavy make-up used by the ladies at Court. On the wall behind her hung a black wooden cross that bore an agonized Christ of polished ivory. Little by little, Victoire adjusted to the brightness and recovered her spirits.

"Why have I been kidnapped?" she exclaimed. "Who planned this shameful act?"

A faint smile flickered over the nun's pale, almost translucent lips.

"For your own good, my child, or rather for the good of your soul."

"I am a Protestant!" cried Victoire indignantly.

"Alas, we know too well how misguided you are.

But the mercy of God is infinite. A holy man has taken pity on you and desires your eternal salvation."

"Father Izard . . ." the girl murmured in terror. "He is not dead, then?"

"For the time being he is abed with a serious wound. Thank Heaven, his life is not in danger. In spite of his suffering, he has had the infinite kindness to entrust you to me and, above all, to our patron saint. You must be infinitely grateful for his solicitude."

With wild indignation, Victoire abruptly stood up. "Gratitude toward a man who murdered my mother, tried to rape and kill me! It was I who wounded him, defending myself against his unwelcome attentions! It is my misfortune that I didn't dispatch him altogether . . ."

"My poor child, you are delirious," replied the Abbess, quite unmoved. "Besides, you are easily excused. What happened last night has disturbed many minds, and stronger ones than yours. We are going to look after you, and I trust that when the holy father has recovered, I shall be able to present him with a candidate for baptism."

"Recant? Never!"

"It will have to be, if you wish to leave here."

"I'd sooner die! Do you imagine that I would be shameless enough to adopt the religion of those who have murdered my father and mother and so many of our religious persuasion?"

"Peace and meditation will do you so much good. You will begin to take a more balanced view of life. God has been pleased to test you in your deepest affections. Give thanks to Him. Your sorrow will serve as a purification."

The Abbess rang a small bell that she wore on a chain about her waist. Two nuns appeared so quickly Victoire suspected them of waiting outside the door throughout the interview, ready to prevent her from escaping had she tried.

She was led to a tiny cell at the end of a dark passage. The room was furnished with a narrow bed, a table, and a wooden chair. The floor was made of bare flagstones and the only decoration on the whitewashed walls was a large wooden crucifix.

"I am Sister Marie-Gertrude," said one of the nuns, "and I will bring you your food. Sister Gabrielle will escort you for a walk in the garden for half an hour a day, and will come and take you to church."

"I don't want to go to church!"

"These are the orders of the Abbess. You must comply with them."

Sister Marie-Gertrude spoke in a soft, even voice. No one in the convent seemed aware that the streets of Paris were flowing with blood, and that the dead numbered in the hundreds if not the thousands. The building gave the impression of being a hundred leagues from the capital.

The nuns withdrew, shoving the bolt in place. For the second time in twelve hours, Victoire found herself a prisoner. But this time there would be no Guillaume to bolster her courage, and no Boris to help her to walk on a roof . . .

On awakening hours later from an exhaustion-induced sleep, Victoire saw a frugal meal on the table: bread, pâté, a piece of fruit and some water. She grimaced, but she was ravenous and resigned herself to eating it. Above all, she must not allow herself to be too weak when the chance came for escape.

From the moment she crossed the threshold of the convent, she had one idea in mind: to get away as quickly as possible and by any means. Except by the recantation which they dared to expect of her!

She took heart from the success of the previous night: if she had managed to outwit ten armed guards, she might well succeed in eluding some nuns. True, she didn't know how many there were, but at least they didn't walk about with pistols and daggers in their belts.

She examined the room carefully. Apart from the door, a high grilled skylight was the only aperture. She climbed onto the table but couldn't reach it. She lifted the chair onto the table and stood on the unsteady combination. She lifted the window and felt the thick strong bars. Without the aid of some type of tool that could bend the grille, she stood no chance.

From her precarious position part of the well-kept garden, which surrounded the convent, was visible. Bushes of red roses brightened the lawns and their scent brought back memories of home. Two men passed by with spades on their shoulders; and a little later, three nuns carrying tubs of washing.

In the distance, behind a row of trees, she glimpsed the entrance gate, flanked on either side by a wall several feet high. Even if she managed to slip out of the building, that would by no means be the only problem.

Depressed by this dismal knowledge, she went back to bed and began some serious thinking. If only someone could rescue her; but who could discover her here? Clearly she would have to rely on herself.

If they allowed her to go out for a short while each day, she would have time to observe the grounds and possibly the nuns' living quarters. At all cost she had to regain her liberty before Father Izard recovered. Now that she was at his mercy he would not spare her. A firm resolve grew in her mind: if desperation drove her to murder again, she would take care to do a good job of it!

Just the same, would Father Izard dare rape and kill her inside a convent? The thought made her whole body shudder. She knew he was capable of anything.

Slowly the cell grew darker, and Sister Gabrielle arrived to take her to evening service. Victoire decided to follow the nun without protest, hoping this apparent submission might lull the suspicions of her jailers. It would give her the opportunity to note the internal layout of the convent.

They went to the end of the passage and up a little staircase, reaching a long hallway with a multitude of doors on either side.

"Where are we?" She had nothing to lose by asking questions.

"These are our cells," Sister Gabrielle explained. "There are about sixty of us."

Victoire fell silent. She hadn't imagined she would have so many to contend with!

They went down a wide stone staircase at the foot of which, behind a table, two nuns held a book between them.

"What are they doing?" asked Victoire.

"They are the extern sisters. They open the gate and receive gifts which the generous faithful bring to our house. Afterward they write their names in the book."

Victoire guessed that at night the sisters left their post in front of the staircase because there would be few gifts then.

On the right, there was a door with a little spy-hole that probably led to the courtyard and the garden. On the left, she could see the glow of lighted candles coming from the chapel.

Just before they entered, the sister gave Victoire a shawl to cover her head with.

"You must genuflect as you enter."

As Victoire imitated Sister Gabrielle, she had an unpleasant feeling of being cowardly and of betraying her true religion.

Carved wooden stalls, arranged in the shape of a horseshoe in front of the altar, screened off the nuns who were singing. Victoire was made to sit on a bench, a little apart. Sister Gabrielle settled herself on one side of her, and a nun she did not know on the other. Thus hemmed in, Victoire attended the Compline Service.

Two priests officiated, and four little boys about ten years old, with lace surplices over their red robes, swung the censer with obvious delight. To the left of the altar was a portal through which the officiants and their acolytes went out when the service was over.

The nuns sang another hymn, and in spite of the circumstances, Victoire enjoyed the choir of well-trained voices, some of which were extremely beautiful. She was then taken back to her room by the same route.

"For the time being," said Sister Gabrielle, "you will only attend Holy Mass and Compline."

"There are other services as well?" said the girl in astonishment.

"Certainly. Matins, Lauds, Benediction, Vespers . . . the bell always rings when it's time to attend chapel. You should not be surprised if you hear it tonight."

Chapter XV

*T*he bell for Lauds, as well as the daylight from her uncurtained window, awakened Victoire from a comforting dream about Guillaume. The abrupt return to reality made her want to cry. She might never see him again. He was not in love with her and would never marry her, but she wanted desperately to be close to him.

The pale morning light gave rise to somber thoughts and terrible memories, of her poor murdered mother, the unknown fate of her uncle and Gilone, and the terror of being confronted by that lustful and fanatic monk . . .

Finally she gave way to the great lump in her throat and tears streamed down her cheeks, which were still pink and fresh in spite of her ordeals. Eventually her tears dried. Afterward she felt relieved and once again full of energy, if not hope, determined to take advantage of any negligence by her jailers.

She got out of bed and turned the door-handle: alas, the diligent Sister Marie-Gertrude had not forgotten the bolt. Would it be possible one day to distract her attention as she was leaving the room? Or even make her an accomplice? That seemed most unlikely, but could it be that Sister Gabrielle, who was more gentle, would prove more open to pity?

Such endeavors would call for a great deal of diplomacy and time. Doubtless much more than she had at her disposal. How many days would it take Father Izard, with his tough constitution, to recover from his wound? How much longer before he would claw her body again? His deep wound might put him out of action for about a week. And perhaps, knowing that his victim was well guarded and within easy reach whenever he wished, he would be in no haste to leave his room. But already a whole day had slipped past . . .

The bolt thudded back and Sister Marie-Gertrude brought in a jug of milk and some dry bread.

Victoire protested violently. "Can you not at least treat me decently since you are holding me prisoner?"

"The Abbess has ordered you do penance."

"Penance for what!" the girl exclaimed bitterly. "For being an orphan after the murder of my mother? For not knowing where I am, or what has happened to my uncle, who replaced my father who was also killed by your people? For the disappearance of my cousin? For the sight of my slaughtered co-religionists? Or simply for being detained against my will?"

"My poor child," said the nun, who appeared moved. "God tests hardest those He most loves."

"Your God, perhaps!"

Sister Marie-Gertrude hesitated. "I am going to see if I can do something for you." She left the room, without forgetting to lock the door, and came back in a few moments with a pot of honey. "Here's something which will improve your meal a little. I am doing this without the permission of our Mother Superior. So don't tell anyone about it, and hide the pot."

"Thank you," said Victoire, smiling warmly. "Don't worry, I shan't give you away."

When the nun had left, Victoire happily put away three slices of bread slathered with the honey. This snack reminded her of others she had enjoyed with Gilone on the farm at Montmaur, and made her think of those happy days which now seemed so far away.

The first step had been made in succeeding to touch the heart of one of her wardens. To some extent, then, these women were accessible to pity.

Soon after Mass, Sister Gabrielle took her to the garden. What joy it was to gaze at trees and flowers instead of the walls of her cell, to hear the chirping of birds and the rhythmic sound of a rake on the gravel in the drive.

Sister Gabrielle performed her rosary while Victoire deeply inhaled the fresh air. The impassive face of her companion betrayed nothing, yet she could have been no older than twenty or twenty-one. The delicacy of her hands, her graceful bearing and gait, were indicative of noble origin. Elegantly dressed, she might be strikingly attractive. Had she really chosen to renounce the world so young, to cut herself off in a nunnery? Victoire could not bring herself to believe it—unless some unhappiness had driven Sister Gabrielle there?

"Sister, may I speak with you?"

The nun dropped the beads which hung from her belt. "I am listening, my child," she said calmly.

Victoire took the plunge. "I'm seventeen. I love life . . . and also a man. My parents have died, both of them most horribly. Is it right to deprive me of my freedom?"

The girl thought she noticed a touch of pain in Sister Gabrielle's blue, childlike eyes.

"We are powerless," the nun sighed at length, "to control our destiny."

"Why should that be? Why should I yield to the desires of a man who wants to rape and then kill me, having first converted me if possible in order to salve his conscience?"

A mixture of terror and amazement spread across the nun's face. "What are you saying? Who are you talking about?"

"Father Izard. Didn't you know?"

She was clearly unaware of the facts. But she paled at the mention of the monk's name. "Shh! You might be overheard! For the love of Heaven, restrain yourself. Wait, we'll go behind the yew trees, where we'll be away from inquisitive ears."

Several nuns, a gardener, and the gatekeeper summoned by the extern sister had passed quite close by.

They sat down on a bench on the other side of the convent where no one was working.

"You mentioned Father Izard," said Sister Gabrielle. "He is the benefactor of our house. Thanks to him, gifts pour in. He has obtained the special patronage of Queen Catherine. Our Mother Superior has the highest regard for him, and we have been ordered to pray for him every day."

"He certainly needs it," said Victoire darkly.

Then she disclosed the evil machinations of the "holy man."

At first the nun was incredulous. "It's just not possible!"

"Your Mother Superior must be completely dominated by him."

Sister Gabrielle was obliged to admit that this was true, that the Abbess blindly followed his instructions. She marveled that the girl had dared to raise a hand against someone so admired and respected by all the sisters.

"How brave you are," she said admiringly.

Victoire, with keen intuition, sensed that the nun was really recalling her own past, and that in order to win her over she must elicit her secret thoughts.

"You are young and pretty," she said. "Forgive my indiscretion, but how did you come to take the veil?"

The nun sighed again. "I was the youngest of five girls," she said. "My father, the Comte de Varemont, having made a settlement for three of us and after the death of the fourth, had nothing left for my dowry. So wasn't it the best solution to send me to a convent where they were good enough to accept me in spite of my slender means?"

"And you are not unhappy?"

There was a long silence. "I am used to it," she murmured. "One has to be."

As they entered the door of the convent, they ran into the Abbess, who sternly rebuked Sister Gabrielle.

"You have exceeded the time for the walk by nearly a quarter of an hour. See that this doesn't happen again."

Sister Gabrielle bowed her head. "Yes, Madame."

"As punishment, you will say another rosary in addition to your usual prayers. You can choose the eternal salvation of Mademoiselle de Montmaur. Now, escort her back to her room until Compline."

She handed Victoire a book. "To occupy yourself,

Mademoiselle, you will do well to read the life of Saint Catherine of Siena."

"As you wish," the girl replied indifferently. It would be useless to confront the Abbess openly.

Sister Gabrielle took Victoire back. "I'll do my best to come and see you sometime this afternoon."

Alone again in her tiny cell, Victoire felt joyful. She had secured an accomplice, and she was sure that quite soon Sister Gabrielle would help her to escape . . . How helpful could she really be, though, to judge from the way the Abbess treated her?

Impatiently she awaited her arrival, not for one moment thinking of opening the edifying volume supplied by the Abbess.

But Sister Gabrielle never returned. As on the previous night, Sister Marie-Gertrude brought her meal.

"I have added a wing of chicken to what they have given you."

"Thank you," said Victoire gratefully. "I'm really very hungry."

"It's natural at your age," the nun sighed. "Our Superior must never know about my misdemeanors."

The Abbess seemed to have her flock quite terrorized.

"The regime is very strict?" asked Victoire as she eagerly chewed on the poultry.

"Yes . . . since the arrival of the new Abbess. I must leave now. If the extern sister doesn't see me go down at the required time, she will report me."

"She would denounce you?" Victoire exclaimed incredulously.

Sister Marie-Gertrude lowered her head and seemed embarrassed. "According to the rule laid down by the Abbess when she arrived, every nun who detects an infringement by one of her companions must report it to her."

When it was time for Compline, an unpleasant-looking nun came for Victoire. This greatly alarmed her. So they were preventing Sister Gabrielle from seeing her. The hawklike eye of the Abbess had perhaps observed that an understanding existed between the prisoner and her young guard.

With nightfall Victoire was not even allowed a candle. Fortunately a pale shaft of moonlight coming through the high window enabled her to pick out the shapes of things in the room.

As she had taken no exercise apart from the short walk and had lain on her bed almost all day, she did not feel at all sleepy. Nothing was more depressing than just lying awake in the dark.

It would take her several hours to get to sleep, her only distraction being the periodic chiming of the bell. Again she felt terribly miserable and despaired of ever regaining her freedom. She began to loathe even more the blind intransigence of the woman who dominated the convent and controlled her own fate. How could the nuns put up with such tyranny and the constant atmosphere of suspicion in which they were obliged to live?

Chapter XVI

A mouse scratched insistently on the cell's floor. In spite of the darkness she thought she distinguished quite clearly its bright eyes and little pointed teeth. She was not in the least afraid. At Montmaur this kind of visit was a frequent occurrence.

The animal was making more and more noise and eventually Victoire woke up with a start. But the scratching continued. It took her only a moment to realize that she was not still dreaming. Someone was outside the door, and was trying as discreetly as possible to attract her attention. "Who is it?" she whispered.

"Ah, you've heard me at last," came the slightly breathless voice of Sister Gabrielle.

"Why don't you come in?"

"I don't have the key anymore. The Abbess took it and relieved me of my duties toward you. From now on, Sister Hildegarde will take you to the garden. There's no hope with her."

Utterly dismayed and on the brink of tears, Victoire thought for a moment. "Isn't there another key you could get hold of?"

"Yes . . . But it's in the bunch kept by the house-keeper."

"I shall never get out of here," moaned Victoire.

"I don't know if I can manage to come back," Sister Gabrielle went on. "I shall try to keep in touch with you through my nephew Raymond, one of the choir-boys. They scarcely ever keep an eye on him."

"Could you make me a floor plan of the convent, showing all the possible exits?"

"Yes, I think so. Don't lose courage. I shall help you, even at my own cost."

Victoire thanked her gratefully. What vengeance would a woman like the Abbess be capable of, especially if pressed by Father Izard? What frightful punishment would she inflict on the poor girl if she was convinced of complicity in the escape of someone entrusted to her by the monk? The thought terrified Victoire, but she had no choice. Without the help of Sister Gabrielle she would be handed over to the monstrous man.

The next day, during Mass, Victoire studied the

choirboys, who were then wearing violet robes. Which was the one who would bring her a message from Sister Gabrielle? Was it the blond boy with that great lock of hair which kept falling down on his forehead, or the little pale one with rather brisk gestures?

Then she took no more notice of them. After all, closely guarded as she was, always flanked by two nuns in the chapel and escorted to the garden by Sister Hildegarde, how could the boy, however artful he might be, succeed in slipping her a note?

However, when Sister Hildegarde, who only spoke to her when strictly necessary, came to take her for her walk at eleven o'clock four boys were playing tag around the lawns.

"They're nice," Victoire remarked, trying again to engage the nun in conversation in spite of the scant success she had so far achieved.

"They would be better off studying instead of wasting their time," declared the nun through her thin lips.

As he ran, one of the boys stumbled over a stone, fell to the ground, and began to whimper.

"They can't even look where they're going," said the nun scornfully.

"He may have hurt himself," suggested Victoire, who saw what the boy was up to.

The sister shrugged. Nevertheless, followed by her prisoner, she moved toward the little group. Victoire was sure that the child's cries grew louder as they approached.

The little blond boy made a swift sign to her and showed her a piece of paper folded in his hand. While the nun was leaning over the casualty, Victoire snatched the message and tucked it in her bodice.

The nun straightened up. "This child has merely scratched himself. He just wanted to attract attention. Now go and play farther away, and don't start again." With a sweep of the arm she dismissed them. "Our Superior should not tolerate their presence in the garden at all hours of the day," she said severely. "Their noisy games disturb the meditation and self-communion of some of our companions."

Having returned to her room and making sure Sister Hildegarde was not outside the door to spy on her, Victoire feverishly unfolded the note. It contained a floor plan of the convent with a few words from her friend. "I think I have found a way to get the key. Will it work? I shall know in a few hours. Be ready tonight, and if I don't turn up, then tomorrow night. Father Izard has said he will come to celebrate Saint Augustine on Sunday!"

Victoire made a rapid calculation and realized with horror that it was already Friday. She only had two nights left to escape!

Very carefully, she studied the plan of each floor of the vast building and memorized it, so as not to pause for a moment in her escape should Sister Gabrielle get hold of the key.

There seemed to be three possible exits, if one ruled out the front door, which would certainly be bolted. Maybe one of these exits would be left open. But Sister Marie-Gertrude had explained that at night, apart from the services which all the nuns had to attend unless they had special dispensation from the Abbess, two sisters, relieved every hour, remained in constant prayer in front of the Holy Sacrament, so the way out through the chapel was barred. There remained the kitchen, a huge room alongside a storeroom where they kept the week's provisions, and the wash-house. Surely these parts of the convent would be deserted between nine in the evening and six in the morning.

The hope of seeing Guillaume again elated her. How she missed him! During her captivity she had striven to recall as little as possible of that evening in the Tuileries when she had belonged to him. Now the memory of his kisses and caresses, of the joy she had experienced, left her almost faint with desire. How long would she have to wait before she was in his arms again?

What was he doing at this very moment? Was he searching for her everywhere? Or had he been trapped again by Monsieur d'Etivey? She knew somehow he must be alive. Of that she was sure.

Once again dusk turned to darkness in the little cell. The vigil began, seemingly endless and possibly pointless. Victoire listened to the ringing of the hours and half hours with growing impatience.

Stretched out on her bed fully clothed, having simply slipped off her shoes, she was ready. The plan of the convent kept running through her mind. What if the doors to the kitchen wash-house refused to open? There were the windows, but most of them had strong, closely spaced bars which would be impossible to slip through.

Even if she reached the garden, how would she get out of the grounds unless Sister Gabrielle had enlisted the aid of the gatekeeper? There were sharp spikes on top of the iron gate, and the walls were at least fifteen feet high. Assuming that she overcame this obstacle, she would still be quite alone in the middle of the night. How would she find her way? She had no money to hire a horse or a carriage.

The clock struck midnight. Would Sister Gabrielle arrive before Matins? Surely in any case before dawn, which at this time of year broke at about five o'clock.

She was sleeping when at last the key turned in the lock. The pale light of a candle threw a shadow on the wall.

"Victoire! Hurry!"

Waking with a start, Victoire quickly put on her shoes.

"No. Take them in your hand."

She caught sight of Sister Gabrielle's bare feet.

"I am going to lock your door so that they only discover you've gone at the last possible moment."

Silent as cats, they tiptoed along the passage and reached the little staircase.

"Avoid the second step; it creaks."

Step by step they reached the long central gallery, the entire length of which they had to cross.

The resounding snores that emerged from some of the cells made Victoire smile briefly. When they passed the Abbess's room, marked with a silver cross, she felt her heart miss a beat. What if the Superior suddenly appeared and roused the whole convent, sending sixty nuns in pursuit of the culprits!

Fortunately they got past without any problem, and soon their bare feet tread the icy flagstones of the main staircase. The glimmer of a night light on a table gave the entrance hall a ghostly look.

"Which way are we going?" whispered Victoire.

"Let's try the kitchen first."

At the end of another passage was the huge refectory, with its long wooden tables and benches and its large fireplace. A few embers glowed in the hearth, and the air was still filled with a strong smell of mutton and cabbage that Victoire found delicious.

The stillness was broken as the room reverberated with the sound of the clock striking two.

"We must move quickly. In scarcely an hour it will be time for Matins." Sister Gabrielle struggled in vain with the handle of the door. "It's quite impossible to open it. Let's try the wash-house."

There were no windows to be seen in the kitchen, nor in the enormous room filled with baskets and drying laundry. Their last hope had vanished. Sister Gabrielle began to sob. "We've failed," she moaned.

"Not yet," said Victoire in an attempt to console her in spite of her own consternation.

They looked desperately for some solution, went back to the kitchen, and then returned to the wash-house.

"What can we do?" exclaimed Victoire, suddenly

dejected. "Wouldn't it be better if I went back to my room? Why should you risk a needless punishment?"

But there was no time left. The bell for Matins was ringing and the convent was coming to life.

"You can't go upstairs again," said Sister Gabrielle in a frenzied state. "You must hide here. Look, underneath here." And she shoved Victoire under a huge heap of unironed washing and covered her up.

"Raymond will bring you food. From noon till two o'clock there's no one around."

She dashed away so as not to miss the service and Victoire was left alone in despair, under a pile of washing, feeling as though she might soon suffocate.

Chapter XVII

*S*he had plenty of time for gloomy thoughts until she told herself it was quite absurd to remain hidden for the moment. It seemed inconceivable that they would come to wash and iron before dawn. She recalled as best she could the layout of the wash-house, which she had scarcely taken in by the flickering light of Sister Gabrielle's candle. She groped her way next door to the kitchen.

She bumped herself several times in spite of her cautious progress, when she collided with the entrance to the storeroom. It was less dark in this room and the air was fresher. Eventually Victoire discovered two ventilation holes, but they were far too small for escape. A four-year-old child would not have been able to get through them.

In the kitchen the fire had gone out. Looking up the great chimney, Victoire saw the light of day as dawn began to break. All of a sudden an idea struck her. It was unthinkable that the rooms where they worked were completely without daylight and that the sisters used candles to do their ironing!

She returned to the wash-house, and when it became a little brighter she did indeed notice the windows: out of reach, just below the ceiling, about twelve feet from the floor. During the day they would have to open the door to get more light and ventilation.

Various movements on the floor above told her that the nuns were getting up, having gone back to bed after Matins. It was time she returned to her hiding place.

Shortly after Mass, Victoire became aware of an unusual commotion in the house, which was ordinarily so silent. Doors banged, people ran about upstairs, hurrying down staircases and even talking loudly, which was strictly against the rules. Clearly her disappearance had been discovered.

The door burst open and several nuns rushed in.

"Search the place," the Abbess ordered in her familiar voice of command. "I want her found within the hour!"

Victoire trembled. Suddenly her cover seemed quite inadequate, and she regretted not having looked for a better hide-out when she was alone.

She could hear the nuns in the storeroom, opening cupboards, moving utensils about, shifting sacks of flour and crates of vegetables. It seemed inevitable that she would be found, and in any case, she couldn't stay under the pile of washing indefinitely. How could she ever get out of the convent if every night the doors were firmly closed?

All the same, when the nuns entered the wash-house

she flattened herself as much as she could. Her heart began to pound. She had never felt so frightened in her life, even on Saint Bartholomew's Night when they threw the Admiral from the window . . . except, of course, when Father Izard had come into her room.

The sisters were bustling about less eagerly now that the Superior had left to issue orders in another part of the building.

"Who is this girl we are supposed to find?" asked one of them.

"It seems she's a heretic."

"Then she has no business to be here."

"They want to convert her."

"Oh! Personally I scarcely believe in conversion by force. I wonder why they simply don't exile all Protestants," suggested one nun, who sounded quite young.

"It would be a good idea. Then the King would be relieved of the problem once and for all."

"In my opinion, she escaped by the tunnel in the crypt."

"Does it really exist, Sister?" exclaimed several voices with great curiosity.

"I have heard so. I was told about it forty years ago by an old abbess who lived here nearly half a century. It comes out in the forest half a mile from here, at the foot of an ancient oak tree. But I never heard of anyone who used the tunnel," she went on, with a little laugh. "Perhaps it's just a legend."

The Superior called the nuns together and ordered them to search the garden, since the investigation of the house had proved fruitless.

"Look in the henhouse, the shed where the gardener keeps his tools and seeds, the outhouse. And don't miss the gatehouse; the fugitive may have taken refuge there."

The Abbess was left alone with the bursar, an old nun whom she trusted completely.

"I am not sure about the gatekeeper," she said. "He

could be bribed. After all, he has only had the job for three years."

"You are right. Even so, I cannot understand how Mademoiselle de Montmaur was able to leave her room with the door locked on the outside."

"That is another matter we must clear up. To think that Father Izard, who entrusted this girl to me, is arriving tomorrow. He will be furious when I have to admit that I have failed to keep her in safe custody."

"We will certainly have gotten her back by then," the nun reassured her in a soothing tone. "How could she get past the gate?"

"Only if someone left it open for her."

The two women moved off to Victoire's great relief. At least she knew that now the search had been switched to the grounds. She could hardly wait for young Raymond to arrive.

When he did arrive she was half asleep.

"Where are you?" he said, followed by a whistle.

Victoire came out of hiding and the boy laughed at her tousled hair.

"I've brought you a bit of food," he said. "It's all my aunt could get hold of."

"That's fine . . . Listen, Raymond, will you take a message for me?"

"Of course," said the boy with a knowing grin.

Could she really depend on this young boy, however bright he might be?

"Tell your aunt there's an underground passage. It begins in the crypt and ends outside the walls of the convent."

"An underground passage!" the boy exclaimed excitedly. "Are you sure?"

Victoire was far from sure, but her last hope rested on that assumption.

"Yes. Your aunt *must* find the entrance to it before tonight. Will she also get me a nun's habit, so that I can enter the chapel without attracting attention? Do you know where the crypt is?"

"It's reached by a little staircase behind the altar," he said. "All the abbesses have been buried there since the foundation of the order in 1334," he added, proud of his knowledge.

"Can you get me a candle and something to light it with?"

"The candle is easy, they're kept in the sacristy. As for the flint, I'll try to borrow that from the gardener."

"Will you leave it on the last step of the staircase to the crypt before this evening? You won't forget?"

"Don't worry, I'll do that after Compline. And I'll help Aunt Gabrielle to find the way into the passage."

Delighted at the prospect, the young messenger jumped for joy and clapped his hands. Hearing a noise, he stopped abruptly.

"Hide quick, they're coming!" Victoire disappeared back under the sheets and towels.

Nuns arrived to prepare the midday meal and others began to sort out the washing. One of them stopped the boy. "What are you doing, young man? You know very well you're not allowed in there."

"I was looking for one of the other boys," he said with studied innocence.

"Be off! Let's hope the Superior doesn't see you. She'd be furious."

Raymond vanished through the open wash-house door.

"Our Abbess is so terribly strict," sighed one of the nuns. "These children are so nice, and they do brighten up the house so much."

"That's just what our Superior doesn't want," said another.

With every hour that passed, Victoire became increasingly pessimistic. Her plan for escape by the tunnel seemed more and more like a flight of fancy. What were the possible chances of Sister Gabrielle's finding the entrance to a passage that had not been used for nearly a century, if indeed it existed at all? Wasn't she asking her friend to expose herself to needless danger?

When the evening meal was finished and the kitchen and wash-house were dark and silent once again, she ventured out to stretch her legs. She could do nothing but wait, having tried in vain to open the doors as she had done on the previous evening. Negligence was surely not a fault of the sisters, no doubt because they feared a reprimand from their dreaded Abbess.

Victoire had to succeed tonight or resign herself to death.

Very soon, just before midnight, a faint sound told her that someone was entering the kitchen with the utmost caution. A flickering light moved toward her.

"Come quickly."

It was Raymond.

"Your aunt?"

"She thinks she's being watched. She's waiting for you in the chapel. Here are the clothes."

Swiftly Victoire put on the white and brown habit, tied the belt round her waist, and arranged the coif so that her face would be seen as little as possible.

"Do I look all right?"

The little boy grinned. "Oh, yes. You look just as funny as the rest!"

She followed him, his warm hand slipped into hers, and he led her to where Sister Gabrielle was waiting.

"You're beautiful," he whispered.

"And you're very brave and clever. I wish I had a brother like you."

"I wish I could go away with you," he said with a sigh. "It's not much fun here."

The entrance to the chapel was darker than usual and the door was half open.

"I've put out most of the candles," the boy whispered.

Victoire marveled at his foresight. Two nuns were kneeling before the altar absorbed in prayer, their heads between their hands.

Sister Gabrielle appeared from behind a pillar and beckoned to them to follow her. The three crept silently along the walls and managed to pass behind the altar without being noticed. They went down twelve steps into the darkness of the crypt, where the air was rank and humid. Raymond struck the flint and lit the candle.

"How did you guess that the passage existed?" asked Sister Gabrielle in a low voice.

"So you've found it?"

"With difficulty, as you may imagine. The crypt is a natural cave. I remembered that in the history of the foundation of the order they described the installation of the first 'enclosed nuns' in a place called 'the stone that turns.' They also said that Saint Joseph was the guardian of the convent. There's a statue of him on the tomb of the first abbess. So I then centered my inquiries there and discovered a rock that can be pushed aside just far enough to let a human being through."

"Wonderful!" exclaimed Victoire. "How can I ever thank you enough for all that you've done for me and all the risks you've taken?"

"Perhaps I will give you the opportunity one day," said Sister Gabrielle quietly.

Victoire sensed that her friend was already beginning to think of leaving this austere and joyless place, where she was bound by no true vocation. But it was too soon for her to make such a big decision.

Victoire kissed her tenderly, and then Raymond, who was quite dejected to have come to the end of his exciting adventure. She took a last look at the rows of white marble tombs engraved with names and dates. Then she took off her nun's habit and squeezed through the narrow opening while her friends held back the stone. Setting off bravely along the passage with the sole aid of a candle and a flint, she could still hear the voice of Sister Gabrielle wishing her good luck. Then there was total silence.

Chapter XVIII

*V*ictoire stumbled repeatedly on the uneven ground. She was forced to slacken her pace because she could barely see. The skill and courage of a nun and a little boy had freed her from the clutches of a lecherous monk and the vengeance of a ruthless abbess, and now she could take her time.

About half a mile, the old nun had said. Allowing for her slow progress, she reasoned it would take her a full half hour. Here and there the rock-face was so low that she was forced to crawl, taking care not to lose her flint and candle. Large rats ran between her feet, but she had reached the point where such creatures no longer frightened her.

She found herself at the top of a stairway roughly hewn from the rock. Cautiously descending the steps, she entered a large chamber with a high vaulted roof. Victoire gasped in horror. Skulls were scattered everywhere, and in one corner two skeletons leaned against the wall as if they awaited some visitor.

Who were these unhappy people who had been denied a decent burial? What sins were they expiating, to deserve such a horrible fate? Distraught with anguish and pity, Victoire was greatly relieved to get away from the charnel house and set off again down a long, straight gallery. By now she estimated she must have covered half the length of the tunnel, so with a little luck she would soon be out in the open air.

What if the other end of the passage were blocked? Surely, after a century or more, stones must have become dislodged and stopped up the exit. The thought made her legs weak, and she was obliged to lean against the wall for a moment. Would she roam this dark tunnel till she died of hunger and thirst? However terrible the prospect, she preferred that to Father Izard's hands tearing her clothes, his wet, greedy mouth on her neck and shoulders. She shuddered with disgust.

The passage had become so narrow and the air so stale that Victoire felt she was going to suffocate. Then she found herself face to face with a dead end.

At first she couldn't believe it. But she soon resigned herself to the frightening fact that she could get no farther. She pushed the stone in front of her from every possible angle, hoping to make it slew around like the one in the crypt. Yet in spite of all her vigorous shoving, the stone did not budge.

Worn out by too much worry and too little sleep, she sat down on the ground and sobbed bitterly. After several minutes it occurred to her that for someone who could normally control her feelings, she had recently dissolved in tears far too often. She must pull herself together, and in any case, she must struggle on to the limit of her endurance. As a country girl who had been brought up in the open air, she was aware of her staying power. But her agony would be prolonged precisely because of it.

Nevertheless, she succeeded in retracing her steps along the passage that only a little while before had so raised her hopes. Perhaps there was another tunnel she had failed to notice in the darkness. She decided to put out the candle, which was burning down dangerously fast, slipped it into her pocket, and proceeded with her arms outstretched on either side so as not to miss any gap in the walls.

It was an exhausting walk and she fell several times, scratching her knees and hands. After what seemed like hours, she reached the big chamber without having come across any alternate route. Again and again she struck the flint before it would catch the damp tinder. She needed to orient herself in the huge room filled with skeletons before going on.

She walked the perimeter and decided that there was no exit, apart from the passage that led to the staircase. There was, of course, the way back to the crypt, but she did not in the least relish the idea of returning to the convent. She was beginning to think she would have to do so, when, as she passed a pile of bones, she seemed to detect an empty space behind them . . .

She had to summon up her courage to climb over skeletal remains of people who died decades ago, because she knew her life depended on it. She managed to overcome her fear and reached the other side.

There she found an almost circular opening, just wide enough for a slim person to get through. She slid into it without much hope, but little by little the roof became higher, and before long she was able to stand up. Her progress was now less arduous, but she was shocked to see the size of the candle. It would not last much longer. Would she succeed in finding an exit before the only light source went out, leaving her again in complete darkness?

After about ten minutes, it seemed that the atmosphere was becoming fresher and less close. Then, all of a sudden, she noticed a scarcely perceptible brightness. To make sure it wasn't an illusion, Victoire put out her light and let her eyes get used to the semi-darkness. There was no doubt now that a very faint glow was filtering through a crack just above her head.

Dawn was just beginning to break. Victoire decided

to wait and rest before she made the final attempt to leave the tunnel, when a little daylight would be of great assistance. She stretched out on the ground, and in spite of the hardness and discomfort, she quickly fell into a heavy sleep.

She awoke to the sound of flapping wings and thrilled at the sight of a bird blithely circling around a shaft of sunlight. The moment for her ascent had come, and suddenly she was seized with impatience at being so near to freedom. But first she had to move away the stones blocking the opening. Sweat trickled down on her forehead and back, her fingernails were broken and her feet bruised by a falling stone. Nothing else mattered: she kept on working till the aperture looked large enough to let her through.

About an hour later she emerged into the open air, surrounded by brambles that ripped her skirt and scratched her hands. She wiped away the drops of blood with her dress. She was in the midst of an overgrown forest and rising majestically before her was the huge oak tree, confirming the success of her wild enterprise.

She reveled quietly in her triumph and pictured with pleasure the anger and discomfiture of the Abbess, who at that very moment might be making her report to Father Izard. Then she tried to find her bearings. She took a winding footpath through the underbrush, not knowing in which direction it led, and silently prayed it would not lead back toward the convent.

She took a turning to the right and walked on till the sun's position told her it was nearly noon. In any case, her stomach was already reminding her that it was high time for some nourishment. In August, alas, there were no more strawberries and raspberries, and it was too early for blackberries and hazelnuts . . .

She reached a clearing where she heard signs of life. She moved stealthily, hiding behind tree trunks. Soon she caught sight of a herd of cows peacefully grazing in the care of a young girl. Victoire walked toward her cautiously.

"Could you let me have a little milk?" she asked. "I'm dying of hunger."

The child gazed wide-eyed at this apparition coming from the woods in stained and ragged clothes whose material clearly identified her as a young lady from the town.

"If you like," she said.

She handed Victoire a pewter goblet, having dipped it in a pitcher of the frothy, lukewarm liquid. Victoire quenched her thirst in long gulps, aware of the curiosity she was arousing.

"Where are we?"

The child burst out laughing at this silly question. "You really don't know?"

"I'm lost."

Still incredulous, the child pointed out some houses that could be seen behind a row of trees.

"The hamlet is called Charmy."

The name meant nothing to Victoire. "Is it far from Paris?"

"Oh, yes," the child assured her. "It's at least two hours away by cart. I've never been there . . . Perhaps my uncle will take me there one day when he goes to market. Look, here he comes!"

A man about forty years old came toward them. He walked slowly, carrying a heavy basket.

"So! I see you have company, my child," he said, but directing his comment to the young woman.

Unsure of what to say, she hesitated. "I fell off when I was riding. My horse galloped away, and I am stranded. Would you be so kind as to show me the road to Paris?"

The man scratched his head. He was puzzled by this stranger who seemed to be a person of quality in spite of her untidy appearance. "You're not hurt?" he asked suspiciously.

She showed him the blood on her hands. "Only here."

His manner softened when he saw her wrists, reddened and scratched by the brambles, and the countless grazes her hands had suffered in the underground passage.

"Come to the farm. My wife will clean you up."

In a large room with a red tiled floor a large woman was busy at the kitchen stove. She turned to face her husband as he came in, surprised that he was not on his own.

"I have brought you a young lady who needs attention."

Her face was flushed by the fire combined with the heat of noon. Having wiped her hands on her apron, she examined Victoire's injuries. "What a state to have got yourself in," she said reprovingly. "My poor girl, sit down there. I am going to fetch a clean cloth and some hot water."

Victoire quickly realized these rough peasant folk had hearts of gold. At ease in their company, she was delighted to eat the delicious meal they offered to share with her.

"My goodness, you were hungry!" the woman remarked. And a half smile appeared on her lips as she handed her guest the big loaf of bread and the salted butter. Victoire needed no encouragement. Now that she was fed and out of danger, her mind turned to other thoughts: the distorted face of her mother, the unknown fate of Anselme and Guillaume, and also of Gilone . . .

Chapter XIX

"*Mademoiselle* Victoire!" exclaimed Cassitère's manservant. "Monsieur le Comte has been greatly distressed. He thought you were dead, even though my master assured him you were not. How happy they both will be!"

Victoire was brought to Cassitère, who was bent over an old book of magic spells.

"My child! At last you have escaped from the evil spell! What joy to find you safe and sound . . ."

"Ah! Safe, but exhausted. I was given a ride to the city gates and then had to walk from there to reach you."

Victoire told him her many adventures and explained how desperately worried she had been about her uncle.

"I can reassure you right away, because he will be here any moment. Every day he comes to beg me to do everything possible to find you. Unhappily this task has proved beyond my powers. I consulted the stars, the cards, the mirror, but you were nowhere to be seen. It was as if a screen had been placed between you and the rest of the world. Nevertheless, I knew that you were alive, thanks to your horoscope. Your uncle feared the worst and refused to believe me. The poor man has hardly slept a wink since you disappeared."

"How did he escape the massacre?" asked Victoire, not daring yet to ask the seer about her lover.

"He will tell you about that himself . . . because he is just arriving."

Cassitère closed his eyes, and a few seconds later there was indeed a loud knock at the front door. Told by the servant that his niece had returned, Anselme rushed into the room and hugged her, laughing and weeping with joy.

"I thought I would never see you again. I was heartbroken . . . first your mother and then you . . . It was altogether too much to bear."

When she was able to study her uncle calmly, she was horrified by his appearance: his ordeals had suddenly aged him greatly. He was terribly thin and lined. "You seem very tired, Uncle."

"Oh! Now that you are here, all will be well."

Cassitère left the room for a moment and came back with a phial of colorless liquid. Handing it to his friend, he instructed, "Take five drops of this elixir morning and evening, and your strength will be restored."

Although she dreaded the thought, Victoire resigned herself to returning to the Louvre. If she were to find her cousin and her beloved Guillaume again, it had to be done.

"My poor child, you *are* in a state," remarked the Comte de Montmaur as Léon, who also had miraculously survived the massacre, drove them through the streets of Paris. The cobblestones were still littered with corpses.

"It's nothing," said Victoire. The spectacle of heaped-up bodies and looted houses still moved her deeply, but she was by now somewhat hardened to the sight. "With a clean dress and Héloïse's help, I'll be the niece you remember within an hour."

The old man could not resist kissing her yet again. "I was so afraid . . . If you hadn't come back I think I'd have died of grief."

The sight of his drawn features, the new wrinkles that had appeared in only a few days, and his trembling hands left Victoire in no doubt as to what to do. It was essential to return to Montmaur as soon as possible so the poor man could rest and recover from his harrowing experiences.

"Uncle, what has become of Monsieur de Louvencourt?"

Anselme beamed at her. "He misses you so much . . . He sends Boris for news of you twice a day."

"He wasn't hurt?"

"Only slightly. He was struck in the ribs by a halberd."

Victoire sighed in relief. How many times since her capture had she pictured Guillaume wounded and bleeding. What bliss to know that he was still alive . . . and still cared for her.

Anselme's face clouded. "Not knowing your fate, I arranged for your poor mother to be buried yesterday. It was not easy. There are so many dead."

"How many?"

He shook his head. "Thousands. And it's not over yet. His Majesty ordered an end to the massacre, but in the Cemetery of the Innocents a fanatic monk claimed that he saw a dead hawthorn grow green and flower again. This miracle was taken as a clear sign of God's pleasure, and so the killings have started up again on a wider scale; not to mention the shameless looting. Now it's spreading to the provinces. In Orléans, five hundred Huguenots died in three days!"

"When will all these horrors stop?"

"At the Louvre, calm has almost been restored."

Suddenly Victoire realized that she hadn't inquired about Gilone.

"Oh! Her . . ." muttered her uncle. "It's bad to be without religion or honor. Belonging to the Flying Squadron has turned her head. She may recant. At least your mother can not witness that."

"Recant?" exclaimed Victoire. "How unspeakable, when they've just murdered our fellow Protestants!"

But on reflection there was no great reason for surprise. Gilone's recent behavior had clearly pointed to such an outcome. "Tell me, Uncle, how you managed to escape from Father Izard."

"Queen Catherine sent for me and, in spite of my protests, kept me shut up until noon the following day. She saved my life."

"Because of her, my mother is dead. And the Admiral, most horribly. And so many others . . . That woman is the devil incarnate." Victoire described to her uncle how she had overheard the plotters in the Tuileries gardens. "Surely it was monstrous to order such a cold-blooded massacre!"

"Most certainly," sighed the Comte de Montmaur. "But surely she was coerced by men she no longer controlled?"

Victoire could not share her uncle's indulgence. "I don't care, I hate her! Although I am glad she saved your life, dear Uncle."

Seeing the somber façade of the Louvre depressed her. It seemed likely that Father Izard, enraged by his setback, would try to kidnap her again. She said as much to her uncle.

"I have already considered that problem," he said. "We shall stop at the Louvre only long enough to pack our bags and pay our respects to the Queen, then we shall go and stay with my friend the Marquis d'Hautemart. I am obliged to remain another fortnight in the capital to straighten out certain affairs. Afterward we shall return to Montmaur, where you will be safe from the various machinations that threaten you."

"And what about Guillaume?" she murmured. "Must I be parted from him forever?"

"Why shouldn't he come and visit us at Montmaur? From now on you will be mistress of the estate, and the running of the house will keep you busy. What's more, you still have to learn about the administration of what land we still possess. Before she died, your mother had time to appoint a new bailiff. Thanks be to God, the Queen has been most generous toward me and we have enough to live on for a good year or more. But certainly the question of your marriage will arise."

"Uncle! I'm in no hurry to marry. I'd certainly much prefer to live with you than with a Monsieur de Mèrande!"

"I am flattered, dear niece, that you derive some pleasure from the company of an old man like myself. Nevertheless, I should inform you of the death of the fiancé your mother picked for you."

Anselme cleared his throat, as if embarrassed by what he was going to ask. "And Monsieur de Louvencourt? Do you have the impression he thinks of marrying you?"

Victoire turned to the Comte de Montmaur with a melancholy smile. "I don't think so, Uncle. Apart from the fact we are divided by religion, I don't believe he really loves me."

"You surprise me. Is it a sign of indifference that he has been utterly dejected ever since you were kidnapped?"

"Really?"

"I went to see him while his wound still kept him in bed. He spoke only of you, of your courage, of the way you walked across that roof. I must confess that when I thought of you in that perilous position, my blood ran cold."

"I wouldn't like to try it again," Victoire admitted. "Any more than roaming about in an underground passage. As for Guillaume," she sighed, "he told me that his feelings for me were no more than those of a close friend."

Anselme remained silent, deep in thought.

As Victoire reached the little gallery that led to her room, she ran into Gilone. She was wearing a sumptuous dress borrowed from Alix, a poppy-red silk with pearls around the bodice.

"Hello. So you're back," she said with no more feeling, as if they had met the night before and nothing special had happened. "Where did *you* disappear to?"

Victoire had no desire to tell her cousin about her adventures. She gestured vaguely. "I'm still alive . . . And what about you? How did you escape the fury of the Catholics?"

Gilone shrugged. "Who would dare attack a lady-in-waiting to the Queen?"

"You are a Protestant, all the same. There's a rumor that you're going to recant. Is it true?"

"So you've already heard," said Gilone, smiling. "Won't I have a better chance of marrying a rich man, as I intend to do, by turning Catholic? What do you think?"

This opportunism sickened Victoire. It was virtually infamous. "Aren't you ashamed to abandon the religion you were brought up in, especially after all that has happened? I'll tell you, in case you don't know, your aunt—my mother—was murdered by those very people you are so keen to join."

"I heard about it, and I am heartbroken for your sake," said Gilone in an artificial tone of voice. "Yet . . . Now, you're as free as I am."

"You're vile!" exclaimed Victoire in disgust. "So that's your funeral oration for a woman who brought you up and treated you like her daughter?" How Gilone had changed since she came to Court! It was hard to believe her childhood friend, who was perhaps a little shallow and anxious to please but affectionate and gay, had turned into this greedy, calculating, unscrupulous creature, this profligate.

"What about Monsieur de Lévis?" asked Victoire.

"I really don't know what's become of him," replied Gilone with indifference. "Anyhow, I hardly see him anymore. The company of his master, the Duc de Cavalade, is more to my liking."

"He's three times your age!"

"So what? His wealth and generosity are ample compensation for such a minor drawback."

Victoire held back a cutting remark. What was the good of it? Gilone had reached the point of no return. "Uncle Anselme and I are leaving for Montmaur," she said. "I feel we shall not be seeing you anymore."

"I have been worried to death," cried Héloïse when she caught sight of Victoire. "I really thought you'd been slaughtered, like Madame." At the thought of her mistress's terrible end, the maidservant burst into tears.

"I said to Monsieur de Lévis' valet, 'Mark my words, Joseph,' I said, 'Mademoiselle Victoire will never come back to us.' He did his best to console me, poor man, and tried to reassure me. He has looked after me so well," she added.

Victoire smiled a little sadly. "Now you must forget those bad times. We are going to leave the Louvre, stay a few days with a friend of my uncle, and then return to Montmaur. You'll see your fiancé again."

Héloïse blushed and started to fidget. "It's just that . . . I've got a new fiancé."

"Joseph?"

"Yes. A Parisian, after all, is better."

Victoire could not resist a laugh.

"He's got nice manners . . . And then he has traveled, accompanied Monsieur Philippe's father to England and Holland. He knows so much! If only you could hear all the things he tells me about. He's not like the other one, who could only stare at me and talk about his cows." Héloïse now felt nothing but disdain for the unfortunate peasant who was patiently waiting for her at Montmaur. Travel had transformed her, too.

"Has he asked you to marry him?"

"Yes . . . Still, I wouldn't like to leave your service, especially now that you are alone."

"I shall be very sorry to lose you, Héloïse. Nevertheless, if you are certain about Joseph, I shall not hold you back. Has he spoken to his master about it?"

"Yes. Monsieur Philippe's sister, who is nearly sixteen, needs a lady's maid."

"In that case," said Victoire, "I wish you every possible happiness. You know that you can always come back to Montmaur if things don't turn out as well as you hope. In the meantime, please help me with my hair, and then we can pack the trunks."

While Héloïse chattered on about the deplorable state of her long hair, Victoire quietly pondered her future.

She could foresee a peaceful, uneventful life in an old castle that would become more and more dilapidated as years went by; a life without much entertainment apart from riding, reading, infrequent visits, and her conversations with Anselme. Formerly, when she knew no other, that austere existence was all she asked for. Even as Gilone and then Héloïse had changed, Victoire herself no longer felt the same either. Dangers and privations, perhaps love as well, had matured her. She was no longer the innocent young girl, dependent on her mother, forced to obey her and to accept a husband she disliked. Having discovered the weaknesses of human nature from observing life at Court, she had learned to mistrust appearances and to judge people on their true worth, and not on their rank, office, or wealth. Her experience perhaps made her less indulgent to herself than to others—even toward Gilone. After all, the girl had hardly been a spoiled darling of fortune. Wasn't it quite natural that she should seek revenge? So much the better for her if she achieved it. Victoire was not, however, convinced that her cousin had chosen the best means. In those depraved surroundings where luxury, greed, and lust for power permitted every kind of baseness and cruelty, would she succeed in finding happiness—and if she did, would she recognize it in time? It could well happen that the unintelligent but cunning Mademoiselle de Glymes would content herself with a brilliant present that would blind her to the future. The Queen might tire of her, and her youth and beauty wouldn't last forever. What would become of her when she was no longer attractive to men, since this appeared to be her sole aim in life?

Having abandoned her cousin to a fate she did not envy, Victoire turned her thoughts to Guillaume, whom she was going to see again as soon as Héloïse had made her presentable.

She despaired at the thought of tearing herself away from him by leaving the capital. Never again, she was sure, would she love a man so strongly, so completely, with her entire being. But alas, even if the young man begged her to become his wife—and clearly that was far from likely—it would be unthinkable and dishonorable to marry a man whose co-religionists had murdered her father and mother! How could she hope that he would become a convert, when the thought of converting was so unthinkable for her.

Yet in the bottom of her heart, Victoire was unable to admit to herself that in two weeks at the most everything would be over between them.

Chapter XX

"*Victoire*, at last!"

With some difficulty Guillaume struggled out of bed and managed to stand up. He was pale, but still as darkly handsome as ever. Victoire threw herself into his arms, speechless with joy. With her face pressed against her lover's shoulder, she reveled in the pleasure of finding him again. Breathing the lemon scent that came from his body, she gazed at him steadily while he held her as tightly as his still-unhealed wound would allow. Victoire dared to hope that Anselme was right, for this surely was no perfunctory welcome.

"Get back in bed, Guillaume. You are still in pain."

"True," he admitted. "It still hurts to stand up. That guard certainly didn't miss with his pike."

With no sense of shame, she lay down beside him. She was too eager for contact with his body to stay in the armchair, as propriety required. She had so little time left to love Guillaume . . .

"Tell me everything that's happened to you," he said, putting his arm around her shoulders. "I looked for you all over the Louvre when we lost each other."

"So did I!" exclaimed Victoire.

"The first wound I received left me unconscious for a few moments. Boris, who was stunned, managed to bring me around. As soon as I could walk, we went looking for you—there were so many corpses . . . Then I wanted to get to your room, hoping you had sought refuge there."

"In fact," said Victoire, "I was trying to find out what had become of my family."

"The Comte de Montmaur, who was kind enough to come and see me, described the horrible way your poor mother died. Until then, I had imagined nothing could be more dreadful than my own mother's end. How awful for you!"

Guillaume kissed her so lovingly that she wanted to cry. Why wasn't it possible to stay with him forever? Life was so absurdly unfair.

He continued telling what had happened to him, pausing to kiss and caress her as he spoke.

"I scarcely had gotten to my feet again before ten halberdiers rushed at me and Boris. He tried to defend me and was wounded. Both of us were drenched in blood. I was in such pain, for a moment I thought I would die then and there. Fortunately some friends arrived, and seeing the state we were in, managed to carry us away from the massacre. And all this time I didn't know what had happened to you and was out of my mind with worry."

Wasn't this a proof, if not of love, certainly at least of very deep affection that she sought?

Victoire then gave him an account of her adventures.

"That filthy man!" cried Guillaume indignantly. "He dared to lay hands on you. I trust . . ."

"No," Victoire replied with a wry smile; even the recollection of those recent events was still painful to her. "Thanks to your dagger and Boris's lessons. If only I'd killed him!"

"I made the same mistake not finishing off Adrien d'Etivey," said Guillaume gravely.

"Has he left you alone since our escape?"

"Since I haven't left my bed, he doesn't know what's happened to me. The moment I recover, we are going to select another weapon to replace the one you've lost. As long as that monster Izard remains alive, I shall fear for your safety."

So as not to cast gloom over their reunion, Victoire did not tell him she was returning to Montmaur, where happily she wouldn't need to use the weapon. She would simply keep it as a precious souvenir.

The young man looked at her and smiled. "Ever since you came in and I was reassured, I've been feeling so much better. I'm going to recover very quickly!" Gently he stroked her shoulder.

Victoire smiled at him. "Suppose I lock the door?" she suggested, getting up. Then she moved back toward the bed. Quite slowly, while his eyes never left her, she took off her dress, her chemise, and lace-trimmed petticoat. For the first time in her life, she showed herself naked to a man she could see was filled with desire.

"How beautiful you are like that," he whispered, dazzled by the slim strong body offered him with such simplicity.

He tore off his shirt and Victoire surrendered herself, intoxicated by the contact of his skin with hers. This time she prepared herself impatiently for the pleasure ahead. She was no longer afraid to give herself entirely to a man—whom she loved completely.

It was most necessary now to tell Guillaume that they would soon be parted. How would he react to the news? Perhaps he would resign himself quite easily to seeing her no more, but Victoire was by no means sure of this. In fact, she strongly doubted it.

"We are leaving the Louvre today," said Victoire as she began to get dressed. "Uncle Anselme thinks we shall run less risk if we stay with his friend the Marquis d'Hautemart."

"He's right. So long as that beast disguised as a man of God has breath in his body, you will never be safe in the palace. In two days I shall be up and about again, and I sincerely hope that your uncle will allow me to visit you frequently."

Victoire smiled. "Of course, he likes you very much.

In a fortnight," she paused, then bravely plunged on, "when he has settled his business affairs, we shall be going back to Montmaur."

"So soon!"

At the sight of his saddened face, for one mad moment Victoire felt that Guillaume was going to propose to her.

"How sorry I shall be to lose you," was all he said.

"I shall be sorry, too," said Victoire. She did not dare add that at Montmaur she would await his arrival every day and would scrutinize every rider she caught sight of in the distance. She couldn't appear more upset than he was, she thought. Besides, she was hurt by his apparently calm acceptance of their imminent and doubtless final separation, when he had just shown her so ardently how much her body pleased him. Did all men behave like this? She wanted suddenly to get even with him, to hurt him.

"You'll soon forget all about me," she said lightly. "There are plenty of other women, prettier and more seductive than a little provincial girl . . ."

Guillaume looked at her with great seriousness. "Don't ever think that, Victoire," he said tensely. "Were I not still smitten with remorse at Marie's death and haunted by her memory, I know in time I would have loved you completely."

Helped by Jacotte, Héloïse finished packing the trunks. Victoire had no regrets about leaving a place where she had risked her life several times, lost her mother and, in another sense, Gilone. And now Héloïse, in tears, was leaving her, too. Who would replace her? Why shouldn't she take Jacotte, if she agreed to leave Paris?

The girl accepted the job at once. What she had seen in one week had terrified her so much that she was delighted at the prospect of living quietly in the country. Besides, being an orphan with no prospect of marriage, she had little reason to stay in the capital.

Victoire went to see her uncle. He was wearing his full dress of pearl-gray doublet with blue facings and cap to match, which gave him a slightly odd appearance. He was awaiting an audience with the Queen.

"I have engaged Jacotte," she announced, "since Héloïse is getting married."

"Are you sure a little girl like her can look after you properly? She is very young."

"Certainly at Montmaur, Uncle. The time of receptions and balls is over."

"Not forever," declared Anselme. "I am going to work very hard, and in a few months' time, when the atmosphere in Paris has calmed down, we shall come back to stay."

In that case, she would not be separated for good from Guillaume. Victoire was overjoyed at the thought. Now she could live for the moment when she saw him again and, who knows, when she might win him over forever.

"The thought of seeing the Queen again disgusts me," she said in a low voice.

Anselme turned to his niece with a look of pity. "My poor child, I understand how you feel. It is not easy to forgive the death of one's mother. But you must realize that this is a formality we cannot avoid."

"Certainly," said Victoire. "I only hope it doesn't last too long."

"You can rely on me to keep it as brief as possible. All the same, do remember that, thanks to the Queen, we shall be able to live for nearly a year without difficulty."

"I'm not likely to forget," sighed Victoire.

Still less would she forget the death of her mother, the poisoned cakes that killed an innocent animal, and her stabbing the night of the fireworks. Who was behind the horrible deeds of Father Izard? But then she had to admit that she could be certain of nothing at all where the monk was concerned.

Clad in her customary widow's weeds, relieved simply by a white ruff, Queen Catherine received the Montmaurs in the room where Victoire had overheard her conversation with the Duchesse de Guise through the attic trapdoor.

"You are leaving us so soon," said the Queen most amiably to Anselme, after he had bowed to her and his niece had curtsied deeply. "We are greatly saddened."

"Your Majesty is kind indeed to set store by the presence of a humble glassmaker. But we only came to Paris to accompany Victoire, who was chosen as a maid of honor by the late Queen of Navarre, and to attend the royal marriage celebrations. Now there is no reason to prolong our stay."

The sovereign studied Victoire with a sharp eye.

"Mademoiselle de Montmaur," she said, "appears to possess all the necessary qualities to become one of my own maids of honor. In this way, I shall also have the privilege of retaining a great artist at Court."

The Comte de Montmaur thanked the Queen profusely and left Victoire to make her own reply.

"Her Majesty has shown infinite generosity in deigning to consider me. Nevertheless, she doubtless has no knowledge of the great sorrow that has so recently afflicted me. I shall therefore be infinitely grateful to Her Majesty if she will consent to my withdrawal to Montmaur in the company of the sole surviving member of my family."

There was a sweet and cajoling expression on Catherine de Medici's face as she gently twisted a ring set with an enormous sapphire.

"I am aware, Mademoiselle, that you have experienced the terrible grief of losing your mother. I am deeply distressed by it, and I respect the feelings that urge you to abandon for the moment the frivolities of the Court. However, consider my offer. It will hold good."

To work for the instigator of such a massacre was unthinkable. "I thank Your Majesty for her kindness," said Victoire, looking her straight in the face.

The Queen dropped the subject and led Anselme to the other end of the room, where there was a cabinet containing glass decanters and sweetmeat boxes.

"Look closely at these and see if you can make pieces of this kind in a dark red, the color of rubies."

While the master glassmaker was engrossed in studying the rare pieces of Venetian origin, the Queen returned to Victoire and caught her trying to determine the position of the trapdoor. She smiled with a touch of mockery and Victoire turned crimson. How foolish to give herself away like that!

"You are admiring the fresco on the ceiling? You are right. It is the work of a very great artist, Niccolo del Abbate, whom I brought specially from Italy."

Ill at ease, Victoire did not know what attitude to adopt. Clearly the Queen was teasing her, but was she also going to make her pay for her indiscretion?

"I like people who are observant," continued the Florentine. "There are not so many of them as one might think. If they combine discretion with observation, they are of invaluable assistance in matters that can sometimes be delicate."

Wasn't she again inviting her, in a thinly disguised way, to join the Flying Squadron?

"My cousin, Mademoiselle de Glymes, already has the honor of serving Your Majesty."

"Dear child, only a few are endowed with intelligence. And it is those alone who can render inestimable services to their country . . . a country we must constantly defend against attack from abroad—and not only on the battlefields."

"By spying on each other in the most deceitful ways and then loyally reporting the secrets overheard?"

"Please think about it," said the Queen as Anselme came over to them.

"I can most certainly produce pieces of that kind for Your Majesty."

"So now, my dear friend, I will allow you to return for a time to your estate with your charming niece. But do not fail to return soon to the Court. There will always be a place for you here. And for you also, Mademoiselle."

In spite of the gracious tone of voice, it was a command. The Montmaurs bowed to take their leave.

Chapter XXI

Informed of the arrival of the Montmaur entourage, the Marquis d'Hautemart's major-domo stood waiting for them at the top of the stone steps in front of the house. As the carriage drew up, two footmen in the Marquis's white and yellow livery hurried to lower the folding steps and open the doors, while the major-domo, somewhat more sedately, walked forward to greet the guests, on whom he had been enjoined to bestow his closest personal attention.

"Monsieur le Marquis welcomes you most warmly. Unfortunately he will not be back until tomorrow and has asked me to place myself at your disposal."

They were escorted to their rooms on the first floor

and were dazzled by the luxury and elegance of the place, which was much grander than their rooms in the royal palace, let alone back home in their old castle. In Victoire's room a maidservant was already opening the wardrobes.

"This is Julie, who will take her orders from Mademoiselle de Montmaur."

The charming brunette curtsied gracefully.

"A meal will be served to you below as soon as you wish," the steward added. "Unless you would prefer to take it in your rooms."

Anselme consulted his niece. "We shall come down as soon as we have refreshed ourselves."

Next to the room and boudoir destined for Victoire, the Comte de Montmaur had the use of a little paneled study, lined with rare books, which led to his own room.

"We shall be more comfortable here than in the Louvre," whispered Victoire, who was more than pleased to have moved from a poorly furnished attic to a vast apartment with walls entirely hung with pearl-gray silk tapestry.

Her feet sank into the plush carpet, whose subtle color schemes enchanted her. The windows opened onto a completely enclosed and private garden that was heavy with the scent of roses.

Jacotte arrived with Victoire's tapestry bag, her eyes popping with wonder. "Everything here is so beautiful, Mademoiselle!"

With a slightly superior air, Julie smiled at such lack of sophistication, and Victorie hoped she would instill into Jacotte the rudiments of her job as lady's maid.

Preceded by a footman, uncle and niece descended a marble staircase with wrought-iron banisters and passed through a room hung with ancestral portraits and into a charming room where the table was laid for supper.

The butler bowed to them. "Monsieur le Marquis thought you would prefer to take supper here rather than in the large dining room." He opened a door to show them a dining table amply large enough to seat twenty guests.

"To be sure," said Anselme with a smile.

Victoire quietly admired the quality of the table-cloth. Clearly the Marquis was a rich man, and this was the sort of establishment where Gilone would love to be invited. The thought of her cousin and their last meeting saddened her for a few moments. But Gilone swiftly slipped from her mind when she was served with lark and thrush pâtés, accompanied by a fine Burgundy that Anselme sipped knowledgeably.

When she awoke next morning in her strange new bedroom, Victoire stretched herself sensuously in the large bed. She didn't set much store by luxury, but it did make life easier and more agreeable. She felt the heavy silk brocade of her counterpane, and the soft white satin eiderdown. Through the shutters she could see it was broad daylight. She pulled a bell rope to call Julie, who soon entered with a tray.

"Good morning, Mademoiselle. Monsieur le Comte wishes to see you as soon as you are ready."

Sun streamed into the room and Victoire felt blissfully happy. What joy it was to be free and safe, to enjoy once again Guillaume's love and Anselme's affection, as well as to be living in such a sumptuous abode! Then she felt a sudden wave of guilt. How could she feel so happy when her mother had been dead for only a week? Should she not frankly admit— and she was shocked by this unnatural sentiment— that she had never enjoyed a close and tender relationship with her strict, rigid mother that normally exists between a girl and the woman who brought her into the world? Victoire's grief at her loss was neither pronounced nor profound. And now the certainty of no longer being compelled to marry Monsieur de Mèrande, or someone like him, was a considerable relief to her. She also knew her uncle was too fond of her to thwart her or to bully her into marrying against her wishes.

With skill and quiet efficiency born of experience, Julie dressed Victoire and did her hair, better than Héloïse had ever done it. Victoire felt bound to compliment her.

"How clever you are with your hands."

Julie went pink with pleasure. "Mademoiselle is most kind to express her satisfaction."

As he waited for his niece the Comte de Montmaur turned the pages of *The Christian Institutes,* a weighty catechism by Calvin, bound in red morocco, bearing the Marquis's coat of arms.

"My dear child, I must have a few words with you before we go to greet our host, who arrived at daybreak. Alexandre d'Hautemart has been converted very recently to our religion. Few people know this, and that is why he and his residence have been spared. Nevertheless, like all new converts, he is a passionate supporter of our cause, and I suspect him of plotting against the Guises. There is no doubt that he is committed to avenge the Admiral's death."

"How well I understand him, Uncle, and approve him!" said Victoire.

She saw again the Admiral, who had scorned so many warnings, clinging to the balcony and then falling to the feet of his murderers before being handed over to the guards. His corpse, or what remained of it, was left hanging for three days from the gibbet at Montfaucon.

Alexandre d'Hautemart turned out to be a strikingly handsome man in his forties. A certain hardness in the eyes and a general look of determination were balanced by his courteous and affable manner.

He held Anselme in his arms and looked at Victoire. "Mademoiselle," he said, "I know well what you have been through."

"It's more than you think," said Anselme. "As if it weren't enough to lose her mother so brutally, she was then twice kidnapped and only managed to escape each time by means of her own courage and, I need hardly say, ingenuity."

"Tell me about it," said the Marquis, gazing at her intently.

A little embarrassed, Victoire gave a brief account of her adventures as her host listened with great interest.

"You have shown as much and perhaps more courage than many men I know."

"I didn't want to stay locked up for the rest of my life," said Victoire simply.

"If our party," continued the Marquis, turning to Anselme, "had a large number of followers of your niece's caliber, we would most certainly get the better of those who are attempting to seize power—including the murder of our leaders."

Victoire longed to offer her services, but she didn't dare to do so in spite of the Marquis d'Hautemart's flattering remarks. After all, who could use a young girl who couldn't even handle a harquebus or a musket, when so many brave men supported their cause?

The Marquis had invited two of his friends to supper. They were the Vidame de Barville and the young banker Becavallo, both of whom belonged to the Reformed Church. Before going in to dinner, they sat in the salon and discussed the deaths of many prominent Protestants.

"So many of our people perished only hours after they thought they were safe," sighed the Vidame de Barville, a large, ruddy man and a staunch fighter, who was wearing his arm in a sling.

"A prominent and reliable person tells me there

were ten thousand victims," said Guy Becavallo, a Venetian banker who had followed the example of his French mother in becoming a convert.

"Others are less pessimistic," said the Marquis. "They put the total number slaughtered at four thousand."

"Not counting the wounded," remarked Anselme, pointing to the Vidame's injured arm.

"For certain people, surely, the massacre was also the opportunity to settle private feuds and rivalries?" Victoire ventured.

"No doubt," agreed the Marquis. "And what about looting? Do you know that Maître Josserand, the Queen Mother's doctor, values the total plunder—that is to say, what was stolen from our brothers and probably from some of the unfortunate goldsmiths—at one million and a half gold crowns?"

"As much as that!" said the banker.

There was a silence during which each of them pondered the vastness of the sum.

"My friends," said Alexandre d'Hautemart, "let us stop brooding on our troubles and turn our minds to action. It must never be said that we left the murder of the Admiral unavenged. Do not forget that after the first attempt, the King of Navarre and the Prince de Condé were already pledged to avenge him and to demand redress from Her Majesty."

"For the time being," said Anselme, "I believe they are powerless. Surely they are being held virtually prisoners in the Louvre in order to compel them to recant?"

"That's true," acknowledged the Vidame de Barville, who had been getting aroused. "What can we do about it?"

Victoire wondered if the King of Navarre, now brother-in-law of the King, would be all that eager to fight his new relatives. And the Queen would surely know some way of keeping her son-in-law in check.

"The moment has not yet come," declared the Marquis, "but it will not be long. Can I count on you, my friends?"

All the men assured their host of their unshakable devotion to the cause. And as they went in to supper, Victoire could not refrain from whispering in the Marquis's ear, "If you ever need me . . ."

As calm was slowly restored to the capital—the King having firmly decreed an end to the carnage—the Marquis d'Hautemart received more disturbing news from the provinces. He told his guests that at Lyon, the Rhône and Saône rivers were carrying away corpses in hundreds, and that following the savage orders of the Duc de Montpensier, the cities of Blois, Saumur, and Tours had been turned into slaughterhouses.

"Will the King be able to stop these killings?" Victoire asked the Marquis.

"Alas, passions are inflamed. We can only hope that the local governors will show tolerance. In Burgundy and Provence, at least for the moment, they are avoiding the worst." The Marquis's face hardened. "A Royal Edict has suppressed all sermons, services, and any practice of our religion whatsoever."

"Since when?" exclaimed Anselme.

"Since August 28th. Now we shall have to gain back our freedom of worship."

"Perhaps it is no more than a temporary measure."

"Temporary measures of this kind have a tendency to last forever."

Everything she was hearing served to strengthen Victoire's desire to fight beside her co-religionists. Was she going to become a fanatic puritan like her mother? She didn't think so. Certainly she was devout in her faith and would never betray it for anything in the world; least of all would she follow Gilone's deplorable example. Nevertheless, among the motives which prompted her to action, she recognized the satisfaction of playing some part, however humble, in opposing the Queen, the Duchesse de Guise, and her execrable son.

She did not discuss these matters with Guillaume, who had now practically recovered and was coming to see her every day. They stayed as a rule in the little garden, where the Marquis had provided seats. They sipped cherry wine and chatted about everything except the future because they both sensed they might never see each other again.

For Victoire, their separation came all too soon. How terribly quickly a fortnight passed in the company of one's lover! When they parted, Victoire did her best to hide her distress as Guillaume promised with passion and enthusiasm to visit Montmaur during the winter, unless the King sent him to fight the Huguenots, a prospect he did not look forward to. There was talk of uprisings in southwestern France. Not that he wasn't brave, but he knew the tension this would create with Victoire.

When she took leave of her host and thanked him warmly for his lavish and friendly hospitality, Victoire had a last conversation with him.

"That offer you made me the other day—did you really mean it?" asked the Marquis.

"Most certainly, Monsieur. I know that a young girl can be of little help in the struggle we are planning, but if ever there is any chance of my serving our cause, I beg you to call on me."

Alexandre d'Hautemart smiled and kissed Victoire's hand. "There are circumstances in which a young woman passes unnoticed, whereas a man would attract attention. I gratefully accept your offer, and when the time comes I shall send you a messenger. You already know him: it will be young Becavallo."

Chapter XXII

Paris was already far behind them. The Montmaurs were traveling home on the same road that, four months earlier, had led them to the city so full of hopes and illusions.

Just four months, thought Victoire. Was it really possible for so much to have happened in such a short time? The inside of the coach had not changed, but whereas it had been uncomfortably crowded on the way to Paris, there was, alas, ample room for everyone. Although Jacotte had replaced Héloïse, there were still two people missing on this return journey.

Anselme and Victoire knew well that in embarking on the journey back to Montmaur they were exposing themselves to serious dangers. Having no escort, they were easy prey to the countless bands of highwaymen who robbed travelers and thought nothing of cutting their throats. That was not the only risk they were running, because if they met a troop of Catholic soldiers, their fate was equally sealed.

While these thoughts were running through Victoire's mind, her uncle, lulled by the movement of the coach, was quietly dozing. Cassitère's elixir had certainly improved his physical condition, but the scars left on his mind by grief and distress would not be as easily removed.

After five days' journey without incident, the Comte de Montmaur and his niece reached Cahors and changed horses. There they heard disquieting news.

175

It was said that Sancerre had risen against the King and that several other towns in the southwest would follow suit.

"The King will not be able to tolerate these defections," said Anselme with concern.

"Which means?"

"That he will send troops to subdue the Protestants."

"Then will there be war?" asked Victoire anxiously.

"I fear once again France will be laid to waste, farms plundered and burned, and that our unhappy country will be reduced to an ever-worsening state of ruin."

Victoire reflected that if war came, Guillaume would be compelled to fight against the Huguenots. How could she continue to love the murderer of her brothers? That would be despicable. Yet tormented as she was by this thought, she knew in her heart of hearts that whatever the circumstances, her love for Guillaume was so deeply implanted that she would never be able to uproot it.

Montmaur had always seemed to Victoire to be a very large house, but now it looked so small compared to the Louvre. Looking at the castle with the eyes of an owner, she noted things that she had scarcely seen before: the poor state of the roofing, weeds all over the courtyard and up the entrance steps, rust creeping along the railings . . . Where would she find the money to put all this right?

Catching sight of Monsieur Charleroi, the new bailiff appointed by her mother during her absence in Paris, Victoire decided to learn as best she could the administration of the small estate she now possessed. By cutting certain expenses it would perhaps be possible to carry out some of the most urgent work.

Quite soon she realized that she would take pleasure in looking after the old house she had been brought up in, and that this new preoccupation might help her to stop thinking perpetually of Guillaume.

She was delighted to see Marguerite, the cook, who came to take her orders each morning. As well as Léon, she had Godefroy, the stableboy, who also sawed the wood, brought in the water, and tried in vain to keep the grounds in reasonable order; and then there were Honoré, the keeper, and his wife, Justine, who took care of the farmyard and the kitchen garden. Including Jacotte, there was now a meager staff of six at Montmaur, whereas in the time when her father was alive there were never less than twelve servants and ten horses in the stables. Gradually the staff had been reduced, lands whittled down, farms sold.

Most of the present staff were born in the neighborhood and had known Victoire since she was born, so she had to tell them first of all of her mother's death. All were deeply grieved because the Comtesse, though strict and sometimes even harsh, had always treated them fairly. Then she broke the news of Gilone's absence, which quite surprised them.

Victoire organized her life as if she intended to live at Montmaur forever. At six every morning, Godefroy led her mare Aloès to the foot of the front steps. He helped her to mount and then watched her as she rode off alone into the country. Once he had shyly offered to accompany her, or at least to follow a little way behind. But Victoire had refused his offer with a smile.

Victoire derived real pleasure from these solitary rides through fields and woods, in the quiet countryside she knew and loved. She no longer shared such simple outdoor pursuits with anyone, since Gilone had preferred the more frivolous activities of the Court. Sometimes certain spots made her think of her cousin: the big oak tree that Gilone had fallen off, grazing her elbow; the farm at Châteauneuf where they paused to drink bowls of lukewarm milk; the river, which froze their legs even in midsummer. But these nostalgic moments didn't last long. As soon as she got back at about nine o'clock, many tasks were waiting for her. It was a delight to be so busy all day long, because this way time scarcely dragged at all, as she had feared it might.

When she came in, her body glowing from the exercise, Victoire ate a meal with her uncle. Since he often spent part of the night studying the stars, he got up later than she did. Both were recovering their strength and well-being, thanks to the quiet, healthy country life. One morning Victoire was delighted to see that the master glassmaker's hands no longer shook, that he walked more steadily, and that he had started to work again.

Later in the morning Monsieur Charleroi joined her in the library, and together they tried to sort out the Montmaur accounts. It seemed that the previous bailiff, whom the Comtesse trusted implicity, had embezzled a bit and that the financial situation was not quite as alarming as he had tended to make out.

During the afternoon Victoire looked after the kitchen garden and the poultry yard. The Comtesse had never taken any interest in such things, so Honoré and Justine were proud to show their new mistress the results they had achieved.

Busily engaged as she was in plans for the estate, Victoire paid little attention to what was going on in the outside world; and at a remote place like Montmaur, away from the main road, any news that reached them was much delayed and often inaccurate. She had quite forgotten the promise she had made to the Marquis d'Hautemart, when, one evening in January, she caught sight of a rider at the end of the drive.

She hurried into the courtyard, her heart beating fast: could it be Guillaume? Her hopes faded as she made out the silhouette of the rider, whose black horse had froth on its nostrils as if it had galloped far and fast.

Guy Becavallo dismounted and bowed to her. "I have come to fetch you, Mademoiselle," he said.

Chapter XXIII

*T*he Comte de Montmaur, sipping his evening cup of rosemary tea, made every effort to dissuade his niece from leaving.

"Haven't you already been exposed to enough danger in Paris? Do you want to be kidnapped, stabbed, raped, and goodness knows what else? It seems to me most unwise, not to say senseless, on your part to travel on the roads in these unsafe times. What do you think, Monsieur Becavallo?"

"I am simply conveying to your niece an appeal from our mutual friend Alexandre d'Hautemart," said the young man, who seemed exhausted by his long hard ride from the capital.

"Uncle, I have offered my services to the Marquis and I wouldn't like to miss an opportunity to help our cause, or to go back on my word."

Anselme shook his head sadly. He knew how stubborn his niece could be, yet how brave and resolute she was. Wasn't it just those qualities which made him love her so?

"What is the precise nature of her mission?" he asked.

"First of all, I must give you a rough outline of what has happened since you left Paris."

"That will be most helpful," said the Comte. "We are out of touch with everything here. People seldom come to see us."

"You should know," the young man went on, "that the Duc d'Albe is advising the King to introduce the Inquisition in France."

When he heard this terrifying news, whose dire consequences he could gauge better than Victoire, the old man went pale. "The Inquisition! My God! Our country will become a gigantic funeral pyre!"

"Exactly. Now we must fight with all our strength if we want to survive. What's more, at this very moment Queen Catherine is trying to arrange a marriage between the Duc d'Anjou and a daughter of the King of Spain, to perpetuate the Catholic line in France. Philip II will probably agree to it."

"And the Spanish influence will be predominant," said Victoire.

"In the Languedoc those of our faith are up in arms. They not only hold Nîmes, but also the port of La Rochelle. The Governor of Languedoc has received orders to retake Florac, Chissac, and Peyre Castle, which have fallen into our hands. In Provence the tolerant Comte de Tende has been replaced by a bloodthirsty monster. They have executed Briquemaut, Coligny's secretary and Cavaigne, even though he was a councilor in Parliament. The King, the Queen Mother, and the King of Navarre came to view the spectacle from a curtained window in the Hôtel de Guise. It took place in the Place de Grève in the evening, by torchlight."

"That doesn't surprise me of the Queen!" exclaimed Victoire. She became more and more convinced of the need for action as Becavallo continued his account.

"Behind the cart where the two victims were chained," he went on, "was a straw dummy dressed as the Admiral attached to a horse's tail. As he mounted the ladder Briquemaut bravely uttered his last words,

'I pray to God, before whom I shall soon be called to judgment, to forgive the King and all those who have brought about my unjust death, as I trust He will forgive the sins which I have committed.' "

"What a noble death," said Victoire, deeply moved.

"Mademoiselle de Montmaur's mission, if she agrees to accept it, will be to try to enter La Rochelle, which has been under siege since November, and take a message to the Mayor, Jacques Henri, promising him help in defense of the town. For we have heard that reinforcements of royal troops are being sent there, under the command of the Duc d'Anjou."

"The victor of Jarnac and Moncontour," said Victoire quietly. She had other memories of the Duc as the man who tried to murder her and Guillaume in the galleries of the Louvre.

Anselme made one last effort to avert the loss of his adored niece. "Couldn't a man take the message?" he asked.

"No," said Bevavallo. "Already it will be difficult enough for a woman to enter the town, even though she attracts less notice and arouses less suspicion. Once the Duc d'Anjou arrives at La Rochelle with all his troops, it will be quite impossible. The Marquis d'Hautemart thinks that if not a minute is lost Mademoiselle de Montmaur still has a chance of getting to the Mayor. He fears that if no news reaches him, the Mayor may become desperate and surrender."

"How soon must she leave?" said Anselme, overwhelmed by the feeling that his niece was determined to achieve the impossible and risk her life to carry out this dangerous mission.

"Tomorrow, at dawn."

Light was just beginning to break when Victoire, wearing her riding clothes and a warm cloak, took leave of her uncle. He had not slept, and he kissed her a despairing good-by. "I shall do nothing but think of you and await your return. From today on I live in perpetual anxiety."

"Please don't worry about me, Uncle. All will go well," said Victoire, far more optimistically than she felt. She too had scarcely slept a wink. Would she be capable of entering that beleaguered town alone?

"If you have any chance of letting me have your news . . ."

"I won't fail to do so."

The Comte de Montmaur turned toward Becavallo. "Monsieur, I am entrusting to you the most precious thing I have in the world."

"Rest assured that I shall do everything in my power to see that your niece comes back to you safe and sound."

Anselme had insisted that Godefroy should go with them.

"But what shall I do with this poor boy?" Victoire had objected.

"It will ease my mind. At least he can look after your horse."

So, followed by Godefroy and Jean Lescure, Becavallo's squire, Victoire and her companion set off for La Rochelle. It was cold, and before long the rain seeped through their clothes. In spite of her outward enthusiasm, Victoire regretted the loss of the soft warmth of her bed, where snuggling under her thick feather quilt she dreamed lazily of Guillaume, whom she never really expected to see again.

The vivid memory of Guillaume and his embrace had become more painful with every passing day. Victoire realized how quickly one could adjust to sensual pleasure and how much she missed his warm embrace.

Becavallo rode at full speed, and even though she had almost been born on horseback Victoire sometimes had difficulty in keeping up with him. They had ridden nearly forty miles before they stopped at a post house to eat and rest their horses.

"I'm exhausted."

"I'm not surprised," said Becavallo. "We've been traveling almost six hours. If all goes well, we'll be able to have supper and spend the night with my cousin Isabelle at Calès Castle.

"I have the impression," he added with a laugh, "that she's bored with the country and misses the parties in Paris—so she's glad when people arrive. Her husband owns vast estates which keep him sufficiently busy to fill his time, and he seldom thinks of taking his wife to the capital for a round of pleasure and gaiety."

The prospect of enjoying an evening's hospitality comforted Victoire, but around them, travelers spoke of nothing but the uprising in Languedoc and the imminent arrival of the royal troops. They were not anxious for renewed conflict, following so many years of civil war between Protestants and Catholics.

The genial innkeeper, thinking that the young couple were on their honeymoon, and possibly influenced by the youth and beauty of Victoire, had given them the best table, near the fireplace.

"You're not too tired?" asked Guy attentively. "Will you be able to do another thirty miles before nightfall?"

"I will have to, won't I?" said Victoire with a smile.

Relaxed by the warmth of the fire, the wine, and by the young Venetian's agreeable company, she let herself be attracted to his flattering attentiveness.

Isabelle was a beautiful woman in her mid-thirties, whose husband had given her five children. She was expecting a sixth, which did not prevent her from being extremely pleased to see her cousin and Victoire.

"You are going to stay for at least a week," she said, "and you can tell us everything that's happening in the capital. It's so long since I've been there!"

Victoire left her companion to make the proper

response, since it was not deemed respectable to be traveling across France in the company of a young girl.

"Dear Isa, we would gladly accept your generous invitation if only we could. Unfortunately, Mademoiselle de Montmaur has just lost her mother, and I am responsible for her safe conduct to Bordeaux, where her uncle is awaiting her. He would worry if we were delayed."

Isabelle was clearly disappointed, but at least she could look forward to one interesting evening when she could feast on the latest Court gossip as well as descriptions of the current Parisian fashions. She had her guests shown to their rooms because they badly needed to rest after their long hard ride.

"I will see you presently for supper. Géraud has not come in yet, but he will not be long."

A chambermaid helped Victoire to take off her muddy riding habit and brought her a large basin of hot water. Having washed, she lay on the bed to rest and was soon sound asleep.

Guy Becavallo knocked on the door to wake her up.

"Come in," she said, thinking that a maid had come to see if there was anything she wanted.

"It's time we went down . . ." The young man was stunned by the sight of Victoire, wearing nothing but a sheer nightdress made completely transparent by the candlelight.

"How beautiful you are," he breathed involuntarily.

Slightly abashed and aware of her provocative appearance, Victoire slipped into a dressing gown as quickly as she could.

"I'll be ready in five minutes," she said as Becavallo went out of the room.

She kept her two dresses in the tapestry bag that Godefroy had fixed behind her saddle. Neither of them was very smart, and Isabelle would find their simplicity rather disappointing. But after all, you didn't need brocade or velvet to enter a town under siege.

The host and hostess and their elder children were waiting in a large drawing room that had been hastily opened in honor of their guests. The fire, which had just been lit, was giving out scarcely any heat.

"My dear," said Géraud to his wife, "I think our friends will be more comfortable in your room, where it is warm."

Isabelle seldom had occasion to use her drawing room, so it was with some reluctance that she led her guests to a smaller room where the temperature was appreciably higher.

"You must be very tired," she said, "so I have asked them to make spiced wine."

"How wonderfully thoughtful of you," said Guy. "We have been riding since six o'clock this morning, so Mademoiselle de Montmaur and I are exhausted."

Isabelle looked at Victoire admiringly. "I couldn't ever manage any more than two hours."

As she sipped the wine flavored with cinnamon, cloves, and nutmeg, Victoire wondered whether she would enjoy being a mistress of a household like this. She imagined that Guillaume was in Géraud's place and that the handsome, charming children were her own, as well as the fine, well-kept castle where nothing was lacking.

Yet in spite of everything she didn't envy Isabelle, who left all the running of the estate to her husband while she simply produced children and issued orders to numerous servants—when all the time she yearned for Paris where she had lived before her marriage. Victoire felt sure she would soon tire of such an existence, even with Guillaume. And suddenly she became aware of a side of her character she hadn't previously realized: her innate desire for action, whether it meant fulfilling a dangerous mission or taking charge of the estate's income.

Chapter XXIV

Well nourished with a hot breakfast, they prepared to set off again into a gray, cheerless dawn. As he helped her to mount, Godefroy asked Victoire whether she was too tired.

She smiled at the ungainly youth who was totally devoted to her. "If I was tired on the second day, we'd never get to La Rochelle! But I'm a little worried on your account. You've left your parents and your quiet life at Montmaur all because of me."

"Oh, Mademoiselle Victoire, don't ever worry about me. I always wanted to travel."

Perhaps you have, thought Victoire, but not under these conditions. As on the previous day, they had to ride as fast as the horses could gallop. How many more days would they have to keep up this pace? Victoire could now think of nothing but staying on her mare, avoiding ruts, and never losing sight of Guy.

"All right?" he shouted from time to time.

"Yes," she called back, smiling as brightly as possible.

That evening they arrived at Bordeaux under a torrential rain. They decided to stop at the first inn they came to, instead of riding on through the town to reach the comfortable hostelry where Guy usually stayed. The inn was not particularly attractive, but at least they were out of the rain. The innkeeper's wife hung their clothes in front of the fire while Godefroy and Jean Lescure briskly rubbed down the horses, who had earned a double ration of oats.

Guy and Victoire ate a very simple meal in the public dining room. A group of soldiers, intoxicated with Bordeaux wine, were constantly clamoring for fresh jugs. As Victoire entered the room they looked her up and down, and one of them made an insulting remark. Guy was about to rush at the man when Victoire firmly held him back.

"Be reasonable; a joke however feeble never killed anyone. Besides, there are nine of them and only one of you. What would happen to me if you got hurt?"

Guy had to agree it would be wiser to ignore the soldiers, who took no further notice of them once a steaming soup tureen was placed on their table.

"I hope these ruffians aren't spending the night here," said Guy anxiously after a while.

"What are you afraid of?"

"They are Catholic soldiers. If they find out our religion, they are quite capable of murdering us in the middle of the night and getting away unscathed."

"My God!" cried Victoire. The memory of the massacres in Paris was so painfully clear in her mind that she dreaded the thought of their spending the night under the same roof as these drunken men, one of whom was already lying sprawled on the table, snoring.

Becavallo got up and went to have a quiet word with the innkeeper. "Surely those rowdy customers over there are scarcely worth your while?"

"You don't have to tell me!" he said. "Last week they started fighting and broke three of my stone jugs and two heavy chairs. And they almost raped the servant girl as well. I had to call the guard!"

"Aren't they going to return to barracks soon?"

"Not likely! They're going to drink here all night, because their company is leaving tomorrow for La Rochelle."

"We must leave before they do," said Guy when they reached the upper floor.

A soldier was reeling about the passage and leaning against the wall to stop himself from falling.

"Guy," said Victoire, "I am afraid to sleep alone. My room has no lock."

"It would indeed be most unwise."

In spite of his drunkenness, the man leered at Victoire with patent approval.

"You go to bed," Guy told Victoire. "I shall wrap myself in a blanket and sleep by the fire. I'll be quite all right."

He turned his back as she undressed and slipped into bed.

"You can blow out the candle," she said.

Firelight flickered in the room, and Victoire stretched her weary limbs between the sheets and reveled in the sense of total relaxation. Then suddenly she thought of her companion, just as exhausted as she was, sleeping on the floor.

"Guy . . ."

"Is there something you need?" He got up and moved toward her.

"It's a wide bed," she said, "and there's plenty of room for two. You're so uncomfortable."

"No . . ." he said with little conviction.

"Come on," Victoire urged him, "we've got another hard day tomorrow."

"We certainly do. But . . . what would your uncle say?"

"That it is the most sensible thing to do."

Tempted by the large bed and stirred by the proximity of Victoire, Guy eventually lay down beside her. She could tell from his breathing that he was not asleep . . . And she, who had been dozing a few minutes earlier, thought only of the body so near to her she could easily touch it. Suddenly dismayed, she realized what she wanted and at the same time dreaded that Guy would take her in his arms. How was this possible when she was still in love with Guillaume?

Two hours before dawn, taking good care not to make a sound, Guy and Victoire left their room and went out into the courtyard without going through the public room, where some of the soldiers were sleeping off their wine.

"Have you found out anything?" the banker asked his squire and Godefroy.

"They are heading for Saint-André-de-Cubsac, where they will be billeted for the night."

"Good. Then we shall follow the Garonne and cross the river opposite Blaye, where there's a ferry."

They rode through the vineyards where rows of bare, wet vine-plants lined the muddy, treacherous road. The horses kept slipping and it was impossible, even dangerous, to gallop under these conditions. Victoire noticed that Guy's brow was darkening.

"We won't do our fifty miles today," he said.

"Are we still very far from La Rochelle?" she asked.

"Unfortunately it's still at least four days' journey from here—and only if we make good headway."

At the moment they were obliged to walk their horses, and so for the first time since they left Montmaur they were able to talk with each other.

"Tell me about the message," said Victoire. "Is it verbal and will I have to learn it by heart?"

"No, it consists of a letter signed by the Marquis d'Hautemart and the leaders—or those of them who are left—of our party. The message entreats the people of La Rochelle to hold on and not to lose heart in spite of hardships that must by now be severe; it tells them the probable date of the arrival of reinforcements, and also how many."

"Where should I conceal it? Perhaps in my boots?"

Guy studied Victoire closely as he wondered in which part of her clothing she could best hide the letter. Their glances met, and Victoire looked away, blushing deeply at the thought that he had seen her in her nightdress and that they had shared the same bed.

At last the rain stopped. In spite of her thick woolen cloak, Victoire felt the moisture soaking through her serge riding clothes; and shivers were soon running down her back. They had covered very little ground since Bordeaux, so apart from a brief pause in an hour or two, there was no question of stopping again before evening.

Victoire dreaded the hours ahead, but nothing in the world would make her complain. Perhaps they would be lucky enough, as on the previous night, to be settled near a good fire. She longed for the moment when she could get off her horse and warm herself.

"How pale you look," said Guy. "You don't feel ill, do you?"

"I do feel rather cold," admitted Victoire, who didn't dare to add that her throat was getting sore and that her feet were icy.

The young man took a small silver flask from his saddlebag and uncorked it.

"Drink this. It'll do you good."

Victoire took two gulps, which burned her throat and made her cough.

"Let's go now," said Guy. "It is essential that we get to the ferry before nightfall, otherwise we'll have to wait till tomorrow to get across."

As she expected, the agreeable warmth was all gone in a quarter of an hour. Victoire clenched her teeth. She would not give in! She could not suffer the humiliation of having to abandon the journey because her strength failed her on the third day. She would never again be able to face the Marquis d'Hautemart, who had put his trust in her.

Fortunately the roads began to dry out and Guy was able to increase their pace. It was dusk when they reached the ferry, but the ferryman claimed it was already too late and that to cross in the dark would be dangerous. After a fruitless discussion with him, Guy pulled a purse from his pocket.

"Look, this will be yours if we get over to Blaye."

The man's eyes glinted. "Get on board," he said. "At your own risk."

The horses were not too happy with this mode of transport. They stared fixedly at the strong current, and now and then they whinnied anxiously. Victoire went over and patted Aloès, and spoke to her softly to calm her. By now Victoire's throat was on fire, her head was throbbing, and she longed to lie down.

Finally the boat drew alongside the opposite bank.

Seeing that Victoire was exhausted and that he and the two squires were not much better, Becavallo decided to spend the night at Blaye. Luckily, at the post house where they stayed, there were no soldiers.

"You will forgive me," said Victoire, who was shivering with fever, "if I don't join you for supper. I really must go and lie down at once."

"You've caught cold," said Guy with great concern. "I'm going to take you to your room and get you some hot soup. Is there anything else you'd like?"

"No, thanks, I'm not hungry."

Guy arranged the warming pan in the bed, and when Victoire had settled down he brought her a cup of chicken soup and a glass of wine.

"You shouldn't have bothered," she said in a weak voice.

Her head was spinning, and soon she was so hot that she threw off the blankets, only to feel frozen a few moments later. Becavallo placed his cool hand on her forehead.

"You have a high fever," he said with deep solicitude. "Go to sleep now. If you're not well enough to leave tomorrow morning, we'll spend the day here."

"Because of me, we may not get there in time," said Victoire with a heavy sigh.

"You mustn't worry about that now."

He paused before he spoke again. "Would you like me to sit beside you for a little while?"

"Oh, yes! Stay here, Guy."

She fell into a restless sleep but was soon awakened by the sound of a carriage arriving. Then she noticed that her hand was holding the young man's, and that he was leaning over her with an unmistakable look of love in his eyes.

"I'm so very happy that you're here," she said.

There was no reply, but she felt Guy's lips on her hand.

Chapter XXV

*T*he following day Victoire was no better. On the contrary, there was no question of her leaving her bed. Guy resigned himself to this delay, telling himself that a day's rest wouldn't do any of them any harm, including the horses. Besides this journey, he and Jean Lescure had ridden flat out from Paris to Montmaur.

He also tried to comfort Victoire, who was depressed by her condition and worried about her responsibilities.

"Everything is going to fail because of me."

"Calm yourself and just think of getting better. They have fetched the doctor."

The doctor prescribed complete rest, a potion of

honey and thyme to clear the throat, and cold compresses on the forehead to lower the fever.

Chatting with a gentleman who had arrived from Paris, Becavallo learned that a man had been caught leaving La Rochelle with a message from some of the inhabitants who begged him to come to terms with the King.

"They're preparing to surrender!" said Victoire when her companion broke the news to her. "One week from now, at the latest, our letter must reach the Mayor. What else did the man tell you?"

"That Montauban and Montpellier are also in revolt."

"That's good. Our position is strengthened."

"It certainly is," said Guy thoughtfully. "And it's also worrying the King, who has appointed Biron, against the wishes of the inhabitants, as Governor of La Rochelle."

"Perhaps he will find it even more difficult than I to enter the town," said Victoire, smiling.

"It also seems that La Noue, who has remained a Royalist although a Protestant, is going to start negotiations with the rebels."

"If both sides are prepared to compromise, surely civil war will be avoided?"

"Too many interests are at stake. Besides, when human passions are inflamed it's very hard to dampen them. Would you believe that a new party called the 'Politicals,' led by Montmorency—who never returned to Court after the massacre—and his brother, is thinking of allying with us against the King?"

"And who would be their figurehead? The King of Navarre, although he has recanted? Or the Prince de Condé?"

"No. A Catholic called François d'Alençon."

This ambitious prince, his face devoured by pox and his heart by impatience, had not yet played any role that was likely to raise him to the eminence of his brothers, one of whom enjoyed power and the other military glory. But the aims of François d'Alençon could still prove as ill-omened as the blood lust of the one, or the religious mania and intrigues of the other.

Victoire spent the rest of the day in feverish slumber, broken by several visits from Guy.

"How good you are to look after me like this," she said, touched by his devoted attention.

"Are you not someone who is most valuable to our cause, and whom it is only fitting for me to deliver safely?" he answered with a smile. "And didn't I promise your uncle to take care of you? Now, how are you feeling?"

"Not very well yet . . . far from it," said Victoire with a little grimace. "All the same, we shall leave tomorrow."

"Yes, we must," Guy agreed. "But as you don't seem well enough to ride, I've hired a carriage for you. At least you will be sheltered from the elements and won't have to exert yourself."

"And what about my mare?"

"Godefroy will lead her."

"It's an excellent idea," said Victoire, relieved that she was no longer the cause of delaying the journey. "We shall not travel quite so fast, but what does it matter so long as we're making progress?"

"I shall be quite well again in two days."

With Victoire in the coach the next day they safely crossed the Saintonge, where the Charente meanders through meadows and rows of poplars; and they passed a group of pilgrims on their way to Saint-Jacques de Compostelle. On the third evening they reached Rochefort. La Rochelle was now only a day's journey away, and Victoire, almost herself again, would be able to ride there on Aloès.

"We're getting there at last," said Guy with relief.

Once again they found themselves sitting down to supper in a little inn. During the journey a great intimacy, a sort of complicity, had grown up between them; and the longer they were together the more keenly Victoire appreciated the intelligence and sensitivity of her companion. However, I am really not in love with him, she would tell herself, because I shall never forsake Guillaume, and the thought of deceiving him is repugnant to me. At other times she felt she might never again see the man who had initiated her in lovemaking and had given her the taste and the need for it . . . So why should she spurn Guy's advances when his eyes alone showed her just how much he desired her? Moreover, Victoire had the impression that Guy, unlike Guillaume, really loved her. Perhaps his relationship with her was like hers with Guillaume. Did she simply wish Guy to share her bed more completely than he had done to protect her from the soldiers? Or perhaps were her feelings deeper than that?

She was surprised at herself for indulging in such frivolous thoughts when she should have been thinking of how she would enter beleaguered La Rochelle.

Jacques Henri and a leading townsman, Jacques Salbert, associated with him in the town's defense, had laid waste to the surrounding country in a radius of twenty-five miles in order to resist attack more easily and to deprive the enemy of vital supplies. Farms were deserted, animals removed, fields abandoned. This desolate countryside, where Victoire and her party met nothing but half-starved stray dogs, clearly showed the resolution of people who were preparing for the worst.

In the distance they could see the massive fortifications that made La Rochelle the bastion of the Reformed Church.

"How will I ever succeed in getting past those walls?" asked Victoire.

"We are being met three miles from here and you

will doubtless be told the best way to proceed from there."

As they approached the town they caught sight of a camp at the foot of the ramparts.

"Thank God for that!" Guy exclaimed. "There's no sign of the royal banner and the number of troops is small. The Duc d'Anjou has not yet arrived." He smiled at Victoire triumphantly. "Good fortune has not deserted us. In spite of everything, we have arrived in time."

Victoire drew a deep breath. The strain of having perhaps to assume some responsibility for the surrender of the town had wakened her several times during the preceding nights. Now for the first time an important enterprise, with incalculable consequences, depended on her, and the realization of this filled her with a certain pride.

Both she and Guy were greatly surprised to find that the Marquis d'Hautemart was at the rendezvous, in an unused barn near a place marked Malparet.

Shyly Victoire walked toward the stern-faced men who stood up to greet her.

"This is our messenger," said the Marquis d'Hautemart, introducing her to the conspirators assembled around a large wooden farm table.

"I never thought you would be here," said Becavallo.

"Nor did I! I am only two days ahead of all the royal forces, who are fully prepared for an immediate assault and are commanded by formidable staff officers: Guise, Montpensier, and Nevers are escorting the Duc d'Anjou and the Duc d'Alençon, and they have enlisted Henri de Navarre and the Prince de Condé . . ."

"Is the King of Navarre going to fight against Protestants?" asked Victoire incredulously.

Alexandre smiled at her indulgently. "Isn't he the brother-in-law of the King of France?"

This surrender of principle by her childhood friend

sickened her. Had he remained neutral, she could have accepted it. But to take up arms with the assassins of Saint Bartholomew's Night was outright treason.

The Marquis spread out a parchment and showed Victoire the plan of the town and the fortifications. "Naturally, the main gates are closed and they will not be opened for you. You must steal inside through a little postern gate on the south side. There, under cover of darkness, they sometimes let in some country-women bringing provisions and seeking refuge. They never refuse them because the provisions amassed within the walls might not be sufficient to feed nearly four thousand people throughout a long siege. Most of the women and children have been evacuated in anticipation of that happening."

He pointed to a package against the wall. "You will change into these peasant clothes and then lead away a couple of sheep that we will provide you with to complete your disguise."

All this sounded relatively easy. Where, then, did the difficulties lie?

"The really dangerous part of your mission will be in getting to the ramparts and reaching the gate without being spotted by the soldiers camping on the perimeter of the town. I want to make it quite clear that you are running a considerable risk, because a moment will come when we shall no longer be able to protect you. And if you are captured . . ." He raised his hands as if to imply that she would have to expect the worst.

Victoire went white. Until then she had simply been dazed at the thought of being picked for this mission, but somehow she had never seriously considered that her life would really be in danger.

"Then again, assuming that you do succeed in your mission, you will of course be unable to leave La Rochelle. You will have to suffer all the privations of the siege for an unspecified time. Perhaps for months . . ."

There was silence.

"That is not all," Alexandre went on somberly. "If we have the misfortune to be defeated—a possible outcome to be faced in spite of all our efforts—and the town is forced to surrender, you can imagine what reprisals will be taken on the inhabitants . . ."

Hearing this cold statement of all the risks that Victoire was going to run, risks that he had not properly assessed either, Becavallo could not conceal his profound anxiety. Their eyes met—and at that moment Victoire was fully aware of a love that would comfort her at a time when she might be obliged to sacrifice her life.

"Now that I have told you everything," said the Marquis, "it only remains for me to ask you one question. Do you accept?"

The reality of the situation was very clear and Victoire was afraid, but she summoned up all her courage and quietly said, "Yes."

"On behalf of us all, I thank you."

The admiration and esteem expressed on his and all the other faces around her made it possible for Victoire to forget for a moment that this cold, drafty barn might well be where she spent her last evening alive.

Chapter XXVI

After a frugal supper of bread and cheese, the Marquis d'Hautemart took leave of Victoire.

"You are leaving already!"

"It has to be," he said with great emotion. "I am leaving you with Becavallo, who will do everything possible to help you tomorrow. He will let me know of the success, or failure, of your venture. Needless to say, my thoughts will never leave you until I am assured that you are safe and sound behind those walls . . . Once again, thank you for risking your life in our cause. Few young people would prove as courageous as you."

If ever he suspected, thought Victoire, how frightened I am and how cowardly I feel . . . It is only pride that prevents me from giving up—since nothing short of a miracle will get me out of this adventure alive.

Godefroy, Lescure, and the Marquis's men, who on the following day were going to cause a diversion and attract the sentries' attention as Victoire stole through the camp, went to sleep in the hayloft. Guy and Victoire stayed in the farm-parlor, lit by a dying fire and two candles that were nearly burned out.

"While we still have a little light, let's try to find somewhere to sleep," suggested Guy.

The room next door was in a state of chaos. The bed was unmade and the owners had clearly left their home in great haste, taking with them only bare necessities.

Victoire found some clean sheets in the cupboard and remade the bed as the candles slowly burned down. In the darkness, she suddenly realized that she could not bear to spend what might be her last night alone, brooding over her fears.

"Guy . . ."

"Yes?"

She noticed that his voice shook a little.

"I'm not sleepy . . . Would you like to stay with me for a while?"

"Victoire! You ask me if I want to stay with you? Perhaps in broad daylight and in other circumstances I would not have dared to say that I want to do nothing else. I love you. Haven't you noticed?"

"Yes," she whispered. "I know."

Guiding herself by the sound of his voice, she moved toward the young man until their bodies met. Instantly his arms clasped her and she could feel his lips searching hungrily for hers.

"My love . . . it's been so long since I first yearned to hold you close to me! What exquisite agony it was to lie beside you the other night—again and again I thought I could bear it no longer!"

Happily and gratefully, her body accepted his embrace and long, passionate kiss. Yet even at that moment the memory of Guillaume came back to her. Was she really going to betray him and give herself to Guy? She longed to do so; physical contact with him had aroused many dormant feelings. She must make a quick decision. Should she remain faithful to a man whose feelings about her were ambiguous, when she might die tomorrow? Shivering with cold and fear, she led Guy toward the bed. "I am yours," she said.

Suddenly he moved away. "You don't love me, I can feel it," he said. "You are moved by pity—that's not what I want."

"If I should pity anyone, it would be myself," said

Victoire. "I don't know if I love you, but you can be absolutely sure that I am deeply fond of you."

"Will you love me one day?"

"Who knows? We may never see each other again."

"That's what drives me to despair."

Why couldn't those words have been spoken by Guillaume? If he had loved her as passionately as this, she would never have now thrust herself so eagerly against the warm naked body whose very presence gave her reassurance and enabled her to forget the future and lose herself in a rapturous present.

Was it merely months of chastity that made her believe she had never in her life experienced such physical pleasure? Or was it that being loved with such passionate intensity made her weak with joy?

She tried to sort out the mixed emotions that were disturbing her. Clearly she had not lost her heart to Guy, but after making love she had slept in his arms and spent a peaceful night. But, alas, the fears he had managed to dispel were growing again as the new day dawned, the day when she must play the role of a heroine. How rash she had been to offer her services to Alexandre d'Hautemart.

Victoire knew from the look in her lover's eyes that the moment had come to get ready. She put on the black fustian skirt, the unbleached cotton shirt, and a woolen shawl, over which she wore her cloak. As she fixed Guillaume's dagger in her belt she said to herself that this time, if she had to strike, she would strike to kill. Then she put into a little bag a change of underclothes and some money given to her by Guy.

"You may have to bribe someone, or buy something."

Finally she slid the letter into her boot.

"There you are," she said. "I'm ready."

In the yard the horsemen were already waiting. Godefroy led Aloès toward her.

"Mademoiselle, what is going to happen to me? What if I tried to go along with you?" he whispered.

"You're mad! You are going to return to Montmaur, where you will tell my uncle that I succeeded. If that is not the case, don't say a word to him. Take Aloès back with you and look after her well. Ride her regularly, so that I find her in good condition . . . if I come back."

"Montmaur is going to be so empty without you," said the boy sadly.

The party set off at a trot and rode as near to the walls as they dared. When they were about a mile away, in a thicket, they left their horses in charge of one of the men. Then, followed by the sheep, which were muzzled to stop them from bleating, they went ahead on foot through the dark, bitter-cold night.

"There's no moon, I'm glad to say," remarked Guy.

A little later one of the clocks in the town struck midnight. There was no trace of light from La Rochelle, which could have well been mistaken for a deserted town. Guy stopped the small band and gave his final instructions.

All the men solemnly shook hands with Victoire and wished her luck. Some of them had daughters of her age and thanked Heaven that they were safely at home.

Becavallo accompanied her southward toward the postern gate. The sheep were walking more slowly and often stopped altogether. No sound came from the tents, which were now no more than a hundred yards away. They could see the sentries around a brazier and soon could hear their voices.

"It's damned cold," said one of them. "My hands are frozen. When are they going to attack this bloody town?"

"Soon, when His Royal Highness the Duc d'Anjou turns up with most of the army—maybe tomorrow. It won't take long to deal with these maniacs. He's a gallant commander—I was with him at Moncontour. In a few days we'll have finished with this siege."

"Good-by," whispered Guy. "In a few minutes our men will attack the guardpost. Then run as fast as you can . . . Tomorrow evening I will come back here to the same spot. From the top of the citadel you will throw me a message wrapped around a stone."

They kissed each other in a last, lingering embrace.

"Don't forget that I love you," said Guy.

Without answering, she held herself closer to him. "I shall try to join you."

"But how can you?" she asked in astonishment.

"I don't know yet, but I shall find a way. I cannot live apart from you."

Suddenly, to their right, there was frenzied activity and cursing. The sentries started to run, firing several rounds on their way. On the ramparts the lookout men came forward to ascertain the cause of the uproar below.

"Away you go!"

Victoire rushed forward, dragging the sheep behind her. Soon she was no more than fifty yards from the postern, and she could distinguish a figure behind the bars of the heavy iron gate. She paused for a moment, out of breath, when a dark shape she hadn't noticed in her haste loomed before her. A hand gripped her wrist with such strength that she almost screamed.

"Not so fast, my beauty!"

The man's menacing face promised nothing but evil. How silly to get caught so close to home! She could have wept with rage . . .

"For a start, you'll hand over those sheep. They'll make a change from our usual rations tomorrow."

Without arguing, Victoire passed him the rope that held the animals. As he took it, he let go of her wrist. Glancing quickly around her, she realized that her attacker was alone and that the nearest of his comrades were at least two or three hundred yards away, fighting with the Marquis's men. As he turned his back to her and stooped to fix the rope to a stake, she drew her dagger and thrust it into his body: in nearly the same place, she noted, that she had wounded Father Izard. The man uttered a cry of surprise and pain. Without giving him time to recover, she swiftly withdrew the weapon and this time stabbed him in the heart. The victim collapsed.

Victoire took her sheep and ran madly to the gate.

"Quick! Let me in," she gasped. "I have a message for the Mayor from the Marquis d'Hautemart."

Realizing they had been tricked, the soldiers now ran toward the postern. Two shots rang out. Just in time, the gate creaked open and closed again behind Victoire and her sheep. Exhausted but triumphant, she leaned against the wall because her legs were giving way. She had succeeded in getting inside. She wondered if she would ever get out.

Chapter XXVII

"*There,* there, little lady, a drink of this will do you good."

Victoire took three gulps of a potent spirit that steadied her nerves. "I just killed a man," she said weakly.

The gatekeeper, a man in his fifties, gave her a look of pity mingled with admiration. "My poor little one . . . That's war. Try not to think about it."

He patted her on the shoulder a little awkwardly, but this friendly gesture helped to calm her.

"Come along," he said. "You're going to catch cold here."

Victoire handed him the rope holding the sheep. The man's eyes shone with satisfaction. He leaned over at once to feel the animals' bellies.

"A couple of ewes!" he exclaimed. "And one of them in lamb!" Marquis d'Hautemart certainly knew how to arrange things well.

"Are you suffering much hardship?"

"Rationing is strict," he admitted. "We don't know how long we'll have to hold out."

Victoire refrained from telling him of the imminent arrival of the royal troops. It was the duty of the Mayor to announce that bad news to the population.

Another man came up to take his turn of guard duty.

"Hello there, Arnaud, I've come to relieve you and freeze in your place."

"And I am going to escort this young lady, who has just arrived, to see the Mayor."

The newcomer whistled. "She managed to get through? Good Heavens! It seems women are better at it, because only last night two men were killed trying to get in . . ."

Victoire shuddered. Fortunately Alexandre d'Hautemart had neglected telling her this fact, which had certainly been reported to him . . .

She followed Arnaud through the dark empty streets, where the only sound came from their own footsteps. The guide must have sensed her first impressions, and he too was affected by the sinister, yet familiar, atmosphere of a place whose starving inhabitants remained willing prisoners because they had pledged their lives to their faith.

"It's not exactly cheerful," he whispered.

"No," Victoire agreed. She was already oppressed

by the thought that she would have to share this secluded existence for an unspecified length of time.

"And it will get worse," said Arnaud, "when the food reserves run out."

In spite of the late hour, the Mayor was sitting up beside a small fire that did not even take the chill off the room. When the messenger from the Marquis d'Hautemart was announced, he leaped to his feet. "At last! I was beginning to give up hope."

Victoire was shown into the room at once, and for a moment Jacques Henri looked at her in amazement.

"What!" he said. "They gave *you* the task of bringing me the news?"

"Yes, Monsieur."

He went toward her and shook her warmly by the hand. "I congratulate you on having succeeded where so many others have failed at the cost of their lives."

"I had a little luck," said Victoire modestly.

"But I see you have blood on your dress. Were you wounded?"

"I had to kill a soldier. Fortunately he was separated from his comrades. Otherwise I wouldn't be here to deliver you this message." She bent down to remove her boot and took out the letter.

As he eagerly read the message the Mayor's strong face, lined by fatigue and anxiety, clouded over. "Alexandre tells me that the Duc d'Anjou and a strong contingent of troops will arrive here shortly."

"He was only two days ahead of the army," explained Victoire.

"Then it will get here tomorrow . . . I must give immediate orders to strengthen the patrols. Arnaud," he called to the man who was still in the next room, "double the guards on the next relief."

"Very good, Sir."

"I am glad to say that Hautemart confirms the

dispatch of reinforcements which will attack the royal forces from the rear."

Dizzy with sudden fatigue, Victoire was starting to nod in her chair. The Mayor looked at her with a paternal smile.

"Forgive me, you must want to go to bed, and here I am keeping you up in the middle of the night. We'll have a quiet talk tomorrow and you can let me know what's happening in the outside world. You'll stay with me, and my wife will look after you."

Victoire looked surprised. "I thought that the women and children had been evacuated."

"That is so, but Emmeline did not wish to leave me."

She was taken to a pretty bedroom hung with almond-green percale. The room was ordinarily occupied by the Mayor's daughter, who was at present in London with her aunt.

Victoire tried for a moment to picture the face of this young girl, who had been safely sent away from the horrors of war and the rigors of a siege. As she slipped into bed under the damask counterpane, a rather darker green than the walls, she began to envy the girl's good fortune. Soon, however, she was carried away by feelings of pride and satisfaction at having accomplished an important mission and overcome both danger and fear. After the events of the past few months and the freedom enjoyed since her mother's death, Victoire thought she might never again get used to a placid, humdrum existence.

She had always been told that adventure was a male prerogative and that a woman's place was in the home, caring for her husband and children. Guy's cousin Isabelle was the perfect example. How, then, was she going to satisfy the deep desire for action that had gripped her since she first left Montmaur for the capital and which had afforded her such violent pleasure, almost as intense as love?

Before she fell asleep, her thoughts turned to

Guillaume. She noticed with dismay that her memory of his physical appearance was becoming blurred, and that she had to make an effort to recall his look, his smile, his figure . . . Had she a sense of guilt toward him? She had to admit that she felt little remorse at having given herself to Guy, and indeed she would do it again—blissfully. His passion had stirred her deeply and she missed his feverish embraces. Had she stopped loving Guillaume? Or had she loved him less than she had imagined, being blinded by first love? Did this mean she was the type of woman she had always despised— someone like Gilone, capable of moving from one man to the next without involvement? No, there was one essential difference between her behavior and her cousin's: Gilone had ulterior motives, while hers were purely for love. But had she not always been told by her mother that a woman who slept with more than one man was a disgraceful wanton?

Although nearly forty, Madame Emmeline was a strikingly beautiful woman of above-average height and stately bearing. Her blonde hair, which fell softly from beneath her well-starched cap, gave her a certain look of gentleness, contrasting with her firm chin and determined features that had been hardened by suffering. Everything about this dedicated woman, who had chosen to stay with her husband in adversity, inspired respect.

Victoire felt these impressions in a confused and incoherent way. She was now suffering the aftereffects of the extreme tension and emotional stress of the previous day. Drained of energy and no longer buoyed up by the excitement of having fulfilled her heroic role, she began to feel almost incapable of thought or action.

"Sit down," Lady Emmeline said kindly as she settled herself beside Victoire. "My husband has told me about your exploit in getting through the enemy lines."

"Oh," said Victoire wearily, "was it one worthy of admiration to have killed a man?"

"It is sometimes necessary to dispose of one's religious opponents," Emmeline Henri remarked with composure. "God will understand your motives and will most certainly forgive you."

Victoire realized that until that moment the thought of divine judgment had scarcely entered her head. Wasn't there something rather surprising about committing a murder and risking one's life for a religion without being in the least concerned with the Deity who inspired it? Had her desire for action motivated her more than concern for the faith in which she had been brought up with the utmost severity? Did she feel any real hatred for the Catholics? Yes, when she thought of Father Izard, or Queen Catherine and the Duc d'Anjou . . . These people had harmed her. But what of the others—Guillaume, Sister Gabrielle, young Raymond?

"Tell me a little of what has been going on outside these walls," asked Madame Henri. "It's been so long since we had any news."

"But surely," said Victoire, "you can still communicate by sea?"

The Mayor's wife smiled sadly and led her to the window. "Look . . ." she said.

Four large ships anchored about a mile from the shore were blocking the entrance to the harbor.

"The Queen of England will have to send a squadron to raise the blockade," said Lady Emmeline. "Will she decide to do so?"

Chapter XXVIII

*N*oticing that Victoire had arrived with very limited clothing, Lady Emmeline took her in hand.

"Aloise is almost exactly your size. Please take whatever clothes you need," she said, throwing open the doors to her daughter's wardrobe.

A little embarrassed by the generous offer, Victoire hesitated. "When your daughter comes back, won't she be annoyed to hear that a stranger has worn her clothes."

"Heaven alone knows when we shall see her again . . . or even if we shall be granted that happiness."

"Isn't she safely in England?"

"Most certainly. But when the siege is over, what will remain of La Rochelle, its inhabitants, and this house? If I am to believe the rumors circulating today, we shall soon be attacked. We shall, of course, hold out as long as possible."

"They say that the walls of the town are impregnable."

"Anything can happen. We are in God's hands," said Lady Emmeline quietly. "Every day I pray for us to be the strongest, for our cause to prevail."

"When did you last see Aloise?"

"Four months ago. It's a long time—and the days drag now that she's away."

How many more months would pass before Aloise came back from exile? Madame Henri persisted in her urgings and finally Victoire relented to borrow the dresses. Although severe in style, they were well suited to the circumstances.

"Thank you, Madame, for being so good to me."

Lady Emmeline's thin lips broke into a faint smile. "Having you here almost makes me feel that Aloise is back."

Touched, Victoire embraced her hostess. "Then treat me just like her, and let me help you in the house since all your maids have gone."

The Mayor's wife nodded her agreement and took Victoire into the kitchen, where one old man was all that remained of the entire domestic staff.

Later in the day Madame Henri offered to take Victoire for a walk around the harbor in the pale winter sunshine.

"It's the first time I've been to the coast," said Victoire excitedly. "Could we go and look at the sea?"

"Of course."

They put shawls about their heads as protection against the wind, wrapped themselves in cloaks, and went out. On the faces of all the people they passed there was a common look of expectation. They were awaiting the conflict that the Mayor had warned them would soon break out. And all were actively preparing for the assault, furbishing weapons and strengthening defenses.

In a huge deserted house in the center of the town, several rooms had been prepared to receive casualties as soon as hostilities began. Supervised by Lady Emmeline, the few women who had refused to leave had gotten everything ready to care for their defenders and dress their wounds.

"If you will allow me," said Victoire, "I will join you."

Her offer was readily accepted, as help was much in demand for the job.

"I'm afraid I'm not very expert."

The women showed her how to disinfect wounds with eau-de-vie, to set a broken limb, and to make a dressing to stop bleeding.

"Is there no doctor?" she asked.

"Three of them have remained in La Rochelle," replied Lady Emmeline. "They will be engaged in extracting shot and sewing up the more serious wounds."

Victoire was introduced to Doctor Malavoine, whose white hair and extreme gentleness inspired confidence. He too was delighted to meet the young new recruit, because many of the volunteers were old people who would only be able to help occasionally.

Afterward Lady Emmeline took Victoire onto the quay, against which large waves were breaking. This unfamiliar sight made a deep impression on Victoire.

"Is there a storm?"

The Mayor's wife began to laugh. "No, no! If there was a real storm, as we all hope there will be, you would see troughs twenty feet deep and the King's ships would be forced to weigh anchor. Then the currents would drive them against the rocks."

The seafront was defended on one side by bastions and on the other by the citadel. Cables prevented entry to the harbor itself, and the outer harbor was blocked by a sunken galleon filled with stones. Meanwhile, the sentinels remained motionless, their guns trained on the shore. La Rochelle was completely encircled.

In a square, a pastor was haranguing a crowd. For a second the sight made Victoire ill because it reminded her of an almost identical scene a few months before. If the tenor of his message was similar, the Protestant nevertheless delivered it in more moderate tones.

"My brothers," he said, "the hour has come to demonstrate our faith. Are you prepared?"

"Yes!" yelled the throng with one voice.

"That is the Reverend Pierre de Cressan," whispered Madame Henri. "He had much to do with my husband's decision to resist, whatever the cost."

Gazing intently at the orator, the people of La Rochelle were drawing a supplementary ration of courage from one of the most eloquent of the town's fifty-five pastors.

"God will not abandon those who fight in a just cause. Brothers, we shall overcome!"

A long ovation followed.

"How well he speaks," said Lady Emmeline, who was under his spell.

In concise sentences the pastor explained to his flock that the sacrifice of their lives was necessary, and that it was fitting to give thanks to the Almighty for this opportunity to serve Him in securing their eternal salvation.

When he finished speaking his audience was galvanized, ready to fight like lions. Victoire was saddened by the thought that most of these honest citizens were undoubtedly going to die, as were the soldiers on the other side, once the fighting began in earnest. So much death . . . and all in the name of God.

After a conversation with the Mayor, Victoire was quite convinced that La Rochelle would not surrender until the last of its inhabitants had perished. She then wrote to Guy to describe to him the state of the people's morale, their determination, and their hope. She couldn't help ending the letter by saying that she missed him.

After dark she went up to the citadel with Arnaud, where they could scan the surrounding plain and see the faint lights of the encampments.

"Tomorrow," said Arnaud, "those tents will stretch as far as the eye can see. We are well and completely surrounded."

Victoire shuddered at the thought of staying a prisoner for many months in a town whose resources were going to dwindle every day. It was something she hadn't anticipated when she accepted her mission. She had hardly been within these walls twenty-four hours before she was already desperate to leave. She was well aware, however, that such an evasion was unthinkable, and knew everyone else there would rather be out of the beleaguered city if they could.

In the distance she thought she could distinguish a solitary figure. Was it Guy?

"Arnaud, you're stronger than I am. Will you throw my message for me?"

She pointed roughly in the direction of the spot where, the night before, she had awaited the moment to break through the lines.

"I will send it with my crossbow."

With a sharp whistle, the message weighted by a stone left their besieged world. Would it reach its proper destination? Victoire doubted whether it possibly could. In any case, she would get no answer.

The next day at dawn, hearing a great commotion in the Mayor's house, Victoire realized with something like relief that the troops were arriving. At last the fight was on. Already the waiting and inactivity were beginning to tell on her impatient temperament.

In the big room she had been shown into on the night she arrived, she found the Mayor, Monsieur Salbert, as well as two captains, and of course Pastor de Cressan.

"Our strength," said one of the officers, "lies principally in our artillery because we are outnumbered by three to one."

"God will provide, my son," said the pastor. "Exactly how many men do we have?"

"Three hundred soldiers and two thousand well-armed civilians. It's not much against several companies—and they are awaiting the six thousand Swiss mercenaries under Monsieur de Bellièvre."

"I sent Arnaud onto the ramparts," said the Mayor. "He will be back at any moment to let us know the number of attackers. Ah, here he comes . . ."

Breathlessly the guard commander made his report. "The troops have halted beyond the ditches and are pitching their tents. There are about five thousand infantry and perhaps a thousand cavalry. The Duc d'Anjou has advanced to within the range of a harquebus with the King of Navarre to reconnoitre the defenses . . ."

Arnaud's report was interrupted by the first bursts of cannon fire.

"The attack!"

The men rushed from the room.

"It's time we went to the hospital," Lady Emmeline told Victoire calmly. "I'm afraid they will soon need our services."

Victoire was furious at having to stay with the women to await the arrival of the first casualties, instead of joining the battle on top of the walls. But Lady Emmeline had made it plain to her that her place was not with the soldiers.

Oh, dear, she thought as she heard the muffled din of battle, if only I were a man, I too could fight. Instead, here I am, listening to this empty chatter.

It was not long before three men staggered into the room, supported by their comrades. Their faces blackened by powder and dust, they looked dreadful. One's arm hung limply as if disjointed, another had been shot through the leg, and the third was losing blood rapidly through a severed artery in his thigh.

One of the doctors quickly prepared while the volunteer nurses cleaned the men's faces and disinfected their superficial wounds. The sight and smell of blood did not make Victoire queasy, but she was horrified by what happened to these once-healthy men. Then a second batch of wounded mobilized all available help, in a situation of indescribable confusion where the sound of groans soon drowned out the sound of guns.

Victoire found herself attending to a young man, still almost a boy, with bloodstained clothes. She cut away his shirt and saw that he had been shot several times in the chest. She called one of the doctors, who was passing. He quickly examined the youth, who had closed his eyes and was scarcely breathing.

"There's no hope," said the doctor with a grimace.

The thought that nothing could be done to save this poor boy, the first victim of the siege, was too much for Victoire. She made him a dressing that she knew to be useless, but which would at least give him the impression that he had not been abandoned. She raised his head to help his breathing. For a moment he opened his eyes, already dimmed by approaching death. His head fell back, and Victoire ran to help the other wounded before she would allow herself to give in to tears.

Chapter XXIX

*T*he first assault did not last long. Both sides were strong; one with equipment and men, the other with determination. The siege would be a long one. Days went by. The soldiers trampled about in the mud, while the inhabitants of La Rochelle settled down to a lengthy, constantly vigilant wait. Rationing became more and more severe. Victoire realized how much weight she had lost from the looseness of her clothes.

Meals usually consisted of a thin soup with bits of bread and sometimes bacon in it.

At first Victoire felt herself impatiently straining at the leash, but now the lack of action did not bother her. Even though she had almost nothing to do, an unaccountable listlessness overcame her. The same was true of Lady Emmeline, who was by now so frighteningly pale it seemed as if all the blood had drained from her very being.

Occasionally Victoire woke up in the middle of the night feeling ravenous, and she would longingly remember the banquets she attended in the days when she lived a hazardous but well-fed existence at Court. Her mouth watered as she conjured up the vision of all those banqueting tables laden with delicious food. She wondered about the chickens and ducks she had begun to rear at Montmaur. Were Honoré and Justine looking after them properly? How she would have loved to have tasted a bit of poultry at that very moment . . .

Victoire was also extremely worried about her uncle. The poor man was weak after everything he had been through, and might find it difficult to run Montmaur by himself. Ever since her mother had died, Victoire felt that Anselme was showering her with even more affection than usual. She could just imagine him waiting for Godefroy to get back, and then, when he arrived, taxing him with questions. Well, at least he would know that she was safe within the walls of La Rochelle.

And what about Guillaume, who had increasingly occupied her thoughts since she had been separated from Guy? Maybe he was among the besiegers, quite unaware that she was only a stone's throw away from him. Did he even remember her? Six months was a long time . . .

Frequently Victoire turned over these gloomy thoughts in her mind, so affected by lack of food and boredom, that she completely lost her sunny nature and became quite morose.

In February the sky remained overcast, but the days began to grow longer. Victoire whiled away the time walking through the streets of the city, which she knew by now like the back of her hand, and listening to the sermons of Reverend Pierre de Cressan, who on each occasion managed to find some new theme to encourage the beleaguered townsfolk. But she found she liked the man less and less, with his hard, clean-shaven face and his exalted, ruthless calls for blood in God's name.

One day when Victoire was sewing with Lady Emmeline in order to pass the time, the Mayor and Jacques Salbert suddenly burst into the room.

"There are traitors among us!"

"I cannot believe anyone could be capable of such infamy," cried Madame Henri, leaping to her feet.

"I'm afraid it's true. Four burghers, whom we thought to be among the most trusted of the town's defenders, had undertaken to betray us to the Duc d'Anjou by letting his soldiers in through the South Gate."

"How did you find that out?" asked Victoire, suddenly roused from her lethargy by such spectacular news.

"From a letter we found after someone had denounced them."

"Just imagine," said Salbert, "if we hadn't, our town would have been occupied by the royal troops tonight."

Lady Emmeline shuddered at the thought of what they had escaped in the nick of time. She imagined the sacking of the harbor, the looting, the fires, the rapes, and the murders that would have ensued. "And what are you going to do?" she asked.

"Mete out punishment to the traitors so that anyone who may be tempted to imitate them will have second thoughts. They will be sentenced and executed in public."

Next day, all the inhabitants except those who were guarding the ramparts assembled in the main square to witness the event. The condemned men were standing in chains on a specially erected platform. Reverend de Cressan, looking more forbidding than ever in his black gown, joined them there and began to address the crowd.

"You are about to witness the punishment of four of your fellow citizens who tried to betray you!"

The furious crowd let loose a sustained roar of hatred and was prevented only by the guards from tearing the four guilty men to pieces.

"But God did not allow their plan to succeed! What further proof do we need that He is on our side?"

As Pierre de Cressan, with bloodshot eyes, continued his diatribe against the abominable crime that was a disgrace to the town and its defenders, Victoire felt a growing sense of uneasiness.

When the four heads, one by one, fell with a blood-chilling thud onto the ground, spattering the nearest spectators with blood, she averted her eyes in disgust. The crowd let out a cry of joy. Justice had been done.

Shortly after the execution, whose swiftness had made a deep impression on the inhabitants of La Rochelle, it was decided to attempt a sortie. The secret was well kept, and the royal troops were taken completely by surprise. They paid dearly for their carelessness. Three hundred men were lost, including three captains, whereas only a score of Huguenots were killed and a few more wounded.

Victoire, like Lady Emmeline, was again needed as a nurse. Since she always managed to remain unflustered, and her movements were neat and unhurried, she was often asked to assist during surgery. To her surprise she realized that she rather enjoyed the job that had been dictated to her by circumstances. It was satisfying to ease the suffering of the poor soldiers with opiates, to see their wounds heal, and to sense that their bones were knitting again.

One day a doctor said to her jokingly, "The job seems to appeal to you."

"Yes," Victoire admitted. "I would like to know more about it."

"You'll certainly have an opportunity to learn some more and get plenty of practical experience here."

The doctor who performed most of the operations was moved by his pupil's eagerness to make herself useful, and he appreciated her patience and efficiency. Increasingly he called upon her services, taught her the rudiments of his art, and even showed her how to sew up a wound. Once, he handed her his razor-sharp scalpel and let her extract a bullet that was not too deeply embedded in the flesh of the wounded man— much to the latter's dismay. But she went about her task with such a gentle touch that the patient was forced to admit that he had scarcely felt any pain. The presence of a charming young woman had certainly made his ordeal easier to bear.

After a hard day's work, Victoire liked to walk back to the Mayor's house through the windy streets of the town. The fresh sea air was a welcome relief after a day of medicinal odors, and, at least temporarily, she did not have to look at blood and torn flesh. The worst of the winter was over, and the days were getting steadily longer.

From time to time she would go up onto the ramparts and visit her friend Arnaud. As she looked down at the enemy camp she wondered how the inhabitants of La Rochelle, whose food was now rationed more strictly than ever, would succeed in holding out against so many soldiers. She scanned the figures moving about beyond the fosses and tried in vain to make out Guillaume.

"You must go home now," said Arnaud in a fatherly

way as soon as night fell. "Madame Henri will wonder what has happened to you."

Meals at the Mayor's house had become so meager, Victoire could no longer allay her hunger. Her stomach felt continually empty, and she found herself dreaming more and more often of stuffed capons, juicy joints of meat, and huge slices of bread and butter.

The townspeople were now reduced to eating dogs and cats, boiled nettles, and the like. Jacques Henri, who was increasingly concerned about the lack of food and its effect on the morale and physical strength of his troops, could often be heard to mutter, "If only the Queen of England were to send a few ships to run the blockade, we would be saved."

"But does she know what a desperate predicament we're in?" asked his wife, who was by now no more than a shadow of her former self.

The Mayor shrugged. How could he know? No news had filtered through since the arrival of the Duc d'Anjou's troops.

One evening, while sharing a rat amongst the three of them, Victoire heard that an old woman was rumored to have the symptoms of the plague.

"We shall have to send an emissary to England," said the Mayor in a low voice, as though he were talking to himself.

Chapter XXX

The plague did indeed break out, and the whole city became terror-stricken. At first the dead were buried unobtrusively at night. The sight of lugubrious processions, lit by only two torchbearers, struck horror into the hearts of the inhabitants, who kept well behind their shutters.

The doctors exhausted themselves rushing from place to place and visiting, at great personal risk, houses with a black cross on the front door—the sign that a member of the household had come down with the plague. Protected by a hood with two holes for the eyes, they could do little but register the symptoms of their patients—a high fever and the appearance on their bodies of blisters containing a liquid that was transparent at first, then opaque and bloodied. Lymph glands grew to tumor proportions on the neck, armpits, and groin, and the patient soon died, usually after having infected his family.

The physicians were less interested in treating the patient, which was virtually impossible, than in trying to contain the outbreak by ordering the destruction of the rats which were responsible for spreading the plague like wildfire, and which freely ran the streets, having become emboldened by starvation.

Victoire began to lose heart. She told herself dejectedly that even if she managed to eat she would die of the plague—the mere thought of the word sent shudders through her body. After having emerged un-

scathed from so many dangerous situations, she was
now doomed to die from a horrible disease she could
not control. Anxiously she plied the doctors with questions.

"My poor child, there's not much we can do except
avoid contact with infected people and maintain extremely strict standards of hygiene, both personally
and in those around us. Wash your clothes each evening and rub your body with vinegar to kill the germs.
That's all that can be done."

"Isn't there the slightest glimmer of hope that one
may survive if infected?"

"It does happen, in about one out of ten cases, that
the inflammations disappear spontanously and the patient recovers. But you shouldn't count on that."

When she thought of the dark, threatening presence
that was enclosed in the town with her, Victoire felt
more and more that she had been caught in a trap, and
that its jaws were slowly but surely closing on her and
would soon turn her to pulp.

Victoire locked the door of Aloise's bedroom and
undressed completely in order to examine every part
of her body in the mirror, craning her neck to get a
proper look at her back. Every morning after that, she
inspected herself meticulously, always dreading that
symptoms of the plague would appear. It was becoming increasingly difficult for her to go on living, or
rather existing, with such a terrible threat hanging over
her head. And she felt so useless. Surely she could be
helping her people somehow outside.

When she had finished scrutinizing her skin, so pale
it looked completely colorless to her, another sad and
depressing sight met her eyes: her thin, almost emaciated body, with its lax limbs and protruding ribs. She
was a veritable walking skeleton. Thank God neither
Guy nor Guillaume was there to see her in such a
sorry state. She stifled a sigh and quickly dressed so as
to remove her own repulsive image from her eyes.

One night when she could not get to sleep because she was thinking sadly of poor Arnaud, the most recent of the plague's victims, Victoire suddenly realized she *had* to leave La Rochelle, whatever the cost. She preferred to be killed by a bullet or a cannonball than to go on rotting away as she was, doing nothing to help win the Protestant struggle.

She was convinced that getting out of the city would prove to be a more dangerous operation than getting into it. There seemed to be only two ways to leave, through the harbor or over the walls. Without the Mayor's help, they would both be impracticable. But he had other things to worry about than the fate of one young girl.

Unless . . . Jacques Henri kept saying if only he could get a message to the Queen of England, she would be bound to send several ships to her allies of La Rochelle to help them to raise the blockade. Victoire decided to be the person who took the message. There was no reason why she should not be able to repeat her exploit, this time in the opposite direction. Some way had to be found of forcing the Mayor to accept her suggestion. He would not be an easy man to convince.

Victoire brightened at the idea she might soon be free again, helping her fellow Protestants, and maybe even see Guy again. Whereupon she sank into a deep, peaceful sleep.

The right moment had to be chosen to bring up the subject with the Mayor. Victoire knew from experience that the success of an enterprise could sometimes depend on trifles, and that everything could be ruined by a passing irritation, annoyance at being disturbed, or poor digestion. Although very impatient, she waited until her host had finished his evening gruel before broaching the subject. His reaction was immediate.

"You must be out of your mind, Mademoiselle!

How do you imagine you're going to get out of a city that is being besieged by the King's army?"

"I managed to get in, didn't I?" retorted Victoire.

"Yes, I know," said the Mayor, smiling, "and that was miraculous enough, heaven knows. You can thank Providence for that, but you should not tempt it. Don't forget that when you succeeded in slipping into La Rochelle, the troops were not yet camped outside the walls."

Victoire persisted. "And by sea?"

"Six large ships are guarding the harbor," he said with a shrug.

"They are anchored some way from shore, beyond the range of the citadel's cannons."

"So?"

"Surely a small fishing boat, on a dark night, should be able to slip along the coast unnoticed?"

The Mayor looked at her with pity in his eyes. "You're talking utter nonsense, my poor child. Don't you realize that if such an expedition were feasible I would have chanced it long ago?"

"Let me try," said Victoire obstinately.

"I refuse to send you to your death—I feel responsible for you vis-à-vis the Marquis d'Hautemart."

"He means nothing to me. Write a letter to the Queen, give me a boat, two brave men who know how to sail, weapons, and enough money to get to England."

The Mayor became thoughtful. "You'd need twelve days to reach Dover . . ."

"I shall make the journey as quickly as my strength allows me."

"I've no doubt about that!" said the Mayor with a smile.

Victoire was relieved to sense that she had found a chink in his armor.

"A week after I arrive in London, a squadron could be in sight of La Rochelle."

As she remembered the thin broth that had served as their supper, she added, "It will bring you provisions—bacon, butter, flour . . ."

When she saw the Mayor's eyes suddenly light up at the mention of food he had not eaten for so very long, Victoire felt that her plan now had some chance of coming to fruition.

"I'll have to think about it and talk it over with the Reverend de Cressan. He'll tell me if I have the right to allow you to run a risk like that."

"I discharge you of any responsibility toward me," she hastened to point out. "Don't you think you ought not to let it be known that I'm leaving? For all your vigilance there may still be one or two spies in our midst. They would lose no time in telling the enemy, which would only make everything more hazardous."

"Why are you so keen to risk your life, if I may be so bold to ask?"

"I want to help our cause," she said quietly. "I'd be happy if I could make any contribution to our victory . . ."

The Mayor looked admiringly at Victoire, who flushed slightly and lowered her eyes.

In the end, it was Lady Emmeline who told Victoire that her husband had agreed to the plan.

"Could you visit Aloise and my sister and give them these letters? I've jotted down the address for you."

"By all means."

"Don't paint too black a picture of the situation here," the Mayor's wife begged. "I don't want them to worry."

"I won't mention the plague," Victoire promised.

"That would be preferable. Don't let them know either how very little food we have left."

Victoire looked at Madame Henri with sympathy. When she had first met her she was still a handsome and dignified woman, with her radiant complexion and her thick, glossy hair. Almost before Victoire's very eyes, she had turned into a feeble old woman who could scarcely stand on her feet, and whose face was covered with a network of tiny wrinkles. She had aged twenty years in two months.

"How brave of you!" Lady Emmeline murmured, her voice hoarse with emotion. "Never in the world would I be able to take such risks."

Deep down, Victoire felt that Madame Henri was showing far greater courage in remaining within the walls of the doomed city, surrounded by a starving and plague-stricken people.

Chapter XXXI

*A*t about two in the morning, Lady Emmeline came to wake Victoire, who had gone to bed immediately after supper. The Mayor reckoned that the lookout men on the bridges of the ships became a fraction less vigilant during the small hours of the morning.

Victoire dressed quickly, putting on the same clothes that she arrived wearing. The bundle she was to take with her felt heavy, for not only did it contain the message for the Queen and letters from Madame Henri to her family, but it was weighed down with a large sum of money that the Mayor had given her to make the journey a speedy one. Victoire calculated that the enormous sum would have enabled her to raise sheep at Montmaur.

But Montmaur and poor Uncle Anselme were miles and miles away. He was probably desperate with worry at not having received news of his niece for so long. If she was ever to see either him or Montmaur again, she would simply *have* to slip under the noses of the King's sailors.

"I shall spend the rest of the night," said Lady Emmeline, "praying that you may arrive safe and sound in England. Your presence here has become such a part of my life that I shall miss you deeply."

Victoire tried to comfort her. "Help will arrive soon," she promised. "And you'll be reunited with Aloise and your sister not long after that."

"May God hear your words!"

As Victoire kissed her good-by, she had the feeling she was seeing her for the last time. Death was gradually stealing over Madame Henri—every day she became more and more ghostlike.

The two men who were to accompany Victoire were waiting for her in the hall, dressed in oilskins and black trousers. The Mayor was giving them their final instructions. "As soon as you leave the harbor, keep going for some distance before coming in to shore. Try to drop Mademoiselle de Montmaur at least four miles away from here, so that when she lands she does not run into the soldiers. As for yourselves, find a hollow in the rocks and hide there in the boat until tomorrow night's tide, then come back."

He turned to Victoire. "Good-by, Mademoiselle. Seeing you off like this is a great wrench to me. From now on, we'll keep our eyes trained on the sea."

Victoire, too, found the parting rather hard on her emotions. But she felt a sense of relief as she left Jacques Henri's house, accompanied by the two men. They padded silently through the pitch-dark streets of La Rochelle. Victoire could hear the groans of the dying coming from behind the numerous doors marked with the dreaded black cross.

Soon she noticed that her companions were far from happy at having been entrusted with such a perilous mission. She tried to gain their good will by talking to one, who seemed to be less ill-natured than the other.

"The Mayor told me you were the best sailors in La Rochelle."

"Yes, I suppose that's what they say . . . But it's folly to try and get through; we won't make it."

"Do you *really* think it's impossible?" exclaimed Victoire.

"Milady, what with the harbor being blocked, the weather just turning nasty, and the King's cannons pointing straight at our noses, I can't for the life of me see how we can do it."

"And there's another thing," the other man chipped in even more cantankerously. "A fellow might have helped us row or bail out if the need arose. But a young lady, I ask you!" He spat scornfully into the night. "You'll get seasick."

"I most certainly shall not," replied Victoire angrily.

But what if she did? She had never set foot on anything but a ferry traveling from one river bank to the other. How would her already weak body react to being tossed by the waves? She tried to make herself as small as possible so that she would be forgotten. Neither of the two men gave Victoire a helping hand when she had to step into the boat. She slipped on the moist wood and almost fell into the water, provoking such sarcastic bursts of laughter she almost wished she had never embarked upon such a wild scheme like this. Then the boat was untied and cast off the moorings, while the other sailor began to row energetically.

When Victoire dipped her hand into the water, she realized it was ice-cold. If she had the ill luck to fall into the sea, she would never survive such a temperature. In any case, she could hardly swim, and her long fustian dress would become weighted down with water, soon dragging her down below the surface.

For the moment there seemed no reason to expect them to be capsized. The two men kept on rowing at a steady pace, and although they may not have been very friendly or talkative, they certainly knew their job. Victoire felt absolutely safe with them.

Straining her eyes, she could just make out the dark, threatening silhouettes of the enemy ships keeping guard in the distance. If she could scarcely see them, there was little likelihood that anyone on the bridge would spot a mere cockleshell bobbing on the waves.

They soon reached the end of the jetty, by the harbor entrance, just short of the open sea. Victoire thought the boat would never succeed in getting past the current, which swept them back into the harbor every time they attempted to leave.

She could sense the two men straining their muscles in concert. Although it was a rather cool April night, sweat was pouring down their weather-beaten faces. In the end they got the better of the current, but then the high seas broke over the boat, soaking Victoire to the skin.

"We'll have to bail out," they grunted.

One of the sailors dropped his oars, picked up a bowl, and began to scoop out the water that was sloshing about at the bottom of the boat. Victoire held out her hand.

"Let me do it."

As she knuckled down to her task, she realized it was not as easy as it looked. The sea was running high, and the boat often shipped a large quantity of water. Her clothes weighted her down and slowed up her movements. Soon her hands were frozen and her fingers numb and clumsy. But nothing in the world would have induced her to stop bailing water, partly because her life depended on it, but also because she was furious with the two males in the boat with her, who had assumed her to be useless and had made no bones about telling her so.

A breeze had sprung up, and soon she found she could not stop her teeth from chattering, even though all the exercise she was taking should have warmed her up. She thought fondly of Guy and the strong, delicious spirits he always kept in his flask. If only he were there to warm her up and comfort her . . . It had been stupid and improvident of her not to have taken a restorative with her instead of relying on someone else to provide it. Lady Emmeline would doubtless have agreed to give her a little of the grape brandy the Mayor offered his more important visitors.

Although she was in an unenviable and precarious situation, Victoire was nonetheless delighted to have left La Rochelle, where everyday life had turned into a nightmare, in spite of the kindness shown to her.

"Look out!"

A faint glimmer in the darkness indicated that a boat was leaving the flagship.

"Do you think they've spotted us?" asked Victoire anxiously

The only answer she got was a shrug. The two men had stopped rowing and were staring at the approaching speck of light. After a few seemingly interminable minutes, to their immense relief the boat changed course and headed for one of the big ships.

"They're paying each other courtesy calls," one of the men chuckled as he picked up his oars.

Victoire did not dare to ask if they were still far from the shore. Her frozen hands were hurting and she was still afraid of getting seasick.

She took advantage of a lull in the weather to look back and try to evaluate the distance they had covered in the two hours or so since they had left La Rochelle. The sea wall and the fortifications were fading into the distance. Almost imperceptibly, the sky was becoming lighter; dawn was about to break.

Victoire still felt as cold as ever, but she no longer needed to be constantly bailing out the boat. When she had a moment, she rubbed her hands together vigorously to try to restore her circulation.

"Are we nearly there?" she blurted out finally, by now at the end of her tether.

"Yes," said the gruffer of the two men, brightening up a little. "You see that spur of land over there? We'll steer around it and land in a cove on the other side."

Victoire refrained from pointing out that it had, after all, been possible to get through the enemy lines.

Now that there was less danger, the sailor became more talkative.

"I must say," h said, "it really beats me why the Mayor got it into his head to send a young woman all alone onto the highways. There were plenty of men . . ."

"People are less suspicious of women. Anyway, it was I who asked him to entrust me with this mission."

"And how far do you have to go?"

"To England, to ask the Queen for help."

He gave a whistle of surprise, mingled perhaps with a touch of admiration, and even saw fit to apologize indirectly.

"I wasn't at all happy at the idea to take you along the coast," he explained. "Three weeks ago, my cousin went out and tried to fish so he could feed his family. A cannonball got him and his boat."

"I hope you manage to get back safely tomorrow evening."

They reached the point just as dawn was breaking. And a few minutes later Victoire jumped onto dry land. She shook hands with the two men, who this time smiled.

Chapter XXXII

After waving them good-by, Victoire began to run toward a hamlet called Percavent, about a half mile to the west. The exercise would quickly make her warm again.

After a time, however, she had to stop and get her breath back. She took great lungfuls of air—the air of freedom, untainted by the stench of the plague.

Soon she could see the roofs of Percavent. But there was something strange about them. As she got closer she realized that no smoke was coming out of any of the chimneys, and although it was by now almost seven o'clock, she could hear no sounds of life. Perhaps the hamlet had been abandoned.

Victoire knocked on the door of the first house she came to; when no one answered she went in. The fire in the hearth was out, and had been for a long time. She went through every room in the house and found no one. Then, not very hopefully, she set about trying to find some food. The larder and storeroom were empty, as was the cowshed next to the kitchen.

Victoire explored the seven or eight small dilapidated houses that made up the hamlet. She would have to rest and eat something very soon or it would be impossible for her to continue. Malparet seemed to be the best place to go, where two of the Marquis d'Hautemart's men were permanently stationed, but she had no idea how many miles she would have to cover by foot.

In the hen roost of the last house she visited, Victoire found a half-starved chicken. Without a moment's hesitation she caught it, wrung its neck, plucked and drew it. A search for cooking utensils was fruitless, and eventually she had to resign herself to eating the bird raw. Satisfying her hunger, she lay down on one of the beds.

About noon Victoire woke up in an unknown room that was nothing like the one in which she had been living for nearly two months. Quickly she remembered where she was, and set off for her destination, orienting herself with the help of the sun.

Heading east, then cutting south, she hoped she would meet someone who could tell her the way across the plains of Aunis, which was so different from the rolling countryside around Montmaur.

Although extremely tired, Victoire strode on and on. The weakness in her legs was exasperating. To think that she once used to spend whole afternoons walking in the woods of Montmaur and would return home without feeling particularly exerted.

In a state of total exhaustion, she reached the edge of a small village as night began to fall. When she saw some soldiers from the King's army crossing the high street, she instinctively kept out of sight. After a moment the silliness of her behavior came home to her: who could possibly suspect that only yesterday she had been in La Rochelle?

Victoire began to follow the troops. At that time of day they were probably going somewhere where they could get supper. Her hunch was right. At the corner of a street she saw a wrought-iron sign that read La Chaudrée. She went in and sat down as far away as possible from everyone else. In any case, they were not ideal company for a young woman traveling alone.

"Would you like some *chaudrée?* It was freshly made this morning." asked a serving maid.

"Yes, Bordeaux wine as well."

It seemed as though she had never tasted anything as delicious as that fish soup made with white wine, chunks of conger, sole, plaice, and whiting. She asked for a second helping and derived enormous satisfaction from a sensation she had almost forgotten—feeling full.

Engrossed as she was in eating, she failed to notice that one of the soldiers was staring at her.

He got up and walked over to her. "Mademoiselle Victoire!"

Victoire whipped around when she heard that familiar guttural voice. "Boris! What are you doing here?"

"Oh, it's quite simple. Monsieur Guillaume is taking part in the siege of La Rochelle, and I am accompanying him."

The knowledge that her lover was so close, almost within arm's reach, made Victoire's heart miss a beat.

"It took me a long time to recognize you, Mademoiselle," Boris went on. "You've . . . changed so much. You look as though you've been ill."

"No, it's not that. I too was at the siege of La Rochelle. On the other side . . ."

"But how," exclaimed Boris, "did you manage to escape from a town surrounded by twenty thousand soldiers?"

"By sea."

Boris obviously found it extremely difficult to believe she could have slipped away under the very nose of the army.

Victoire tried to sound as casual as possible while she asked the question that was most on her mind. "And what about Monsieur de Louvencourt? How is he?"

"Fine. He received a command, and we arrived at La Rochelle last month. In any case, he should be here very soon. He asked me to reserve a room for him here. He feels like spending a night in a real bed with nice dry sheets. So do I for that matter. At the camp we live in mud and rain."

"But you can at least eat as much as you want. Do you know what I had for lunch today—and I can tell you it was a feast compared with the rats and nettles of La Rochelle—raw chicken!"

Boris looked at her wide-eyed with a mixture of horror and amazement.

"And *you* don't have to worry whether you're going to catch the plague," Victoire went on.

The Mongol stiffened. "So what they're saying is true? The plague? So close to us?"

Victoire nodded. "A dozen people die of it every day."

"You lived there?"

"For two months. I was lucky to get out again."

Suddenly the tall figure of Guillaume appeared in the doorway and her heart bounded wildly.

Unlike Boris, Guillaume immediately recognized Victoire, and an expression of tremendous happiness spread over his face, which showed signs of fatigue from the long siege. Boris unobtrusively left them so they could be alone. Guillaume sat down next to her.

"Oh, Victoire, my darling, I had given up hope of ever seeing you again." His blue eyes hungrily examined her face.

"So had I," admitted Victoire, thinking a little guiltily of Guy.

But maybe Guillaume, too, had had some love affairs, she thought. She found it difficult to imagine him devoting himself solely to her memory all those months. She felt understanding, even indulgent. Besides, now they really were in enemy camps.

"What have you been doing since we last saw each other?"

When she had finished her story, Guillaume chuckled admiringly and said, "It really seems as though you've chosen to live dangerously."

"I can't say I had any choice. My task is not over yet; I have to go to England as soon as possible."

Guillaume looked at her with concern. "You're in no condition to undertake such a long trip. You'll fall ill. Be reasonable, Victoire, and listen to me. I can stay here for three days, and I suggest you spend them with me. You'll get your strength back if you take some rest in this peaceful inn, where there is plenty of good food."

He smiled at her with a teasingly affectionate expression. "Just look at you, my poor girl, you're nothing but a bag of bones!"

Although tempted, Victoire had her doubts. "Surely I would be betraying the trust of those who sent me if I put off my departure, for however short a time? The people of La Rochelle are starving to death."

He took her by the hand. The moment he touched her she knew she would give in. She was unable to resist Guillaume when he looked at her with glowing eyes.

After a time she asked, "Can you do me a great favor? Would it be possible to get a message to my uncle?"

Guillaume thought for a moment. "Yes," he said. "One of my friends has to go to Cahors soon. He will arrange for your letter to be delivered from there."

"You've taken a great weight off my mind. I'm so afraid he is worrying about me."

"I've no doubt about that," Guillaume agreed. "He loves you as he would a daughter. Perhaps even more."

While Guillaume de Louvencourt was telling the innkeeper to prepare the best room for Victoire, she remembered another somewhat similar evening, in another inn where there had also been soldiers . . .

As she lay in her large bed, which had been specially warmed for her, Victoire felt both euphoric and on the brink of a nervous collapse. On top of all the stress she had undergone recently, there had been the tremendous effort she had made since the previous day to withstand the cold, fatigue, and hunger of her journey and the emotional shock of being reunited with a man whom, at the bottom of her heart, she had never forgotten.

But that evening she wondered whether Guillaume would understand that all she wanted from him tonight was his presence and his affection. Of course she wanted to belong to him again; but not now, later on, when she no longer looked like a waif. Victoire knew he was going to come into her room, yet even so, she was half asleep when he did.

He sat down on the bed and gently caressed her face. "In three days you'll be recognizable. You'll have gotten your color back, your smile, your appetite for life. My poor little half-starved girl from La Rochelle . . ."

"Will the siege continue much longer?"

"I've no idea. The town is so well protected by its location. We're trying to tunnel through the counterscarp, but the building of the bridge across the fosses has been held up by bad weather."

"We're still on opposite sides," sighed Victoire.

"But that doesn't seem to change much between us, does it?" murmured Guillaume.

He bent over and kissed her with greater passion than he had ever done before. To her great surprise, she could feel awakening in her a thirst for lovemaking that she would never have thought possible.

"Do you want me to stay? Or to leave you to get some sleep?"

"Stay," she murmured and clasped her hands more tightly around his neck.

Chapter XXXIII

"*I* was watching you sleep," said Guillaume. "You look like a child."

Victoire stretched herself and sighed. "I feel as though I'm a hundred years old."

"You don't look it. It's high time you had a good meal. I'm going to get them to send food up to you. I hope you're hungry?"

"Are you joking? I could eat anything."

The chambermaid placed a table in front of the fire, which she revived with a pair of bellows, and brought in half a loaf of fresh bread, a small jar of salted butter, some clover honey, a six-egg ham omelet, and a hare pâté. Guillaume and Victoire devoured it all amid much joking and laughter.

"I must say I feel better," said Victoire.

While Victoire lazed a little longer in bed before getting dressed, Guillaume went off with Boris in search of a horse for her.

The two men traveled about two miles out of the village where, according to the innkeeper, a gentleman had two saddle horses for sale. One of them was a superb chestnut. After a careful inspection of its teeth and legs, Guillaume tried trotting, walking, and galloping the horse. Then he made it jump a gate. He found the animal so well trained, obedient, and strong that he bought it with no further delay.

"What a beauty!" cried Victoire delightedly when

she set eyes on the horse. "I know we'll get along perfectly. What shall we name him?"

"How about Igor?" suggested Boris. "It's a common name where I come from."

Now that she had found Guillaume's love again, Victoire also found she wanted to regain her former attractiveness as rapidly as possible. She was ashamed of her clothes, which were very drab and nearly in tatters. Guillaume, who had known a properly dressed Victoire at Court, must have been surprised to find such a ragamuffin.

She asked the chambermaid about the possibility of getting some clothes made quickly by someone in the village.

"You could try Madame Germain, on the road to Niort. Of course, it won't be as smart as anything you'll find in Paris."

Madame Germain, a young woman who had three children to rear in addition to her dressmaking activities, promised to make her a plum-colored serge skirt within a couple of days.

"I've just finished a woolen cardigan, and the person it's for won't pick it up until next week, so if it fits you, take it. I'll have time to make another one."

Victoire tried it on. It would keep her warm under her cloak during her journey. It would also be suitable for London, where the climate was said to be damp. She also bought two pairs of stockings: one silk, the other cotton. For the moment, that was all she needed. Once she got to London, she would have a silk dress made up for her with the money the Marquis d'Hautemart had given her. It would be delightful to have fine clothes again after the experiences in La Rochelle.

She could almost feel her strength returning with the passing of each new hour; her circulation revived and swept away her feeling of weariness. That evening, when she went up to her room after a supper of mussels, lark pies, snails and rib steak with shallots cooked in wine, she found herself waiting impatiently for Guillaume to join her.

The next morning Victoire took advantage of the fact that Guillaume was away to try to sort out her feelings. She had spent the last two days enjoying herself and had scarcely given a thought to the future. Now she realized that she still loved Guillaume to distraction and that she had been attracted into the arms of the young Venetian more because of circumstances than as a result of a deliberate choice. But she could not help wondering how she would react were she to meet Guy again. Would she have the strength of mind to spurn his advances?

She would be sleeping with Guillaume again that night. Then they would have to part—for how long this time she did not know. Certainly until the end of the siege, anyway. That might go on for months.

After carrying out her mission, she would return to Montmaur. Guillaume had promised to join her there as soon as possible But last September, when she left Paris, he had also said he would come; and she had waited in vain, her hopes diminishing a little every day. Instead, it was Guy who appeared one evening at the end of the driveway.

Somehow Victoire felt certain that Guillaume was attached to her. Yet he had not told her he loved her. Had he asked for her hand in marriage—she would have immediately accepted, despite the problem of religion standing between them. Yet, how could she marry a Catholic while she was fighting so hard for the Protestant cause?

She resigned herself to the fact that she would have to be satisfied with what she had at present. But she did not entirely lose hope of eventually being with him forever.

Time passed so quickly Victoire found it hard to

realize that she had arrived exhausted at La Chaudrée only three days before. Up to the very last moment she would do her best not to think of their parting, to remain in high spirits, and to stop from worrying about a future without Guillaume.

They devoted their last night together to lovemaking and pillowtalk, as though sleep would have cheated them of the few precious moments of the time remaining to them.

At dawn, Victoire was overcome by a sadness she did not even attempt to fight. She was suddenly tempted to give up her mission and stay on at the inn, where her lover could come and see her often, or dress as a man and follow him to the camp of those who were besieging La Rochelle. Nothing counted in her life, she realized, except Guillaume.

He soon noticed how downcast she was. "I hate the thought of leaving you," he said tenderly. "We get on so well together."

"Will we ever meet again?" sighed Victoire.

He caressed her bare shoulder affectionately with his strong hands, then kissed it gently.

"I'm sure we will."

She had to stop herself from asking him whether he loved her, just a little at least. That was a question you should never ask a man—or so she had been told by Héloïse. Victoire's mother had never talked to her about any of the problems of being in love; all she had been concerned with was finding her daughter a proper husband. A relationship certainly existed between husband and wife, the Comtesse had said, but it should be of an extremely distant nature.

At last the moment came when Victoire had to rise from her warm bed and prepare herself for the long journey. That morning, she did not feel in the least eager for adventure. Morosely she got dressed while Guillaume went down to pay the innkeeper and saddle the horses.

She put together her bundle, which was heavier by now, and looked at herself in the mirror. Although her eyes still looked sunken in her emaciated face, she had gotten her color back. She felt physically capable of undertaking her long trip on condition that she did not make her stages too long and tiring at the beginning. She thought of her mission. Would she be able to get across a war-torn France and find her way to the British Queen?

Igor was pawing the ground in the courtyard. She already preferred her new mount to Aloès, because it had been chosen by Guillaume. Boris helped her up into the saddle.

"I trust you haven't forgotten the lessons I gave you," he said. "You still know how to use a dagger?"

"I certainly do. I've killed a man."

A smile flickered across the face of the delighted Mongol. "You're a good pupil. Next time I'll teach you something else."

Victoire burst out laughing.

"Boris, I've no intention of spending my time killing people."

"Sometimes one has to . . ." he said, shaking his head.

Guillaume and his groom escorted Victoire as far as Malparet. During the journey they kept up a brisk gallop—the two men were in a hurry to get back to La Rochelle and exchanged not a word. When he saw two horsemen in front of the barn, Guillaume reined his horse to a halt.

"I shall leave you here. It would hardly be fitting for a captain in the King's army to enter his enemy's lair."

Victoire held out her hand, which he kissed.

"I shall wait for you at Montmaur. Don't be too long . . ." Abruptly she spurred her horse so Guillaume would not be able to see the tears welling up in her eyes.

Part II

Chapter I

*W*ith the back of her hand Victoire de Montmaur wiped two large tears from her cheeks. She must not give way to her feelings. What would the Marquis d'Hautemart's men think if they saw her crying? They had thought her very heroic for having taken on the dangerous task of entering the beleaguered port of La Rochelle. But if they saw her now, they would lose all respect for her, and rightly so. For the time being she must banish all thought of Guillaume de Louvencourt from her mind, and try to forget that she did not know when—or even whether—she would ever meet him again.

She reined in Igor's gallop to a trot and affectionately stroked the horse's sweating neck. She sighed heavily. Every time she rode her beautiful chestnut horse she would be reminded of Guillaume, who had chosen him for her with such loving care. But this was not the moment to think nostalgically about the past, though it was so recent that she could still taste her lover's kisses on her lips. As she approached the two men by the side of the road, they suddenly started toward her.

"Mademoiselle de Montmaur! How in God's name did you manage to get out of La Rochelle?"

"How thin you are, Mademoiselle," said Jean Lescure, seizing her horse's bridle as Victoire leaped nimbly to the ground. "I hope you're not ill?"

The three days she had spent at the La Chaudrée

inn with Guillaume had obviously not been enough to put the flesh back onto her body. She hated to look so emaciated. And after only an hour on horseback she felt completely drained of energy. Normally she was quite capable of spending eight hours straight in the saddle without turning a hair.

"At least I was lucky enough not to catch the plague," said Victoire. At this dreaded word Lescure and his companion shuddered, though they were tough men and well accustomed to danger.

"So it's true what they say," said Jean Lescure, lowering his voice. "People are being buried every night?"

"It's quite true," replied Victoire.

"Come to the farm with us. We can't offer you much in the way of comfort or food, but at least it's safe, and Monsieur Guy will be back tomorrow."

"Is he still here?" exclaimed Victoire with a mixture of delight and foreboding; seeing him again was going to present a problem.

"He didn't want to go very far from La Rochelle. He was still hoping that he might manage to slip in to see you."

From the vast bed in the farmhouse's only bedroom, by the smoky light of a candle, Victoire contemplated the sideboard, the linen chest, and the rickety chair that were the shabby room's only furniture. The last time she had been there she had scarcely had time to notice her surroundings. Guy had been there with his tender yet urgent need for her, and at the same time she had been terrified at the idea that she might die in La Rochelle.

Guy . . . she was going to see him again tomorrow, and from Jean Lescure's remarks she was sure that she had been constantly in his thoughts since they had separated nearly three months before. She dreaded having to explain to him that she could no longer give herself to him. Of course he would be expecting her to, after that passionate night when their mutual anguish had thrown them into each other's arms.

Nevertheless, she particularly needed the young Venetian banker's help just now if she were to successfully carry out her new mission entrusted to her by Jacques Henri. She was well aware that the journey to Calais would be difficult and dangerous, regardless of the large sum of money she had been given to cover her expenses. She would be crossing a country laid waste by the incessant war between Catholics and Protestants, not to mention the danger of attack from the many criminals who were taking advantage of the breakdown of law and order within the country to pillage, kill, and hold ransom innocent travelers.

Soon Victoire's tiredness proved stronger than her worries and she slid into sleep. Suddenly she had the impression that someone was watching her; at the same time she sensed daylight through her closed eyelids. She opened her eyes. Guy Becavallo was there, looking down at her with such a happy look that Victoire was touched.

"Guy!"

"My love, at last I have found you again! I have been so afraid I'd lost you . . ."

"Everything went off all right . . . or almost," she added, remembering her terrible ordeals.

He sat down beside her and covered her with passionate kisses. At first Victoire was slow to respond, but soon she found it impossible to resist the sweetness that flooded over her when she realized that her lover of one night was more captivated by her than ever.

"I love you."

She found it difficult to reply without either lying or hurting him. Fortunately Guy was not expecting her to say anything. All he desired just then was to hold Victoire in his arms and embrace her. She could explain later.

When his ardor had calmed down a little he demanded, "Tell me all that happened. I want to know."

Once again Victoire told the story of all her trials, though she said nothing about the three days she had spent at La Chaudrée with Guillaume. She hadn't said anything about Guy to Guillaume either. She didn't want to hurt either of them. If circumstances were different she would be perfectly candid with both.

"And now," she concluded, "I must somehow get Jacques Henri's letter to Her Majesty Queen Elizabeth of England."

"I'll come with you!" Guy cried.

"What about your business?"

"That can wait. I am so happy at the idea of traveling with you."

During the afternoon Guy Becavallo wrote to Alexandre d'Hautemart to tell him that Victoire had gotten out of La Rochelle safe and sound, and that they were both setting off for London.

"Alexandre will really be relieved to know that you have come out of this mission safely. He was very concerned about you. He felt responsible to the Comte de Montmaur."

"I offered him my services."

The truth was that when she had made the offer, she had had no idea of what she was letting herself in for. This time, on the other hand, she had encouraged the Mayor of La Rochelle to entrust her with this new mission, but now she was far more aware of the risks involved.

"When do you want to leave?" asked Guy, staring at her anxiously.

"As soon as possible. Tomorrow."

"Are you capable of it? You're still in a very weak state."

"I've got to be."

"Wouldn't it be more sensible to wait for a few days?"

"I'm sure it would. But the people of La Rochelle can't wait. For them it's a matter of life and death. Have you ever eaten rats and boiled leather?"

"No!" Guy exclaimed, horrified. "Were you really driven to that?"

Victoire nodded. She preferred to forget that throbbing pain called hunger which twisted like a knife through her stomach and the shadowy figures wandering through the city in search of food, many of whom must surely have died since she left.

"All right," Becavallo conceded. "We'll leave tomorrow. But in short stages."

"I know I can't manage more than eight or ten leagues a day as yet," sighed Victoire.

Guy looked at her tenderly. "You'll soon be better. I'll see to that. I've sent Antoine to find some fresh game for our supper this evening. There's nothing much left to eat anywhere around here now, even for gold. The King's armies are plundering the farmyards and cowsheds. But tomorrow evening I promise you we'll have a feast. We'll toast our reunion with champagne."

Victoire thanked him. He was always so kind to her, so attentive to her slightest wish. And so devoted, too, to their common cause.

At nightfall Antoine returned triumphantly, brandishing two ducks and a huge loaf of bread.

"I'll roast them," said Jean Lescure immediately, for the time being combining the functions of both squire and cook.

When the time came for Antoine to set the chipped plates and tin goblets on the table, Victoire realized with growing unease that the moment was approaching when her vow to remain faithful to Guillaume would be tested. She would have to refuse Guy access

251

to her bed. When she said farewell to Guillaume she had naively thought that she would find it easy to explain, kindly but firmly, to Guy that their relationship must henceforth not go beyond the bounds of friendship. But Guy's whole attitude—his enveloping presence, his looks—revealed how impatient he was to be alone with Victoire again.

She herself could not help being affected by the waves of passion emanating from her former lover. Though he controlled his desire, he could not completely hide it. She felt her own determination weakening; she too was desperate for his touch. It would cost her dearly to sleep alone, knowing that Guy was so near. However, a secret instinct warned her heart that this was an effort of will that she *must* make. But would she be capable of keeping to her resolve every night during a journey that would last perhaps two weeks?

Victoire insisted that Jean and Antoine must dine with them. They sat down with a certain embarrassment, which Victoire's gaiety and verve soon banished. As the red wine gradually began to take effect, they all enjoyed the meal very much. All four of them were to leave Malparet at dawn. Jean Lescure was to accompany his master and Victoire, while Antoine took Guy's message to the Marquis d'Hautemart in Paris.

When the meal was over, Jean and Antoine retired to sleep in the barn. Like the previous time they had been together at the farm, the young couple found themselves alone in front of the dying fire. Guy did not dare to formulate his desires immediately, but his shining eyes told Victoire all she needed to know. She must take the initiative.

"Guy, I want you to understand . . ."

He stopped her with a gesture. "I understand." His face darkened with terrible disappointment, almost anger.

Victoire came up to him and took his hand with her most winning smile. "Give me a few days . . . Can't you see what a miserable state I'm in just now?"

He pulled her tightly to him and murmured, "If you only knew how much I love you . . . All right, I'll wait. But I'll be thinking of nothing but that moment. Remember that."

Chapter II

*A*ntoine had already been gone more than two hours when the other three set off on their journey.

"We don't need to set off at dawn as we're doing the journey in short stages," Guy had quite rightly remarked.

"Even so, we mustn't be too late."

Victoire was haunted by the thought of her friends starving in La Rochelle. The previous night she had dreamed she saw Lady Emmeline dying, a white, motionless figure on a magnificent state bed with pink brocade hangings.

"As soon as you feel stronger we'll travel farther each day," Becavallo promised.

So Victoire was off on her travels again, after a last, long glance at the Malparet farm. The fields this time last year had shoots of wheat thrusting strongly upward. Now they were uncultivated and gradually giving way to wild scrubland. It was hardly a year since she had left her home at Montmaur together with her mother, Anselme, Gilone, Héloïse, and pet dog Triboulet. Within a few short months her childhood world had been destroyed.

Her life had hung by the weakest of threads on so many occasions since then. Victoire asked herself whether perhaps she had developed a taste for taking risks, or whether she had been born with an innate love of danger. It was really very pleasant to be traveling to England and not only because it might help her fellow Protestants. The prospect of visiting a new and unknown country was exciting.

When they stopped briefly to water the horses, Victoire said to Guy, "Tell me about England. I know nothing about the place, or of Queen Elizabeth."

Guy smiled. "She's very difficult to describe. She must be about forty and is very conscious of being a woman. She always wants people to find her attractive —they usually do."

"Yet she has never married?"

"No. Although the King of Spain himself asked for her hand, as well as the Archduke Charles. People are saying that the Duc d'Alençon is interested, now that the Duc d'Anjou is no longer in the running."

"That horrid, stunted little man, with his pockmarked face!"

"Queen Catherine is very much in favor of the idea. It would have the additional advantage of annoying Philip II, the Spanish king."

"Her former son-in-law!"

"Also Queen Elizabeth's brother-in-law. You remember he married Bloody Mary, her older sister."

"What a horrible nickname!" exclaimed Victoire. "What dreadful things did she do to deserve that?"

"She was a fanatic Catholic and had many Protestants burned at the stake."

Victoire sighed. "So we have been persecuted in England, too?"

"She even threatened Queen Elizabeth herself, can you imagine? Toward the end of her reign, Mary, out of her mind with an imagined pregnancy, locked her sister up in the Tower of London. Elizabeth's mother, poor Anne Boleyn, already knew the inside of this gloomy prison beside the Thames only too well. She only left it to lay her head on the block on the orders of her husband, Henry VIII. He was tired of her, and wanted to be rid of her in order to marry again."

"What a charming family!" Victoire exclaimed. Suddenly she felt frightened at the idea of asking for help from a woman so closely related to such ruthless people. Suppose the Queen were like them?

At the end of the first day's journey, Victoire was so exhausted she could hardly stand up. All she wanted was to go to bed immediately. But she could not possibly disappoint Guy, who was so looking forward to this evening to celebrate their being together.

"How long will it be before you're ready?"

"Can you give me an hour?"

"Of course. I shall get busy ordering our supper."

Victoire went upstairs to her bedroom in the prosperous-looking inn, followed by a pleasant-faced servant girl.

"Will Madame need me?"

With a shock Victoire realized that everyone here thought she was Guy's wife. She knew, though, that it would be safer if she let them believe it.

"Will you bring me a jug of water, please?"

At Malparet, Victoire had found her riding clothes and the two dresses she had brought with her from Montmaur. Though they were not very elegant, at least they were decent. But alas! They were both much too loose for her now.

The maid helpfully adjusted her dress so that it fitted her as well as possible.

When she had gone, Victoire carefully inspected her

face in the mirror, as she had done three days previously in her room at La Chaudrée. Exercise and a day spent in the open air had brought back some of the color to her cheeks. She thought the candlelight would be more flattering than the daylight. In any case, the dark shadows around her eyes were beginning to fade, and her eyes were beginning to sparkle once more. The maid had brushed her blonde hair until it shone. She so much hoped Guy would like the way she looked.

But even as she formulated the thought, Victoire sensed how illogical she was being. She had no need at all to make herself look attractive for Guy when she did not wish to accept his attentions.

The staircase smelled of polish; everything in the inn had a clean, well-cared-for look. How different it was from the verminous hovels where Guy and Victoire had been obliged to stay during their previous journey together! Then they had been tormented by fleas, cockroaches, and bugs, and dirty linen.

Through a half-open door at the bottom of the stairs Victoire caught sight of the kitchen where the owner presided, helped by busy-looking boys. A delicious smell wafted through the door; it would have tempted even the most jaded appetite.

In the dining room she immediately saw that her companion had taken great care with his dress. Over his pearl-gray, heavy Genoan velvet doublet and his shirt of the finest cambric glittered a chased-gold chain; his breeches were smoke-gray. Victoire was well aware that his elegance was intended for her alone. The other customers at the inn were hardly a worthy audience for such magnificence.

"You do look handsome, Guy!"

His eyes gleamed with pleasure. "Allow me to return the compliment."

"I'm sorry," sighed Victoire, "I don't have an outfit with me to rival yours. I intend to buy some clothes in London, otherwise I shall not really be able to appear at Court and ask Queen Elizabeth for help."

Guy seemed to hesitate a moment before speaking. "You will need to go very carefully."

"What do you mean?"

"The French Ambassador, M. de la Mothe Fenelon, is very much in favor in London and has many spies there. He acts as an agent for Catherine de Medici and sends her all the information he can obtain."

"Do you mean Queen Catherine will rapidly be informed about my intervention on behalf of the Protestants?"

Guy nodded. Victoire pondered the matter. It would be very difficult to obtain an audience with the English Queen without the French Ambassador knowing. In theory, at least, she would need to request an introduction through the intermediary of her country's official representative, and he would, of course, want to know the reason for her request. The problem seemed insoluble for the moment, and Victoire decided to tackle it more seriously when she arrived in England. For the time being she would concentrate instead on the magnificent pheasant pâté baked in pastry and flavored with Armagnac that was being placed before them.

Although their table had been placed as far away from the others as possible, the other guests were watching in wonder as one dish succeeded another. Victoire began to have the uneasy feeling she was being watched. Several times she turned around to see who might be looking at her. What was the reason for what she was sure was a close scrutiny? Envy at the delicious food being served to them or simply curiosity. Eventually Guy noticed her unease and asked whether anything was wrong.

"No," said Victoire, though without much conviction.

"I can see something is. Doesn't the meal suit you?"

he asked with such a doleful air that she burst out laughing.

"Don't worry. This meal would make up for the whole siege without food. You must think me disgustingly greedy."

"I'm happy to give you pleasure."

Nevertheless, he continued to watch Victoire with a questioning and solicitous air.

Finally she admitted, "I have the impression we are being spied on. Isn't it stupid of me?"

But Guy did not laugh at her fears. He looked carefully around the room several times. "There are an awful lot of people here," he whispered. "But I'll try to see who's watching us. Act as if nothing was wrong."

They went on talking and laughing together like a young, newly married couple. But Guy did not relax his vigilance for a moment.

As they were finishing their meal he said in a low voice, "There are six men drinking wine together by the door. I think they were already there when we arrived. It could be one of them who is staring at you. He's only interested in you, not in me."

Victoire shuddered at his words and gave way to panic. What new danger was threatening her now? For she was very conscious of some threat hanging over her.

"When we get up, drop your handkerchief. While I'm picking it up you'll have plenty of time to look over toward the door."

Victoire did as he suggested. As soon as she looked toward the table where the six men were by now a little the worse for drink, one of them turned his head quickly away. But not before Victoire had seen and recognized his face. Where had she seen those bushy brows, that thick mane of reddish hair, and that broad, sensual mouth?

Chapter III

"*Well?*" Guy Becavallo asked Lescure as he brought the horses into the innyard.

The previous night Guy had escorted Victoire back to her room and made sure that the bolt on her door fastened properly. Then he had returned and asked his squire to get into conversation with the six men and find out who they were, if necessary buying them drinks.

"All I can tell you, Monsieur, is that they have a lot of money," the squire answered. "They offered me some of their own wine, and it was good quality. They were obviously suspicious of me. They asked me if I knew you and Mademoiselle. Of course I told them I didn't." Lescure concluded apologetically, "That's all I managed to find out."

"On the contrary, you have obtained some very important information," said Guy, whose face had clouded over with anxiety.

"What's that, Monsieur?" inquired Lescure with some surprise.

"They *are* interested in us."

Guy turned toward Victoire. "You were quite right."

"Do you think they are the Queen's agents?" she asked.

"No, I don't."

"Nor do I, Mademoiselle," said the squire after a moment's thought. "One of them started to talk about their master, though unfortunately he didn't mention his name, saying he was waiting for them somewhere, when the others shut him up straightaway."

They set off, though somewhat uneasily. But nothing happened either that day or the next. Victoire began to feel easier in her mind, and to feel she had perhaps been mistaken. Her strength was returning, and she felt quite capable of riding an extra two or three leagues a day.

"If we go on like this," said Guy, "we shall reach Alençon within two days." As they were riding through a forest close to Alençon early in the afternoon, two days later, they were suddenly surrounded by a score of ferocious-looking armed men.

"Mon Dieu!" exclaimed Guy. "An ambush! We're done for!"

Victoire thought so, too. She had already recognized one of their attackers as the bushy-browed man she had seen at the inn. Suddenly, in a flash, she remembered where she had seen him before: at the house where she, Guillaume, and Boris had been held prisoner by Adrien d'Etivey.

One man grabbed Guy's bridle, another Victoire's. A masked man, who seemed to be the leader of the gang, pointed a pistol at them and threatened, "Follow us without trouble or else . . ."

They were obliged to give in. The three of them were powerless against twenty armed men. The men grouped themselves around the young couple and watched them closely. Victoire and Guy set off slowly, their hearts taut with fear.

"Where are you taking us?" Victoire asked the man riding closest to her.

He laughed unpleasantly. "You'll soon see."

Victoire whispered to Guy, "I know who's behind this ambush . . . M. d'Etivey."

Guy shrugged his shoulders. "Who's he?"

Victoire had to duck a low branch, and did not

reply. Why had she been taken prisoner? she wondered. Perhaps their attackers had thought Guy was Guillaume de Louvencourt. But the two men did not look at all alike. Guillaume was a good two inches taller than Guy for one thing.

Perhaps Adrien d'Etivey was taking revenge against her because his enemy had escaped just when he thought he had Guillaume at his mercy. Guy was probably being taken along with her just because he happened to be there, like Boris and herself the previous time. Suddenly she remembered Jean Lescure. She looked carefully around the group as they entered a clearing, but could not see him.

"Jean," she whispered to Guy, who was again riding alongside her.

He managed a feeble smile. "He is our only hope now."

Night was falling as they came to a long flagged walk edged with chestnut trees. It led up to a château flanked with two towers and surrounded by moats filled with stagnant water. The drawbridge was lowered as they approached, and they rode into a courtyard where some grooms were rubbing down their horses in the flickering light of torches fastened to the walls. At the sight of this apparently peaceful scene, Victoire felt terror rising slowly but inexorably within her. Though she was not at all cold, after so many hours in the saddle, she could not stop herself from shuddering.

Her attackers ordered her to dismount. She obeyed, but had to make a huge effort to rally her strength and control her shaking limbs. Her only comfort in this terrible situation was the presence of Guy beside her, though he, too, was for the moment as powerless to act as she.

Six men escorted them inside the château into a huge vaulted room whose ceiling was supported by stone columns. In one corner a group of men were drinking and playing dice. Adrien d'Etivey stood alone, warming himself before the fire. He turned to greet them as they approached.

"Here you are at last, Mademoiselle de Montmaur," he said, smiling sarcastically. "It's taken me quite a time to lay my hands on you!"

Victoire retorted, "You still haven't managed to recapture M. de Louvencourt."

"I shall, in time. I shall use you as bait."

For a moment Victoire was dumbfounded by this Machiavellian scheme; then she found her voice again and exclaimed indignantly, "What an unspeakable trick! It's no more than I would have expected of you!"

"All's fair in love and war. As for this gentleman," he said, examining Becavallo, "he looks very rich. He can always be ransomed."

"I am ready to pay any sum to free Mademoiselle de Montmaur," said Guy in a determined voice.

Victoire knew quite well their captor would not agree to this. He was bent on revenge and his only aim was to capture Guillaume.

One of Adrien d'Etivey's men came up to him and whispered in his ear. He paled with fury. "You band of fools! You've let one of them escape!"

At this Guy could not prevent himself from smiling quizzically, which made the bandit even more angry.

"Send ten men after him immediately. Bring him back dead or alive. Otherwise you'll pay for it!"

The messenger rushed outside. Soon afterward shouts and neighings could be heard in the courtyard.

What was to become of them? M. d'Etivey did not leave them long in doubt. He sat down comfortably in an armchair whose oak back echoed the color of his copper hair, which framed a sly-looking face with a receding chin. He left his captives standing, as though it gave him pleasure to do so.

"Now we'll deal with you," he said slowly, in a way which boded ill.

He called over two of his men who were playing dice. "Robert! Jeremie!"

They came and stood, one at each side of the prisoners.

"You will remain in prison until I lay my hands on M. de Louvencourt."

Turning to Victoire, he continued, "You can hasten his arrival, Mademoiselle, by giving one of my men a letter for him. It will be given him as soon as possible."

"Never!" exclaimed Victoire, revolted. "Do you think me capable of such a shameful act?"

Adrien d'Etivey replied, "Suppose your life depended on it?"

"Nothing would force me to draw someone into an ambush!"

He gestured nonchalantly. "It doesn't matter for the moment. We have plenty of time. Perhaps you will change your mind. Take them to the underground dungeon."

Victoire's mind flew back to her frenzied search in the dark for a way out of the convent's underground passages, and terror chilled her blood. But Guy's presence and her own pride gave her the courage to restrain her cry of despair and revolt. Mademoiselle de Montmaur was determined not to give her kidnapper the pleasure of her weakness!

They were each seized in a strong grip and dragged into the courtyard.

"I thought we were being taken to an underground dungeon."

One of the men deigned to reply, swearing as he did so. "The entrance is by the stables; they are under the moat."

Victoire raised her head to look at the stars and the moon, which tonight was almost full. How long would it be before she saw them again? At a first-floor window a woman stood wearing a white shawl, her long dark hair spread loosely over her shoulders. The blood pulsed through Victoire's temples in shock. Surely that was her cousin. No, it couldn't be possible. And yet she could not stop herself from crying out, "Gilone! Gilone!"

The woman left the balcony and disappeared.

Chapter IV

*T*hey were hustled down a dark staircase. By the flickering light of a candle they could see the damp oozing through the walls, which were spotted and stained with saltpeter. At the far end of an underground passage they saw a door fastened with a heavy iron bar. One of their captors, a fearsome-looking brute called Robert, opened the door with difficulty and shoved the prisoners into a cell with no other windows or doors.

"See how nice I am," he snickered. "This evening I'll leave you the light." He stuck what remained of the candle into a hole in the wall. "I've no orders to bring you any supper, so you can wait until tomorrow. If you're thirsty there's a jug over there in the corner."

Dumbfounded by the horror of their situation, the captive pair watched him go. They heard the key turn in the lock, the sound of a grating being opened—presumably to give them a little air—and then the sound of his heavy footsteps receding along the passage. Soon they could hear nothing but their own breathing.

"Short of a miracle, I can't imagine how we can possibly get out of here," said Guy, inspecting every square foot of their prison.

"And remember, we're underneath the moat."

The idea of the enormous mass of still water above her head terrified Victoire more than anything else. Suppose the water started to drip into their prison through some crack in the walls? She imagined the water gradually rising . . . It had reached their knees . . . their stomachs . . . their shoulders—soon they would die a horrible death. Guy looked so downcast that she kept these dreadful thoughts to herself. She even tried to comfort him. "Jean will do all he can to rescue us."

Guy shrugged his shoulders, completely disheartened. "Even if he manages to find out where we are being held—and knowing him, I think he probably will —it will take time for Alexandre d'Hautemart to get his men together and organize an attack on the château."

"We can hold out until he arrives," Victoire reassured him.

"Even if he gets into the château, he'll never find this dungeon. They'd never hear us even if we shouted until we were hoarse."

"Surely one of d'Etivey's men would betray his master . . . at a price."

"Perhaps," said Guy without conviction.

But she knew that he did not believe her.

The guttering candle gave a final flicker and went out. They were now in total darkness. For them the dawn would not come . . .

They huddled together on a heap of straw, trying to fight the cold that was inexorably chilling their blood. Victoire had already sneezed several times in the cold, damp air.

"If only they'd give us some food, it would warm us up," said Guy bitterly.

"From what I know of Adrien d'Etivey, we shouldn't count on it."

"Yes, wherever did you come across that vile specimen?"

"At Court."

"What a place it must be!"

"Oh, there are lots worse than him," said Victoire, thinking of Father Izard, in whom a narrow and intolerant faith coexisted with a taste for blood and debauchery.

"Who is this M. de Louvencourt? Why should he come to your rescue when he finds out you're here?"

This time she would have to say something about her relationship with Guillaume. But Guy sounded so worried that she decided to tell him as little as possible. The last thing she wanted was to plunge him into alarm and perhaps even despair. This was not the time or place for a frank confession. She would have plenty of time to tell him the truth later . . . if they ever got out of their prison alive.

"There's been a feud between the de Louvencourt and d'Etivey families for a long time, I believe. They both come from Lorraine. Guillaume suspects that Adrien's father strangled his mother and then drowned her."

"D'Etivey obviously learned a lot from his father!"

"While I was the Queen of Navarre's maid of honor they fought a duel. M. de Louvencourt seriously wounded Adrien d'Etivey."

"I don't quite understand how you are involved in all this," said Guy.

Victoire was very glad that he could not see her face. She went on, trying to keep her voice quite steady.

"M. de Louvencourt has been a good friend to me, even though he is a Catholic. He tried to help me save my mother on Saint Bartholomew's Night. Unfortunately we arrived too late. The fact that both our mothers died a violent death created a bond between us."

"Poor Victoire!" said Guy, very touched by her story. "I didn't know the Comtesse de Montmaur died such a tragic death. I know so little about you."

He put his arm tenderly about her shoulders. Victoire gratefully pressed herself against him. She could not even begin to imagine what a state she would be in if she were alone in this dungeon. And he was there only because of her.

As soon as they awoke, hours later in each other's arms, the complete darkness reminded them of their desperate situation. It must be daylight outside.

"I'm so hungry," moaned Victoire, overcome by this sudden return to reality. Once again she was having to face the bitter prospect of starvation.

Now it was Guy's turn to try to cheer her up. "They'll bring us some food soon."

They waited for what seemed like an eternity before they heard heavy footsteps in the corridor and saw a faint light gleaming through the grating.

"At last," whispered Guy.

"Here's your lunch, my turtledoves! And it will have to be your supper, too."

He did not even open the door, either because he was afraid they would try to escape, or because he was under strict orders not to do so. Instead, he handed them their food through the grating together with a lighted candle. Then his grimacing face disappeared. Guy hurried to place the candle where it cast the most light across their cell.

They were so famished they threw themselves on the food without ceremony. To their surprise it wasn't too bad, and there was plenty of it.

"We must keep some for this evening," said Victoire.

At the siege of La Rochelle she had learned to survive on a very small amount of food and to chew slowly to make it last longer. She thought of Lady Emmeline, who would have considered their scanty rations a feast. She must be watching out for the English fleet even now with an impatience bordering on despair. But now she would wait in vain.

They paced up and down the cell to stretch their numbed limbs a little and then threw themselves down on the straw once more.

"How long do you think this infamous creature will leave us here to rot?" Guy lamented.

"God alone knows!"

But Victoire could hazard a guess. They would remain here until d'Etivey got his hands on Guillaume again. Then he would kill both his enemy and Victoire too. Perhaps he would agree to release Guy for a huge ransom.

They began to review the possibilities for escape. Without tools they were quite powerless to break down the door. It was at least an inch thick, and reinforced on the outside with metal bars.

"If only the guard would come into the cell when he brings our meal. I could easily take care of him while you escaped," said Guy.

"Where could I go? Even if I got through the door at the top of the steps—and it might well be locked— I should only get as far as the courtyard before I was seized. In any case, I refuse to escape without you."

In reply Guy kissed her. "I could not feel completely unhappy so long as you are with me."

She was extremely fond of Guy—his crumpled clothing and the straw in his brown hair touched her—but she could not love him whole-heartedly. Was it because he loved her so very much?

"I've got some gold. Do you think we could bribe Robert?"

"It's worth a try."

However, Victoire did not really think they had much hope of success. Adrien d'Etivey's men seemed completely devoted to their master—they must be paid well.

The long day dragged by with nothing to break the silence or lighten the blackness, once the candle had gone out. The ate their supper in the darkness and drank straight from the jug, one after the other.

"Who were you calling to yesterday as we crossed the yard?" asked Guy.

Slightly embarrassed, Victoire explained, "I thought I recognized my cousin Gilone on the balcony."

Guy was surprised. "Do you think it's at all likely she'd be with such a wicked man?"

"Not at all," replied Victoire quickly. "She's at Court. It must have been an illusion."

And yet the mysterious figure had been the same size as Gilone, with the same hair and the same detached way of watching the grooms bustling around in the courtyard in the evening light, though she knew quite well they were staring at her. But, of course, Victoire caught only a momentary and distant glimpse of the figure on the balcony.

A second night went by, more depressing, if possible, than the first. There was no reason why they should not spend many more nights there before M. d'Etivey decided to murder them. Victoire decided she must fight her depression.

"At least they haven't caught Jean Lescure," she said.

"Who knows?"

"If they had, Adrien d'Etivey would have lost no time in telling us."

"Perhaps you're right," Guy admitted. "By now he should be close to Paris."

They vacillated between extremes of hope and despair as they pondered how they could best tempt Robert.

"How much should we offer him?"

"Enough to make a big risk worthwhile. Judging by the way his henchmen were enjoying themselves at the inn, d'Etivey must pay them well."

"Suppose he tells his master about it?"

"What could he do that would make things worse than they already are?"

"Separate us."

Guy stretched out his hand in the darkness. Victoire took hold of it and squeezed it tight.

"If you weren't here," murmured Guy, "I think I'd bang my head against the wall until it cracked open."

They heard Robert's heavy footsteps approaching. His pockmarked face appeared at the grating.

"Let's try to get him talking first of all."

"Here's your food, my little lambs!"

Victoire rushed forward. "Could you possibly get us some candles?"

He scratched his head and gave a sly smile, revealing a few yellow stumps of teeth.

"But I don't know how to make candles, you see."

"We'd buy them."

"Oh, that's different."

Guy came forward, a gold coin glittering in his hand. "I'll go and get some."

He had left the upper door open and a draft of fresh air blew into the cell. The prisoners breathed it in nostalgically.

"Well, we've got something out of him," said Victoire, pleased.

"Do you think we should go on with it now?"

Victoire hesitated. "Let's wait until tomorrow."

Chapter V

*T*he thought that they would not have to spend another day in total darkness gave Victoire and Guy some small comfort. They washed themselves perfunctorily in the water from the jug, and Guy tried to straighten out Victoire's tangled hair.

"I wonder who was in this cell before us," she remarked pensively.

Guy took the candle and they went around the cell deciphering—though with some difficulty—the inscriptions on the walls. They were mostly dates, some of them from a long time ago: May 13, 1484 . . . December 6, 1521 . . . August 3, 1502. Some of them were more recent, doubtless put there by M. d'Etivey's prisoners. The date January 17, 1568 was followed by a pathetic message: "I have been here 123 days. I'm going to die." Underneath were small dashes for each day.

Victoire shuddered. "I couldn't possibly stay here for four months without air or light."

"Don't worry," said Guy. "We'll kill ourselves before then."

Victoire did not dare ask him how. They had no weapons.

From an inscription on the wall by the door they found out where they were: Eglimont Château.

"I'm sure I've heard something about this château," said Guy, racking his brains. "That it was the haunt of a particularly ruthless band of robbers who held travelers for ransom and practiced various kinds of extortion. But I never knew where it was. If I had I should have avoided it like the plague."

"Our fate was sealed as soon as one of d'Etivey's men recognized me at the inn. We could only have escaped if we had had a powerful escort with us."

"That's my fault," Guy reproached himself. "I thought we'd travel faster this way."

"It wasn't your fault at all. We are in this situation because of me alone."

Once more they tried to calculate how close to Paris Jean Lescure must be by now.

Robert turned out to be incorruptible, though his small eyes glittered when he heard how much they were offering. But his fear of his master was far stronger than his greed.

"If things went wrong," he said, terrified, "he'd kill me . . . or even worse."

"What could be worse?" Guy asked.

"Last year one of us betrayed him. He cut off his hands and feet, took him into the middle of the forest, and left him there as an example to the rest of us. He told us that if anyone helped him he would be punished in the same way."

Victoire turned white with horror at such cruelty.

"I don't want that to happen to me."

Nevertheless, he was quite ready to do all he could to improve conditions for them, providing, of course, that he was paid. He brought them two blankets, as much water as they wanted, and a bowl for them to wash. He even found a comb for Victoire and brought them wine with their meals, which became much more plentiful.

"That's already something," said Victoire. "By now Alexandre must be organizing our rescue."

"If Jean's gotten to Paris safely."

They settled down to wait again. The small comforts they had managed to obtain for themselves seemed like a miracle after the misery and cold of the first few days. Their worst problems were lack of air and the fact that they had nothing at all to do.

Days and nights went by. They lost all idea of time since they never saw the daylight. One day they asked Robert the date and were amazed to find they had already been captive for a week.

On the ninth night they were awakened not by their usual jailer but by two masked men dressed in black. They entered the cell, and before Victoire and Guy, still dazed with sleep, realized what was happening, they bound their hands behind their backs and blindfolded them.

"Where are you taking us?"

For once her question received a reply.

"To a party that M. d'Etivey is giving."

"But why have you tied us up and blindfolded us?"

"Those are our orders."

It was all the information they could get. Their captors led them upstairs, gripping them tightly by the arms to stop them from stumbling. When they reached the courtyard Victoire took a deep breath of air with a feeling of exhilaration. The exceptionally mild April night almost made her faint with pleasure. If ever she managed to escape from the clutches of this bird of prey, she knew she would always in future be aware how lucky she was to be able to breathe in th evening air.

As they approached the château a joyful uproar reached their ears. D'Etivey's guests seemed to be enjoying themselves, and the drink was flowing freely. Through her blindfold Victoire could just make out an area of light toward which they were walking. As they entered the château the uproar of the party grew louder. They climbed a staircase and entered a huge room that seemed to contain at least fifty people.

As they made their appearance the guests gradually became aware of their presence and fell silent. They must, thought Victoire, make a strange sight with their pale underground faces and tousled clothes. Why had M. d'Etivey brought them here? she wondered.

His slow, ice-cold voice rang out across the crowded room. His guests, flushed with food and drink, were all, Victoire sensed, turning toward her and her companion.

"Here is my latest prize, and an important one at that. You see before you Mademoiselle de Montmaur, a former maid of honor of the late Queen of Navarre, and M. Becavallo, a well-to-do banker who, if my information is correct, represents the famous Fugger house in Venice."

A murmur of approval rose from the guests. Victoire wondered who the Fuggers could be; their name alone seemed to arouse an immediate response.

"For your amusement," went on the master of the house, "I have thought out a little game."

His guests exclaimed with pleasure. Victoire guessed that she and Guy were likely to be pawns in this game.

"Messieurs, you will throw dice for Mademoiselle de Montmaur. The winner will spend the rest of the night with her."

"The monster," hissed Guy from between his teeth.

It was a few seconds before Victoire realized that d'Etivey was talking about her, and that one of these degenerates would have the right to abuse and rape her. Immediately her mind was filled with terrible images from the past, as though to confirm the horror of the present. Father Izard watching from behind the door, advancing cautiously in his sandals, then, like a wild animal, throwing himself onto her bed which was, luckily, empty. And yet another occasion when, taken by surprise, she had suddenly felt, pressing down on her, the body of this man of God who had sold himself to the Devil. Even then she had managed to escape with her honor intact. But this time she had no weapon to defend herself. She had left the second dagger Guillaume had given her in the body of a Catholic soldier outside the gates of La Rochelle.

"Remove the prisoners' blindfolds. I want them to watch the game."

At first Victoire's eyes were blinded by the unfamiliar light. But soon she made out a long horseshoe-shaped table laden with a vast assortment of food and drink. Around it were sitting a score of men and half as many women whose disordered dresses showed they had already been receiving attentions from their companions. Shortly one of the men would have the right to rape her. Victoire looked eagerly—with a sudden wild hope in her heart—at the women. And sure enough, she recognized Gilone sitting on Adrien d'Etivey's right, queening it over the party in a bright red dress she liked so much because it set off her white complexion and her thick black hair. She stared at Victoire with an evil, taunting expression on her face, as though she was excited by her cousin's fate.

Gilone leaned over and whispered something in Adrien d'Etivey's ear. He agreed to her request with a smile.

"Let the woman's hands be untied; she may approach."

As the servants cleared part of the table for the dice game, Victoire came forward, trying to hide her emotion. "Gilone."

It was inconceivable she should make no attempt to save Victoire, whose family had always been so kind to her. Victoire's mother had presented her at Court, where her beauty and worldliness had won her the attentions of several noblemen. Catherine de Medici had taken her under her wing, despite her Protestantism.

But Gilone's eyes betrayed no hint of any desire to save her cousin.

Adrien d'Etivey turned to her in surprise. "Do you know Mademoiselle de Montmaur?"

"She's my cousin."

D'Etivey was taken aback for a moment.

"In that case," he announced, "I shall choose another prize for the dice game. Of course, there can be no question of freeing your cousin, at least not until I capture Guillaume de Louvencourt."

A flicker of hope arose in Victoire's heart, but it was soon extinguished.

"Please don't change your plans for me, darling," said Gilone with studied indifference. "I, too, shall find the dice game amusing."

Her lover stared at her, perplexed. Her wickedness surpassed even his own, and he found this disturbing.

He poured out a glass of wine and handed it to Victoire with a smile verging on embarrassment. "Have a drink, Mademoiselle."

She took the drink and had a sudden impulse to throw the wine over, at least making sure of spoiling both her cousin's dress and her evening. But her intuition told her that something was at work in her captor's mind which would make her gesture out of place. So she drank some of the wine and hesitantly took the rest to Guy and held it to his lips as though he were a child because his hands were still bound.

"Thank you," he whispered.

The guests had gathered around the table, where a cloth had been laid to muffle the noise of the dice. The game began. The women seemed as excited as the men, Victoire noticed. How could they be so pleased to see one of their own sex in such a situation? Observing them more closely, Victoire was sure that they were the kind of women who exchanged their favors for food, drink, and gowns. Apparently Gilone had been reduced to this level as well, otherwise she surely would not have wanted to share Adrien d'Etivey's life. Perhaps she had been forced into this situation after incurring the Queen's displeasure.

Half of the sixteen players were eliminated on the

first round. Somewhat piqued, they returned to console themselves with drink. One of the men still in the game seemed more eager and passionate than the rest. His regular features and his intelligent, kindly expression made him stand out from the rest. He looked less brutal than d'Etivey. In her misery Victoire began to hope that he would win.

Fascinated despite herself, she watched the game— in which she was the prize—take its course. She was furious now to think that she had so often refused to give herself to Guy, who was so sensitive and loved her so dearly. She could see he was close to despair now that he was powerless to save her. As soon as she returned to their cell she promised herself she would give herself to him—if he still wanted her.

The guests who had already lost were criticizing her appearance—sneering at her looks and her tousled clothes. Victoire was aware that she must cut a wretched figure alongside the other women who were dressed up for the occasion, covered in make-up and jewelry. But it might be a good thing that she looked so unattractive—perhaps no one would want her.

At last the terrible uncertainty was over—but the game ended in disappointment for her. The man she had wanted to win had lost. He gave Victoire a sad smile that expressed something more than frustrated desire.

He refused to be beaten, however. He turned to the winner, whose face was already bloated with drink and his doublet stained with sauce. "Edmond, I'll buy Mademoiselle de Montmaur from you."

The winner laughed, thinking it was a joke.

"Not a hope, old friend, she's mine. Aren't I right, Adrien?" he asked in a somewhat slurred voice.

"Of course. But you can sell her to Renaud if you wish."

"You hear, Edmond? How much do you want?"

"Much more than you want to give."

"Tell me anyway."

Victoire became increasingly convinced that she had heard Renaud's voice somewhere before. Perhaps she was imagining it in a desperate hope that her fate would be somehow less dreadful with him. In any case, it was very unlikely she had met any of M. d'Etivey's friends before. Though perhaps it might have been in the house where she had fled with Guillaume on Saint Bartholomew's Night? She searched her memory in vain.

How much would they price her at? she wondered. It was impossible to guess. But she found it extremely unpleasant to be haggled over like some animal at market.

Before he replied, as though to give himself time for thought, Edmond swallowed another mouthful of red wine. His round, already rosy face grew even redder.

"Five hundred crowns."

She had no time to feel frightened. Renaud's voice rang out immediately. "Agreed! Come on, Mademoiselle."

He grabbed her by the arm, while the guests laughed and applauded.

"Bravo, Renaud!"

"He's in a hurry!"

"Edmond's got a good bargain!"

The latter began to laugh heartily and pulled one of the women onto his knee, where she let herself be freely fondled.

"Pretend to fight a little," Renaud said so softly she could hardly make out his words.

He dragged her after him.

Chapter VI

*R*enaud gestured to her not to ask questions until they were well out of the guests' earshot. As she followed him through a maze of corridors and staircases she wondered at the bizarre situation that she found herself in. Earlier she had dreaded her fate, but this man seemed more like an accomplice than an enemy. She was not frightened of him nor repulsed by the touch of his hand. He clutched her as though he was more afraid of not being with her rather than of her escaping. Was it possible there was a human being capable of pity among this band of unscrupulous people?

Perhaps, though, she was unreasonably trying to reassure herself about him and had been wrong to imagine that, because he had better manners than the rest, this man might be her ally. He wanted to make love to her, there was no doubt of that.

But what could be the reason for his warning to her and his silence since they left the banqueting hall? He kept turning around. Did he suspect they were being spied on?

Finally he showed her into a bedroom where a torch was warming up the damp air. Renaud pointed to an armchair. "Sit down and get yourself under control. I've got just what you need."

He poured some colorless liquid from a silver-gilt flask into a goblet. "Do you like eau de vie?"

"I've never tasted it."

The brandy was very strong, and did her good. With a jolt she realized he might be trying to get her drunk so that he could do what he wanted with her more easily.

"Victoire . . ." He came close to her, smiling mockingly. "You don't recognize me?"

She hesitated; her Christian name hadn't been mentioned earlier. "Perhaps your voice."

"Yes, that's true. You've never seen my face. Don't you remember one evening at the Louvre when I consoled you? You weer so unhappy, though I didn't know why."

"The masked ball!" she remembered suddenly.

"I have often thought of you since then," he went on. "You were so beautiful, so young, so innocent among those worldly women. You softened my heart. Then I saw you again in this den of thieves!"

"You don't think I came here of my own free will!"

She told Renaud how she had been abducted and held prisoner.

"What a scoundrel!"

Renaud began to pace up and down the room, muttering obscure threats to himself. Victoire was perplexed at this sudden fury.

"What are you doing in such company?" she asked.

His face looked anguished. He smiled sadly. "Can you imagine!" he said. "Adrien d'Etivey is my brother-in-law!"

Victoire was stunned by this revelation. She felt quite unable to speak or to move from her armchair. One thing was certain. She could expect no more from Renaud than a little commiseration at her predicament.

He had turned his back on her and was looking down at the courtyard, which was quite deserted at this hour. He went on in a tired voice. "Yolande d'Etivey was an angel. Despite the disgust I feel for her brother, I sometimes come to Eglimont Château, where she spent part of her youth. From time to time Adrien talks to me about her."

"I understand," Victoire said softly. "You must have loved her deeply."

"Passionately, the way one loves when one is young. She died in childbirth, my child, a boy. I don't know why I'm telling you all this. Maybe I've drunk too much wine, and you are so different from the women I usually meet here. But I'd rather talk about you . . ."

He broke off and his voice suddenly changed. He dragged Victoire toward the bed. "Will you stop fighting!" he shouted.

Victoire immediately entered into the spirit of the game. She started to scream. "No! I don't want to! Leave me alone!"

They were rolling about on the counterpane. Renaud's lips brushed her ear. "We're being watched! The door."

Victoire continued pretending to resist fiercely. Renaud was tearing at her clothes, trying to disrobe her. This was going too far, she thought, but when she remembered it would probably save her life, and Guy's, Victoire knew she would have to continue with the pretense. Renaud lay on top of her, and over his shoulder she saw the partly open door gently close. She waited for a few seconds, then whispered, "They're gone. Do you know who it was?"

"One of Adrien's men. He'll report on what he saw."

Victoire stretched out on the soft bed alongside Renaud to catch her breath. She felt so comfortable there. It was so much better than the straw bed in the dungeon that seemed like part of a nightmare from which she might never wake up. She felt so much safer here and wanted to abandon herself to Renaud's irresistibly sweet lips out of gratitude. But then she thought of Guy. What had become of him?

"Renaud," she begged, "please help us to get out of here."

"It won't be easy. But we'll manage it, never fear. You don't think I intend to leave you in the hands of these bandits!"

Calmed by his promise, and exhausted after so much excitement—the first light of dawn was already beginning to glow through the curtains—she did not have the strength to resist Renaud's insistent caresses that helped her for a few minutes to forget the hideous reality of the situation.

"You are exactly as I imagined when I held you in my arms on the Louvre balcony the night of that party." Renaud spoke softly into her ear.

Once again he drew her to him as though he wanted to make the most of the little time they had left. "I'll get you out of here within two days!"

An insistent knocking on the door awoke them. They had finally dozed off under the warm eiderdown, though the fire had gone out. Victoire went pale. "They've come to take me back to the dungeon."

"I'll have to let you go," whispered Renaud, kissing her for the last time. "If I am to succeed no one must suspect anything. Rely on me!"

Victoire gave him a sad smile. "You're my last hope, Renaud." She paused thoughtfully for a moment. "Renaud, thank you for not taking advantage of me last night. It would have been easy for you to do so. I will always remain grateful."

Hearing heavy footsteps outside, she hardly had time to dress before the guards dragged her away. In the courtyard the horses were being brought out in the pale early-morning light, whinnying with impatience after being fastened in all night.

She breathed in a last lungful of pure air before she was hustled back down into the damp, underground confines. Guy would be waiting for her anxiously, and she looked forward to telling him that they would soon be rescued. As the days slowly passed they had gradually lost hope in Jean Lescure. Perhaps he had been killed or wounded by other brigands. Even if he had reached Paris safely, Alexandre might have been away, in which case it would take him some time to get together sufficient men to rescue them.

Guy would doubtless question her about what had happened in the room upstairs with Renaud. She wondered if anyone would believe her, especially Guy.

She was shoved so roughly into the gloomy cell that she almost fell over.

"Guy," she called.

But there was no reply.

Victoire collapsed onto the mattress and, shivering, wrapped herself in the blanket. What had they done with Guy? The hostile solitude of the cell drove her to distraction, preventing her from even ordering her thoughts. There was nothing she could do but wait for Guy to return, persuading herself that at any second footsteps would echo along the corridor, the door would open, and he would be there.

Minutes went by, each one seeming to last an eternity. The minutes turned into hours, and nothing happened. Finally, overcome by tiredness, Victoire dozed off.

She dreamed of Montmaur, but, far from calming her, the familiar scenes only increased her anguish. Sitting nodding by the fireside, Anselme was drinking his infusion of rosemary, as he did every evening. Then his head fell to one side, the cup dropped from his hands, and she knew he was dead. From below she heard the hammer blows of the carpenter making his coffin. The noise awakened her, mingling with the noise of the grating being opened. She leaped to her feet.

"Robert, where is M. Becavallo?"

But instead of the jailer's face, which was at least familiar if not friendly, she saw an unknown head crowned with a mop of red hair. He made signs to her to explain that he was dumb, then gave Victoire her rations and the lighted candle and slammed the grating shut.

For how long had she been hoping in vain in her dungeon? She tried to think of Renaud. He had promised to free her "in two days." But her thoughts constantly returned to Guy. Perhaps he was lying somewhere buried in a hastily dug grave. Or, though this was far less likely, perhaps he had been set free. If so, perhaps he too was planning to rescue her.

She would never, thought Victoire, see Guy again. He must surely have been cruelly killed by d'Etivey. Never again would he look at her so tenderly, with that hint of controlled passion in his gaze. Never again would she be comforted by his presence at her side. Huddled in a corner of the cell, like a sick animal close to death, Victoire gave way to tears. Even if, with Renaud's help, she managed to escape from this fetid dungeon, she would be haunted as long as she lived by the thought of Guy's death; these wounds would never heal. If she had not met Guillaume, she would have loved Guy, she was sure of that.

Victoire's thoughts turned to Gilone. What a shock it had been to see her as the mistress of Eglimont! When Victoire had last seen her she had been an ambitious and greedy woman, exploiting her attractions, and willing to abjure her Protestant faith in order to prosper in the service of Catherine de Medici, who was responsible for the massacre of so many Protestants. Now, only a few months later, her childhood companion had turned into a monster who took pleasure in the suffering and humiliation of others, even—perhaps especially—when the victim belonged to the family that had looked after her for so long.

What could have happened to change Gilone so radically? Anselme de Montmaur would not have been surprised to see how she had changed. He had never liked Gilone, sensing a flaw in her character that no one else did.

Victoire tried to analyze her memories honestly. She was sure that, from the moment when Gilone had come to live in her home, she had treated her like a sister. Since they had come to Court, they had certainly seen less of each other. Court life had brought out a new—and rather unattractive—side of Gilone. Disappointed in her cousin's behavior, Victoire had taken her distance from her. Maybe this had upset Gilone. Before Victoire had left the Louvre, she had frankly shown Gilone how disgusted she was at her dissolute, self-seeking way of life. Perhaps ever since then Gilone had been brooding over her anger, waiting for an opportunity to take her revenge. Now she had that chance, which must have succeeded even her wildest dreams. Victoire shivered.

Alone, she was allowing panic to get the best of her. Without Guy's warm body to snuggle up against and comfort her, she felt the damp cold was gradually turning her body to ice. In the next instance, she was immediately aware that she was being watched.

Gilone de Glymes was looking at her through the spy-hole with every sign of pleasure at what she saw. Victoire leaped to her feet. "Why have you come here?"

"To look at you," Gilone replied. "To enjoy the sight of Mademoiselle de Montmaur lying powerless on a pile of straw."

"You're just filth," Victoire said angrily. "A dirty whore!"

Gilone sneered. "What a nice way to talk! But for the moment I am mistress of Eglimont."

"It's just the right place for you. You could hardly sink much lower! I suppose you were banished from Court. That must be why you were obliged to share Adrien d'Etivey's bed."

Gilone's nostrils flared in anger; she bit her lips.

Victoire knew she had touched her cousin on a weak spot.

"You must have done something very wicked for Her Majesty to decide to dispense with your services."

"I left of my own free will," Gilone retorted.

"That *would* surprise me! You were so proud to be maid of honor to Catherine de Medici. Anyway, it doesn't matter. Since I don't imagine you came here to set me free, we can have no more to say to each other."

"That's what *you* think. I've got something rather unpleasant to tell you."

Since Victoire did not deign to reply, Gilone went on, "I hope you are not expecting to see M. Becavallo again?"

"Why?" Victoire cried out despite herself, expecting the worst.

"Adrien had him strangled this morning."

Victoire felt complete despair, but she tried desperately to hide her feelings. She had no intention of revealing her sorrow to Gilone. She would have been only too delighted to see Victoire suffer.

"Have you nothing to say?"

Victoire shrugged her shoulders and went to lie down on the straw to prevent Gilone from seeing the tears glittering on her lashes.

Then Gilone began to scream, in a sudden fit of hysteria. "I hate you, do you hear, I've always hated you! Life at Montmaur was one long humiliation. I was treated like a poor relation who had been taken in out of charity. You always had the best of everything and I was given the leftovers!"

But by now Victoire was so absorbed in her grief that she was quite indifferent to Gilone's curses. Indeed, she hardly heard them; all she could think of was Guy. Never again would he take her in his arms, nor look at her with the burning gaze that troubled her to the depths of her being, even though she was in love with someone else. And how could she ever forget that voluptuous, anguished night they had spent together before she slipped furtively into La Rochelle? Poor Guy, and it was entirely her fault that he was now dead.

Victoire hid her grief while Gilone remained watching her through the grating, the incarnation of jealousy, hatred, and envy.

When she finally closed the opening and went away, Victoire gave way to despair and terror at being alone in the dungeon . . . alone until she died. Renaud had not been able to help.

Chapter VII

*I*t was highly unlikely that Renaud would be more successful than Guy in bribing the guards or risk making Adrien angry on behalf of someone he had only met once before at a ball. He had already paid dearly enough to satisfy his passing desire for her. Victoire began to hate Renaud, and the pleasure she had felt in his arms just when Guy was being put to death. Her thoughts constantly returned to Guy. She was responsible for his death. Sometimes she wondered if she after all had not been in love with him—although not as much as with Guillaume, and not in the same way.

Now there was nothing left for her to do but to prepare for death. She knew that alone she would not hold out for long in this dank dungeon with no one to talk to, for even the jailer was a deaf-mute. She had heard stories of prisoners who had lost their minds in this way.

During the evening—or was it the night, she did not know—she gave way to a fit of black despair which left her exhausted, incapable of movement. Alone in the dark, the cold, and the terrible desolation, she felt her mind beginning to go. She plumbed the depths of despair, her only consolation being that Guy, at least, was now beyond suffering.

She was tempted to end her life, but the only way she could do so was by starving herself. She doubted whether she would have the strength of mind to push food away. She would need to persevere for a long time before she actually died. When she was at La Chaudrée, Boris had told her he had gone without food for twenty-five days before Guillaume's father had taken him in.

At long last she dropped off to sleep. She dreamed Guy was alive, and was fighting a duel with Adrien d'Etivey. Half-naked, bound to a post, Gilone watched the fight. Now *she* was powerless in her turn. Guy plunged his sword into his enemy's body. D'Etivey fell to the ground in a pool of blood.

Another twenty-four interminable hours went by. The jailer appeared at the cell earlier than usual and tried to explain something to Victoire. At first she could make nothing of his clumsy gestures, but eventually it seemed as though he was trying to say someone would come to fetch her at midnight.

Her first reaction was one of wild joy. Renaud had kept his promise. She had misjudged him after all. To-morrow she would be free to continue her journey to England. No one had thought of searching her, so she still had her gold hidden in her belt. She would obviously need to buy another horse; she had no hope of getting poor Igor back.

She hungrily devoured the meager meal, abandoning the idea of self-starvation. Tomorrow evening she would have a feast, but Guy would not be there to celebrate with her. How would she manage to carry out her mission successfully without someone to guide, advise, and guard her against the hazards of the road? And yet, she reflected sadly, Guy and Jean Lescure together had been unable to prevent her from being captured. Perhaps it would be wiser to make a detour through Paris and borrow a few men from Alexandre d'Hautemart. He would certainly be willing to help her. When she had put a few leagues between herself and the château of Eglimont, she would reconsider the matter. She tried to stop her mind from running ahead. After all, she still wasn't sure of being rescued. She might have misunderstood the deaf-mute. She had thought he was telling her that someone was coming to fetch her, but who? This jailor seemed kinder than his fellow servants. Perhaps he had taken pity on her and wanted to warn her that Adrien's men were coming to fetch her. Adrien might well have captured Guillaume. If so, he would have them both executed as rapidly as possible. Even if the message really was from Renaud, things might go wrong at the last moment. And there was always the possibility that she might be recaptured as she was trying to escape. Wavering between doubt and hope, Victoire spent the day in torment. Would the coming night bring freedom or death?

Victoire made herself ready well in advance. Without a watch she had little idea of the time. Was freedom close at hand, she wondered, or would she have to wait still longer, straining her ears in the total darkness and silence that had already driven her to the edge of madness? She had nothing to take with her since Jean Lescure still had her tapestry bag containing all her belongings. She tried to concentrate her thoughts on frivolous things to take her mind off the present moment. Time was passing by, and still nobody came to fetch her. Would Renaud come to fetch her himself? It seemed more likely that he would stay with his brother-in-law in order to distract his attention and make sure he didn't go down into the courtyard.

Despite all her efforts at self-control, Victoire was in a state of intolerable anguish when at last she heard the sound of muffled footsteps in the corridor. The door opened slowly and she got to her feet.

"Come with me," whispered an unfamiliar voice in the darkness. She went toward the cell door. A strong hand took hold of hers and guided her carefully up the staircase. Her rescuer made sure the courtyard was deserted and then led her into a building opposite the stables.

"Don't move. You might hurt yourself."

A spark flashed, and the man lit a small light. Victoire found herself in a shed cluttered with tools and furnture of various kinds. She noticed a workbench and some planks of wood, and deduced that this was where the château carpenter must work.

"So the first part of the plan has been successful," the man said, smiling. "The next part will be more difficult."

"That doesn't surprise me at all," said Victoire. "But how am I to get out of here now?"

"In the coach," her companion replied simply. "Look." He pointed to the other end of the room.

"I don't understand."

"Tomorrow morning Mademoiselle de Glymes is going to Alençon to look at some velvet cloth which has just arrived from Lyon. She wants to have some dresses made. At sunrise you will get into the box underneath the coachman's seat. I shall get you out of there at the first possible opportunity, since I shall have the honor of accompanying Adrien d'Etivey's mistress to Alençon."

He uttered the last words disdainfully.

"Who are you?" Victoire asked.

"A friend of Renaud's, Mademoiselle."

"Monsieur, I must thank you from my heart for taking so many risks on my behalf."

"I should wait until our plan has been successful," he said thoughtfully. "You haven't got out of Eglimont yet."

Victoire shuddered with fear. Renaud's plan seemed foolproof at first sight, but there was one unforeseeable factor that might thwart their hopes: the temperamental Gilone might decide to postpone her trip to Alençon.

"Where is Renaud?" asked Victoire.

"He left this morning so as not to arouse suspicion. He will be waiting for you a league from the town. Now you must try out your hiding place. I put a blanket in there to make you a little more comfortable."

The box was very short and narrow. Victoire curled up, but even then it was a tight fit.

"I hope the journey won't last too long."

"It should take us about an hour and a half to get from here to Alençon. I've made two holes in the bottom of the box so that you will have some air."

"When must I get in?"

"Around five o'clock. From then on, someone might come into the shed. We are due to leave at eight. I'll leave you my watch. I don't think you have one."

"That's true. Thank you again for all you are doing to help me escape."

"What would I not do for such a charming young lady?" he smiled.

Victoire looked into his eyes in which the flickering candle was reflected. His expression showed her that he found her attractive, despite the sorry state she was in. The realization cheered her up when she found herself alone once again in the dark shed. She sat down in the coach, where Gilone would sit the next day, and settled down to wait for the dawn.

Victoire was gradually losing her battle against sleep. She shook herself with fierce determination. She must not go to sleep now; soon dawn would be breaking. The prospect of seeing sunlight again filled her with joy. Even the very simple things of life seemed marvelous after her long imprisonment underground.

Soon the first sounds that heralded the dawn could be heard. Birds began to sing in the trees in the courtyard, and a horse whinnied. She heard voices in the stable. Quickly she got into the box and pulled the lid shut after her. Once again she was in darkness, and she soon began to feel uncomfortable. She could not move either her legs or her arms. But she would have to endure the discomfort even though it seemed intolerable. Her freedom depended on her powers of endurance. She began to get cramped, so she raised the lid a little and changed her position, but this did not improve matters much.

Eventually the shed door opened and she heard snatches of conversation.

"Don't forget she wants the coach at eight."

"Don't worry. I know."

"I hope you've cleaned it up. Remember the fuss she made last time because the windows were dirty."

"I'm not going to wear myself out for a whore like her," a voice replied with irritation. "I think it's shameful that we should have to cart a slut like that around."

Clearly Gilone was neither liked nor respected. Victoire could not suppress a certain feeling of satisfaction that her cousin was held in such contempt. What would happen when Adrien was tired of her? she wondered.

The sound of horses being brought to be harnessed could be heard in the courtyard.

"Pass me the bit. There, my beauty! Calm down!"

Victoire prayed that none of these men would think

of lifting the lid. Once discovered, she would be taken straight back to the dungeon and then her only way out would be to starve herself to death. She felt herself trembling until the grooms had finally finished with the horses. Then someone sat down on top of the box, the coach jolted slowly into motion, and she realized they were going out of the shed.

"Mind the door. You scraped it last week."

"Don't worry. We'll get through."

The coach came to a halt after a short distance.

"Go and tell Mademoiselle Gilone we are ready. I hope she won't keep us hanging around. Last time she made us wait an hour."

The possibility that she might have to stay even longer in the box caused Victoire even more torment. Already her limbs were almost numb.

Soon Victoire heard Gilone's voice. "Let's go," Gilone said, eager for her new dresses.

Victoire's heart beat faster as they crossed the drawbridge. She was almost free. She wondered how many of Adrien's men were in the coach, apart from the coachman. For the moment it was impossible to tell because of the bumpy road which was jolting her mercilessly. The horses broke into a gallop. Another hour and a half of this torture!

Chapter VIII

*A*fter what seemed an interminable time the coach began to slow down, and Victoire guessed that they had reached the outskirts of the town. About ten minutes later the coach stopped, to Victoire's great relief. She was not sure she would even be able to stand upright when she finally got out of the box. She told herself to be patient yet again. Surely the moment of release could not be far away.

Suddenly she heard Renaud's friend close at hand.

"Here, my friends, go and drink my health."

"We won't say no to that!"

The seat creaked above Victoire's head as the coachman jumped to the ground. Victoire didn't move an inch. She had been warned not to make any move until told to.

A few minutes later the lid was raised.

"Come quickly."

Painfully Victoire extricated herself from the box.

"We must be quick!"

She was hurried into a nearby street. He led her into a modest-looking house where a young woman was sitting beside a feebly burning fire mending linen. "Camille, this is the person I told you about. Are the clothes ready?"

"Yes, Monsieur."

Victoire's rescuer explained, "You must disguise yourself a little. We shall have to walk through part of the town."

Camille led Victoire into a nearby room, sparsely furnished with a wooden bed and a cupboard, and helped her to put on a simple gray dress which made her look like a prosperous townswoman. Then she gave Victoire a mantle with a hood to hide her blonde hair and part of her face. "It's not enough," she said, examining her carefully. "You might still be recognized." From a metal saucer she took a small piece of charcoal and rubbed it over Victoire's pale eyebrows.

"That's better."

Victoire looked at herself in the mirror. Her black brows heightened the pallor of her face. She had very obviously not seen daylight for a long time, she thought.

"Shouldn't I wear a little rouge?" she queried.

Smiling, Camille rouged her cheeks. "I think you will look healthier like that!"

They returned to the other room, where Renaud's friend was standing with his back to the fire, impatiently waiting for them. He looked Victoire up and down with a slightly mocking smile. For the first time Victoire had the chance to get a good look at him. He was very handsome.

"Excellent. Well done, Camille!" he said.

He threw her a purse which she caught with obvious satisfaction, opened the door, and looked up and down the street.

"Those fellows are still at the inn," he said. "The coast is clear. Walk about fifteen paces behind me. If I stop to speak to someone I know, overtake me and keep going until I catch you up."

She followed his instructions and they set off. Without incident they reached the outskirts of the town, where a small closed carriage was waiting. He helped Victoire into it. "Now I must say good-by to you, and wish you good luck."

Taking a final look at her, he kissed her hand respectfully.

"I can never thank you enough," said Victoire.

"It is I who am in your debt," he replied. "It has given me great pleasure to get you out of Adrien's clutches. Perhaps we shall meet again one day in more pleasant circumstances."

"I hope so with all my heart," replied Victoire, giving him one of her most winning smiles.

Victoire was happy to be continuing her journey alone so that she could savor her freedom to the full. It was hard to believe that she was free, and she kept turning around to make sure no one was following her.

Gilone would never guess that her frivolity had helped her detested cousin to escape from Eglimont. Victoire was still stunned by Gilone's explosion of hatred. Until they arrived in Paris, she had always considered her to be her sister. She racked her memory for old incidents that might account for Gilone's bitter hostility.

It was true that the Comtesse de Montmaur had been a cold and undemonstrative person who had not overwhelmed Gilone with any outward display of affection—but then she had behaved exactly the same way to Victoire. As for Uncle Anselme, he had never made any attempt to hide his low opinion of Gilone, who had always taken second place to her cousin in his affections. But surely there was nothing unusual in that. After all, it was a stroke of pure luck that had put Gilone in the position of daughter of the house. It must have rankled with her more than Victoire had ever suspected.

How was it, though, that Gilone, who was usually so cunning, should have been so stupid as to lose a good place at Court which in the normal way of things would have ensured her a good position in life? Never before had the Queen Mother abandoned one of her maids of honor to her fate, even when she no longer required her services.

The conclusion was obvious. Through some vile, indelicate, or clumsy action Gilone must have incurred Catherine's deep displeasure.

But did her disgrace mean that she had to lower herself to the level of becoming Adrien d'Etivey's mistress? Once the attraction of the novelty had worn off, she would become no better than a soldier's whore, on the level of the women Victoire had seen at Eglimont who were used by one man after another, as the fancy took them.

Try as she could, Victoire could not understand what had led her cousin to choose a man who would not provide her with what she most desired: a rich marriage and a brilliant life at Court. Surely she could not be in love with D'Etivey?

The coach came to a halt in front of a slate-roofed manor house on the edge of a small oakwood. It was a beautiful spot, and in no way austere. Victoire got down from the carriage and a servant led her into an unpretentious residence that, she felt, perfectly suited what she had already glimpsed of Renaud's personality.

Renaud was awaiting her anxiously, pacing up and down in a drawing room whose paneled walls were decorated with gold leaf.

"Here you are at last!" he cried out in relief. "Right up to this moment I have been afraid that things had gone wrong. The plan could so easily have miscarried. Yesterday morning Mademoiselle de Glymes caught a chill out hunting and went to bed in the afternoon. The only thing that gave her the energy to drag herself out of bed this morning was her fear that all the best material would have been snapped up early by the ladies of Alençon!"

"Thanks to you and your friend, everything went off without a hitch," said Victoire. "The only trouble is I am black-and-blue from my trip in the box!"

"Unfortunately it was the only possible way to get

you out. I have had a room prepared for you here. You must relax now and refresh yourself."

He pulled on a bell rope and an elderly woman servant entered the drawing room.

"Madame Leone, would you please look after my guest and find her some clean linen. And find a suitable dress for her, too."

The woman hesitated. "One of those belonging to Madame? There aren't any others."

"Yes," said Renaud, looking into the distance.

"But I can easily keep this one on," said Victoire, somewhat put out at the idea of wearing a dead woman's clothing.

Renaud came toward her and tried to smile. "Mademoiselle de Montmaur must start to dress fittingly again."

Victoire soaked herself at leisure in a copper bathtub filled with warm, perfumed water. Her tiredness disappeared, to be replaced by a delightful sense of well-being as Madame Leone energetically massaged her back.

Then the servant sprinkled her with *eau de Hongrie,* wrapped her in a warm towel, and took her into an adjoining bedroom where the bed was ready for her.

"Mademoiselle must rest now. Monsieur insists."

After a long, refreshing sleep Victoire awoke in the unknown bedroom with red silk hangings on the walls. For a second she stared around the room, with no idea of where she was. Then, voluptuously, she stretched out her limbs, which were still somewhat numb from her trip in the box, and remembered how she had escaped.

She rang for the servant, who hurried in with some refreshments.

How lucky she had been to meet Renaud at d'Etivey's dice game—and to make such a strong impression on him. To her horror she suddenly realized she did not even know her rescuer's full name. She could not possibly ask the servant. What would she think of a guest who did not even know her host's name?

Toward the end of the afternoon Madame Leone came to do her hair and help her dress.

"Do you think I should really wear this dress?" asked Victoire in embarrassment.

Laid out on an armchair she saw a beautiful plum-colored brocade dress embroidered with pearls.

"It's such a long time since poor Madame passed away," sighed the servant. "Her dresses really should be used."

"I don't want to awaken unhappy memories," said Victoire, undecided.

She longed to wear the brocade dress. It had been so long since she had worn clothes that flattered her. Giving in to the impulse of the moment, Victoire asked Madame Leone to help her put on the gown.

Before she went downstairs, Victoire looked at herself in the mirror. She saw an image of herself she had not seen for some time, not since she had left Court. She was once again a beautiful girl, attractively dressed. Madame Leone—with a little help from powder and make-up—had restored all her former beauty; her gray eyes glistened, though a hint of darkness could still be detected beneath them.

She perfumed herself with iris water and then felt ready to face Renaud. At the same time, she didn't want him to be *too* taken with her appearance. Her heart was loyal to Guillaume, and if she let Renaud continue to bestow his attentions on her, he would only be hurt. Besides, she would have to leave very soon to carry out her mission. By now she should already be in England, kneeling before the Queen with her request.

Her host was waiting for her, elegant in a claret-colored velvet doublet. He received her in a smaller, more intimate room than the large room she had seen him in that morning. Nearby she saw a table laid for two.

Victoire's eyes shone with pleasure when she saw, by the light of the candles in their silver sticks, the opulent splendor of the crockery and the gleaming cutlery. It was a long time since she had seen such elegance. How pleasant it was to savor Cyprian wine in a silver-gilt goblet instead of drinking water from a tin mug.

"I think it's time you told me your full name, dear Renaud."

He smiled. "It's true, I'm still a stranger to you. Well, then; my name is Renaud de Surlemont, and this modest manor house where you are staying has been in my family since the time of Louis XII."

"I like it a lot better than your brother-in-law's château!" said Victoire.

"He must be beside himself with fury at this moment!"

"And he will be sending men out to look for me. Won't he think of coming here?"

"He has never been to Surlemont," said Renaud. "Not even when Yolande was still alive. Frankly, my wife had no desire to entertain her brother. She got on so badly with him."

"But what if he does come all the same?" said Victoire anxiously. "Surely he'll suspect that you organized my escape?"

"The deaf-mute promised not to reveal you'd gone until this evening. That gives us a little respite."

"I owe it to you to tell you this. I am a Protestant."

Renaud smiled. "Do you know, I had already guessed that! However, I'm grateful to you for trusting me with your secret."

"That isn't all. I have just come from the siege of La Rochelle."

"You must tell me about your adventures . . . I'm sure you've had many. But let us sit down to eat. We mustn't keep the pike mousse waiting for long—it's one of my cook's most successful dishes."

During the meal Victoire told Renaud briefly what had happened to her during the last few months, and explained that she must leave for London as quickly as possible.

"The only trouble is," she concluded, "that I have no horse. He's still at Eglimont."

"We'll arrange that," Renaud promised.

"And my escort, Guy Becavallo, has been killed by your brother-in-law."

"Are you sure of that?"

"Alas, yes. Gilone de Glymes took the trouble to come and tell me about it."

There was a moment's silence.

"What exactly did Becavallo mean to you?"

"He was a friend, a fellow Protestant, the man who was going to look after me on my journey."

"I could escort you as far as Le Havre with a few men," Renaud offered, after a moment's thought. "You could set sail from there to England."

"Would you really do that for me?"

"Yes, *ma petite* Victoire. Since that night we spent together I feel a little less sad, a little less lonely, thanks to you."

He was gazing at her attentively. She misunderstood his meaning. "I am ashamed to be wearing this dress. It was Madame Leone who . . ."

"She was quite right."

Victoire was gradually getting to know two very different facets of Renaud's character. He was at the same time a lighthearted, attractive, pleasure-seeking young man and a man who had never recovered from the death of the only woman he had ever loved. Perhaps it was his grief that had made him so sympathetic and ready to help others. Without it he would perhaps have been simply an egoist, interested only in his own comfort and pleasure.

After they had finished their supper Renaud's somewhat melancholy mood gradually changed. He began to watch Victoire almost greedily, making her feel somewhat uncomfortable, though he remained very courteous.

Renaud had drunk heavily during the meal and Victoire began to wonder if his urgent attentions were for her alone, or whether he had encouraged her to wear a dress belonging to his dead wife in order to create the illusion, however brief, that she was still alive.

These vague feelings killed any enjoyment Victoire might have felt in Renaud's attentions. The other night at Eglimont she had found pleasure in his arms. Though she was quite determined to repay the debt she owed him, she felt no genuine impulse toward him this evening. She was slightly shocked when he began to kiss her shoulders wildly.

Her thoughts constantly returned to Guillaume and Guy, and she imagined that Renaud too was thinking of someone other than the woman in his arms.

Renaud's expert hands had already more than half undressed her when a horse's galloping hooves echoed across the courtyard.

"Do you hear?" she whispered.

But he was already on the alert, listening. "Come through here."

He pushed her into a small closet where she straightened her clothing as best she could.

Rapid footsteps mounted the stairs. Through the half-open door Victoire saw a man enter, wet through with sweat, and panting from his race against time.

"I've been sent to warn you. M. d'Etivey and

all his men are on their way here. I am scarcely an hour ahead of them."

"Thank you for coming so quickly. Go to the kitchen and get something to eat and drink."

When the messenger had left the room, Victoire returned, her limbs trembling.

"We haven't a moment to lose," said Renaud. "We must be on horseback in ten minutes."

Chapter IX

Followed by only ten men—all that Renaud de Surlemont had been able to get together at such short notice—they galloped at top speed beneath the starry April sky.

Victoire had changed back into the gray dress and Madame Leone had given her a bottle-green woollen cloak from Yolande's wardrobe.

Her horse took the obstacles of the road in its stride without any difficulty. If she had not been so terrified at the thought that Adrien d'Etivey was on their trail, Victoire would have enjoyed the reckless ride through the night.

"Do you think he'll follow us for long?" panted Victoire when they stopped for a moment to give their horses a brief rest.

"Who knows? He must be mad with rage. He'll soon realize there's no one at Surlemont. Does he know you intended to make for England?"

"No."

"Then he won't know which direction we've taken. At least we have a chance of escaping him. I shall send four men off toward Paris, telling them to leave as many traces of their passage as possible."

"Is it a good idea to weaken our strength?"

Renaud shrugged his shoulders. "In any case, he must have at least twenty-five of his cohorts with him. We can't risk meeting them face to face."

"I am really sorry to cause you to quarrel with your brother-in-law."

"It had to happen sooner or later. I shan't lose much by it," said Renaud nonchalantly.

Except, thought Victoire, the chance to go to Eglimont Château, where the pale ghost of his young wife still wandered.

At dawn they halted at a dilapidated-looking inn so that both horses and men could take food and drink. They sat down at table in a room with smoke-blackened beams and were served with pea and bacon soup—its delicious smell made them even more hungry, if that were possible—and a huge jug of cider. Even despite her hunger Victoire could not take her eyes from the door, imagining that d'Etivey might appear at any moment.

"We've covered a lot of ground, you know," said Renaud to reassure her.

"He could have ridden as fast as us," murmured Victoire.

Renaud took her hand and squeezed it gently. "Don't be afraid. That fool won't catch up to us."

But Victoire was far from sharing his certainty. The memory of her imprisonment was still too fresh in her mind, and her horror at the thought of returning to rot in that vile dungeon was so powerful that each minute they remained at the inn was torture.

They set off again, minus the four men who headed toward Paris. There were only eight of them left, in-

cluding Renaud and Victoire herself, and d'Etivey
would have at least twenty-five men!

"My friend who helped you escape will do all he
can to delay Adrien and put him off the scent," said
Renaud again.

"I'm sure he will."

What was Gilone doing just now? Victoire wondered. She was probably alone at Eglimont, looking
at the velvet she had bought that morning, perhaps
thinking with loathing about her. Did she guess she
had helped Victoire to escape? Could she in her fury
be pursuing Victoire along with her lover?

They passed through Argentan to change horses.
Their own were exhausted, their nostrils streaked with
foam. Victoire too felt very tired by this race which
had started at midnight and would not end before
dusk. Toward the end of the afternoon she fell from
her horse, for no other reason, she felt, than that she
was worn out.

Renaud leaped from his saddle and helped her to
her feet. "I hope you haven't injured yourself," he
said anxiously.

Though her knee hurt dreadfully, Victoire fought
back the tears and reassured him. Weakened by the
combined effects of the many hardships she had en-
dured in La Rochelle and her long underground imprisonment, Victoire was simply not capable of riding
thirty leagues or more on horseback.

Realizing this, Renaud promised her that they would
soon halt. "We're less than a league from the Château
de Cuisery, which lies off the main road," he said.
"The people there won't turn us away."

Victoire had to yield to his wise decision. She
barely had the strength to hold the reins, and yet the
idea of stopping for a whole night was a terrifying
prospect. She would only feel really safe once she was
at sea, separated from her pursuers by the English
Channel.

The sun was just sinking beneath the horizon when they reached Cuisery. The Chevalier du Harmel and his sister Alice both seemed overjoyed at an unexpected visit which promised to enliven their monotonous lives. Mademoiselle du Harmel ordered the rooms to be prepared for the guests and added extra courses to the normal fare.

"You must be dying of hunger!" she exclaimed. Her heavy figure showed clearly enough that good food was her main interest in life, after religion.

"We're more exhausted than hungry," said Renaud, realizing with annoyance that both brother and sister were looking forward to a convivial evening. "And Mademoiselle de Montmaur has fallen from her horse," Renaud went on.

"My goodness! Come with me, you poor child. Why, I see blood on your dress."

"There's just a slight cut on my knee," said Victoire, who by now could hardly walk from the pain shooting through her leg, which was beginning to swell. Weakly she sat down on the bed and let herself be examined by her hostess, who then cleansed the wound with alcohol. Victoire bit her lips to stop herself from screaming. Mademoiselle du Harmel's blue-gray eyes showed satisfaction at a job well done as she gently bandaged Victoire's leg.

"You must rest until supper," said Mademoiselle Alice benevolently. "I'll send the chambermaid in to you in a while."

Then she glanced around the bedroom and said in surprise, "But they haven't brought your bags up!"

Victoire explained that her luggage had been stolen and that all she possessed were the clothes she wore.

"It can't be possible!" exclaimed Mademoiselle Alice indignantly. "You've had so much trouble! But don't worry, we'll arrange things as best we can!"

And with that she went off down to the kitchen to make sure her orders were being carried out.

The chambermaid soon appeared, bringing a simple yet tasteful dress of about Victoire's size. "It belongs to the steward's daughter," said the old woman.

"I'm sorry to cause you so much trouble," she said.

"Mademoiselle is only sorry not to have found anything better."

"It will be perfect," said Victoire, starting to get up from the bed. But as soon as her foot touched the ground a spasm shot through her leg, forcing her to sit again with her leg stretched out before her.

"I can see Mademoiselle is in great pain," said the maid. "I know an excellent cure for inflammation."

Victoire sank back onto the bed. When the chambermaid returned she brought a wet compress which she applied to Victoire's knee, cooling her burning-hot skin.

"What is it soaked with?" asked Victoire curiously.

"Plants gathered at dawn, when the moon is waxing. Hawthorn, ivy, sage, and thyme."

"It seems to be effective," said Victoire a few minutes later. Soon she was able to limp slowly across the room.

"You must apply a fresh compress before you go to sleep. I'll leave you the bottle."

"I don't know how to thank you," said Victoire gratefully.

In a huge, formal, and chilly room the four were approaching the end of a delicious but lengthy meal. During it Mademoiselle Alice and her brother had asked a number of very awkward questions about Victoire and Renaud's journey. Renaud invented a story to satisfy their curiosity. At the same time he had taken great care not to arouse in these fervent Catholics any suspicion about Victoire's religion.

The conversation turned to recent events, including the war in the southwest. The name of the King's brother, the Duc d'Anjou, was of course mentioned, since he was still besieging La Rochelle.

"The Duc d'Anjou is bound to get the better of these terrible people," said the knight bitterly. "It's only a matter of days now."

Chapter X

*I*n the middle of the night, Victoire was overcome with an attack of fever. Bathed in sweat, half-unconscious, she imagined that she was back in the dungeon. The water from the moat was gradually seeping in through a crack in the wall. The thing she had most dreaded during her imprisonment had finally happened. And yet, she felt this terrible death was in some way her destiny.

The water was lapping around the bottom of the cell. It swirled around her ankles, then rose to her knees. There was no furniture, nothing at all to climb onto. There was no purpose in prolonging her death agony. When the water reached her neck she began to scream, struggling with all her strength against the engulfing tide. As she fought against the water she tumbled out of bed and woke up with a start.

At first the sound of her own heartbeats deafened her. She had no idea where she was, or what was happening. Her hand touched the soft fabric of the eiderdown, which had fallen to the floor with her, and she realized she was not lying on the hard straw of her cell.

The door opened quietly and she heard a voice, which seemed to come from a great distance. She was relieved to recognize the maid.

"Mademoiselle cried out in her sleep."

"I had a nightmare," Victoire stammered.

The maid lit a candle, and the light finally banished the images of horror.

"I'm so hot," Victoire moaned, wiping sweat-soaked strands of hair away from her face. No sooner had she spoken than chills coursed through her. She felt the maid's cool hand on her burning forehead.

"Drink some orange-blossom water, Mademoiselle. It will help you to sleep more peacefully."

Victoire drank the sweet smelling potion, and her head suddenly began to feel very empty.

"Do you want me to leave you the candle?"

"Yes, please."

How comforting Victoire found the small, flickering flame! Perhaps her terrible experiences had made her afraid of the dark. She hoped she was not becoming what she most despised in all the world: a coward, unworthy of the Montmaur name.

Victoire slept for a while, until she was awakened by the throbbing pain in her left leg, which the maid's potion had only temporarily relieved. She did not want to wake her again, so she prepared a new compress herself as well as she could.

What a stroke of bad luck that she should be incapacitated just now! She had often fallen from horseback when she was jumping over a ditch or hedge, but so far her tumbles had not had serious results. And now, when she was fleeing for her life, she was almost unable to move.

Failing a miracle, she knew that she would not be able to bear riding. She had the feeling that for some time now the fates had been against her, almost as if they were forcing her to pay for her happiness with Guillaume.

The window did not close properly, and through the crack she could hear the wind howling in the forest outside. The noise rose to a crescendo and the sinister roaring made her fear worse. From the past—the recent past, less than a year ago—rose up into her mind the evil features of those who had persecuted her. First came the most terrifying of all, the Italian woman whose penetrating gaze, full of unformulated questions, had last rested on Victoire when she had gone to take her leave of Queen Catherine before leaving the Louvre.

Then she saw the image of Father Izard, whose austere appearance belied his base appetites, and that of his accomplice, the Abbess, her green eyes like pools of stagnant water where no creature could live, and no human being find solace.

Then came Adrien d'Etivey's hawklike face. His image spanned both the past and the present and was more threatening than the rest because he might well be close at hand. At his heels she saw a tall, slender figure: Gilone too was now a monster.

Finally she saw an equivocal, mysteriously charming figure. It was Henri d'Anjou, who had tried to kill Victoire in the Louvre.

How lonely and vulnerable Victoire felt after this parade of devils!

Guillaume was far away and Guy was dead; only Renaud was left to defend her. She had not known him for long, and yet he had managed to get her out of that gloomy prison. Would he be able to keep these shadows at bay, though they were now gradually disappearing from her mind as the potion took effect?

At daybreak Renaud came into her room.

"How do you feel?" he asked.

Victoire grimaced "Not too well."

"Try to get up. Lean on me."

Cautiously she lowered her foot to the floor and was amazed to find that she could bear the pain. "I'll be all right."

Seeing Victoire's frail figure in the filmy muslin nightdress which probably dated from Mademoiselle du Harmel's youth, Renaud could not resist taking Victoire in his arms and pressing her tightly to his body. The unexpected tenderness comforted her.

"I'll get dressed and be straight down," she said.

"I'll have the horses saddled meanwhile."

The old chambermaid hurried in as soon as Renaud had gone. "Why must you leave so early in the morning?" she exclaimed. "This won't do your leg any good."

Victoire hesitated for a moment before replying. "I am in great danger," she finally admitted.

The shrewd eyes looked her up and down. "I thought as much. I could feel the danger around you."

"Is it coming closer?" Victoire asked anxiously.

"Yes, but I think you'll escape. The hand of death is not on you."

Could this woman, like Cassitère, foretell the future?

"You must take the potion with you."

The maid gently massaged Victoire's leg with some cream that penetrated her skin and made her leg burning hot. Then she rubbed on it a brownish ointment that smelled of woodland thickets, and bandaged the knee with lint.

"There you are," she said. "You should be able to ride until nightfall without too much difficulty."

"I don't know how to thank you," said Victoire, touched by the old servant's devotion.

She went slowly downstairs to the courtyard. The knight and his sister were already up, watching the preparations for their guests' departure.

"We are so grateful to you for your hospitality," said Renaud. "Thanks to you, Mademoiselle de Montmaur is now fit to continue her journey."

"We should have liked you to stay longer," sighed Mademoiselle du Harmel, sorry to see her guests leave.

One of Renaud's men helped Victoire to mount her horse, and soon the Château de Cuisery was disappearing behind them into the distance.

To her great surprise, Victoire found she could gallop without too much difficulty. The elderly chambermaid must have magical powers, she thought, to be able to soothe the pain so successfully.

Renaud had told her that if all went well—that is, if she managed to stay in the saddle all day—they would reach Lisieux late in the evening.

During that day they rode across the Dives River on a shaky and dangerous-looking bridge. Next they came to the Vie River, whose bed was almost dry. After riding across an interminable flat plain they reached the Touques River, after which they would be in the outskirts of Lisieux. When they were in sight of Saint Peter's Cathedral with its facade topped by twin towers, Renaud stopped.

"Now I think we are out of danger," he said. "The bandits must have lost our trail by now."

"Are you sure?" asked Victoire, who could not really believe that the nightmare was over.

Renaud nodded. "I was still a little uneasy this morning, but now we can sleep in peace. I have sent my squire ahead to look for a suitable inn to have supper and spend the night. Here he is now!"

Renaud de Surlemont's squire galloped up.

"Well?"

"There's a coaching inn close by."

"Let's go, then," said Renaud.

Victoire was relieved to be able to rest. The pain in her knee was starting to hurt again, and she was eager to apply the old maid's potion and to recuperate after the long journey.

The Ramparts Inn was sheltered inside the walls of the little town. There was a hubbub of excitement in the courtyard caused by the arrival of an elegant carriage drawn by four white horses.

"These travelers must be very rich, judging by their turnout," said Renaud anxiously. "I hope they haven't taken all the rooms."

But there were still some rooms free, and Victoire was very glad to go upstairs and rest. On the staircase she met a strikingly beautiful young woman, escorted by an older man who moved back to let Victoire pass, smiling kindly at her as he did so.

The servant who was warming the bed told Victoire that the important travelers were Lord Craighton, a wealthy English nobleman, and his niece Lady Philippa.

A little later, after she had arranged her hair and perfumed herself with iris water, Victoire joined Renaud in the big room downstairs, which was brightly lit by scores of candles in honor of the English visitors. All the inn servants were bustling around these important guests who, seated at the best table in front of the fire, were doing justice to their meal.

"They seem to like our wine," said Renaud, smiling. "They are into their second pitcher already."

The servant brought them thick slices of underdone leg of mutton well seasoned with garlic. Meanwhile, Victoire was covertly scrutinizing Lady Philippa, whose flaming red hair and milky-white complexion made her the focus of all eyes.

"She's incredibly beautiful, don't you think?" said Victoire in a low voice.

Renaud carefully examined Lady Philippa.

"I don't like her expression," he said after a moment. "There's something pitiless about her."

"You think she's wicked?" asked Victoire in surprise.

"It's quite possible. Look at that determined chin!"

"It's no different from mine!"

"That's true," said her companion, smiling. "But I

like you a hundred times better than that cold and probably calculating Englishwoman."

"She's more beautiful than me."

"Perhaps. But she has no charm, at least not for me."

At first Victoire thought that Renaud was saying this out of politeness. Her own feeling was that Lady Philippa's emerald-green dress admirably set off her pale skin. But then, as Lady Philippa glanced disdainfully at the other guests and at her homely surroundings, Victoire was momentarily reminded of Gilone, a thought that made her uneasy.

"You are right," she said finally. "There is something unpleasant in her face. On the other hand, I like her companion very much."

Lord Craighton was an elegant and good-looking man of about forty, with perfect manners. His face, surrounded by a halo of graying hair, and slightly flushed with red wine, was a kindly one, unlike that of his niece. He seemed to have a hearty appetite, and to be enjoying his food, while his niece was hardly touching her food.

Then the young couple stopped observing their neighbors and began to talk about themselves and the following day's journey.

The end of the journey was in sight. Lisieux was only eight leagues from Honfleur, where they would take the ferry across the Seine to Le Havre.

"I shall be sad to leave you," said Renaud.

"And I to leave you!" exclaimed Victoire. "I owe you so much. Why don't you come to London with me?"

Renaud hesitated. He was visibly tempted. "I think it would be better for me to return to Surlemont."

"What are you afraid of?"

Renaud gestured evasively. "Everything and nothing. With my brother-in-law . . ."

"You think he may have taken reprisals against you?"

"I'm absolutely sure he has," he said mournfully.

"What do you think he might have done?"

"Set fire to the house maybe, or killed the guards."

"Good Lord!" cried Victoire, appalled to think that she might be responsible for such tragedies in her friend's life.

Renaud saw her consternation. "Perhaps he's done nothing at all," he went on quickly. "But I'd like to know as soon as possible. Once you are safely embarked on a good ship, I shall return home."

Victoire took hold of Renaud's hand and squeezed it affectionately. "I'll never forget you."

The sun was setting as they reached Le Havre. Renaud took Victoire to an inn, where she again rubbed the potion onto her aching knee. The condition of her knee had improved miraculously. She was in much less pain, although she still felt a twinge from time to time.

An hour later Renaud returned from the harbor looking pleased with himself. "You will leave tomorrow morning on the *Marie-Charlotte*. It seems to me a sturdy boat, and the captain strikes me as trustworthy."

"That's wonderful," she said.

So she would be able to carry out her mission after all, despite having been delayed for so long.

"Where shall I land?"

"At Eastbourne, where you will take the coach to London. And now," said Renaud rather sadly, "if you are willing, let's have supper together for the last time."

Chapter XI

Victoire walked with a determined step up the gangplank of the *Marie-Charlotte,* a sailing-ship big enough to carry about a dozen passengers in relative comfort.

She paid the captain for her crossing, and a sailor showed her to a tiny cabin barely furnished with a narrow bed, a single chair, and a table.

"Try not to be seasick," said the sailor, a friendly Breton.

"Will the crossing be rough?"

"It often is, by Our Lady!"

He put on the table the bag containing the few things Victoire had hastily bought that morning. She had two pairs of stockings, a linen chemise and a woollen one, and a red shawl with long tassels to keep her warm during the journey. She could not wait to get to London, where at last she would be able to buy some decent dresses.

When she went up on deck to watch the boat set sail, she saw that Lord Craighton and his niece were on board, too, and she felt even more vexed at the poverty of her wardrobe. Lady Philippa gave the tall, badly dressed Frenchwoman a scornful look and snuggled deeper into a black cloak lined with squirrel fur which Victoire coveted. She decided to have one like it made as soon as she could.

The sailors hoisted the sails and the boat slowly edged away from the quayside. It was the first time

Victoire had left French soil, and she felt apprehensive. How would she make out in an unknown land whose language she could not speak? Would she even be able to make herself understood?

The *Marie-Charlotte* made good speed, and by midday the French coast had disappeared from view. Almost all the other passengers kept to a room, somewhat pompously called the "salon" by the crew, but Victoire stayed up on deck beside the helmsman, who had taken a liking to her and confided that he had already been shipwrecked four times.

"And you see," he concluded, "I'm still here."

"You must have been very lucky, and you must be a good swimmer, too," said Victoire, full of admiration for his exploits.

The sight of the gray mass of water rising and falling alarmed her.

"Sailors are well advised to learn how to swim," said the helmsman.

Sometime later the sea began to get rough, and the waves grew bigger. "You really should go below now, otherwise you'll get soaked through," said the sailor.

Victoire did as he suggested; she did not look forward to the prospect of getting her only dress wet.

She joined the seven passengers in the salon who were sitting around the only table, and a sailor brought them some ham and boiled potatoes seasoned with beer. Apart from Lord Craighton, who was placed next to Victoire, and his niece, there was a young English gentleman returning from a long trip to Italy, and a Protestant printer and his wife and two children who had been forced into exile to escape persecution. At first Victoire was pleased to meet some fellow Protestants, but she soon came to the conclusion that they were not very interesting people.

The three English passengers spoke enough French to make general conversation possible. The young man described his trip to Italy and was particularly enthusiastic about his visit to Venice, whose prosperity and luxury had greatly impressed him.

"You can't imagine," he cried, "the pomp with which the Doge is surrounded, the ostentatious display with which people entertain, and the gold everywhere."

The printer's two children, a boy of about twelve and a girl of about thirteen, listened entranced to every word uttered by the young man as he described the fabulous splendor of the courtesans' jewelry and their gondolas carpeted with white bearskins. As for the parents, their severe expressions clearly revealed their disapproval at such an excessive display of luxury.

After this indifferent meal the wind rose and the sea became increasingly stormy. The passengers all retired to their cabins, except for Victoire and Lord Craighton.

"We're in for a storm," he said. "Hadn't you better lie down?"

"There's more air here. My cabin feels rather stuffy."

"In that case, may I offer you a glass of port?"

"With pleasure."

"An admirable drink!" said Lord Craighton enthusiastically. "We should be grateful to the Portuguese for having invented it."

A sailor brought them tin drinking cups containing the amber-colored liquid.

"How strong it is!" said Victoire. "I quite like it."

"May I be so indiscreet as to ask what you are going to do in England?" asked Lord Craighton.

"I'm going to see some kinsmen who are in exile in London," she said. Guy had advised her to keep her mission secret as long as she could.

"There are many of your fellow countrymen in London, particularly since Saint Bartholomew's Night."

"My mother died that night."

"My poor child!" exclaimed Lord Craighton, looking at Victoire sympathetically, "Religious persecution is a terrible thing," he went on. "I lost my brother too; he was burned alive by the previous Queen."

"How terrible! Was that Queen Mary?"

"Yes, it was toward the end of her life. She was madly in love with her husband who cared little for her, and to please him she embarked on a reign of terror. She used to say that she would rather lose ten kingdoms than imperil her soul. She had hundreds of people burned."

"In France our custom is to cut people's throats or to hang them," murmured Victoire. Though sometimes, she thought to herself, people were simply flung out of the window . . .

"But we have been lucky since Her Majesty Queen Elizabeth came to the throne: calm has been restored to our country."

"How fortunate you are," sighed Victoire. "I wonder whether we shall ever have peace in France?"

When Lady Philippa came back upstairs, she found her uncle and the young Frenchwoman in the middle of an animated conversation. And though she was civil to Victoire, it was quite clear from her glacial look that she was thoroughly displeased at their tête-à-tête.

As she clung to her seat, which fortunately had been clamped to the floor, Victoire tried hard to forget that the *Marie-Charlotte* was swooping from the crest of one wave down into the trough of the next, and then back up again, as though it were no bigger than a nutshell.

"You've had bad luck for your first crossing," observed Lord Craighton, fighting the effects of the heavy seas with glass after glass of port, which heightened the flush of his already rosy cheeks.

Lady Philippa was stoically trying to hide the gradual onset of seasickness.

"If I were you, my dear," her uncle said to her, "I'd go and lie down. You're very pale."

But for some reason Lady Philippa seemed determined to stay with the other two in the little salon.

What a curious reaction, thought Victoire. Anyone would think she was in love with her uncle and jealous of me. And yet she must have plenty of suitors.

A heavy sea roared in through the hatchway and swirled about the salon floor, soaking everything as the boat heaved up and down.

"They might be more careful!" yelped Philippa Craighton, lifting her feet off the floor to protect her fine glacé-kid boots and ivory taffeta skirt.

"The poor things must have their work cut out just to keep us on course!"

Suddenly Philippa turned green and fled toward her cabin, moaning.

"I can see you're a better sailor than my niece."

"But perhaps I'll be as ill as her in time," said Victoire apprehensively.

He examined her carefully "I don't think so. You've still plenty of color in your cheeks. Have a spot more port. There's nothing better for preventing seasickness. Philippa always refuses to drink any, but she's quite wrong."

Victoire did as he suggested, reasoning that Lord Craighton must know what he was talking about.

"Your niece is very beautiful," she remarked.

Lord Craighton's face brightened at once. "Isn't she?" he said, obviously delighted. "Wherever she goes she wins admiration. I took her in after the death of my poor brother. Since then she has lived with me." He sighed. "But not for much longer, alas!"

"Why is that?"

"She'll soon be twenty, and it really is high time she was married. This little trip of ours to France is doubtless the last we'll make together."

"Lady Philippa must have plenty of young men to choose a husband from."

"That's true. But she's proving very difficult. She really will have to decide now."

As night fell over the stormy sea, Victoire's anxiety increased. The violent storm was tossing the *Marie-Charlotte* about in the darkness. How would the captain manage to steer his frail craft safely to port? Surely the *Marie-Charlotte* was doomed to founder on some unseen rock, far from civilization.

By now Lord Craighton had finished a whole flagon of port and was happily broaching a second. He was in the best of spirits. His manner became increasingly friendly, and there came a moment when he even began to take Victoire into his confidence.

"I shall be very lonely when Philippa has gone."

"Have you never married?"

"No, I spent my youth hunting, traveling, and amusing myself in all kinds of ways, never giving a thought to the future. Now I regret it."

"But it still isn't too late," said Victoire politely.

She wondered how old he was; around forty-five, she guessed. He would make an excellent match for a young widow of slender means. Particularly since he seemed charming, easy to get on with and highly cultivated, not to mention the attraction of his wealth.

Victoire wondered whether Philippa had a large fortune as well.

Chapter XII

The ship rolled violently during the night, twice throwing Victoire out of her bunk onto the floor. Each time she thought she was in for an attack of seasickness, like the printer and his family whose moans could be heard from the other side of the partition.

But the next morning she was quite well enough to go up on deck, where she drew in deep breaths of the fresh, invigorating air. The sea was calm, and Eastbourne harbor could be seen in the distance.

"You've survived this time," said her friend the sailor cheerfully. "You'll be landing safe and sound, my little lady."

"Thank goodness! I must admit there were times when I doubted it."

Sometime later Lord Craighton appeared, muffled up in a greatcoat of Flemish wool.

"How is your niece?" inquired Victoire.

"Oh! the poor thing. I don't think she'll feel better until she steps onto dry land. Still, it won't be long now."

And it was not until they drew alongside the quay that Philippa emerged from her cabin, looking pale and out of sorts. The arrogant, imperious girl of the previous day seemed to have disappeared.

The printer and his family were in an even more wretched state. They swore they would never again set foot in a boat. No matter what happened to them, they vowed they would remain in England.

"I simply couldn't go through all that again," the printer's wife confided to Victoire.

"Was it really so awful as all that?"

The printer's wife gave Victoire a look of horror. "Didn't you think you were going to die a hundred times over?"

"To tell the truth, no." Perhaps Lord Craighton's port had immuned her against seasickness.

The passengers took their leave of the captain and walked down the gangplank. The sailors unloaded the passengers' luggage and placed it inside a waiting coach. Then the group set off for London.

This was the year 1573, the fifteenth of Elizabeth I's reign. She had succeeded to the throne at the age of twenty-five on the death of her half-sister, Mary Tudor. As the daughter of Henry VIII and Anne Boleyn, she had long been considered illegitimate. Her father, in order to counteract opinion, had had Parliament declare his previous marriage invalid.

For the first part of her life, Elizabeth was not really recognized as legitimate, despite Parliament's decree. It was only in 1544, when she was eleven years old, that she had taken her place in the order of succession after her young brother Edward and her sister Mary.

An extraordinary chain of events had in fact been necessary before Elizabeth finally came to the throne, the goal of all her hopes, ambitions, and efforts. Her lively natural intelligence had been developed by a careful education at the hands of the most capable teachers. Her Majesty could discourse in Greek and Latin, and was fluent in Italian and French.

The Queen had been brought up a Protestant, but her sister's intransigent Catholicism had strongly influenced her, making her a relatively tolerant person, whose dearest wish was a truly English church.

No one was sure what the Queen truly believed in. Though the Established Church was Protestant, she was careful not to reveal her own innermost convictions—if she had any, which many people doubted.

So a more peaceful atmosphere had now returned to England, after the upheavals of the previous reign. On her accession, the Queen had prayed to God to enable her to rule without spilling blood. But though she was temperamentally inclined to mercy, circumstances had not always allowed her to show it.

The coach drove through the charming Sussex countryside, intersected by numerous rivers and streams, and Victoire was struck by the greenness of the countryside.

Lord Craighton dozed for most of the journey and Philippa was sulkily silent, but Victoire looked attentively at all the peaceful villages through which they passed. From time to time she caught sight of a magnificent dwelling in the distance. She tried to imagine what kind of life was lived in these grand houses, and wondered how different it might be from life at Montmaur.

How long would she have to be in England? It was impossible to say. However, Victoire found the idea of spending a few weeks here quite pleasant. She wished to make the most of her opportunity, perhaps the only one she would ever have, of getting to know a foreign country. This new experience could not fail to enrich and extend her mental horizons, which had for so long been limited to her little village in Béarn.

They changed horses at Pembury, and the passengers had a quick meal. Then they set off again through the night, with drizzle softly falling. The coach was not very comfortable and the passengers were often jolted against each other as it bumped along.

Philippa was sleeping soundly with her mouth hanging slightly open. In a shaft of bright moonlight that lit up the inside of the coach for a moment, Victoire saw that even in sleep Lady Philippa's expression was no more kindly than it had been the previous day. Why was she so morose and hostile? To all appearances she had everything she could desire.

The night seemed endless to Victoire, who was completely exhausted, particularly since she had hardly slept at all on the boat. But the excitement of the journey kept her from falling asleep, even for a few seconds.

Just before lunchtime the travelers reached their destination and took leave of each other. Lord Craighton took Victoire's address and gave her his own, making her promise to come to supper shortly. Lady Philippa said good-by in a forced manner, and Victoire guessed she would do all she could to prevent her uncle from seeing Victoire again.

Philippa's attitude struck a spiteful chord in Victoire and she decided to see Lord Craighton again as soon as possible. Perhaps this great nobleman would be able to get her an introduction to Court. He had even given her to understand that the Queen honored him with her friendship. Victoire could not count on getting any support from the French Ambassador, M. de la Mothe Fenelon, who wholeheartedly served the interests of Catherine de Medici. And the Mayor of La Rochelle's kinswoman probably had little influence in London. So her meeting with Lord Craighton was probably a godsend.

Victoire went to the address Madame Henri had given her and found it was a very modest-looking house in a quarter that had no pretensions to elegance. As she went through the center of London she had seen coaches drawn by splendidly harnessed horses in which beautiful women were lounging, dressed in the very latest fashions. When she caught sight of them, Victoire grimaced. It was going to be difficult to match them.

An old woman came to the door, and Victoire asked to be taken to Genevieve Le Blachet, Lady Emmeline's sister. She was ushered into a small salon with nondescript furniture. It was obvious that the room had been hastily furnished with whatever had happened to be available, by someone whose mind was on other things.

The mistress of the house appeared and was surprised that her visitor was so young.

"Madame, I bring you news from your sister and brother-in-law,"

"Mon Dieu! It can't be true!"

"I have come from La Rochelle. Here are the letters given me for you and your niece Aloise."

"How wonderful they are alive! Mademoiselle, I was in a state of terrible anguish, which you have relieved. And Aloise has been pining away without news of her parents for so long. Allow me to call her."

"I shall be glad to meet her," said Victoire, smiling. "I lived in her room for several weeks."

A dark-haired girl hurried into the room, whose pale skin reminded Victoire of her mother's. Both women plied their visitor with questions, and Victoire tried not to paint too gloomy a picture of the hardships of the siege. She was true to her promise not to say anything about the plague that was ravaging the city when she left. But in spite of Victoire's silence on the subject, Madame Le Blachet was shrewd enough to suspect the truth.

"My poor fellow citizens!" she lamented. "How long will they be able to hold out in such terrible conditions, without even the bare necessities of life?"

"I have come here in order to help them, Madame."

Victoire explained that the Mayor of La Rochelle had sent her to England to ask the Queen for help.

"The Queen!" exclaimed Madame Le Blachet. "But how will you ever get an audience with her?"

"I have a letter of introduction to Sir William Glanville, who is a faithful supporter of our cause."

"It's all so complicated!" said Madame Le Blachet, overwhelmed by the difficulties involved.

"First of all," went on Victoire, "I must find somewhere to stay."

"But you must stay here! We have a spare room."

"I don't want to inconvenience you."

But Aloise had already picked up Victoire's bag and was already climbing a narrow staircase.

Chapter XIII

*T*he next day Victoire's first task was to order some dresses. In the present state of her wardrobe, even if Lord Craighton were to invite her to supper, she could not possibly think of accepting his invitation.

She had quite a lot of money at her disposal as she had hardly touched the money given her by the Marquis d'Hautemart and by the Mayor of La Rochelle. Her only large outlay had been on poor Igor, who unfortunately had been left behind at Eglimont. So she asked her hostess to recommend a dressmaker who would be able to make her—as quickly as possible— the clothes she so urgently needed.

During their six months in London, Madame Le Blachet and Aloise had learned enough English to make themselves understood. They took Victoire to a Hampstead dressmaker, Mrs. Cross, who was just beginning to acquire a reputation.

In her premises looking onto a courtyard, the customers were jostling each other in two tiny rooms next to the workshop where half a dozen seamstresses were trying hard to sew in the semidarkness. Mrs. Cross's son, a blond, pimply young man who spoke with a stammer, was displaying fabrics to a crowd of elegant young ladies who seemed in no hurry to choose from among the Genoese velvet, Florentine brocade, Lyon silk, and Alençon lace. Victoire could not understand a word of their rapid chatter and cries of admiration.

With the help of her companions, however, she managed to attract the young man's attention. He showed her some very tempting lavender-blue brocade that could be trimmed with *passementeries,* a particularly flattering violet-colored velvet, and an exquisitely worked piece of gold cloth, which she found quite irresistible.

Madame Le Blachet inquired about the price and was told a figure that she considered exorbitant. She began to haggle with the young man, to Victoire's great amusement, and obtained a substantial reduction.

"Since you have my interests so much at heart, please let me buy a dress for Aloise. It would be only fair since I wore hers for so long at La Rochelle."

Overjoyed at this unexpected windfall, Aloise blushed with pleasure and gave Victoire a grateful look.

Next they paid a visit to a shoemaker, where Victoire ordered some delicate court shoes with silver buckles to go with her dresses, and some boots to replace her own, which were almost completely worn out by now.

Then she asked to be taken to Sir William Glanville's house. It was time to think of serious matters.

Sir William lived alongside the Thames, near Saint Andrews. It was an expensive quarter, worlds away from the dilapidated street where Madame Le Blachet and Aloise lived. The brick houses were large and wide-fronted and the streets were full of luxurious-looking carriages. Victoire asked Madame Le Blachet if she and her niece would return to fetch her later.

While she was visiting Sir William they would be able to explore this quarter of London, which was quite unknown to them.

Victoire knocked on a high wooden door which was promptly opened by a solemn servant wearing the green and black Glanville livery. It was only at this moment that Victoire suddenly realized she was totally unable to explain in English that she wanted to see Sir William in person. She began to get angry at herself, but could only repeat over and over again, "Sir William Glanville! Sir William Glanville!" waving her precious letter of introduction about in the air. The servant, misunderstanding what she wanted, kept trying to take the letter from her to give to his master.

They made such a noise that a tall, heavily mustached man appeared from a nearby room to find out what was happening.

"Monsieur!" exclaimed Victoire. *"Parlez-vous français?"*

Smiling, the man looked her up and down. *"Un peu, Mademoiselle."*

"Alors, be kind enough to lead me to Sir William Glanville."

"I am he. *Veuillez me suivre."*

He took Victoire into a small smoking room lined with beautiful light wood panels where, in front of a cheerfully crackling fire, he had been reading and drinking port.

"Monsieur, the Mayor of La Rochelle asked me to deliver this letter to you. Please would you read it."

Sir William glanced through the letter in which Jacques Henri described the situation in the besieged city, and the terrible privations being undergone by its inhabitants.

"Les pauvres gens!" exclaimed Sir William. "How they must be suffering!"

"More than you think, Monsieur. And the situation must have gotten much worse since I left."

He looked at Victoire incredulously. "Were you really in La Rochelle?"

"Yes."

"It's almost a miracle that you managed to get out."

Victoire detected a hint of suspicion in Sir William's tone. So she decided to tell him about her escape from La Rochelle in detail.

"You're very brave," he said admiringly when she had finished. "And now you want to see the Queen?"

"I have come to implore Her Majesty to help her fellow Protestants."

Sir William became thoughtful. "I'd better tell you honestly that you have not come at a very favorable time."

"Why not?" asked Victoire in surprise.

"Queen Elizabeth, who has remained unmarried until now, is at present seriously considering marrying the Duc d'Alençon."

"But he's twenty years younger than her!"

Sir William shrugged his shoulders. "I know. Nevertheless, I wonder whether Her Majesty will feel ready to vex Catherine de Medici by helping a faction in rebellion against the King of France."

"So you think my mission is doomed to failure?"

"I didn't say that. But you must be aware of the difficulties involved."

"I'm only too aware of them," sighed Victoire. Sir William showed her out, promising he would do all he could and would be in touch with her.

As Victoire got to know her hostess better, she realized that Madame Le Blachet was in very difficult financial straits. Nobody had expected their exile would have to last so long. Realizing her stay would be an extra burden, Victoire insisted upon contributing as much as she could to the household expenses.

Madame Le Blachet, a widow of about forty with no children of her own, had her sister's kind and gentle nature, but without Lady Emmeline's down-to-earth practicality. She had not managed to organize her new life to make the best of their difficult situation. She had only one elderly servant with her in exile, and she could not come to terms with her reduced circumstances. At La Rochelle she had lived in her sister's comfortable and well-provided house, with no cares or responsibilities of her own. In London she spent all her time bemoaning the many problems facing her, but made no attempt to put them right.

Aloise had a contented nature, but she had been badly spoiled by her parents. She did all she could to help, but did not have the force of character to change matters much. She was still very much a child, unaware of the realities of life. Sometimes, faced with her naïveté and lack of experience, Victoire found it hard to believe they were almost exactly the same age. Yet, she had experienced life at Court, from which she had learned much, and she had been forced to make do on her own and make decisions for herself in all kinds of situations. Victoire found herself treating Aloise like a younger sister.

As she regained her strength and put on some weight, Victoire began to find her life in London very boring. She could not understand how her hosts could give in to events as they did, without making any efforts to alter their destiny.

Victoire fretted at her inactivity whereas Genevieve Le Blachet was content to wait passively, though she complained all the time. She was looking forward to so much: the end of the siege, their return to France, the day when they would be sent money. But the days went by, and nothing new happened.

Her bordom with this uneventful life made Victoire particularly thrilled to receive an invitation from Lord Craighton to a grand evening party two days later. The intervening days were spent in feverish preparations.

Mrs. Cross was urgently asked to have at least one of the dresses ready in time. The whole household was in a state of feverish agitation. Aloise seemed the most excited of them all; she was well aware that what happened that evening might change the course of events for the city of La Rochelle and, of course, for her parents, too. Victoire was to make her entry into English society. If she were successful, support might be forthcoming for the Protestant cause from those who were displeased at the idea of an alliance with France through Elizabeth's projected marriage. At the same time, Victoire had to be careful not to arouse the suspicions of M. de la Mothe Fenelon's numerous and energetic spies.

Chapter XIV

Victoire made her way serenely—to outside appearances at least—through the spacious salons of Lord Craighton's London residence, but she was concealing a feeling of utter panic. She did not know a single person in the huge throng of people, apart from her host and his niece, and not many were likely to speak French.

She recalled another, but in retrospect less frightening, ordeal: her presentation at the Louvre when she had gone to make her bow before Catherine de Medici and King Charles IX. But on that occasion her family had been present, too.

She made her way toward Lord Craighton, who was holding forth in the middle of a group of guests. Beside him stood Philippa, wearing a very low-cut dress of Tyrian pink that showed off her firm white bosom. She was welcoming the guests, playing the role of mistress of the house. A crowd of young gentlemen clustered eagerly about her, and she was replying gracefully to their attempts to attract her attention.

The rooms where the reception was being held were brightly lit with crystal chandeliers and silver-gilt candlesticks. Outside the weather was chilly on this spring evening in London, but the numerous flames inside had warmed up the air.

At length Lord Craighton caught sight of Victoire. He welcomed her warmly, obviously genuinely pleased that she had come, and this lifted her spirits a little.

"How pleased I am to see you!" he exclaimed.

Philippa too smiled at her, but with no genuine warmth in her eyes. Her crowd of young suitors stared inquisitively at this young Frenchwoman who had come without an escort.

"My dear Pemberley," said Lord Craighton to one of them. "You speak French so well, would you escort Mademoiselle de Montmaur this evening?"

The young man bowed. "I shall consider it an honor."

He offered Victoire his arm. "Have you just arrived from France?"

"Yes. I had the pleasure of crossing the Channel with Lord Craighton and his niece."

Richard Pemberley was an easy young man to talk to, and Victoire quickly learned that his greatest interest in life was breeding horses for fox hunting.

"Do you like hunting?" he asked.

"I do indeed," Victoire assured him. "When I was at Court we went hunting at Saint-Germain or Vincennes at least once a week."

"In that case," Pemberley went on, "our host will

certainly invite you to one of his famous hunting parties. He owns a magnificent estate about twenty leagues south of London called Cranmore."

All the guests had by now arrived, and Lord Craighton ushered them toward an enormous horseshoe-shaped table with places laid for two hundred people. As he went past Victoire he stopped. "You're looking very beautiful this evening. I hope you're not feeling too out of place?"

"Not at all, thanks to Mr. Pemberley."

"I was just telling Mademoiselle de Montmaur about your hunting parties at Cranmore."

"I do hope she will give me the pleasure of her company at one of them."

"I should be delighted," replied Victoire.

The supper was a feast, the like of which Victoire had not seen since she left the Louvre. An army of servants brought in Colchester oysters, lobsters, turbot, Scottish salmon, lampreys, pike, and trout, washed down by Chablis and Macon wines, which in England were considered a great luxury. But the refinements of the French court were missing from Lord Craighton's table, and the dishes were prepared much more simply.

"Does Lord Craighton often give parties like this one?" asked Victoire.

"At least once a month, except when he's abroad. From now on they'll doubtless be more frequent because he has decided it's time his niece was married."

"She must have at least ten suitors this very evening!"

Pemberley smiled. He was quite pleased to be a little indiscreet about his host's niece. "Lady Philippa is not such a fine match as appearances might suggest."

Victoire looked at him questioningly. He went on, "Her father was executed in Queen Mary's reign, and all his goods and possessions confiscated by the Crown."

"I'm surprised Queen Elizabeth hasn't returned them to his daughter," said Victoire.

Pemberley made an evasive gesture. "It's difficult to get something back once the Crown has its hands on it."

"So Philippa is poor," said Victoire thoughtfully.

"Yes, and what is more, she is used to a very expensive way of life. Her uncle never refuses her anything. Did you notice her jewels?"

"Yes, I saw them," said Victoire. "Has Lord Craighton any children?"

"He has no heirs apart from Philippa," said Pemberley. "At least, not for the moment." He seemed to hesitate.

"But he's still young enough to have some. Is that what you mean?" asked Victoire.

"Exactly. He might make a late marriage."

"What would happen to Philippa if he had children?"

"She could expect nothing except a dowry when she marries."

This amply explained Philippa's behavior to Victoire. Doubtless she acted the same with any young woman who might be dangerous.

"She should marry her uncle," she suggested jokingly.

Pemberley lowered his voice. "Some people say she's thinking of it."

"What about him?"

"I don't think he would."

As they savored their grouse, Victoire discreetly examined the guests sitting nearby. She wanted very much to find out which was the French Ambassador, M. de la Mothe Fenelon. After all, he would be likely to do everything in his power to thwart her mission, if he knew of it. But she could not pick him out from the English guests, and indeed she was not even sure he was there. "Is M. de la Mothe Fenelon here to-night?" she asked her escort.

"He doubtless will be," said Pemberley. "He is a habitué of the house, and one of Lady Philippa's admirers. Yes, there he is, sitting on her right."

Even at first glance he looked like a formidable adversary. He was a mature man, whose eyes sparkled with intelligence. His witty remarks were obviously amusing everyone within earshot. The chances of Victoire's achieving her objective without his hearing of it seemed very slender. She knew he had informers everywhere, perhaps even among some of the guests tonight.

It was Lord Craighton himself who introduced her to M. de la Mothe Fenelon. "Your Ambassador will surely be happy to make the acquaintance of such a charming compatriot," he assured her.

Victoire doubted whether that was true. What interest could she possibly have for a man whose sole concern was politics? But, of course, he would be surprised to discover she was all alone in London. She must invent a story quickly.

"He is a very shrewd man. How would you say that in French? Subtle, I think."

This description of the Ambassador did not reassure Victoire at all. She was not at all sure she would be capable of lulling the suspicions of a man who saw it as his duty to serve the monarchy wholeheartedly and to combat those who opposed it.

M. de la Mothe Fenelon greeted her graciously and begged her not to hesitate to ask for his help if she should require it. When the initial exchange of courtesies was over, Victoire tried to avoid his questions, but in vain. "Our mutual friend tells me that you crossed the Channel together," he said.

"Yes, in a terrible storm."

"And where are you staying in London?" he asked in a casual tone.

She could not lie in front of Lord Craighton; after all, he had sent her his coach.

"Goodness, what a strange place to stay!" exclaimed the Ambassador.

Victoire was dismayed to feel his interest in her growing.

"Such an out-of-the-way quarter can't be very convenient or comfortable for you," he remarked, observing Victoire closely.

She hesitated, ill at ease under his penetrating gaze.

Luckily Lord Craighton got her out of difficulty. "When people arrive in an unknown city they stay just anywhere at first, and afterward they become set in their ways."

"Obviously. Is your family happy here?" asked the Ambassador. This apparently harmless question contained a trap, but Victoire did not see how she could avoid it.

"My aunt complains a little about the climate," she finally said, smiling. "But surely it *must* soon be summer?"

For a moment Victoire thought the Ambassador's suspicions had been lulled, but she was disappointed. "May I request the pleasure of being introduced to your aunt?"

"She is indisposed, and was unable to attend the reception," said Victoire, turning so that her host could not hear her reply. Lord Craighton most likely would have immediately suggested inviting her next time. The last thing Victoire wanted was to be escorted by Madame Le Blachet, who would, of course, reveal her relationship to the Mayor of La Rochelle.

"Do you intend to stay long?" asked the Ambassador.

"As long as possible!" said Victoire, trying hard to

look naive. "You see, Excellency, it's the first opportunity I have had to travel abroad."

To her great relief Victoire saw that the Ambassador's attention was wandering elsewhere. She would report the conversation to Sir William when she returned to London.

Chapter XV

*O*n a number of occasions during the evening, Victoire caught Lord Craighton looking at her. His duties as host, however, kept him very busy, and he was not able to devote himself to her as he would clearly have wished. But the next morning, when Victoire had hardly woken up, a footman dressed in his livery brought her basketfuls of different kinds of delicacies. There were dragées, violet pastilles, bilberry and plum jam, Welsh honey, and little frangipane and almond paste cakes.

Dazzled by this munificence, Genevieve Le Blachet could at first say nothing but, "What a lot of things!" Then she asked timidly, "Did Lord Craighton send you all that?"

"It appears so."

"He must be very taken with you."

"Come now! They're only a few sweetmeats." Secretly, however, Victoire felt very flattered to have attracted the attention of Lord Craighton, whose intelligence and character she so much respected.

"Take all you want."

Her hosts didn't have to be asked twice. They were eager for sweet things, having been deprived of them for so long.

Victoire left her hostess to unpack the baskets, and read the note that came with them. It said, "Yesterday evening you eclipsed all the other women. Will you honor me by accompanying me for a ride tomorrow morning? The best mare in my stables shall be at your disposal."

Victoire's spirits rose at the prospect of a day out in the open country, and she hurried to the hall where the footman was waiting.

"Is there a reply for my Lord?" he asked respectfully.

"Please thank His Grace for his kindness, and tell him I shall be very pleased to accept his invitation."

When the valet had gone, Victoire returned to her room. She had preferred not to write to Lord Craighton, fearing that Philippa, who kept tabs on everything her uncle did, might find it. As far as possible, she thought it was wiser to leave her in ignorance of their growing friendship.

Victoire and Lord Craighton were galloping together in the crisp but sunny morning air. Their horses were well fed and full of energy. Like their riders, they were finding the exercise so pleasant they were hard to hold back.

They met a flock of sheep jostling some newborn lambs along with them, though they were still unsteady on their feet. As they approached a farm some poultry fled cackling out of their way. A hare ran out from a thicket across their path, and a flight of plump quail rose from a clump of trees.

"They would be good to eat," remarked Lord Craighton. Then he asked solicitously, "You're not tired, I hope?"

"Oh, no. I'm so enjoying the ride."

How could she explain to her companion how happy she felt to be riding through the woods, at one with her mount as it cut through the crisp air, and to breathe in deeply the invigorating country air, far from the sickening smells of the city where, like Paris, the streets were strewn with refuse, rotting meat, and rubbish of every kind.

Victoire stroked her horse's neck.

"I can see you love horses. Would you like to keep this one when you come hunting or would you like to try another?"

"I'd prefer to keep this one. We get on so well together."

"Then I'll have it brought to Cranmore."

"I am looking forward so much to visiting your house."

"It's a modest residence, but I hope you will enjoy staying there . . . as long as possible."

She wondered how to ask whether M. de la Mothe Fenelon would be there without her question seeming too obvious. After waiting a little while she said, "I found the French Ambassador a charming and very shrewd man."

"You're quite right, he is," said Lord Craighton in a delighted voice. "Our sovereign has a high opinion of him. He is on very friendly terms with her. Unfortunately his duties keep him in London just now and he will not be able to come hunting."

Victoire sighed with relief.

"However, the Queen's principal adviser, Sir William Cecil, will do us the honor of being with us."

Victoire pricked up her ears at the name, though her ignorance of English politics prevented her from gauging Cecil's exact importance in the country. She decided to ask Sir William Glanville about that too when she returned to London. But since he was a member of the government, it would almost certainly be helpful to be on good terms with him.

They stopped for a meal at a little farm belonging to Lord Craighton. "It will be very simple," he said, apologizing. "But this side of London there is no inn where one can take a lady."

"I shall be delighted to eat at a farm. At Montmaur, when I was out riding, I often stopped like this to eat a bacon omelette and drink fresh milk."

"I do so like people like you who enjoy any pleasure, however modest."

Perhaps he was thinking of Philippa, who was so difficult and demanding, for whom nothing was quite right. He obviously was, for he went on, "I'm afraid I've spoiled my niece. I have always given her everything she wanted. I've tried to do all I could to make up for the cruelty of fate that deprived her of her father. But from what little you have told me about your own life, the fates have been even more cruel to you in depriving you of both your parents so brutally."

"Yes, my father was hanged after the conspiracy of Amboise, like so many other Huguenots," Victoire confirmed sadly.

When she saw how affectionately concerned Lord Craighton was about her, Victoire had an urge to confide in him about her mission and ask him for support, even though he was friendly with M. de la Mothe Fenelon. But instinct told her this would be premature. She knew she would do better to wait until she knew him better. Lord Craighton gave her his hand to help her down off her horse, grasping it in his a little longer than was necessary.

Perhaps, thought Victoire, he would approve if the Queen helped the French Protestants, providing, of course, that he was not a strong supporter of her marriage with the Duc d'Alençon. A lot of English people regretted that Elizabeth had not decided to marry before now. At her age it was becoming somewhat unlikely that she would be able to provide the country with an heir to the throne.

If the Queen were to die without any direct descendants, the throne would go to her cousin, Mary Queen of Scots, who had—though for less than a year—been Queen of France, too. Mary Stuart was the adored niece of the Guise family. She was herself a fervent Catholic, and was already the mother of a son. If she came to the throne, the Protestants could expect to continue being persecuted and harried.

The farmer's wife ran up and curtsied deeply, welcoming them warmly, though Victoire unfortunately could not understand a word she said. She took them into a room with a beaten earth floor and they sat down at the long walnut table laid with earthenware plates and tin goblets. She brought them roast, crackling duck, and rye pancakes still warm from the oven. One of the squires served them while the other uncorked a flagon he had brought with him in the pocket of his saddle.

"I hope the claret hasn't suffered too much from the ride!" said Lord Craighton.

When she had satisfied her hunger a little, which had been sharpened by the fresh air and exercise, Victoire became aware that Lord Craighton was staring at her passionately. She smiled.

"I so much like to look at you," he murmured. "You're so . . . natural, at ease in every situation, whatever your surroundings." He gestured toward the whitewashed walls whose only ornament was a side of ham hanging from a nail.

"I feel happy here," said Victoire.

She felt like adding, "I'm free, I'm neither hungry nor cold, no danger threatens me for the moment, how could I possibly not be happy in this situation?"

Scarcely a fortnight before she had been lying in a dungeon, a prisoner of Adrien d'Etivey. And now she was eating a delicious lunch, after which they would gallop off together in the afternoon sun, and she could look forward to the prospect of staying at Cranmore in the near future, where she would be meeting an adviser to the Queen.

And then suddenly she thought of Guy, and all her joy melted away. Since she had escaped from Eglimont she had hardly had time to think of him; first she had had to make quite sure of staying out of Adrien's clutches; after that she had been full of the excitement of the journey and her discovery of a new and foreign country. Her grief had been dormant within her. But now it reawoke until she felt her heart would break; she imagined a thousand torments for Guy's assassin. She would herself willingly have torn out his eyes, cut off his ears, or even worse than that. No chastisement, no punishment seemed terrible enough to punish him for the murder of her dear friend. What would she not have given at that moment to have had Guy riding beside her instead of Lord Craighton?

Chapter XVI

"So William Cecil is going to Cranmore," said Glanville reflectively. "What an unexpected stroke of luck!"

Sir William paced up and down his comfortable smoking room, where ladies were usually not admitted, while Victoire sat beside the fire awaiting his instructions.

"I have requested an audience with the Queen for you," he went on. "I tried to be as discreet as possible, but M. de la Mothe Fenelon will almost certainly find out about it. He may well know already."

"Already!" exclaimed Victoire in alarm.

William Glanville shrugged. "That man is devilishly clever. He has spies everywhere."

"In that case, I don't see how Her Majesty's adviser will be able to help us."

"Oh, yes. He could speed up your introduction to Court, and use his influence to support your cause with the sovereign. That way he would at least counterbalance the influence of your Ambassador."

"That's already quite a lot," remarked Victoire. "Tell me a little about him and the best way to approach him."

"Yes, there are some things you really ought to know."

He sat down in front of her and she concentrated hard, determined not to lose a single word of what he said.

"You see, unlike most previous sovereigns, the Queen has not chosen her ministers from among the nobility or the members of her own family. From the very first moment when she came to power she realized how vitally important it was for her to have around her intelligent men who were good administrators, with an instinct for government. So she has chosen as her ministers men whose fathers or grandfathers had made their fortunes from trade or the dissolution of the monasteries and the distribution of their treasures. When she became Queen she made William Cecil Secretary of State, and I don't think she has ever regretted her choice since then. He is a simple man who dislikes any ostentatious display of wealth. For example, his favorite mount is a mule!"

Victoire tried to recall whether she had met anyone like that at the French court. She thought not.

"He is an extremely cautious man," went on Sir William. "When Mary Tudor was persecuting the Protestants, he did not scruple to observe the Catholic rites in order to save his life. Queen Elizabeth herself had done the same thing when her sister imprisoned her in the Tower of London."

"He abjured his faith!"

"You *could* put it like that. One does sometimes have to be ready to put aside one's principles," said Sir William cynically. "But now he is quite ready to persecute and execute the Catholics."

"So he should be favorable to us?"

"Yes, to a certain extent. But there's always the problem of the Queen's marriage, which I mentioned to you the other day. Recently William Cecil even dared to write to the Queen: 'God will demand of you a severe reckoning for the time you have lost.' "

"He favors the match with the Duc d'Alençon?"

"As a last resort. Particularly since the matter is so serious that Parliament itself has now begun to interfere. It sent the Queen a petition recently. Her Majesty has already refused so many suitors over the last fifteen years."

"So, in fact, the Duc d'Alençon is her last opportunity to provide an heir, considering her age?"

"That is more or less the situation," Sir William confirmed.

Everything Glanville told her made Victoire curious to meet this all-powerful Queen who was said to be both beautiful and learned, who was surrounded by favorites, and yet who refused, to the despair of all her subjects, to marry and provide an heir to the throne.

Cranmore was an imposing building dating from the reign of Henry VII, its facade flanked by four thick-walled towers. It stood in the middle of a forest whose trees were almost a century old, alongside the river Crew. Around it stretched a pleasant park.

Indoors the estate was somewhat spartan. It was much less comfortable than most of the noble residences that Victoire had visited during her travels. To make matters worse, it was very cold, much colder even than the French châteaux.

An army of servants greeted the guests, under the watchful eye of a major-domo, taking their horses and their luggage and showing them up to their rooms. Victoire was delighted to catch sight of Richard Pemberley among the guests.

"I'm feeling a little lost," she admitted, smiling.

"I'll look after you. I know the place well."

"It's such a nuisance not to be able to understand the simplest remarks," she exclaimed.

Preceded by two servants carrying Victoire's chest, they climbed a huge stone staircase.

"I suppose Lord Craighton will have accommodated you on the first floor."

"Why?"

"Because he usually reserves that floor for guests he particularly wishes to honor."

He inquired of the footman, who confirmed that Mademoiselle de Montmaur was to occupy Lady Mary's state bedroom.

"Who was she?"

"Our host's mother. She died of grief when her younger son was executed."

"Philippa's father?"

"That's right."

He added, with a slightly mocking smile, "I won't hide from you that it's the finest room in the whole house. There you are, I'll leave you. A woman will come to look after you. Dinner is at six."

"Thank you for escorting me this far."

"If you wish, I'll come and fetch you when you're ready," Pemberley offered.

"Willingly," said Victoire gratefully. "If I got lost, I wouldn't even be able to ask my way!"

The chambermaid appeared and launched into voluble speech. Victoire gestured to show that she could not understand. The woman laughed gaily. She led Victoire to the open chest and asked her which dress she wanted to wear that evening. After a moment's hesitation Victoire chose her blue dress with gold trimmings.

While the maid was dressing her and doing her hair, which was highlighted nicely by the gold in the dress, Victoire had time to admire at leisure the splendid tapestries of hunting scenes lining the walls which, apart from being decorative, did warm up the damp atmosphere a little. Above the fireplace hung a portrait of a young woman.

"Lady Mary?" questioned Victoire.

"Yes, Milady," confirmed the maid with a happy smile. She added an explanation which remained incomprehensible to Victoire.

There was no doubt Philippa looked very like her grandmother. She had inherited her large luminous eyes and her thick auburn hair. But there the resemblance ended. Philippa's most characteristic expression was hard, almost pitiless, while her grandmother looked gentle, even resigned. She looked as though she had had an unhappy life, even before her son's death.

Victoire sent the chambermaid away once she had finished her duties, and examined herself in the mirror with a satisfaction she had not felt for some time. Her cheeks were once again rosy and her eyes bright. The traces of her imprisonment and hardship had disappeared. Her shoulders, which her dress left completely bare, were as soft and rounded as before. Her long blonde hair, which had been dull and lifeless when she had left La Rochelle, was now shining and growing with renewed vigor. Victoire thought she looked at her best, and only regretted that Guillaume was not there to see her.

She followed Richard Pemberley along a gallery where the servants were just lighting the candles, banishing the shadows. The faces of Lord Craighton's long-dead ancestors rose up out of the gloom.

"Did you notice the portrait of Lady Mary in your room?" inquired Pemberley.

"Yes, I did."

"It is the work of Holbein, the Court painter under Henry VIII."

"He must have been very talented. But why did he make her look so sad?" Victoire wanted to know.

"She had good reason to look sad, believe me!"

Victoire did not dare to ask why as they were now entering the great hall, at each end of which log fires were burning. Lord Craighton came forward to greet them. "I was longing to see you again," he said to Victoire as soon as Pemberley left them alone. "I'm so pleased to have you staying under my roof."

"You have treated me royally!"

"Nothing is too good for you. I'm so pleased you like your room. It was my mother's . . . Ah! here is Lord Burghley."

A man in his fifties came forward to greet them. William Cecil was of average height, his hair receding to reveal a high, bulging forehead. His simple black apparel looked out of place in this room thronged with richly dressed ladies and gentlemen. The expression of his regular features revealed a somewhat rigid and mistrustful character, but more attractive qualities of patience and steadfastness could be glimpsed there, too. His small gray beard completely failed to conceal his determined chin.

All of the fifty guests clustered around the Queen's adviser. He accepted their tributes to his office goodnaturedly. Victoire realized how insuperably difficult it would be for her—an insignificant little French girl —to approach such a highly important person. The other guests would never leave him alone for a moment!

Victoire found the idea of speaking to Lord Burghley more awe-inspiring than escaping from Eglimont, though for the moment, at least, she had no choice but to wait and observe him. The evening gathering would be short as they were to rise before dawn the next day.

After some time Philippa finally deigned to appear. Victoire detected a hint of annoyance in the look her uncle gave her when she made her entrance. No doubt, thought Victoire, he was angry at her for keeping the guests waiting so long.

She greeted everyone haughtily before finally condescending to notice Victoire's presence.

"Well!" she said, pursing her lips. "I didn't know my uncle had invited *you*."

"Yes, he was kind enough to do so," replied Victoire. She realized that Lord Craighton must not have told his niece they had been out riding together.

"I hope you will have a pleasant stay," Philippa went on. But it was obvious to Victoire that she was very peeved.

It was still dark when the chambermaid came to wake Victoire next morning. Still bemused with sleep, she put on her riding clothes and boots, washed and brushed her hair.

Breakfast was being served in the great hall. At first the guests were taciturn and drowsy with sleep, but as soon as they had eaten, their spirits began to lift and they joked and laughed heartily together until Lord Craighton said it was time to set off.

The horses were waiting for them in the courtyard, pawing the ground, impatient to be off. The stable boys were having difficulty in holding their bridles and dogs were running about everywhere, trying to bite the horses' hocks despite the whip readily wielded by the master of hounds.

The hunting horn rang out and they all set off in the gray, damp early morning.

"I suppose you've never been fox hunting," said Pemberley to Victoire. He seemed by now to consider himself her regular admirer, and to feel at home in his role. "I don't think you do it in France."

"No indeed. How is it different from hunting boar or deer?"

"Well, the larger animals usually hide in the thickest part of the forest, while the fox will lead the huntsmen into open country, either flat ground or hills. It's good sport, you'll see!"

"I'm sure it will be!"

Pemberley's forecast proved correct. The wily fox led them for miles over hedges, streams, and ditches.

Around eleven o'clock the hunt was over and the party rode slowly back to the house. In front of her, but quite inaccessible, Victoire could see Sir William Cecil. Half a day had already gone by and she was no nearer to finding an opportunity to speak to him, despite Sir William's confidence in her.

As they came in sight of Cranmore she turned to Lord Craighton, who was riding alongside her, and making sure no one was within earshot, she revealed to him why she had come to England.

Chapter XVII

*A*t last Victoire had her chance to speak to the great Lord Burghley. He sat very still in his chair, listening to her very attentively, but without any special good will toward her. Victoire felt very intimidated now that the moment to speak was at hand, but she made every effort to present her cause as persuasively as possible. Lord Burghley did not speak French very well, so Lord Craighton interpreted when necessary.

Sir William had first of all perused the letter from Jacques Henri. He had turned it over several times, as though trying to make sure it was genuine.

"My Lord," said Victoire, "you cannot imagine the destitution within La Rochelle. For some months now there has been no food in the city and the people are dying of hunger all the time. What is worse than that, the city is infested with hordes of rats that are spreading plague and disease. Weakened by starvation, the people are dropping like flies. Soon the city will have no more defenders."

"Mademoiselle, you plead the cause of your friends very eloquently," said Lord Burghley.

"My friends are also England's allies!" exclaimed Victoire.

'That's true," said Lord Burghley reflectively. "Like the Dutch, who are also begging us to intervene and rescue them from the destructive mania of the Duc d'Albe and the Spanish armies. Our country has a lot of burdens to bear."

"That's true, but it is nevertheless important for the strategic base of La Rochelle not to fall into hostile hands," intervened Lord Craighton. "Our ships would be sunk as they passed by on their way to trade with the African coast and the Indies."

"Her Majesty certainly attaches great importance to England's mastery of the seas."

"If the Catholics get possession of La Rochelle," said Victoire, "the Spaniards would have access to the harbor."

Lord Burghley grimaced. He obviously found this eventuality unpleasant, even though his sovereign was still flirting with her former brother-in-law, the King of Spain.

Lord Craighton had been very helpful during the interview. His hatred of the Catholics had animated him to some extent, it was true, but he had also been influenced by his strong growing attraction toward Victoire.

She felt powerless to intervene in the discussion between these prestigious men. They evaluated the problem, weighing the advantages and the disadvantages of taking action. If the country intervened, the consequences would be very serious. Perhaps, thought Victoire, she would have been more successful at persuading them if she had been a man.

"M. de la Mothe Fenelon will take it very badly," sighed Lord Burghley.

"But he must know nothing about it!" exclaimed Victoire hastily.

The two men smiled at her naiveté.

"Very little happens at Court without the Ambassador knowing. He makes everything his business, even what happens in the Queen's bed!"

"Particularly just now," added Lord Craighton.

"Nevertheless," went on Lord Burghley, "I shall report to the Queen on this important matter. And we shall see if it is possible, at the present stage of negotiations, to send a few ships to La Rochelle. Providing, of course, they can manage to get through the blockade!"

Victoire had done everything within her power to influence the course of events. All she could do now was to await developments. Until now she had been able to think of nothing else but persuading Lord Burghley to assist her starving friends. She had not really been in the mood to appreciate Cranmore's many amenities. But now she felt ready to make the most of the amusements Lord Craighton arranged for his guests. For a few short days she would perhaps be able to be a carefree young girl like any other.

The evening following her talk with Lord Burghley, Victoire put on her gold dress for the first time. Every time she looked at it, the delicate workmanship of the cloth never failed to thrill her. It was by far the most beautiful dress she had ever owned.

Just as she was getting ready to leave her room to join the rest of the company for supper, Victoire suddenly felt dizzy. For a few moments the room seemed to spin about, and if she had not grabbed the bedpost she would have fallen to the floor. As she lay down she began to worry because nothing like this had ever happened to her before. Perhaps it was simply from too much hunting that morning. And yet she had often exerted herself just as much, and more, in the past without feeling any ill effects.

She got up carefully. Lady Mary's portrait was again in its place above the fireplace, and the tapestry animals, which had been dancing wildly about the room, were again quite still. Though her legs still felt shaky, she risked going downstairs, desperately hoping she would not faint during the evening in the presence of Lord Burghley. He would think her a weak creature and would despise her.

"You look very pale," said Richard Pemberley. "Are you ill?"

"Just a little tired."

"In that case, a glass of brandy will make you feel better."

This was a remedy poor Guy had often resorted to. In memory of him Victoire accepted a generous glassful of brandy and sipped it slowly. "I do feel better," she said, smiling. "I felt very dizzy."

After supper three musicians sang old ballads for the guests, accompanying themselves on the lute. Their songs dated from the long-drawn-out Wars of the Roses, when so many English noblemen had died a cruel death. Victoire loved the old melodies, which were sometimes gay and stirring, sometimes infinitely sad. After the musical interlude, the lute players were applauded and allowed to finish up what remained from the feast, which they fell on voraciously. Victoire went close to the fire, which had been deserted by the other guests.

She was shivering in spite of all the food and claret she had consumed. The other women, she noticed, had rosy cheeks. Some of the men had bloodshot eyes, and others even seemed on the verge of apoplexy. If a doctor had been present, thought Victoire to herself, he would have bled quite a few of them immediately.

To her great surprise Lady Philippa came up to her in her most kind and gracious manner.

"What a beautiful dress!" she complimented Victoire. "Who made it for you?"

"Mrs. Cross."

"I thought so. I recognized the workmanship immediately. But you look cold, my dear."

"I am a little," Victoire confessed.

"I'll have someone bring you a shawl."

"Thank you for being so kind," said Victoire, touched to see her hostess so considerate.

It was possible she had been wrong about Philippa.

A footman preceded Victoire along Cranmore's interminable corridors, bearing a three-branched candlestick. He went into her room, placed the heavy silver candelabra on a table in the middle of the room, lit a small candle to light his own way back, and bowed. "Good night, Milady."

Victoire smiled at the blond, blue-eyed young man who was staring at her as though dazzled.

"Good night," she said in her turn.

"John, to serve Your Grace."

"Thank you."

Victoire had decided to make an effort to learn English. Each day she learned about five words, which at least enabled her to greet and thank people.

A few moments later Nelly the chambermaid came in to undress Victoire and get her ready for the night. Victoire took off the magnificent cashmere shawl from her shoulders that had been given to her earlier and held it out to the woman. "For Lady Philippa, please."

Nelly nodded her assent and then carefully hung up the gold dress in the wardrobe, though not without first admiring it at length, exclaiming her delight at its beauty. Finally she went away, and the exhausted Victoire was at last able to stretch out in the enormous bed, hidden away in an alcove upholstered in gray velvet.

She blew out the candle and pulled the covers up to her chin. She still felt uncomfortable, though she could not locate any specific pain. She wondered whether she had a touch of fever. She might well have caught a chill out hunting, or perhaps her interview with Lord Burghley had upset her more than she had realized. At last, however, she fell asleep.

When she opened her eyes the white, almost unreal light of the full moon was shining into the room through the window, which Nelly had left partly open. Its rays shone directly onto the portrait of Lady Mary, which seemed animated with some strange nocturnal life. Victoire had the impression that the young woman's dark eyes were staring at her with extraordinary brilliance, as though they were trying to pass on some mysterious warning. Though she was wet through with perspiration, Victoire forced herself to get up and make sure that this was only a hallucination. She pushed the shutters wide. They creaked mournfully as they opened and the room was flooded with light.

Lady Mary wore her usual peaceful, slightly resigned expression, her eyes lost in a distant and melancholy dream. Victoire shrugged her shoulders. Was she going to start being afraid of the dark like a stupid girl when she had withstood the ordeal of prison for so many long days and nights?

She was dying of thirst, so she drank a little water from the jug. It tasted rather brackish, as though it hadn't been changed for some time. She reminded herself to mention it to Nelly the next morning.

Chapter XVIII

*W*hen daylight came, Victoire felt in good form and her anxiety had quite disappeared. She looked at Lady Mary's portrait with equanimity. Except for the fact that it was by Holbein—which must make it very valuable—she found nothing to distinguish it from the dozens of other pictures hanging on the walls of Cranmore. How could she for a moment have imagined that the eyes had moved? Her nerves must be in a very fragile state.

When she saw only two horses waiting in the court-yard, Victoire realized that Lord Craighton intended to ride out alone with her.

"At last I can enjoy your presence here a little," said Lord Craighton. "Yesterday evening Lord Burgh-ley monopolized me the whole time. I couldn't even snatch a moment to come and speak to you—though you did retire very early, I thought."

"I was exhausted by the long day," admitted Victoire, smiling.

"We'll go gently today. We're not in any hurry."

Before they set off, Victoire turned in the saddle to get a view of the front of the house. At a window she caught sight of Philippa watching her uncle riding off with the young Frenchwoman who had been clever enough to get into his good graces.

"Perhaps your niece won't be too pleased at our little escapade," she could not refrain from remarking.

"Surely I'm old enough to choose when I go out, and with whom!" exclaimed Lord Craighton. "But it's true Philippa pays far too much attention to what I do. I suppose she feels involved in my life. After all, I'm her closest relative and have always made much of her. But I do hope she'll finally decide to marry. There are three of the best matches in the kingdom in my house at the moment, and they'd all be only too glad to marry her. All *she* has to do is choose the one that suits her best!"

They plunged into a forest of oak trees, following a path that twisted through the thickets. Spring seemed much later here than in France. The new spring vege-tation could hardly be smelled at all, though a few buds were bursting open in the weak sunshine. At last new life was coming to these huge trees, which the interminable English winter had held transfixed for so long.

"Do you think Lord Burghley will speak to the Queen?" she ventured to ask.

"Certainly. I heard him say there was a fleet of eighty ships ready to put to sea—no one knows in what direction. M. de la Mothe Fenelon apparently heard about the fleet and told the Queen the French monarchy would be very annoyed if it was used to help the rebels."

"What did Elizabeth say?"

"Our sovereign is highly skilled at giving assurances without promising anything specific."

Victoire turned her grateful face to Lord Craighton. "I don't know how to show you how grateful I am to you."

"By coming to Cranmore as often as possible."

He took Victoire's hand and kissed it devotedly.

Toward the end of the afternoon Lord Burghley returned to London together with various other guests whose duties forced them to leave. The remaining guests were staying on until the following day.

Supper that evening was a far simpler and more relaxed meal, in the absence of the Queen's adviser. The assiduous Lord Craighton was able to devote most of the evening to Victoire, to Pemberley's great disappointment. Philippa was ensconced at one end of the salon, surrounded by her usual group of admirers. She appeared to be enjoying herself very much, as the frequent peals of laughter from the group showed. But despite appearances to the contrary, Victoire had the impression that she scarcely took her eyes off the couple formed by Victoire and her uncle.

"May I ask a favor of you?" asked Lord Craighton.

His gleaming eyes made Victoire a little uncomfortable. However, she replied, "Certainly, if it is in my power to grant it."

"Please, will you come back here to hunt next week?"

"I'd love to!" she cried, relieved. She had been half

expecting another type of request that she would not have felt able to grant.

Lord Craighton's face beamed with joy. "Your presence gives me untold happiness."

When the evening was over Victoire went up to her bedroom reflecting on the behavior of her hosts. Like the previous evening, she was escorted by John.

She had only just arrived in her room when she felt overcome by terrible exhaustion, and asked Nelly to undress her as quickly as possible. She could not understand why she suddenly felt so drowsy; her eyes were closing and all her limbs were sluggish. Nelly gently tucked in the covers, wished her good night, and retired noiselessly. Victoire sank into a strange state; she felt incapable of movement but remained fully conscious that her body was sometimes burning hot, sometimes freezing cold, and sometimes very heavy as though it had been crushed by an enormous weight. She was aware of strange feelings within her body, perhaps in her stomach or her abdomen. She began to twist about, tormented by terrible pains in her intestines; they quickly spread all over her body, as though she had fire running in her veins. She had no idea of the time, no idea how long she remained like this, incapable of getting up or calling for help. She cried out, but no sound passed her parched lips. Then, little by little, the shooting pains and the burning sensations subsided and finally disappeared, and a deep sleep overwhelmed her.

Chapter XIX

*L*ord Craighton had offered Victoire, Pemberley, and two other guests one of his coaches for the return journey. The horses moved forward slowly and with great difficulty in the pouring rain that had already soaked the roads and dug deep ruts through the mud. Victoire was feeling desperate at their slow pace; she had not yet fully recovered from her nightmare of the previous night.

She searched in vain to discover what could have made her so ill and caused her such pain. It had been far, far worse than anything she had ever felt before. She went through in her mind the food she had eaten the previous day, but could find nothing out of the ordinary.

She hadn't dared to tell anyone about what had happened, because she felt unable to explain to herself what had caused her such pain. By now she could no longer separate her dreams from the reality of the night; her nightmares and the pain had become inextricably confused in her mind. She was still quite certain she had felt so ill she thought she was dying, but would not have been able to describe what she had suffered in detail.

She remembered she had had a headache when she woke up, but it had gradually disappeared. She had gotten out of bed and breathed in deep gulps of fresh air at the window as though to rid herself of the foul memory of the night. Looking at herself in the mirror, she had been shocked to see her drawn features. Even after her imprisonment at Eglimont, her face had not looked so strained.

But for the moment Victoire only felt impatience. She wanted the interminable journey to be over so that she could climb into her bed at Madame Le Blachet's house. From time to time she tried to make some reply to Richard Pemberley's remarks. He had been talking to her ever since they left Cranmore, but she would have been quite incapable of saying what he was talking about. On one occasion, after the coach had jolted about violently and almost overturned, she again felt dizzy. But since she was sitting down, her companions did not notice anything.

"When shall I have the pleasure of seeing you again?" asked Pemberley hopefully.

He really was taking his role as her faithful admirer very seriously.

"Soon, no doubt," said Victoire, embarrassed at the attention her arrival was causing.

The coach had stopped in front of Madame Le Blachet's modest residence, and already a group of idlers and ragged children was forming about it. The poverty-stricken neighborhood rarely had the chance to see such a fine vehicle.

"Will you allow me to call on you tomorrow?"

"If you wish," Victoire conceded, wishing to get rid of her traveling companion as quickly as possible. If she still felt as bad tomorrow, she thought, she would send him a message that she couldn't receive him.

At last she was able to shut the door behind her. She leaned against the wall of the corridor that, with the small closet where they kept their cloaks and capes, was all the entrance hall the house could boast. She was at the end of her tether.

"Mon Dieu!" exclaimed Aloise, running up at the sound of the coach. "What's wrong with you?"

Victoire's legs had given way beneath her and she

sank down onto the floor, though without completely losing consciousness.

"Aunt! Come here quickly and help me carry Victoire to her room."

With great difficulty they lifted Victoire by themselves since the servant was too old to be of any help.

"Take her legs," ordered Aloise with sudden authority, taking hold of Victoire's shoulders.

Victoire did not even have strength enough to speak. She let herself be carried upstairs to bed like an inanimate object.

"What am I to do?" lamented Aloise.

"I'm cold," Victoire managed to whisper through her chattering teeth.

The old woman ran off to heat some water while Aloise undressed Victoire.

"Go and fetch all the blankets you can find," Aloise ordered her aunt.

Soon only Victoire's head could be seen above the covers. Aloise leaned toward her. "In the name of Heaven, what's happening?"

Victoire could barely make out her anguished face; it seemed to be surrounded by a kind of halo.

"I think I've been poisoned!"

When Victoire awoke from her semicomatose state, Madame Le Blachet was by her bedside, her worried face looking for the moment very like her sister's. Now that she was confronted with a serious situation, she faced up to it calmly. She no longer complained, but concentrated on being an efficient and sympathetic nurse.

Genevieve Le Blachet gently raised the sick girl's head and wet her lips with an infusion made of dried herbs she had brought with her from France and stored preciously for an emergency.

"I've called the doctor. I don't think he'll be long.

Do you remember eating any food that you thought had an unusual taste?"

"No, I don't think so," moaned Victoire.

"What did you have to drink?"

Suddenly something clicked in Victoire's mind. She saw the jug in her room at Cranmore. "The water," she murmured.

"Would anyone have reason to want to poison you?"

Who could desire her death? Victoire immediately thought of Philippa. But there was another possibility that couldn't be completely ruled out—M. de la Mothe Fenelon.

The doctor, an emigré from Lille, began to bleed Victoire almost as soon as he crossed the threshold, to Genevieve Le Blachet's silent disapproval. The immediate result of this treatment was to weaken the sick girl even further. Victoire had the impression her life was ebbing away together with the blood that flowed from her body into the basin, but she did not have the strength to protest.

"Mademoiselle de Montmaur has reason to think she may have been poisoned," said Madame Le Blachet timidly.

"It's possible, but highly unlikely," said the doctor in a peremptory tone.

He prescribed a potion to restore Victoire's strength, and went away very satisfied with himself. When Madame Le Blachet returned from seeing him to the door, she found Victoire unconscious.

"Aloise! Bring me some brandy!"

With the aid of her niece, Madame Le Blachet tried to pour a few drops of brandy between Victoire's set jaws.

"Is she going to die?" asked Aloise, her voice full of tears.

"Of course not, you little silly! She just fainted.

That stupid ass has exhausted her with his bleeding. Rub her feet. I'm sure they're icy."

"Yes, they are, despite all the blankets."

"She needs to be warmed from inside," murmured Madame Le Blachet.

Finally Victoire regained consciousness.

"You must take some nourishment, my child. I've had some chicken broth made for you."

Victoire obediently swallowed the scalding-hot liquid.

"I shan't have that doctor back again," said Madame Le Blachet. "I don't think he has any idea what's wrong. Bleeding is a ridiculous way of counteracting poison. But tell me, are you sure you've got rid of all the poison?"

"Do you mean . . .?"

"Yes," said Madame Le Blachet firmly. "Have you vomited?"

"Oh, no."

"Then you must!"

Her hostess sat up with her for most of the night and only went to bed herself at dawn, when she was sure Victoire was sleeping peacefully.

When Aloise entered Victoire's room the next morning, she shouted with joy to find her sitting up in bed. "You're better?"

"It looks very like it to me," said Victoire, smiling. "Though, of course, I still feel tired."

And yet she managed to get up, wash and tidy herself a little, and, with Aloise's help, put on a dress.

"Don't you think you ought to go back to bed? Aunt Genevieve won't be pleased to find you've gotten up."

"Don't worry. I'll take it easy."

She was determined to see Pemberley and ask him one or two questions. She must find out as quickly as possible who was responsible. It was a matter of life and death for her. There was nothing to prevent the would-be murderer from making another attempt. Pemberley was very young. He would give himself away in one way or another if he had had anything to do with the crime. She must prove herself clever enough to trip him up.

Pemberley arrived around three o'clock, elegantly dressed in a well-fitting raw silk, pale blue doublet braided with silver.

Victoire had taken care to place herself so that the light from the window fell on his face, while she herself remained in shadow and looked him full in the face.

"I was poisoned at Cranmore," she said directly.

Pemberley seemed flabbergasted. "My God! Can that be possible?"

"I almost died," went on Victoire without taking her eyes off him.

"But who was it?"

"I'm counting on you to help me find out . . . if you don't already know."

He looked sincerely surprised. "How should I know about it? What a terrible thing to do!"

"Isn't it?"

He remained silent for a few moments as though trying to convince himself of what she said. "That's a very serious accusation you're making," he said finally. "Are you quite sure?"

"Yes," said Victoire firmly. "I even know how it happened. Some powder had been added to the water in my jug."

"Why?" he murmured, overwhelmed. "Who would want to kill you?"

If he was acting, Pemberley was very good at it. By now Victoire was ready to swear he was innocent.

"I don't see which of the men . . ."

"Who said it was a man?" asked Victoire gently.

Pemberley's eyes opened wide in surprise, then a glimmer of understanding appeared in them.

"A woman. You're not thinking of Philippa?"

Victoire did not reply.

Chapter XX

*I*n the late afternoon Victoire heard the noise of a coach and went to the window to see. Usually only carts laden with goods went past their house. She saw Sir William Glanville struggling manfully through the mud, trying hard not to dirty his clothes, and her heart beat faster. Something important must have happened to bring him to this out-of-the-way quarter when they had arranged to meet two days later.

She was so impatient to find out that she ran down the wooden staircase without even glancing at herself in the mirror.

"What has happened?" she asked, still panting from her rapid descent.

Glanville smiled. "Lord Burghley seems to have succumbed to your charms. He has asked the Queen to grant you an audience."

"That's wonderful!" exclaimed Victoire.

"He painted the Queen a terrible picture of the suffering within La Rochelle and it seems to have impressed her."

"What did she say?"

"Oh, Her Majesty is not in the habit of compromising herself with ill-considered words or promises. She simply consented to receive you."

"Surely that's a great victory already!"

"Of course," said Glanville, smiling. "Nevertheless, the hardest part remains still to do. The Queen is quite ready to admit that the Huguenots in La Rochelle are undergoing terrible suffering, but it will be much more difficult to convince her that *she* must help them."

Victoire's elated mood disappeared.

"I wanted to give you the news so that you can be ready."

He was preparing to leave when Victoire detained him with a gesture. "I must tell you that someone has tried to do away with me."

Sir William's chubby face looked incredulous. "You?"

"Are you surprised?"

"I must admit I am. Do you suspect anyone?"

"It seems to me there are only two possibilities. Lord Craighton's niece, or one of the French Ambassador's men."

"Why should that charming girl, whom I have met on several occasions at her uncle's house, try to kill you?" asked Sir William.

Slightly embarrassed, she explained that Lady Philippa was doubtless very annoyed at her uncle's marked preference for Victoire herself.

He reacted in the same way as Pemberley. "She wouldn't go so far as to murder you! One of M. de la Mothe Fenelon's spies, on the other hand . . . If so, he hasn't wasted any time!"

"What would you advise me to do?"

"Not to leave this house, by God!"

"Lord Craighton has invited me to return to Cranmore. How can I refuse when he has been of such service to me?"

Glanville reflected, pulling at his reddish mustache with a vexed air.

"If you go there again, you will be in serious danger. In the midst of such a crowd of guests and servants, it would be only too easy for someone to add poison to your food without being seen. And you can't stay there without eating or drinking anything!"

"Suppose I announce I am leaving shortly?" Victoire suggested.

"That would very likely put Lady Philippa off the scent if she is involved, which I very much doubt. But I fear that strategy might be unsuccessful in the case of another enemy."

"And when do you think Her Majesty will receive me?" asked Victoire.

"Next week, no doubt. I'll let you know straightaway."

Night was falling and the room gradually filled with shadows. But Victoire sat on in her chair, weighing the arguments in favor of Lady Philippa or some unknown person as her would-be murderer.

The servant came in, hardly disturbing her train of thought. "You mustn't sit in the dark," she muttered. "It will give you gloomy thoughts."

She lit two candles, which dispelled only a few of the shadows, and then went out, leaving Victoire alone again to her thoughts.

Through the partly open door she could hear Madame Le Blachet and the servant preparing the evening meal, while Aloise was laying the kitchen table for supper. These homely noises reassured Victoire in a way that all Cranmore's luxury could not. As Sir William had quite rightly said, in this modest dwelling she was safe.

She was just getting up—it was nearly suppertime and she wanted to see if she could help in the kitchen—when a violent pain riveted her to her seat. She stopped herself from crying out, for she did not want to worry her hosts. For a few seconds she thought she was going to die in this shabby room in a foreign city, without ever seeing Guillaume again.

As though from very far away she heard someone come up to her, and a scarcely audible voice saying, "The soup is ready."

Not receiving any reply, Aloise came closer and went on: "Victoire, you must . . ."

Then she caught sight of Victoire's face, which was rigid as though carved out of stone, and her eyes empty of all expression, staring without seeming to see. "Aunt Genevieve, come quickly!"

Unable to utter a single word, Victoire watched the scene as though it didn't concern her at all. She heard the noise of a chair scraping on the floor, then the sound of a metal object falling onto the tiled kitchen floor as the two women rushed to help her. She was aware of their hands touching her and shaking her, but her body remained totally without feeling: she was paralyzed.

"Mon Dieu!" exclaimed Madame Le Blachet, distraught.

"What is it?" asked Aloise.

"The poison must still be in her body. I've heard there are some that are very difficult to get rid of. Whoever did this did not want to take any chances."

"Yes," whispered the servant. "Look at her eyes."

Suddenly, without any warning, Victoire was again able to move her limbs and to speak.

"It's over," she murmured incredulously.

"God be praised! How you frightened me!"

Victoire's mind gradually began to function normally.

Chapter XXI

*T*wo days went by without any further feeling of discomfort. Victoire's great day was now at hand: today she was to have her audience with the Queen. Through the intermediary of Lord Burghley, Her Majesty had intimated that she would receive the emissary from La Rochelle at Greenwich Palace, where she was currently in residence.

Now that the time to act was near, Victoire was haunted by the fear that when she found herself in the Queen's presence, she would be paralyzed with terror and unable to move or utter a word. She felt very apprehensive, too, about putting forward her case to such an enigmatic and all-powerful woman. What sort of person was Elizabeth really? she wondered. Was she a learned sovereign with a quick, intelligent mind capable of stimulating people to give of their best, whose reign had inaugurated a new era for England? Or was she a Queen still haunted by the memory of the little girl she had once been: whose father had had her mother executed, and had declared her herself to be illegitimate, though he had given her the same upbringing as her brother, the legitimate heir to the throne?

Surely she must feel a desperate need for revenge after all those childhood humiliations. After them had come yet more horrors: her imprisonment in the Tower of London on the orders of her fanatic sister whose mind was crazed with religious passion.

Victoire had thought for a moment of borrowing Madame Le Blachet's modest jewels for her visit to the Court, but then changed her mind. After all, her objective was to plead her cause with the Queen, not to make an effect on the Court.

She was trembling with emotion when, wearing her gold dress, she climbed into the coach where Sir William Glanvill was waiting. She waved good-by to her hosts, who were all very excitedly watching her departure from the doorstep. They had particularly wanted to see her off to Greenwich Palace and wish her good luck.

"You must help me to be brave," said Victoire. "I'm so frightened."

Glanville patted her hand in a fatherly way. "Pull yourself together," he said. "It will be all right. Her Majesty won't eat you. However, though she is well inclined toward you, thanks to Lord Burghley, it is by no means sure she will grant your request."

"I know that," sighed Victoire. "Especially if M. de la Mothe Fenelon interferes."

Victoire de Montmaur sank into a deep curtsey. When she at last dared to raise her eyes, she saw a woman of above-average height, rather thin, with a slightly olive skin and an oval face surrounded by a halo of curly reddish-blonde hair. The sovereign's small dark eyes were examining Victoire with interest mixed with curiosity. Then the thin lips, which she had vainly tried to enlarge with lipstick, opened. Much to Victoire's surprise, she spoke in a rich contralto voice. "Rise, Mademoiselle," she said. "And tell us why you have come into our presence."

The Queen spoke in fluent, though heavily accented French. Beside her stood Lord Burghley who gave Victoire an encouraging smile, obviously guessing how ill at ease she must feel.

About twenty ladies and courtiers were gathered in the vast room, whose windows looked out onto the gardens. Victoire was anxious to know whether the French Ambassador was present, but she didn't have the time to look around.

"Your Majesty," she began somewhat hesitantly. "I have come from La Rochelle to throw myself at your feet and beg your help for my unfortunate countrymen."

"Lord Burghley has described the suffering of the besieged citizens to us," said the Queen. "We are, of course, full of pity for those brave defenders of our faith."

"Alas, their strength is ebbing away with every day that passes. Without food, they will soon be unable even to hold their attackers at bay, however strong their courage. That is why I implore Your Majesty to come to their aid."

"Mademoiselle, you plead the cause of your people very well," said the Queen, without revealing in any way what effect Victoire's speech had made on her.

She turned toward her adviser. "My Lord, what is your opinion?" she said.

Lord Burghley answered in English and Victoire had the impression that he was supporting what she had said. The sovereign listened to him attentively and then said, "We shall examine his serious matter, Mademoiselle."

"I thank Your Majesty from my heart."

Victoire curtsied and left Greenwich Palace with Sir William Glanville.

"You see," said Sir William when they got into the coach, "Her Majesty was very pleasant."

"Indeed, but that is no proof I have succeeded."

"We shall soon be informed about that."

"I did not see M. de la Mothe Fenelon at Court," said Victoire hopefully.

"He himself was not present at the interview. However, he will hear all the details from Lady Ashbury, who is wholeheartedly in his service."

"So women spy for him as well," said Victoire indignantly.

Sir William's face broke into a slightly mocking smile. "And you yourself, my dear," he said. "Aren't you conspiring against the King of France?"

When she arrived back at Madame Le Blachet's house, Victoire had to report in full detail how the interview had gone, and describe Greenwich Palace and, of course, Her Majesty's appearance and dress.

"How lucky you are!" exclaimed Madame Le Blachet a little enviously. "Now you know both the King of France and the Queen of England."

"It must have been very awe-inspiring" said Aloise, who blushed when anyone looked at her.

"Yes, it was," admitted Victoire.

She had been quite convinced she would faint away when she found herself obliged to speak before the Queen and the assembled courtiers, all of them staring curiously at this unknown French girl who had dared to come to plead her cause before their Queen.

During the afternoon, Lord Craighton came to inquire what result his service to Victoire had had.

"Did my friend William Cecil prove cooperative as he had promised?"

"Indeed," said Victoire, to whom Glanville had translated the adviser's words. "I can never thank you enough for the support you have given me."

"If my modest efforts have been of help to you, I am quite content. You know there is nothing I wouldn't do for you," he murmured, looking at Victoire very tenderly. "You have conquered my hardened old heart, which is now wholly yours. I hope you will permit me to offer you a small token of my affections."

Victoire felt very ill at ease, and uncertain of how to react. She did not want to cause pain to this man who had been such a wonderful friend to her, but she did not want him to cherish impossible hopes about her. While she was hesitating, Lord Craighton opened a green morocco-leather jewel case with his arms on it, and took out a beautiful sapphire and diamond necklace.

Despite herself, Victoire exclaimed, "How beautiful it is!"

Lord Craighton smiled delightedly. "I am so pleased you like it," he said.

Victoire went on, regretfully, "I cannot accept such a magnificent present. It would not be right of me."

"My dear, I ask nothing of you in exchange," said Lord Craighton quickly. "Just your presence and the sound of your voice are all I desire."

Victoire hesitated. She was very tempted to accept. What would Uncle Anselme advise her to do? He would say she must refuse, she knew quite well. But how could she do that without offending Lord Craighton?

"Philippa must know this necklace exists. She would be surprised and perhaps indignant if . . ."

"My niece has nothing to do with this. Please do not imagine I encroach upon her rights in any way by giving you this present."

Lord Craighton fastened the necklace around Victoire's neck. "It suits you perfectly."

She decided to wear the gift at Cranmore, but when she left England she would discreetly return it to Lord Craighton. In this way she would have the pleasure of wearing the jewels without offending her own principles or giving false hopes to Lord Craighton.

"Don't forget I'm expecting you at Cranmore the day after tomorrow," said Lord Craighton as he said good-by. "I'll send Pemberley with a coach to fetch you."

"I am enchanted to be returning to your beautiful house."

Lord Craighton pressed her hand affectionately. "You have only to say the word and it will be yours."

Chapter XXII

"*Y*ou really are flagrantly neglecting me," said Pemberley somewhat sulkily. "I came to see you twice, but you were out both times."

Victoire laughed. "Richard, dear, you musn't be angry. You know quite well I had the honor of being received by Her Majesty."

"I also know you have been seen riding with Lord Craighton."

"I don't deny it."

"The whole of London is talking of nothing else but this hardened old bachelor's sudden passion for you."

"Really!" exclaimed Victoire in vexation.

This meant Philippa must have heard about it, too. If she was indeed responsible for the poisoning, she would stop at nothing to get rid of her rival when Victoire returned to Cranmore. The previous night, just before dawn, Victoire had again felt ill. The sensation had only lasted for a few seconds, but it had been so intolerable that Victoire had had to bite the sheet to stop herself from screaming with pain like an animal.

"Richard . . ."

She examined the young man's honest face as he sat opposite her, bouncing up and down like a ball on the upholstered velvet seat as the coach jolted along.

Could she completely trust him? He seemed loyal and brave, but she had known him only a short time. She absolutely needed an ally on the spot. On her own she would never be able to get her hands on the fatal drug that was gradually undermining her strength.

"Yes?" He looked at her with a questioning and slightly worried air. "Have you felt ill again?"

"Richard, I am in danger of death. Are you willing to help me?"

"I think you'd better tell me what's happening."

"The other day I told you I thought I was being poisoned."

"Has it happened again?"

"No, not exactly."

She told him of her sufferings.

"Of course, I've *heard* about that kind of thing," cried Pemberley incredulously. "But I always thought it was all old wives' tales."

"I must admit that until now I had no personal knowledge of this type of thing either. However, the evidence is overwhelming."

"That's true," murmured Pemberley. "So how can *I* be of help?"

"As I told you, I must get my hands on the poison, which, if my suspicions are correct, will be in Philippa's room."

"And suppose it isn't there?"

"Then we'll have to look elsewhere. Perhaps we won't find it in time. Of course, I count on your absolute discretion."

"I can't understand why you don't inform Lord Craighton about the actions of this . . . this . . ."

"What if I am wrong?" said Victoire. "For the moment I have no proof at all. How can I accuse our host's niece?" Silently she pondered the possibility that the culprit might not be Philippa at all, but the French Ambassador. That would be a much more difficult and dangerous thing to prove.

The sun was shining when they reached Cranmore. In other circumstances Victoire would have been thrilled to watch the English countryside awaken from its long winter sleep, and to stay in a residence where everything was calculated to please and amuse the guests fortunate enough to be invited there.

She was given the same room as before, presided over by her guardian angel, the melancholy Lady Mary. John placed her chest in the corner of the room. As he straightened up again, she was struck by his intelligent face and his obvious desire to please her. Perhaps she could ask his help. But how could she explain to him what was happening?

Philippa was often haughty and arrogant with the servants, and they obviously felt little affection for her. Victoire had often caught glimpses of looks and smiles that explained eloquently enough how they felt about their young mistress.

"Can I help Your Grace with anything?"

Before Nelly, whose hurried footsteps could be heard approaching along the corridor, came into the room, Victoire said very quickly, "Yes."

He must have realized from her tone that she had a somewhat unusual service to ask of him. "What?" he whispered.

"Tonight."

He nodded assent and then retired, and in came Nelly, who was obviously delighted to see Victoire again. She launched into a long monologue as she unpacked.

Victoire got ready for supper halfheartedly and resigned herself to wearing the necklace, despite the danger it might lead to. She hoped that it was at least not part of the family jewels. How would Philippa react when she saw a stranger wearing jewels that she quite justifiably expected would be hers one day?

That evening there were only about fifteen guests present, so they used a smaller, warmer, and more intimate salon. The other guests were due to arrive the following day.

Dressed all in yellow, Philippa came forward to greet Victoire. Immediately her attention was caught by the necklace, but she took care not to mention it.

"What a pleasure to see you!" she said in her most gracious tone.

Her excessive kindness put Victoire on the defensive. "The pleasure is all mine," she replied.

After this exchange of civilities, Philippa returned to her circle of suitors, who were still waiting patiently for her to decide on one of them.

"I'm pleased to see you and my niece have become friends," said Lord Craighton.

It was not for the first time that Victoire was amazed at how naive men could be. They were really incapable of seeing anything, she reflected. She would do all she could to preserve Lord Craighton's illusions. If possible, she would keep from him that the girl he had brought up as his own daughter was evil.

Only too soon the moment came when the company retired to rest after the day's exertions. Lord Craighton, who had had eyes only for Victoire all evening, said to her with such visible tenderness that it must be obvious to everyone around, "Sleep well, my dear, so that you can be in top form tomorrow morning. If you like, we can take a gallop together to a part of the forest you haven't visited yet, close by the lakes. The scenery is particularly beautiful there at this time of year."

"Willingly."

Philippa was standing alongside, taking leave of her suitors. Victoire was sure she was watching and straining her ears to catch every word that passed between Victoire and her uncle, though she went on talking gaily.

As she said good night, Philippa gave her a nasty

smile. This time there could be no possible doubt: her smile amounted to a declaration of war.

"Well, I wish you a very good night," she said with a challenging air that made Victoire fear the worst. "What a lovely necklace you're wearing! I don't remember seeing it before."

Victoire was ready. "I had to take it to the jeweler's to have the catch mended," she explained as naturally as possible.

"Let's hope it has been properly mended, and that you won't lose it!"

Victoire realized that, whether or not she recognized the necklace, Philippa had in any case guessed who had given it to Victoire, and she was furious with rage. Victoire could not hope for more than an hour's respite, while the other guests were getting ready for bed, before her enemy launched another and more terrible attack that might well kill her victim on the spot.

In the antechamber the footmen were waiting with torches to conduct the guests back to their rooms through Cranmore's maze of corridors and staircases. Among them Victoire was relieved to see John's familiar face.

When they reached her room she signaled to John to shut the door. She had at the most a few short minutes before Nelly arrived. And in that time she had to explain to John the very complex situation in which she found herself, in a language she couldn't even speak!

She led him over to the desk and drew a rough outline of a woman. John watched her attentively, but he obviously had no idea what she was leading up to.

"It's me," she said.

He looked at her questioningly.

She took some water from the jug and pretended to drink it. Then she clutched her stomach and simulated writhing in agony.

From his fiercely concentrating expression Victoire could see that John was trying hard to see what all this meant. She then pierced the drawing's heart, saying, "Danger! Death!"

A flicker of understanding showed in his eyes. Victoire was relieved to see he was beginning to understand.

"Death," he repeated thoughtfully. Still fumbling to understand, he tasted the brackish water. Suddenly he realized what Victoire was trying to explain. His face went white. "God!" he said in a terrified voice.

Then a moment later he asked, "Who?"

"Lady Philippa."

When he heard this name, John reacted immediately and violently. His normally mild, peaceful features contracted into an expression of ferocious hatred, and he spat out some words in a voice which left no doubt about his feelings.

Victoire breathed again. She had succeeded in her plan. Now all that remained was to explain to him that he must get hold of the drug as soon as possible.

She took the drawing of herself and hid it, successively, in a drawer, under her pillow, and inside a vase, watching her would-be accomplice's face all the while. Then she grabbed hold of his hand, gave him the drawing, and had him hand it to her. Then she tore it up, saying as she did so, "No death."

He nodded. "Lady Philippa," she said again.

Then he explained to her in gestures that what she was asking was very difficult, but that he would try the following day when Philippa was out.

Chapter XXIII

She would not drink the water in her room, but who knew to what other means Philippa might resort? Trembling with apprehension, Victoire got into bed and asked Nelly to leave her the candle. She felt she would be less frightened than in total darkness. Tonight there was not even a moon to reassure her.

She lay there, unable to sleep, her body tense with expectation, as the house gradually sank into silence around her. At the slightest noise in the walls or the wooden floor she jumped. She imagined she heard a scratching noise in the small room that separated her bedroom from the corridor. Was it only a mouse foraging for food, or was someone trying to get into her room?

Perhaps Philippa might send someone to strangle or suffocate her with the pillow.

Nelly entered the room, and with her came the bright sunlight. It hurt Victoire's eyes so much that she hid her head under the sheets. She had only just dropped off to sleep and felt no desire at all to get up, much less to go riding. For the moment she was quite incapable of movement.

If she could only doze off for a few hours, she might feel sufficiently recovered to come down to lunch, though for the moment the idea of eating made her feel sick. She wrote a short note to her host, which the chambermaid delivered, apologizing for not being able to ride to the lakes with him.

She was just thinking about Pemberley, who had apparently not been at all worried about her the previous night, when he appeared in the doorway, inquiring how she was.

"I might have died a hundred times during the night," she said to him with an edge of bitterness in her voice.

He seemed quite sincerely upset. "Why did you not call me?" he said.

"I couldn't. You would never have heard me."

He had only just left when Lord Craighton was announced. Victoire had to receive him, though all she wanted was to sleep. "Nelly tells me you are ill," he said worriedly.

"No, not at all, although recently I've had a recurring pain from an old injury. I just feel a little tired."

"I'm so sorry. We'll go riding another day. I have asked Doctor Jacobson to come and see you. You must have seen him about the house."

"It really isn't necessary."

"Oh, yes, Philippa insisted on that."

A skinny little man appeared in the doorway. He had a hunched back that gave him an appearance of humility, though this was false, Victoire quickly realized.

"I'll leave you," said Lord Craighton. "Doctor Jacobson speaks a little French."

Victoire felt a sudden and violent aversion toward the doctor. She profoundly disliked his two-faced expression and his obsequious manner. How could Lord Craighton possibly have chosen a man like him to watch over the health of the inhabitants of Cranmore?

"So you have been indisposed?"

How did he know? she wondered. "Yes," she said, suddenly suspicious.

"Pains in the intestine, a burning feeling?"

He described her sufferings in detail before she herself had said anything at all about them. His small cruel eyes stared at her insistently, as though he were making sure the treatment was having the desired effect. She detected a hint of disappointment that his victim was still in fairly good health.

She sat up straight in the bed and stared defiantly at him. "Lady Philippa is really too kind to trouble herself about me."

Doctor Jacobson began to stammer incomprehensibly.

"You can tell her that I am very well, except that I feel slightly tired. That's quite natural, surely?"

Realizing that Victoire had seen right through him, the doctor lost face completely.

She dismissed him without ceremony. "I don't need your services anymore," she said.

Philippa's messenger backed out of the room, bowing at each step, and visibly put out that the drug had not been more successful.

Doctor Jacobson's visit left Victoire so wild with fury against Philippa that she found it impossible to rest at all. The doctor would doubtless hurry to warn Philippa of their failure. Victoire could expect a new attack very shortly. There were so many opportunities of contaminating her food without being detected. She feared the next time she would not be able to hold out against it, since she had not completely recovered from the earlier dose.

Despite her tiredness she decided to get up and look for John. Nelly came in to help her dress and do her hair. In the meanwhile, Victoire tried hard to compose her face. She wanted to look as resplendently healthy as possible to prove to Philippa that the poison was of little avail. Her uncle's now overt passion for Victoire must exasperate her the more since she knew quite well there were no real obstacles to their union: they were both free, and of the same religion.

Victoire found out where Philippa's suite was. With luck John would be somewhere near, watching for an opportunity to get in without attracting the attention of the other domestic staff. Since he was not attached to Philippa's service, he had no valid reason to enter her room. Nor had Victoire any reason to be in that part of the house. Whenever a servant went past, she pretended to be admiring the pictures. Finally John came, and she looked at him questioningly.

"Nothing," he said with a depressed air.

"Jacobson," she said, to warn him to watch out for the sinister doctor.

The name seemed to give him an idea, for he shot off like an arrow from a bow to the other end of the corridor, gesturing to her to wait. Very anxiously, she kept watch up and down the gallery, fearing that at any moment Philippa or one of her followers might appear.

Hearing a noise, she hid behind the curtains in a window recess. A couple was coming toward her, clasped tenderly in each other's arms. She recognized one of Philippa's friends and one of her suitors. They stopped for a moment, made sure the gallery was deserted, and embraced at length. Then they went on, to Victoire's great relief.

After an interminable wait she heard hurried and yet cautious footsteps. It was John. She saw at once from his radiant face that he had been successful.

"I've got it!" he exclaimed. He held out a small package of powder.

Though she was unable to express her infinite gratitude in words, she took hold of John's hand and squeezed it hard. She searched hard for some words to describe her feelings and finally managed to get out, with an awful accent, "You save my life!"

Chapter XXIV

"*Well?*" demanded Madame Le Blachet, in a state of great excitement.

Before the coach had even drawn up before the house, she had rushed out onto the doorstep in her slippers with her bonnet on sideways.

"I'll tell you everything," promised Victoire, smiling. "But first of all, give me five minutes to straighten myself up."

She felt in high good humor, although during the coach journey, for the first time in her life she had felt her stomach was a little upset. But this was probably the result of too much self-indulgence at the lavish hunting banquet the previous evening.

Holding the packet tightly in her pocket, she had gloried in her victory in front of Philippa, until the moment when she realized that her enemy could quite easily get more with Doctor Jacobson's help, and begin her wicked spells again. But then when she saw Philippa's distraught face as she greeted the guests at suppertime, Victoire realized that she had nothing more to fear from her.

She continued to be wary, however. Though Philippa was beaten she was still dangerous. Her bitterness might lead her to find some other, more rapid, way of getting rid of her rival. The hangers-on at Cranmore had sized up the situation and Victoire quickly found herself the center of her own small court of admirers. Though she still could not understand their words, their intentions were all too clear. They had concluded she would soon be the mistress of Cranmore, and to her great amusement, they were all eager to establish a place for themselves in her favor. They would be very disappointed. The high point came at the end of the evening when the proud Lady Philippa came humbly up to her.

"You won't say anything to my uncle?" she begged, wringing her hands. She knew well that Victoire could easily have had her resoundingly banished from Cranmore forever. "I'll do anything you want in future."

Sickened that she could sink so low, Victoire allowed herself the luxury of replying, "I'll see."

The following day, when she had gotten her emotions under control, Victoire went to see Sir William Glanville.

"Well," she said, "have you had any news?"

Sir William's face creased into a huge grin. "Our affairs, or rather yours, seem to be progressing very well," he said. "Lord Burghley has informed me that it is now certain a fleet will be sent to help the besieged city."

"How marvelous!" exclaimed Victoire.

After so many ordeals and so much suffering, she had managed to attain her objective. Out of curiosity she asked, "And what has happened about the idea of Her Majesty marrying the Duc d'Alençon?"

"Oh! that match was only part of a remarkable series of projects thought up by Catherine de Medici. She wanted to make the Duc d'Anjou King of Poland, and see the Duc d'Alençon established in England. This would have considerably strengthened His Majesty Charles IX's position."

"How?"

"Well, Charles would then be the Emperor's son-in-law, the brother of the King of Poland, and the brother-in-law of both the Queen of England and the King of Navarre. Just imagine how all those alliances could be brought into play against Philip II's diplomacy!"

Once she was reassured about the fate of La Rochelle, Victoire began to get ready to leave London.

After more than four months' separation from him, she was very much looking forward to seeing her uncle again and telling him about her adventures, including the most recent: a proposal of marriage from Lord Craighton.

At first Victoire could not see how she was to get out of this difficult situation without causing pain. Lord Craighton was passionately in love with her, and for the first time in his life, it seemed.

"You know how very fond I am of you," said Victoire. "And how grateful I am for all your kindness to me."

"You could make me so happy. You only have to say the word."

"Your proposal both honors and touches me. But I regret to say that I am already engaged to another. There is a sacred bond between us. My heart is not free, although I esteem and admire you immensely and am very honored at your asking my hand."

"Is there no hope?" exclaimed Lord Craighton in despair.

"Alas," she said very gently, "no."

"Victoire, I love you so much. I cannot agree to lose you in this way! I'll go to see your uncle and . . ."

"It is useless," said Victoire firmly. "I'm truly deeply sorry."

She hated to see him suffer so because of her. It was not her fault that she still loved Guillaume so desperately, and preferred above all else to cherish the hope that one day he might love her in return.

Pemberley too came to say good-bye to Victoire. She

asked him to return the necklace discreetly to Lord Craighton after she had left England.

"You ought to keep it."

"That would be dishonest of me. He gave it to me, hoping to marry me. He will present it to the woman who will one day become his wife."

"He won't forget you as quickly as that!"

"More quickly than you think. Now that he has once had the idea of taking flight from the nest, he'll soon do so . . . but with someone else. Philippa will have to get used to the idea of having an aunt."

Then it was time to take her leave of Genevieve Le Blachet. She too was in despair that Victoire was leaving. Once again Victoire urged her to gather the other exiles around her in London.

"I could never manage that alone!"

"Aloise will help you."

"Of course," said Aloise. "We must do something."

Victoire invited the whole family to stay at Montmaur, and then tore herself away. It was time to get into the coach.

She found a boat without any difficulty at Dover. During the crossing she at last became quite certain of something she had for some time been suspecting: she was expecting a child.

Chapter XXV

T hroughout the return journey Victoire's thoughts kept turning to the child she was to bear. Since she had given herself to Guillaume de Louvencourt the day before the Saint Bartholomew Night massacre, she had known she ran the risk of pregnancy. But her fear had remained at an abstract level. It was quite another thing to be faced with the reality of a child.

She was so glad now that she had heeded her innermost instincts when they told her not to give herself to Guy after her escape from La Rochelle. Otherwise she would not now have been sure which of the two men was the father of her child. But now she could be quite certain that she had conceived this child with Guillaume during the three nights they had spent together at La Chaudrée.

She was not as yet quite sure what she felt about this child yet to be born, who had intruded himself so suddenly into her life. For the moment, she was mainly worried about how Uncle Anselme would react to the news. She decided not to spoil their reunion by telling him immediately, though she would have to break the news to him sooner or later.

As soon as she stepped onto French soil again, Lord Craighton, Philippa, Pemberley, and all her English acquaintance, who had been so important in her life during the past few weeks, began to fade from her memory. She had no regrets at all at turning to a new page in her life, particularly since the day before she left England she had been told the fleet had set sail for La Rochelle. Now her duty was done, and she could concentrate on her own future. At the moment it looked none too rosy. She could see no alternative for herself but to return to Montmaur and embark on a retired life there with her old uncle—and very soon a little child. She could at least devote her energies to making money from livestock rearing, and use the proceeds to repair the tumble-down old château.

Despite this gloomy perspective, as she came closer to her home and began to hear the accent of her native region spoken around her, Victoire felt impatient to see Montmaur again. There no danger would threaten her. Perhaps later on she could set off again for some new adventures.

At first sight nothing seemed to have changed since she left Montmaur. But as she came closer she was delighted to see that the château was looking much more prosperous: the roof and the courtyard had been repaired, and the moss had been cleaned off the old flight of steps that led up to the front door. She resolved to congratulate her steward for his good work during her absence.

Anselme rushed out of the house at her approach, and Victoire ran into his embrace. How sweet it was to feel herself again warmed by the old man's watchful affection, and to see the joy lighting up his face!

"I have been so terribly worried about you," he admitted at once.

He never seemed to tire of looking at his niece, as though he could not quite believe she was indeed there before him, radiant with youth and good health.

"All that is over now," she assured him, smiling.

"I hope we shall never be separated again. It was so upsetting not to have any news of you, not even to know whether you were still alive."

"Didn't you get my letter?"

"Yes. But it didn't reassure me very much to think of you all alone in England!"

"I saw the Queen while I was there!"

"I shall want to hear about all that later. Now you must go and rest after your journey."

"I'm not tired. First of all I want to inspect the property," she said, smiling.

She couldn't wait any longer to stroke Aloès, count up the ducks and chickens, and embrace Marguerite, who had been present when she was born. She wanted to run everywhere at once, to take possession of her own home again, to breathe in the air of Montmaur that smelled so sweet on this wonderful May day.

"Well, then, I'm coming with you. I'm not going to let you out of my sight again."

They set off together, but before they had even gotten as far as the stables, all Victoire's good resolutions flew to the winds. "Uncle Anselme," she said. "I've something to confess."

The old man stopped short with a worried look. "Is it serious?"

"*Very* serious."

"What are you making all this mystery about?"

"You're going to be a great-uncle."

Anselme stared at his niece, completely dumbfounded. He seemed not to have taken in what she said at all.

"You mean that . . ."

"I'm expecting a child."

"Oh, my goodness! Who's the father?"

"Guillaume de Louvencourt."

"I didn't know you'd seen him again."

"Before I left for England."

Oddly enough, the Comte de Montmaur did not seem very angry at Victoire's news, though he did seem rather put out.

"You're not too angry at me?" asked Victoire timidly.

"I know I *should* be," sighed Anselme. "But I don't have the courage to be angry. What do you intend to do when the child is born?"

"Bring him up."

"Well, then, I'll help you. If it's a boy . . ."

"You're really quite pleased, aren't you? Admit it," Victoire interrupted.

"I would have preferred you to have a husband all the same. What are people going to say around here?"

Since Victoire had left, the keepers had taken great care looking after the livestock entrusted to their care. Victoire was surprised and pleased to see dozens of chickens and ducks contentedly clucking in the poultry yard.

"We get twelve dozen eggs a week," said Justine proudly. "Some young ones have hatched. Look!" In another enclosure, protected from the wind with bales of straw, she showed Victoire about a hundred young chickens just out of the egg, staggering about on their shaky legs, covered with soft ruffled down.

"They're four days old."

Victoire was thrilled. "We could sell some at the market."

"Yes, we could. We've already sold some eggs. And with what we earned we bought some more ducks," said Justine, adding hastily, "after first asking the Comte for his permission, of course!"

"You have done very well."

"It all makes a lot of work," groaned Justine, who was not in her first youth and often complained of her "aches".

"Of course," said Victoire thoughtfully. "You need a young girl to help you."

She wanted to count up how much money she had left. While she was in England she had spent most of the money Jacques Henri had given her. But she had hardly touched the money given her by the Marquis de

Hautemart, which he had implied she could keep. She felt this was a suitable time to carry out her long-standing ambition to rear sheep.

"Does the idea seem reasonable to you?" she asked her uncle.

"My dear, I cannot advise you. I have no experience in that kind of thing."

"Neither have I!" exclaimed Victoire.

"Oh, you're different!" said Anselme, smiling. "I really believe you would make a success of anything you took on."

"Well, then, we'll buy a few sheep and a ram. We can sell the skins."

"And where will you graze the animals? They'll need quite a lot of room."

"What do you think of that small meadow low down, close to the Caloire? Godefroy could fence part of it off."

"That will be fine for the summer. But you'll need to bring them indoors in the winter."

"That's the problem," said Victoire. "We'd need to build a stable."

"You do run ahead so quickly!"

"If we don't get started on something, you know quite well we shall be paupers soon."

"Don't exaggerate. Queen Catherine's gold has been used to have the roof done, and some other urgent work. There is still some left."

"How much?" asked Victoire, rapidly calculating how much a stable was likely to cost.

"Oh, don't ask me that kind of question!" cried Anselme. "I don't want to get involved in the accounts. That's your responsibility from now on. Take the money and do what you like with it."

"That's very good of you, Uncle."

"Not really," sighed the old man. "I should so much like to end my days here."

"Where else would you think of going, anyway?"

"We shall have to go back to Paris again one day."

"I'm not particularly anxious to do that! It would mean seeing the Queen again."

M. de la Mothe Fenelon surely must have told Queen Catherine what she had been up to in England.

"Anyway, you must try to put some money aside for the child," added Anselme grumpily. "He'll need a horse."

Victoire burst out laughing and threw her arms around her uncle's neck. "I think that can wait a few years. And by then, who knows?"

At the beginning of June a rumor reached the village of Montmaur that an English fleet had tried to force the blockade just off La Rochelle. Two royal men-of-war had attacked the English, and the English fleet had had to raise anchor without being able to disembark provisions for the city.

Victoire lamented to think of the danger she had been through to achieve such a miserable result. It must have been small comfort to the besieged to see help being snatched away from under their noses.

On May 26 the Duc d'Anjou had ordered a major attack, trying to scale the walls using Swiss mercenaries, while the royal fleet bombarded the harbor. The attack failed.

Two days later came confirmation that the King's brother had been elected King of Poland. But La Rochelle had still not been taken.

"If the Duc d'Anjou leaves the siege without taking the city, his prestige will suffer," remarked Anselme.

"If I know the people of La Rochelle, they will persist to hold out."

"If they can for just a little longer, a compromise solution will have to be found."

At the end of June they learned that on the 12th the King of Poland had tried to take La Rochelle simultaneously in two places, the Boulevard de l'Evangile and the Vieille Fontaine. This attack had been no more successful than all the others. The Poles were getting impatient for their King to arrive, so it was decided talks must take place. The Duc d'Anjou sent emissaries to negotiate with the besieged city.

On June 18 a peace treaty was signed with the Huguenots. The latter were to retain three strongholds: La Rochelle, Nîmes, and Montauban. Moreover, they were allowed freedom of their religion throughout France, and the right to retain their goods and charges. Victoire prayed fervently that peace had been achieved at last!

Chapter XXVI

*T*he summer went by without any very important or dramatic developments in the world outside Montmaur. On July 6 the peace treaty was ratified by the Edict of Boulogne, and on August 19 the Polish Ambassador arrived in Paris, to be welcomed with lavish celebrations.

Victoire showed her pregnancy more visibly and had to give up riding, which was her only amusement at Montmaur. She began to get very bored. Even the sight of her sheep grazing peacefully in their meadow was not enough to occupy her.

Victoire's child was born shortly after All Saints' Day. When she looked at Guillaume's son for the first time, she said, "I want him to be a scholar."

"Book learning is not enough," said Anselme. "In order to achieve happiness a human being must be complete. The education of the mind and that of the body are two essential and complementary parts of the whole man."

He inspected his great-nephew and was happy to see how delighted Victoire was that her child looked so like Guillaume. And now he regretted never having had any children of his own.

Victoire, well aware of his mixed feelings—reflected clearly in his melancholy look—declared, "Since he has no father, I hope you'll take his place."

"What will you call him?" Anselme asked, trying to fight back his tears.

"Emeric, after my own father."

Soon after his birth they had an unexpected visit from the Vidame de Barville, who was traveling to Albi and asked if they would put him up for the night, which they were delighted to do. The Vidame had just come from Paris and knew all the latest Court gossip, which he was very happy to pass on to his friends.

"Tell us about the Polish Ambassador," said Victoire. "What are these foreigners like?"

The Vidame smiled. "I don't think His Majesty the King of Poland was exactly thrilled when he saw his new subjects. They shave their necks, wear mustaches and long blond beards, and walk about in gold-embroidered dresses with scimitars at their side. Can you imagine that?

"There were great celebrations in their honor, with balls, tournaments, and illuminations," went on the Vidame. "Despite being in poor health—he's now spitting blood quite often—the King received them with the two Queens, his mother and his wife, the Duc d'Alençon, and the King and Queen of Navarre. Laski made a speech in Latin to which the Queen of Navarre replied most elegantly."

"And what has happened at Court?"

"The Duc d'Alençon almost died of typhoid, though he did not let this stop him from claiming the position of Lieutenant-General of the kingdom in place of the Duc d'Anjou. But the King refused to grant him the post. His Majesty declared to the Council that if he died without children, the King of Poland should succeed him. The King of Poland himself seems in no hurry to set off for his new kingdom. The Ambassador left without him in September: the Duc claimed he had not finished his preparations for the journey. People are saying the King is impatient to get rid of his brother, and is furious he is taking so long to go. But the Duc cannot tear himself away from Marie de Condé."

"I saw her at Court," said Victoire. "She's very beautiful."

"Finally His Majesty forced the King of Poland to leave, and personally accompanied him as far as Vitry-le-François, where King Charles caught smallpox!"

"And is the Duc d'Anjou not afraid that his brother the Duc d'Alençon will seize the throne if the King dies when he is away?" asked Anselme.

"That might well happen. Monseigneur is very active. He's trying to ally himself with the Bourbons, it seems. The Guise, of course, would be very pleased to be left alone at the head of the Catholic party."

"In short, everyone seems pleased the Duc d'Anjou has gone, except the Duc himself," Victoire concluded. "Has he already arrived in Poland?"

"Not at all, far from it!" cried the Vidame. "Though it's true you can't travel very quickly with a train of five hundred people. At present he must be breaking his journey with his sister the Duchesse of Lorraine in Nancy. Alexandre d'Hautemart was saying to me only the other day . . ."

Anselme interrupted him, "Talking about Alexandre,

I must tell you I am very angry with him for leading Victoire into so many terrible dangers."

"Yes, I've heard some of them from Guy Becavallo."

"You don't mean Guy is still alive?" cried Victoire excitedly.

"He is indeed," said the Vidame calmly. "I saw him less than a fortnight ago."

Victoire felt deliriously happy to think that Guy had managed to escape from Eglimont. She had so often reproached herself for causing his death.

"Becavallo was worrying about you, Mademoiselle," said the Vidame, who had not been told about Emeric. "When I return I shall be able to reassure him that you have never looked more beautiful."

The Vidame's visit and his news from Paris left Victoire feeling disturbed and dissatisfied, even though she had resumed her normal way of life again and had the satisfaction of seeing her sheep safely in their fine new stable before the winter. To add to her discontent, the winter promised to be a hard one. And now that Victoire's son was safely born, she found her thoughts turning increasingly to Guillaume. She did not even have any definite information about what had happened to him. He must have left La Rochelle several months ago, she supposed, unless, of course, he had been killed during the siege, like so many thousands of others. Had he, she wondered, returned to his native Lorraine, or was he still at Court, a prey to its many temptations? Perhaps he had forgotten all about Victoire and the time they had spent together at La Chaudrée. He could have no idea what important consequences their time together had had for her.

Victoire decided that if ever she saw him again, she would not tell him about Emeric. She did not want him to feel obliged to marry her in order to recognize the child. She would have nothing to do with that type of marriage. If Guillaume ever returned to her, he must do so of his own free will.

Anselme was fully aware of Victoire's gloomy mood, and did all he could to amuse her. But he could not give her what she needed most: a young man to share her life.

The old château rarely heard Victoire's cheerful laughter. Instead, she sighed heavily to herself as she sat by the fire in the evening, when her uncle tried to cheer her up with amusing stories.

Victoire realized her uncle was attempting to pull her out of her unhappiness and made great efforts to hide her sadness during the dark winter days when it rained so much she could not even go out with Aloès. At five o'clock it was already dark, and they had to light the candles and settle down by a big fire for the evening. Then they would eat a light supper and wait until the time came to retire for the night. Victoire would kiss her son good night and then go to her snug room from which all the insidious winter drafts had been shut out.

One day Anselme finally plucked up his courage and said to Victoire, "This isn't a very gay life for you, my dear."

"I'm very happy to be with you."

"But at your age you need amusement."

He was almost relieved when one evening a messenger appeared with a letter from Queen Catherine saying she would like the Comte de Montmaur and his niece to present themselves at Court.

"It seems to me it's more an order than an invitation," said Victoire, suddenly apprehensive.

"I'm sure of it!"

"I wouldn't have thought Her Majesty would have remembered two poor people like us from such a distant province."

"She never forgets anyone, or what they can do to carry out her plans. It would appear, Victoire, that she remembers you from the days at Court and knows about everything you have done since then. I suspect she has plans to use you now for her own purposes."

Chapter XXVII

*T*he messenger left, bearing a promise from the Comte de Montmaur and his niece that they would set off for Paris as soon as possible. But there was so much to do before they could leave. The vases and carafes which Anselme had made for the Queen's favorite château at Saint-Maur had to be wrapped up very carefully. And, of course, they had to make arrangements about Emeric.

"I'm very apprehensive about taking him," said Victoire. "He's so tiny."

"If I were you, I wouldn't risk taking him on such a long and tiring journey in this bitter December weather. He would be better off here, where he has plenty of people to look after him."

"You're quite right, of course," said Victoire, though she was sad to be leaving Emeric behind.

After their initial surprise when it became obvious that Mademoiselle de Montmaur was expecting a child, the staff at the château—who adored her—had made the best of the situation. Marguerite and Jacotte had made some swaddling clothes out of old sheets, and Godefroy, who was very skillful with his hands, had made a wicker cradle. Honoré had tanned the hide of the first sheep they had slaughtered to make the baby a warm bedcover. So Victoire knew she would be leaving her son in good hands. If she was still at Court when spring came, she would send for him.

Just now her feelings were very mixed. She had exhausted Montmaur's resources for the moment, so she felt pleased to be leaving, though she still loved the place as much as ever. Quite naturally she hoped she would meet Guillaume again in Paris, but at the same time she felt very apprehensive about facing the Queen Mother. The sovereign was bound to consider her actions in England as treason.

These anxious feelings, which sometimes woke her up in the middle of the night, did not prevent Victoire from organizing their departure as efficiently as possible. She conferred at length with the steward and examined the accounts, noting with secret pride that they were now making quite considerable profits from poultry rearing.

"The sheep will begin to be profitable next year," he said. "And then, of course, you will be receiving your farm rents."

All this added up to quite a reasonable amount of money by local standards, but in Paris it would not go very far. Life was so expensive there and money seemed to disappear like magic.

"I don't want to live in the Louvre," said Victoire to Anselme. "I have such awful memories of it."

"I've already written to our friend Alexandre to ask him to put us up when we arrive. He owes us that at least!"

Victoire found the idea of returning to live in the Marquis d'Hautemart's magnificent residence very attractive. She would have all the comfort of Cranmore, without Philippa's unpleasant presence.

Godefroy polished the old coach, and Léon took the horses to be shod. Jacotte, who was to accompany them, packed her mistress's dresses in chests while Marguerite prepared food for the journey. These busy preparations reminded Victoire of the first time they had set out for Court. What a lot of changes had taken place in her life since then. She refused to anticipate the changes this visit could bring.

At last it was time to climb into the coach, which Godefroy had polished so hard that it looked quite respectable. Victoire and Anselme got inside, together with Jacotte, who was delighted at the prospect of seeing Paris.

Léon and Godefroy climbed up onto the box. Emeric and his nurse came to say good-by, then came the steward, who promised to send regular news about Montmaur, the people, the animals, and the land. Then Léon cracked his whip and they trotted through the gate.

"I do hope nothing happens to Emeric," sighed Victoire.

"You can be quite sure he won't lack for anything," said Anselme. "Though he may be a little spoiled from having his every whim satisfied."

Victoire smiled, almost reassured. "You're right. I would do better to worry about how the Queen will receive me."

"You will have plenty of time to get upset about that in Paris. Why think about it now?"

"I just hope she doesn't take it into her head again to enlist me as one of her maids of honor! I wouldn't want to, yet I'd have no way of refusing."

"I understand your feelings," said Anselme. "Though personally I take great pleasure in making for her what she is kind enough to call works of art. No one appreciates careful workmanship like she does."

The two travelers fell silent, each deep in their own thoughts as the coach bumped painfully forward over a badly surfaced road.

"I wonder what terrible crime Gilone can have committed to have been banished from Court," said Victoire a little later.

"She might well have left of her own free will."

"For someone like Adrien d'Etivey?"

"Who knows?"

"It would surprise me very much," said Victoire. "She was so happy and proud of her position."

When evening came they stopped at a little inn on the outskirts of a village.

As she sat gazing into the fire, Victoire's thoughts turned to Guy Becavallo, with whom she had stayed in so many inns similar to this one. Would she be able to tell him she had a child by another man?

Everywhere they went they saw terrible ruin and desolation. So many of the villages and small towns through which they passed had been burned or plundered by the rival armies.

Whenever they stopped, Victoire and Anselme heard complaints about how hard life was for the people, many of whom were faced with imminent famine. In some places bread was already short. They came across hordes of haggard, emaciated children, with equally starved-looking dogs at their heels. The children were begging, and threatening any passerby who refused them charity. The freezing-cold wind whistled through their wretched hovels, where no fires burned. All the weaker members of the community—the old, the sick, and the newborn—were beginning to live under the shadow of death's approach. It was just before Christmas, and in front of the churches the beggars were appealing to the public for charity. Just behind them stood the outcasts, those who had been driven from their homes by cold and hunger. But they stretched out their arms in vain for charity.

"What a horrible sight!" said Victoire, sickened by so much misery. "How could one possibly help them? There are so many."

"This is only the beginning," predicted Anselme.

"Wait until the middle of the winter when the granaries are completely empty."

"Why doesn't the King do anything?"

"All he does is to increase the taxes," said Anselme. "He doesn't know which way to turn himself to get money to feed his troops."

"War is very costly."

"Particularly the results of war," said Anselme. "Both Catholics and Protestants pillage the land in the name of God."

They changed horses at the Black Horse Inn near Blois. Meanwhile, Anselme, Victoire, and their servants consumed a hurried meal.

"Take care on the road," said the innkeeper as he served them. "Travelers say there is a band of brigands on the rampage around here who are burning and killing everything in their path."

"We have no escort," said Anselme apprehensively.

"If you are making for Paris, you would be wise to wait a little and go on with some other travelers. You would run less danger together."

"Even worse than the brigands," added a peasant who was having a drink to warm himself up, "they say there are ruthless German soldiers wandering about in the countryside."

"They're quite merciless," added the innkeeper's wife. "They have even attacked religious processions, and people going to worship."

"Of course! They can find what they want in anyone's pockets."

"They have their own ways of making people tell them where they hide their gold coins."

"The other week they hung a priest upside-down from an oak tree until he told them where he kept his money."

"I don't like it. We'll spend the night here and join with some other travelers," said Anselme.

"I think you would be wise to do so," said the inn-keeper.

The Montmaurs were lucky. The next day the Duchesse de Bouillon passed by on the road. She had a large mounted escort with her and was quite willing to allow them to join her.

Chapter XXVIII

As she entered the courtyard of Alexandre d'Hautemart's house, Victoire felt she had stepped back into the past. It all looked exactly the same as in September 1572 when she and Anselme had fled from the Louvre. The steward was still at his post, and in the courtyard to greet them was Alexandre himself, looking very attractive in a black doublet embroidered with gold.

"My dear Anselme, what a pleasure to see you again! I beg you and Mademoiselle de Montmaur to consider my house your own for as long as you please."

While the maid was busy unpacking and putting away her things, Victoire went downstairs with her uncle to take some refreshment after the journey. Their host was waiting for them, standing in front of a brisk fire.

"How comfortable your house is!" exclaimed Victoire, holding out her hands to the warmth of the fire. "We were so cold during the journey."

"I imagine you were even colder in La Rochelle,"

said Alexandre d'Hautemart in that deep voice that Victoire remembered so well.

"The cold was no more than a minor inconvenience compared with the hunger and fear of the plague," she replied quietly.

"I've never had the opportunity to tell you how very much my friends admired your courage, as I do myself."

Victoire, embarrassed by his praise, lowered her head slightly.

"Alexandre, I so often cursed you for having enlisted my niece's help during those interminable weeks when I was without news of her," said the Comte de Montmaur. "If you only knew what I suffered!"

"I can well imagine," said the Marquis d'Hautemart quickly. "Please believe me when I say that I too was very concerned about her. Mademoiselle de Montmaur has every reason to feel proud. Her bravery certainly helped to bring about the signing of the peace treaty. But," the Marquis went on, turning toward Anselme, "I am not responsible—or at least not directly so—for your niece's trip to England, and even less for her abduction by that bandit here in France. Becavallo has told me that you were held in terrible conditions."

"Did he manage to escape, then?" Victoire wanted to know.

"No. When Jean Lescure brought me the news, I set off for Eglimont with a small army to free Guy. To my great surprise I encountered virtually no resistance. The château was empty of defenders except for two guards, who were completely drunk."

"That must have been when Adrien d'Etivey set off after me with all his men."

"How did you manage to escape on your own?" the Marquis asked with interest.

Victoire told him she had believed Guy had been assassinated by d'Etivey and explained how she had been freed by Renaud de Surlemont.

"But can you explain to me why d'Etivey hates you so much? I can't imagine you'd done him any harm."

Anselme sighed. "That, my dear Alexandre," he said, "is yet another story."

Victoire blushed. She had no desire at all to tell the Marquis d'Hautemart about Guillaume. People said he was completely devoted to the Protestant cause, that he no longer gave a thought to anything else at all, and she was not sure how he would react if he knew Guillaume was Catholic.

"It's all the result of Saint Bartholomew's Night," she said finally, not daring to meet the Marquis's penetrating gaze. He could sometimes be quite patronizing, though always in an exquisitely courteous way.

"I hope at least that your trip to London went off smoothly," he said.

"You don't know Victoire!" exclaimed Anselme, who was by now a little under the influence of the Burgundy. Victoire began to tell him all about Philippa's attempts on her life, until some guests arrived and interrupted her with their greetings.

Victoire was very pleased to find they were people she had known at Court. Perhaps, she hoped, one of them would be able to tell her what had happened to Guillaume de Louvencourt.

Victoire felt very apprehensive about appearing before the Queen, though she was obliged to pluck up the courage to do so the following morning. Yet her fear did not prevent her from looking at the crowded Paris streets with interest and amusement as they trotted along from the Rue Saint Jacques, where Alexandre's house was, to the Louvre. They passed the poultry market, where hares, young goats, and young wild boar were also sold. Next came the wine market, selling products from Orléans and Burgundy brought to Paris by barge.

As they crossed the Ile de la Cité, the coach had to move aside to let a mounted guard go past carrying a cloth effigy. A priest followed, his hands manacled behind him and his feet chained as well. As he laboriously moved forward he kept tripping on his ragged brown robe.

"Whatever is that?" asked Victoire in surprise.

Anselme leaned over to see. "An enemy of the Crown who has been condemned to be executed. The Queen has used this method before to get rid of her enemies and their followers.

As the priest passed their carriage he turned his head to look at them. Victoire gasped in horror. Their eyes locked in a challenge of hatred.

In the next moment one of the guards pushed him forward, but the priest glanced over his shoulder and gave Victoire a parting leer.

Her whole body trembling with terror, Victoire turned her frightened eyes toward Anselme. "Uncle, that was Father Izard!"

"Yes, I know. I'm sorry that you ever had to see him again. It seems, though, that the Queen has decided he was more concerned with his own self-interests than hers. She must have decided he had gone too far . . . He won't be able to torment anyone anymore now."

The image of the man who had caused her so much anguish remained only too clear in Victoire's mind as they continued past stonecutters, second-hand clothes dealers, and illuminators' shops before crossing the Seine by the Pont au Change.

Léon, whose thoughts were too occupied with Juliette, ran into another coach on the bridge. The Comte de Montmaur apologized profusely to the occupant for his coachman's clumsiness. He was particularly annoyed since the man in the other coach was the Venetian Ambassador, Sigismondo Cavalli.

As their coach drew up beside the Louvre, they saw river barges being unloaded by the palace gates. Victoire stared up at the enormous, gloomy building, which held so many unhappy memories for her. She felt her resolve weakening as repulsion overwhelmed her. Would she, she wondered, have the strength of will to get out of the coach and enter the palace she hated so much? Seeing her reaction, Anselme said to her, "Be brave! The Montmaurs do not flee in face of danger. It's not so long since you were in a far worse situation than now."

"Yes, I know that," Victoire sighed.

But secretly she still felt apprehensive as she climbed the steps. Catherine de Medici must have a reason for summoning her as well as her uncle. Otherwise the Queen would surely have been content to have her master glass-smith at her beck and call. There was no real need for his niece to come with him. The most likely motive for Catherine's action was that she still intended to enlist Victoire as one of her Flying Squadron.

This was something that Victoire would hate more than anything else in the world. She would rather die than become like Gilone or Mademoiselle de Chabrière. But she could not possibly refuse to obey the Queen Mother's orders. As the King grew weaker with every day that passed, so Catherine's power grew.

As they were waiting in the antechamber for the Queen to summon them, Victoire recognized Mademoiselle d'Aillanges among the crowd of courtiers, ladies, and pages. They exchanged a few remarks, but as soon as possible Victoire plucked up courage to ask after Guillaume de Louvencourt.

"I've no idea what became of him," said Mademoiselle d'Aillanges, arranging a ribbon on her dress. "I think he was at the siege of La Rochelle."

"You haven't seen him since?"

"No, I haven't."

"What about his brother Gontran?" If she really had to, she would find out about Guillaume from him.

"I haven't seen him either. They must have returned home."

The doors opened. "Her Majesty the Queen!"

Gentlemen bowed and ladies curtsied. Catherine advanced, followed by her daughter, the new Queen of Navarre, who looked more beautiful than ever. The Queen addressed a few words to various people present, and then went to sit down by the window.

Victoire learned that the Court had just returned from Saint-Germain, where they had spent most of December. The Queen disliked the Louvre more and more, and preferred to stay at Saint-Maur or Montceaux.

Then Anselme and his niece were summoned to greet the sovereign.

"Ah! Comte de Montmaur, I am very glad to see you in Paris again. I do hope you have brought me some fine glassware."

"I shall be honored to show Your Majesty the fruits of my modest work whenever you please."

"I should like to see them as soon as possible. Come and see me later when we shan't be disturbed. You will stay for supper together with Mademoiselle de Montmaur."

Her dark eyes rested for a moment on Victoire, who felt paralyzed with fear.

Chapter XXIX

"How did your visit go?" inquired Alexandre d'Hautemart.

"Her Majesty was most gracious," replied Victoire. "But alas! She has invited my uncle and myself to supper this evening."

"Why do you say alas?"

"I have no desire at all to return to the Louvre. I honestly don't feel very safe there."

"I know how you feel. I'm in a very difficult situation."

"What about?" asked Victoire, surprised to find her host confiding in her.

"About you. I need your help."

Victoire hesitated before replying. This time she was more able to judge what risks she would be running if she agreed.

"You know full well that I shall always willingly help our cause," she said at last.

"I don't doubt that."

Why was he so embarrassed if he was sure she would agree?

"But this time," said Alexandre, coming closer to Victoire, "I speak to you as to a different person. For me you are no longer just the niece of my old friend Anselme. Your courage has won my admiration, and much more than that too . . ." He took Victoire's hand and raised it to his lips.

"Victoire," he murmured, "you must remember as

well as I do that old barn with the wind whistling through the cracks in the walls where you so calmly accepted to carry out a mission which—though I did not know at the time—would almost inevitably end in your death. That evening an anguish was born in my heart which never left me so long as I knew you were still behind those walls, condemned to a life which I could only too well imagine. When Jean Lescure brought me the terrible news about your capture at Eglimont, I hastened there immediately. We freed Becavallo quickly. We searched in vain for hours to find some trace of you. I made mincemeat of the two guards without being able to get anything out of them. Guy was sure you were alive. He kept on saying, 'A woman like Victoire can't die like this!' I shared his feelings. Yet I could not find you anywhere in the fortress, even though my men and I combed it foot by foot. How relieved I was afterward to meet M. de Barville, who told me about your escape. But he could not tell us what had happened to you after the fire at Surlemont."

"The fire?" said Victoire, horror-struck.

"Yes, the scoundrel set fire to his brother-in-law's château. By a miracle, Renaud de Surlemont was away at the time."

"He was escorting me to Le Havre."

Renaud had paid dearly for helping her and Victoire was absolutely powerless to make any amends. Poor Renaud! His action had cost him his last remaining link with his lost love, Yolande.

"Adrien d'Etivey should be killed," Victoire murmured.

"I *had* thought of it. But he's gone into hiding since then, and no one can find a trace of him."

"He'll turn up again before long."

"You can be sure that when he does, I will exact a terrible revenge," promised Alexandre. "There is no one I loathe as much as him, not even the Queen Mother."

A strained silence fell between them. Finally she said, "You still haven't told me what you want me to do," she said.

"You have access to the Louvre. It would be extremely useful to us to know what the Duc d'Alençon and the King of Navarre are up to just now. I'll tell you what is happening."

Alexandre told Victoire that a new party had been formed called the "Politicals," who were allied to the Protestants and to be led by the Duc d'Alençon.

The Marquis had promised to help the new party because of his hatred for the Guise family, the Duc d'Anjou, and the Queen Mother. The party was seen as the last chance to save the kingdom from sinking under a weight of misery and general discontent, which the royal authority seemed to have lost any power to halt.

"And what will the King of Navarre's role be in this operation?"

"Both he and his wife have promised to help us."

Aided by Juliette and Jacotte, Victoire dressed for her supper with the Queen, without much enthusiasm. She was feeling very apprehensive about their meeting with the Queen beforehand, when Anselme was to show her his glassware away from the crowd and pomp of the morning's gathering. Nothing in the Queen's expression had so far revealed whether she knew about Victoire's expedition to England, but Queen Catherine was adept at hiding her feelings.

Through the window Victoire caught sight of her uncle watching his boxes being loaded into the coach. It was time to go down.

Juliette held out a beautiful madder-red velvet cloak that matched Victoire's dress. It was warmly lined with squirrel fur and edged with ermine. Victoire wrapped herself up in it snugly. The evening was chilly and the gray skies threatened snow.

In the entrance hall, where the torches had not yet been lit, she met her host. Alone in the gloom with Alexandre close by her side, Victoire felt a strange sensation of imminent danger . . . but a danger which fascinated her.

"Mademoiselle, I pray your fears prove to be without foundation."

"I hope so too, Monsieur."

A footman approached. "The Comte de Montmaur is waiting for Mademoiselle."

"I'm coming." She went out, lifting the hem of her dress to keep it out of the mud and dirt. A servant helped her to climb into the coach where Anselme came to sit beside her, grumbling because the cold, damp weather brought on his rheumatism.

They went the same way as that morning, though this time without incident.

Two of the Queen's servants were waiting to carry the boxes into her apartments. Anselme was already busily calculating how much he would be paid for his work. "Let's hope she's as generous as last time," he murmured.

"We'll extend the stables," decreed Victoire firmly.

"All you think about are your own affairs!" exclaimed her uncle, laughing.

They were ushered into a salon where Victoire immediately noticed some new acquisitions. The Persian rug, which the Queen must have been tired of, had been replaced by a superb carpet from Flanders, and there was also a particularly lovely rosewood chessboard inlaid with ivory.

Catherine de Medici made her entrance followed by an escort of about ten courtiers. She was still in mourning, offset by a few handsome diamonds.

"We wish to offer a present to our dear cousin the Queen of England through the intermediary of M. de la Mothe Fenelon," she said without looking at Victoire. "Let us see if you have something suitable."

Victoire blanched, unnerved by this direct attack. How cleverly the Queen Mother had instantly made clear that she knew all about what Victoire had been up to. After all, thought Victoire, her intervention had been an act of high treason. She could now expect to be arrested, imprisoned, or even executed. She was probably only alive now because she was the niece of a man whom Catherine admired for his artistic skill.

The Queen examined the glassware carefully as Anselme held it out to her, exclaiming with pleasure in Italian. Victoire began to feel faint. She wondered what would happen when the Queen's heavy silhouette, which was leaning over one of the boxes of glassware, turned toward her. Would the Queen berate her with anger and bitter reproaches?

"A woman of taste could not fail to be moved by the delicacy of this glass and its subtle red color, at the same time dull and vivid. The next messenger shall bear it to the Queen of England!"

"Your Majesty does me infinite honor in deigning to choose something I have made," said Anselme, bowing.

The Queen smiled. "You know how much I appreciate perfect workmanship. No doubt she for whom this glass is destined will feel the same!"

"I don't know how to thank Your Majesty."

"By staying with us for some time . . . with Mademoiselle de Montmaur, of course."

Uncertain of the direction the conversation was taking, Victoire curtsied.

The Queen turned toward her. "Mademoiselle de Glymes was a relative of yours, wasn't she?"

"Yes, Madame."

"Some unfortunate occurrences obliged us to separate ourselves from her. You will replace her."

Her decisive tone left no room for argument. So now

Victoire was to be obliged to seduce men the Queen wanted in her power. She could sink no lower, she felt. She must have looked completely dismayed, for the Queen said with a quizzical smile, "Of course, I shan't expect you to provide the same kind of services as your cousin . . . she had done nothing to require my pardon."

This enigmatic speech left Victoire completely bewildered.

"We'll see about it later," said the Queen. "Let's go to supper now. I'm ravenously hungry."

Huge fires were crackling in every fireplace, but they hardly even began to warm the vast, high-ceilinged rooms into which the cold from outside seemed to have penetrated. Among the chattering throng of distinguished guests Victoire recognized the Queen of Navarre and the Duc d'Alençon with his new favorite.

Was there any difference, thought Victoire, between this supper party and those she had attended in the past? Though the surroundings had not changed, the atmosphere was subtly different: the air was heavy with intrigue; laughter seemed more forced. The Duc d'Anjou's restless, inventive mind was noticeably absent. His younger brother was a gloomy, uneasy man, quite incapable of enlivening a group he was with. None of all those present would be able to give her news of Guillaume de Louvencourt.

After supper, she went to ask Mademoiselle de Chabrière why Gilone had been banished.

Alix was still trying to outdo the highest ranking ladies, with regard to dress at least. At first she stared at Victoire condescendingly. "Well! So you're back from your province," she said.

"It seems your friend Mademoiselle de Glymes will have to remain there," said Victoire.

The Queen's maid of honor pouted scornfully. *"My*

friend!" she exclaimed. "I hardly knew her. In fact, I could never stand her."

Victoire smiled at this sudden change. She replied mischievously, "Well, you often lent her your dresses. Maybe you could tell me why she was banished from Court?"

"She disobeyed Her Majesty," was all Alix de Chabrière would reply, and then she turned her back on Victoire.

Chapter XXX

*O*ne rainy January morning the Comte de Montmaur and his niece went to see Cassitère. Anselme had no great expectations from their visit, but Victoire was feeling at once curious and a little apprehensive. So far all the seer's predictions about her future had proved accurate. This time she had a specific question to ask him. She wanted to know whether Guillaume de Louvencourt was still alive. But it was by no means sure that Cassitère would be able to answer her question.

Victoire had been a member of the Flying Squadron for almost two weeks now, much against her will. When she had told Alexandre d'Hautemart about it, he had been delighted. She was now in a much better position to observe the Court. She saw the royal family and the most important personalities at Court almost daily. But Victoire herself was still completely in the dark about what special services the Queen Mother was expecting her to perform. All she had done so far was be present when told, and perform a few very unimportant tasks. Catherine seemed to be taking pleasure in keeping her guessing.

When they arrived at Cassitère's house, they were greeted by his servant, who said, "My master is waiting for you," and showed them into the library.

Even before she was aware the seer was in the room, Victoire felt his presence. "My dear friends, I am so happy to see you again," he said.

He examined Anselme, his cap ornamented with marten fur slightly awry.

"You look very pale, my friend. You need an elixir."

"I'm getting old," sighed Anselme. "You, on the other hand, seem to be immune to the effects of time."

Cassitère came up to Victoire. "I can see you don't need any remedies," he said, smiling.

"If you only knew what she has been through!" exclaimed Anselme. "It's a miracle she's still alive."

"Your niece possesses a robust constitution and an exceedingly resolute spirit."

"I would like to ask you a question," said Victoire.

"Are you anxious about your future?"

"The future of someone dear to me."

"Well, then, let us go upstairs and look into the future."

All three sat around a circular table, and the servant brought in a smoking incense burner. Into it the magician poured a drop of mercury and a phial of reddish liquid. Then Anselme and Victoire sat silently in the dark room lit by a single candle as the sage concentrated.

"I can see a little child alongside you," he said.

"I have had a son," said Victoire, slightly embarrassed.

From the burner came a slightly sickening smell of an overripe peach. Cassitère's staring eyes gazed into the liquid and from time to time he stirred it with a hazel wand.

"You will cross the mountains," he said. "I can see snow. Two men are laying a fortune at your feet. One fortune is plain to see, the other is hidden."

Two men—Victoire was puzzled. Who could he mean?

"I see violence . . . a fantastic animal which I cannot identify." The smoke had cleared a little, and Cassitère seemed tired. Yet Victoire plucked up all her courage and asked, in a scarcely audible voice: "Is Guillaume de Louvencourt still alive?"

The seer remained motionless for a few moments and then replied, "I see nothing more."

Victoire was very downcast as she left, though the seer had reassured her that the fact that he had not been able to see Guillaume in the magic smoke did not necessarily mean that he was dead.

"Don't be so upset," said Anselme, trying to comfort his niece.

"Cassitère wanted to spare me the truth! Don't you find it surprising that no one knows what has become of Guillaume? He had so many friends among the combatants."

"My dear child, in the confusion of the battlefield it's very difficult to know what has happened to everyone."

That day Victoire's time was her own—she was not needed at the Louvre—and she spent it deep in thought. Her mind inevitably turned to Guillaume and to their little son, but she also thought about Guy Becavallo: she was looking forward to seeing him again when he returned to Paris from Venice.

That evening she went with her uncle and Alexandre d'Hautemart to supper at the Vidame de Barville's house in the Marais. Everyone present was a sworn adversary of the Guise family. There was the Marshal de Montmorency, the Admiral's nephew, who had for a short time been a member of the Council, with his brother M. de Thoré. They were all doing everything they could to bring down the arrogant Guise family, whose power was growing with every day that passed.

"Don't forget, my friends, that the Duc and the Cardinal de Lorraine are certain of both military and financial support from Spain," said Thoré.

"Our only hope is a general uprising," murmured Alexandre d'Hautemart. "If we were properly organized we could abduct the Duc d'Alençon, Navarre, and Condé."

"They could take refuge in the fortress at Sedan. The Duc de Bouillon and our nephew Turenne have offered it to them," said Thoré. "They would be in a very strong position there."

"We shall have to ask La Noue for his support," said the Marshal. He was quite ready to plan for the operation, but was unwilling to take more than a moral responsibility.

"But who could be put in charge of this surprise attack?" asked Alexandre. "Whom would you honor with your confidence, gentlemen?"

The Marshal and his brother looked at one another.

"It seems to me M. de Chaumont-Quitry would be the obvious choice. His courage has been tried and tested."

"But is he smart enough?" asked Alexandre.

The Montmorencys gave him a surprised look. Surely that was obvious.

"The weak point of the whole plan is the behavior of the most important person in it," remarked the Vidame. "He has a weak character and is very afraid of his mother. This must inevitably strengthen the hand of our adversaries."

"You're right," Alexandre broke in. "That's why the information Mademoiselle de Montmaur is able to pass on each day is of vital importance to us. With her help we should be able to foresee a possible change of heart. It's always possible!"

"All the same, you don't really think . . ."

"My dear friend, we must be ready for anything."

"Fortunately we can count on the King of Navarre's support."

"Up to a certain point," said Alexandre. "Don't forget that his father spent his whole life going from one side to another."

"That's true," Thoré conceded. "Poor Antoine had no strength of character."

Victoire observed the conspirators. Despite appearances to the contrary, the moving spirit behind the plot was not the Marshal, who often retreated into a discreet caution, but the hotheaded Alexandre. He was quite ready to compromise himself, and to risk his own skin if need be. The others implicitly recognized him as their leader.

All three returned home together. Victoire wanted to borrow a book from the library, so she remained downstairs for a moment with their host, while Anselme went straight to bed. As he went he said ominously, "There are too many people mixed up in this plot."

A few days later, on January 16, as Victoire made her way along the great gallery of the Louvre she smelled a hint of drama in the air. The courtiers were whispering together in small groups, some of them looking completely dumbfounded. Victoire realized something serious must have happened.

She joined the Venetian Ambassador and a few other ladies and gentlemen who were listening to Mademoiselle de Sauve describing an attempt on the life of M. de Ventabren that had taken place within the Louvre itself.

"Really!" she exclaimed. "The Duc de Guise seems to think the Louvre is the Pré aux Clercs! I ask you, is it proper to try to run someone through with a sword as they come peacefully down a staircase?"

"What was the pretext for the attack?" asked Sigismondo Cavalli, the Venetian, with a worried look. He would have to make a report on the incident to the Doge, who was passionately interested in everything that happened at the French court.

Beautiful Charlotte de Sauve lowered her voice. "People are saying Duc Henri suspects that M. de Ventabren wanted to enjoy his wife's favors."

"But had he already been successful?"

Mademoiselle de Sauve shrugged in ignorance.

"Is M. de Ventabren wounded?" Victoire asked.

"No, he managed to escape. He has taken refuge with his master, the Duc d'Alençon."

Victoire had to leave at this point to go to the Queen. Sigismondo Cavalli followed her in a state of great excitement.

"Mademoiselle, please forgive me for not having greeted you in all this confusion. I am overwhelmed by this assassination attempt. Some people may think it is no more than the result of a personal animosity. But if the King's brother takes it into his head to avenge his servant . . ."

"I understand your fears, Ambassador, and I share them," said Victoire.

If an open rift developed between the Guise family and the Montmorency family before the date they had planned for the revolt, all Alexandre's plans would be called into question.

Chapter XXXI

"*The* time has come to make use of you, Mademoiselle de Montmaur."

Victoire went pale. She had been in the Queen Mother's service for almost a month now, but her past conduct had never once been mentioned. At the beginning she had been continually on the alert, but recently she had begun to feel more reassured about the Queen's reaction to her rebellion. She believed the Queen Mother must have decided to act indulgently toward her because of her marked affection for Victoire's uncle. But now M. de la Mothe Fenelon had presumably denounced her, and she was going to have to pay for her visit to the Queen of England.

"I am ever ready to help Your Majesty," she managed to utter, though her throat was constricted with emotion.

"I should hope so," the Queen grumbled.

She led her, trembling, to a window recess, where the other maids of honor could not hear.

"After yesterday's incident, I have every reason to think that the Guises and the Montmorencys will take further action. Of course, I don't want things to go any further. I want you to report to me everything you hear about this from whatever source, whether from the Queen of Navarre or the Duchesse de Nevers. Don't worry about the King of Navarre and the Duc d'Alençon; Mademoiselle de Sauve will deal with them."

This meant that Victoire was going to be in the position of spying for both the Queen and Alexandre.

"I'll do my best to satisfy Your Majesty."

She dared to look directly into Catherine's eyes, though she was so terrified of her. To her great surprise she saw the beginnings of a smile on her heavy features, which Catherine's love of good food had thickened.

"Do you love your country, Mademoiselle?"

"Indeed I do, Madame!" exclaimed Victoire.

"Well, then, try to serve it instead of fighting it. I do not doubt you are brave and daring."

A servant in the King's livery ran up.

"Madame, His Majesty feels very ill. He's spitting blood again!"

"Tell Madame Marguerite and the Duc d'Alençon to join me immediately at his bedside."

The Queen hurried off after the servant as quickly as her dignity and stoutness would allow.

"Do you think the King is going to die?" Victoire asked Alix de Chabrière.

Mademoiselle de Chabrière had been more gracious to Victoire since the Queen had chosen her as a maid of honor.

"Do you remember what I said to you just before Saint Bartholomew's Night, about what had been predicted," she asked, "that this is the year Charles IX should die?"

"I often think about it," replied Victoire. "But now that the Duc d'Anjou is King of Poland, surely the Duc d'Alençon will succeed his brother if anything happens to the King?"

"He would be more than willing."

The maids of honor were somewhat at loose ends, having no idea when the Queen would return. They began to talk together and, almost inevitably, to speculate about the Queen of Navarre's affair with M. de la Mole. All the Court was talking about it.

"M. de la Mole is certainly most attractive," said Mademoiselle d'Aillanges dreamily.

"I'd prefer him to the King of Navarre, wouldn't you?" asked Alix, watching Mademoiselle de Sauve. "At least his armpits don't smell!"

"That's a disadvantage, of course, but I prefer the King of Navarre to the Duc d'Alençon. His nose is so horribly swollen since he had smallpox," remarked Henriette d'Aillanges.

Victoire agreed. Monsieur had not been good-looking even before he had the smallpox, but now he was really horrible with his dark complexion, his red eyes, and his deeply pockmarked skin. To think he aspired to the hand of the Queen of England! The King's face had been less marked by the terrible smallpox—in fact, both brothers had been lucky to survive. But the King had scarcely recovered from the disease before he had been struck down by a recurrence of an old malady, aggravated by the long hours he spent out hunting.

"There's no doubt at all that the King's activities last night brought on this attack," said Charlotte de Sauve mysteriously.

"Last night? What happened?" asked Mademoiselle de Chabrière.

The maids of honor were now clustered around Mademoiselle de Sauve, who was obviously highly pleased to have aroused their curiosity. She went on in a low voice, "They say the King is very annoyed by his sister's obvious interest in M. de la Mole. Particularly since he is in the Duc d'Alençon's service."

It was common knowledge that Charles IX detested his brothers. He had not attempted to hide how pleased he had been to get rid of the Duc d'Anjou by sending him to the other end of Europe.

"Last night, with the Duc de Guise and a few other gentlemen, the King lay in wait outside the Duchesse de Nevers' apartments, where he knew M. de la Mole was."

"Why did he do that?" asked Mademoiselle de Chabrière.

Mademoiselle de Sauve lowered her voice. The Spanish Ambassador had just come into the room.

"To strangle him."

The other girls cried out in horror.

"Are you sure?"

"M. de Brangle was there, and assures me of it. But when he came out, instead of going to the Duc d'Alençon's apartments, as the King was expecting, he went straight to the Queen of Navarre's door. His Majesty hesitated to attack him then, as it would have caused a scandal and his sister's honor would have been compromised."

"What are you talking about that is so interesting, ladies?" asked Don Diego de Zuniga.

Like his colleague from Venice, the Ambassador was constantly on the alert for news. Philip II was even more avid for the latest Court gossip than the Doge.

"We were talking about the King's illness, Ambassador," said Charlotte de Sauve with an angelic smile. "Did you know His Majesty is at death's door yet again?"

Victoire told Alexandre d'Hautemart all about the attack on M. de Ventabren and the King's unsuccessful ambush.

"So the King is making himself look ridiculous by hanging about in a corridor waiting for his sister's lover!" exclaimed the Marquis scornfully. "Has His Majesty no more urgent problems to deal with, at a time when the whole country is seething with unrest, than the love affairs of a young woman who does not care for her husband?"

Victoire tried tò defend the King's sister, who had always been kind to her.

"I can quite understand that in some ways the Queen of Navarre prefers M. de la Mole to her husband. Yet she should not associate so openly with an ordinary gentleman, even though the Duc d'Alençon has honored him with his favor."

"I don't know exactly what I would do if I were Madamé Marguerite," replied Victoire. "But she could at least be a little more discreet. If *I* were a Queen I shouldn't like the whole Court to know about my private life." Everyone, down to the lowest footman, knew where M. de la Mole spent his nights.

Alexandre went on, "They're a fine pair of conspirators."

"What pair?"

"M. de la Mole and his friend M. de Coconat, the guards captain and the Duchesse de Nevers' lover."

"I don't know him."

The Marquis reflected, leaning on the mantelpiece. "We must make use of these gentlemen since they are there. Mademoiselle, be good enough to go on keeping watch. You are doing us great service."

Victoire did not dare to tell him that she was doing the same for the Queen Mother. She was surprised to find she felt qualms of conscience at the idea of betraying the Queen. After all, she had always fought against her, within the limited range of her capabilities.

But the Queen's magnanimous behavior troubled her, and she was too straightforward to work for both sides. She would perhaps be forced to select which piece of information to give to one or the other side. She much disliked the idea of playing a double game, which ran counter to her honest nature. But she was not sure what to do now. If she concealed vital information, whom should she conceal it from: Alexandre or the Queen? Where did the interests of her country really lie?

The Court was in residence at Saint-Germain, and Victoire, to her great annoyance, was obliged to stay there. But she still remained in close contact with Alexandre. He sent a servant to her almost every day to collect her messages.

Among the courtiers close to the royal family a controlled restiveness could be felt. Some important project was being hatched, there was no doubt. Victoire tried hard to deduce what was happening from the snatches of information she managed to get hold of. Madame Marguerite and her brother the Duc d'Alençon were definitely closer as a result of M. de la Mole's influence on his mistress. Madame Marguerite must also have been well aware that she could dominate this neglected little creature more easily than the King or the brilliant Duc d'Anjou.

The new intimacy between brother and sister might well lead to an argument between the two brothers-in-law, with the Queen of Navarre as the link between them. The two men were increasingly seen together, often accompanied by M. de la Mole, though it was known that Henri de Navarre disliked him.

The name of M. de La Noue was often on people's lips, too. He was still at La Rochelle, where he had replaced the Admiral at the head of the Protestant party. He was expected to take some decisive action.

On Shrove Tuesday, February 23, the expected action materialized. At his instigation there were Huguenot uprisings in Saintonge, Poitou, Dauphiné, and Guyenne. When the news arrived at Court, there was terror at Saint-Germain. Everyone expected that Montgomery would seize the opportunity to spread the revolt in Normandy with the help of the English.

While all this was happening, M. de Chaumont-Quitry became impatient to act. He could not bear to wait until the date they had set for the abduction of the Duc d'Alençon.

In the middle of all these dramatic events, only the

Queen Mother remained calm. More than ever she kept a close watch over her son, her son-in-law, and the latter's cousin.

On the evening of February 27 catastrophe struck. Victoire and Mademoiselle d'Aillanges had just begun their service with the Queen. They were alone with her, helping her to get ready for supper, though it was to be a simple one, as Lent was just beginning.

Suddenly the Duc d'Alençon burst into the room, followed by M. de la Mole. He threw himself at his mother's feet.

"Ah, Madame! Something terrible is happening!"

Panic had given his face a greenish tinge that made it even more unattractive. He trembled convulsively and huge drops of sweat were forming on his brow.

"What is it, Monsieur?"

The Queen had risen to her feet, her face white. She completely forgot to dismiss the two girls, who had stepped back into a corner of the room.

"We're lost!"

He began to sob and lament hysterically. His fear had made him totally lose control. Victoire watched him disintegrate before her eyes. He was obviously incapable of going through with the role he had intended to play.

"Well, will you explain?"

"Madame, I'll tell you everything, but I beg you to forgive me."

As Victoire listened, amazed and disgusted at his cowardice, the Duc revealed the whole plot. His mother was furious, and even more so as she began to realize its extent. To ingratiate himself with her again, he denounced everyone involved, beginning with his brother-in-law and M. Condé, and including the Montmorencys and Turenne. He was careful to lay special blame on Montgomery, since he was well aware that Catherine had never forgiven him for fatally wounding Henri II at that tournament so many years before.

"That infamous man!" murmured the Queen. "Nothing would surprise me coming from him!"

Her dark, glittering eyes terrified her son, who backed away from her fearfully. She raised her voice. "Do you realize, Monsieur, how serious an act you have committed? At a time when your brother is on his deathbed, you are doing all you can to ruin the kingdom."

For two days Charles IX had been bleeding through the pores of his skin. The doctors were quite powerless at this new development in his disease. It could only mean that his death was imminent.

"I beg you to pardon me! Never again, I swear to you, will I attempt anything against the King!"

Catherine began to snarl with rage. Her fury smote her unfortunate son like claps of thunder.

"You worthless creature! Remember the terrible fate Philip II inflicted on Don Carlos for much less than this! You deserve worse than that! You are a hundred times more guilty!"

"Pity me, Mother, I beg you."

During all this time M. de la Mole had been keeping very quiet alongside his master, in the most humble posture. Nothing at all remained of the proud courtier who only yesterday had been sure of his master's favor, and who today was in danger of death.

Victoire thanked God she had witnessed this betrayal, which she would report to Alexandre. He would be able to judge for himself if this Son of France was worthy of the confidence his followers had placed in him.

"Follow me to the King," ordered the Queen. "And you too, Monsieur."

Chapter XXXII

$\mathcal{A}$t two o'clock in the morning the Court fled from Saint-Germain in complete panic; the King on a litter, the Queen Mother in a coach with the conspirators so that she could personally keep an eye on them. Surrounded by a strong escort, the procession made for Vincennes to the east of Paris. It was an almost impregnable stronghold with its strong outside walls, its keep, and its nine towers. Unfortunately it was a very uncomfortable place to live in. Slightly disheveled, their clothes hastily thrown on, the maids of honor piled into a wagon which set off after the royal coach.

Victoire tried to listen to what the others were saying. Mademoiselle d'Aillanges' description of what had happened in the Queen's cabinet proved a great success. Victoire did not try to add to her account at all. She still felt disgust at the Duc's behavior and had no desire at all to comment on it.

She was very curious, however, to find out what had happened afterward. Alix de Chabrière had been there some of the time. She was very friendly with one of the King's gentlemen and had been talking to him and a few other people in the sovereign's antechamber when Catherine de Medici had burst in, literally dragging her youngest son along by the scruff of the neck. He cut a most sorry figure, she said.

"We could hear the King moaning, 'Can't they let me die in peace!' and then the door was shut. Her Majesty sent for the King of Navarre and his cousin.

They were all closeted together, and from time to time shouts could be heard from the room. Finally the Queen Mother came out of the bedroom and announced we were all leaving for Vincennes immediately."

Victoire wondered what punishment these conspirators against the state would be given. Would the King pardon his brother for trying to oust him at a time when he was in terrible pain, battling against the disease that would kill very soon in the opinion of the many doctors who were called to his bedside.

A few days later Victoire was strolling in the gardens at Vincennes when she heard a piece of news that, she felt, completely devastated her. She was with M. de Surgy, one of the Duc de Nevers' gentlemen, who had remained behind with the Duchesse while the Duc was away. He gave her the fatal information quite by chance, not intending to cause her pain.

Victoire asked her companion how he had lost three fingers she noticed missing from his left hand. He replied philosophically, "It was at La Rochelle. I managed to come through the battles of Jarnac and Moncontour safe and sound, but during the attack on the Protestant stronghold a shot from a harquebus carried away half my hand."

"So you were at the siege!" said Victoire. "In that case, maybe you met M. de Louvencourt?"

"Indeed, I knew him very well. He was in the same company as me, poor man!"

Victoire's heart contracted with apprehension. "Why do you say that?" she asked in a voice she could hardly recognize as her own.

"Because he was unlucky. He didn't return from the attack. And the siege was over a week later. Mademoiselle, why are you so pale? . . . You're going to faint!"

He rushed forward and caught Victoire as her legs gave way beneath her. "Here, come and sit down on this seat. You must pull yourself together, Mademoiselle."

M. de Surgy was a brave soldier, but he had no idea what to do under such circumstances. He looked around desperately for help.

"It's nothing, Monsieur. Give me just a moment."

She felt as though someone had dealt her a violent blow. All her strength vanished. She still could not believe the terrible news that M. de Surgy had, in all innocence, told her so brutally. Perhaps, she thought desperately, he was confusing Guillaume with someone else.

"Mademoiselle, I'm sorry to have made you so unhappy. Excuse me for being indiscreet, but was he a relative of yours?"

"No. A friend. Tell me, I beg you, how he died."

"M. de Louvencourt was hit by a bullet in the stomach and another in the shoulder. He was cared for, and for a while it was thought he would live. But his temperature rose, and the stomach wound became infected."

"Did he suffer very much?" asked Victoire tonelessly.

"Toward the end he became delirious."

She hesitated before inquiring, "Did he say anything before he died?"

"I wasn't present, so I can't say."

She would so much have liked to know whether Guillaume had thought of her at the end. It would have been a consolation, a small one perhaps, but it would have helped her to bear the pain. And Guillaume had died without even knowing she had borne his child.

"Do you feel better now, Mademoiselle?"

She saw the concerned face of this man who had so unwittingly broken her heart as he leaned over her solicitously. She got up and tried bravely to smile. "Thank you. I'll be all right now."

"Take my arm. We'll walk back very slowly."

She only had one desire, and that was to fling herself onto her bed and sob her heart out over a happiness destroyed before it had even had time to exist. From now on, nothing could touch her that deeply again, she was sure.

Perhaps luckily for her, Victoire did not have much time to give way to her grief. During the following weeks she had hardly any time to herself. In March the Court learned that on February 18 the King of Poland had finally reached Cracow, and before the month was out, the Comte de Montgomery did indeed move on Normandy.

Though he was exasperated at the Duc d'Alençon's behavior, Alexandre d'Hautemart had not given up his plans. He plied Victoire with questions about first one person then another. Victoire was amazed to see him so determined to go on with a plot that had begun so badly. How could he, she wondered, put his trust in a man who had so resoundingly proved his cowardice?

"Is it wise to base your hopes on him?" she asked worriedly.

"We have no choice," the Marquis replied. "If we're to have any chance of success in our struggle against the Guise family, we need a prince of the blood royal on our side. After all, the Duc d'Alençon has given various pledges of his good will toward us."

M. de la Mole and his devoted follower, M. de Coconat, were increasingly active. It was obvious to everyone that they were plotting something. Rumors were rife about a second abduction attempt of the Duc d'Alençon and the King of Navarre in which some new conspirators were implicated.

At the beginning of April Mademoiselle de Sauve, whose two lovers had very rashly confided in her, and who detested M. de la Mole, revealed the whole plan to the Queen Mother. La Mole and Coconat intended, she said, to abduct the princes and take them to Sedan.

This time the Queen Mother went into a blind rage. The King shared her feelings: he was exasperated that his generosity to the conspirators had been rewarded so meanly.

On April 10 the Duc d'Alençon and the King of Navarre were confined to their apartments, with a strong guard on the door. Alexandre d'Hautemart managed to escape. La Mole was arrested. A little while later his friend Coconat joined him in prison— the Duchesse de Nevers had managed to hide him for a while in the Grands Augustins convent—together with the Marshals Montmorency and Cossé. The Prince de Condé slipped over the border into Germany.

Charles IX did not want to bring the affair before Parliament, as this would discredit members of his own family, so he set up a special commission to judge the accused. Yet again the Duc d'Alençon gave proof of the most base cowardice. He accused his own accomplices without a qualm, his favorite in particular.

Madame Marguerite abandoned her lover to his fate and concentrated on helping her husband. She wrote a very clever speech in Henri de Navarre's defense, in which he justified his own conduct without implicating anyone else, unlike his brother-in-law.

Charlotte de Sauve was triumphant. And, of course, she was more and more in favor with the Queen Mother. She took a cruel pleasure in M. de la Mole's downfall, though Victoire had no idea why she hated him so much.

"M. de la Mole will never seduce anyone again in the state he must be in now," she said with a nasty smile that gave her a fleeting resemblance to Gilone.

"What has happened to him?" inquired Victoire.

"He has been given the water torture and the torture of the boot."

"Has he confessed?" Mademoiselle d'Aillanges asked.

"No," Charlotte admitted regretfully. "Even when he was shown the Duc's statement he remained silent."

Chapter XXXIII

All these intrigues succeeded in distracting Victoire's mind from her grief. When she began to reflect on the dramatic series of events she had witnessed since her return to Paris, she became aware that her view of life had imperceptibly changed. Close proximity to such important developments among the leaders of her country had matured and sharpened her mind. She no longer judged people in the same way as before. This was particularly true of her view of Alexandre d'Hautemart and the Queen Mother.

She still admired the Marquis and found his intelligence exciting and stimulating, but she was no longer quite sure she fully supported his cause. Previously she had never so much as questioned its justice and even its legitimacy. But now that she knew what the Duc d'Alençon's true personality was like, she found herself unable to hope for the success of any plan in which he was involved. She believed the Protestants had everything to lose and nothing to gain from their association with such a contemptible person. She even began to feel that any cause he supported must be automatically discredited. With this new slant on the situation, she was unable to understand how his followers could go on blindly considering him as the head of their faction. How could they fail to be aware of the Duc's mean, treacherous spirit?

Though in the past Victoire had always energetically supported any plans to thwart the Queen Mother's schemes, now she increasingly had reservations about doing so. She confided to her uncle how her thinking had changed, and he admitted he shared her feelings.

"I really do believe that our people have nothing to gain by acting so recklessly. I had already warned Alexandre before he went into hiding that information about his plans was leaking out, even before the bubble burst definitively. Conspirators can never resist boasting and acting a part, particularly in front of ladies. Their own lack of responsibility is the main reason for the plot's failure, though I must admit I do not really regret it. They would have led the country into a foolhardy adventure. The only people who would have ultimately profited from the operation would be the Guise family: they would have seized power with the help of Spain."

Victoire hesitated a moment and then asked, "Do you think Alexandre is lacking in judgment?"

"He wouldn't be the only one," replied Anselme.

This conversation left Victoire very thoughtful. She felt she had to revise her opinion about the Queen Mother. She could now understand how exasperated Catherine must be at the internal unrest within the country at a time when France was threatened from without on every side. The Queen wanted to retain her power, that was undeniable, but at the same time she was trying to reestablish civil order, without which ordinary life was impossible. Brigands were ravaging the countryside, and even the streets of Paris itself. Soldiers were setting fire to the crops. Trade was in jeopardy, and finance was a serious problem which the King could solve only by borrowing money from all sides. Honest people were overwhelmed by crippling taxation and harried from all sides. They were often short of bread, and could not even travel about safely to do their business.

Victoire had been living in close contact with Catherine for some time now, observing and getting to know her better. She had to admit the Queen rarely acted from narrow personal motives, except when her maternal love for the Duc d'Anjou clouded her judgment. What she was trying to do, in the face of opposition from all sides, was to preserve the unity of the kingdom that Henri II had confided to her care. She had continued this policy without ever once weakening throughout the adolescence of both François II and Charles IX. Her second son's feeble health and lack of authority had forced her to begin playing one adversary off against another. This policy had so far been successful. She had avoided what everyone most dreaded: France's annexation by Spain. Philip II was a very greedy and ambitious man.

Yet the past was still clouded by the Saint Bartholomew's Night massacre, for which Victoire could never forgive the Queen. Though, as time passed, Victoire found she was able to be more detached and rational about what had at first seemed a gratuitously cruel act; she was beginning to see that things had not been so simple as she had imagined at the time.

One fine May evening Victoire and Anselme were walking together in the gardens of Alexandre's house, smelling the sweetness of the rose-scented air. Uncle and niece recalled a little nostalgically their arrival in Paris two years previously.

A footman came up to them. "M. Becavallo is here. He asks if the Comte and Mademoiselle will receive him despite the late hour."

Victoire gave a cry of joy. "Guy!"

"Tell him to come and join us," ordered Anselme.

The servant went to fetch Guy, and Anselme turned toward his niece. "You seem very pleased at this unexpected visit."

"I shall be happy to see Guy again," Victoire confessed. "And yet I had thought I could never find any pleasure in anything anymore."

Anselme observed his niece at some length, his troubled expression revealing his concern. When she had learned of Guillaume's death, Victoire had refused to eat anything for almost a week.

Guy rushed up to them. He could hardly contain his happiness, apparent in every line of his face. Anselme noted this with satisfaction. He liked Guy very much and saw no reason why Victoire should not marry this charming Venetian now that Guillaume was dead. After a few moments' conversation with the young man, which only served to confirm this idea in his mind, he withdrew, leaving the young couple alone together.

"Guy, I can't tell you how I suffered when I thought that terrible Adrien d'Etivey had killed you!"

She saw in his eyes the same unwavering tenderness that had so comforted her during their imprisonment together.

"And I was so desperate when I found no trace of you after Alexandre had freed me."

"So you haven't forgotten me?"

"How could I?"

Guy took her hand and raised it to his lips.

"Since I learned you were alive, I have so often imagined this moment when I would see you again. At last the time has come."

He led Victoire behind some bushes in a dark corner of the garden and pressed her tightly to him. "Victoire," he murmured, "I still love you."

She was surprised to feel such happiness in his arms. She hadn't forgotten Guillaume, but her grief at his death was less painful now. She hurried to speak first, guessing that Guy was about to ask her a question to which, for the moment at least, she did not wish to reply.

"I went through hell in that dungeon without you," she said.

Once again he embraced her with a passion that their separation had only served to intensify. "I don't ever want to leave you again. I can't live without you."

"Guy . . ."

"I know you don't love me: I can feel it," he said sadly.

She could not bear to hurt Guy. The ordeals they had gone through together had created an indissoluble bond between them. And yet she refused to be dishonest with him by pretending to love him. She could never love anyone again. So why should she not try to make Guy happy? He was more worthy of her love than anyone else could be.

"I need your love."

"Is it important for you?" he asked, surprised and hopeful.

"Yes," said Victoire in a scarcely audible voice.

"Set your mind at rest. You shall be loved as no other woman has ever been loved before."

Guy Becavallo's almost daily visits did Victoire good. Her uncle was delighted to see her smiling and taking pleasure in life once again. He encouraged the young man, with whom he had struck up a close friendship, and told him to come as often as possible. Victoire realized that Guy was becoming more attached to her with each day that passed, and felt he would soon ask for her hand. The only thing holding him back was his fear of a refusal. She was confused about her own feelings and intentions. She was still in the grip of the aftereffects of her shock at Guillaume's death. She had always loved Guillaume and deep down had never stopped hoping that one day she would meet him again and make him love her once more. And after all, he was the father of her child. If she decided to marry Guy to make a home for her child, Emeric would present a problem. She could only marry a man who was ready to accept the child as his own. As yet she had not dared to tell Guy about him.

If she was to tell him about Emeric, she would have to mention Guillaume as well. How would Guy react to the news that Victoire had been the mistress of another man? Though she did not love him with the passion she had felt for Gillaume de Louvencourt, she was afraid to lose him. He was her dearest and closest friend.

She badly wanted advice about what to do, and quite naturally thought of Anselme. But she hesitated, fearing her uncle might be somewhat ignorant about love. However, he brought up the subject first.

"You're seeing a lot of Guy. It would be dishonest of you to allow his hopes to develop if you do not intend to go on with your relationship at another level."

"You're right," sighed Victoire. "But what can I do?"

"You need not be in any hurry to make a decision that will change your own life and that of Emeric, too, but it would be a good idea for you to be clear in your mind what you want."

"But that's the trouble. I don't know!" cried Victoire.

"Guy would be a very honorable match for you. I have found out . . ."

Victoire interrupted him. "That doesn't surprise me!"

"But I must take care of you. You have no father or mother."

Victoire kissed Anselme tenderly. "You're everything to me, you know that. What should I do without your affection?"

Not wishing to show how touched he was, the Comte de Montmaur went on, "On his father's side, his family is allied to the Doge Alvise Mocenigo, who has governed Venice since 1563. When his father died, Guy replaced him as head of the family firm. He is not only the accredited representative of the Fuggers . . ."

"Who are these Fuggers?"

"They are a rich banking dynasty from Augsburg who founded their fortune during the last century in the spice and fabric trade. But their main claim to fame, for which they were in fact awarded a coat of arms, was when they assured Charles V of the Crown of the Holy Roman Empire. This meant that François

I, the grandfather of our present King, was supplanted."

"How did they do that?" asked Victoire.

"The elections to the imperial throne are often no more than large-scale bargaining campaigns. The person who offers most—who is the richest—wins. I'm telling you all this to show you that the Fuggers don't put just anyone in charge of their agencies. The man they choose must be both prosperous and honorable."

"So Guy owns a fortune?"

"A large one. And in addition, his father left him a very prosperous business with ships trading all over the Mediterranean. If you married Guy, you would provide for your son's future. Bear that in mind."

"I shall never marry out of self-interest!" exclaimed Victoire. "And in any case, livestock of Montmaur brings in enough money to provide for his needs!"

"True," said Anselme approvingly. "But not enough to give him a suitable position in the world."

Chapter XXXIV

The King's doctors were becoming increasingly pessimistic about his health, which had been undermined still further by his annoyance at his brother's behavior.

With the aid of his wife, who on this occasion had unexpectedly given proof of conjugal solidarity—a death threat from the Guise seemed likely—the King of Navarre had defended his cause very ably with his brother-in-law. He seemed to have extricated himself from his difficult situation without too much unpleasantness. However, he still remained a prisoner at Vincennes.

Montmorency-Damville, the Governor of Languedoc and brother of the Marshal who had been thrown in prison, was now in disgrace. Because of this he signed a truce with the Protestants, thus bringing the "Politicals" even closer to the Huguenots and weakening the Queen Mother's position. She was being squeezed in a vise, whose two arms were the Guise and Montmorency families.

Queen Marguerite was distraught with grief and mourned her lover quite openly. She wore black with death heads hanging from her necklaces and bracelets. This was her revenge on her mother and brother, who had refused to pardon her lover, and on the King of Poland, who, from distant Cracow, had expressed his pleasure at La Mole's imprisonment in a letter.

Meanwhile, no one except the Queen Mother seemed to be worried about the serious dangers threatening France. The Duc de Bouillon was pressing forward in the north, Damville in the south, and the Comte de Montgomery in Normandy.

Montgomery was finally captured at Domfront, to Catherine's great satisfaction. She promised herself to have him beheaded at the earliest opportunity, which was not long in coming.

Her eldest son was completely indifferent to the news. As one hemorrhage followed another, his only concern was his imminent death.

The King died on Whitsunday, May 30, at the age of twenty-four, after reigning for thirteen and a half years. He left no son to succeed him, only a daughter, Marie-Elisabeth.

Together with all the members of the Court, Victoire went to Vincennes to pay her last respects to the sovereign before he was embalmed. It was rumored that his death agony had been terrible, and that the memory of the Saint Bartholomew Night massacre had haunted him like a nightmare to the very end.

Parliament sent some Council members to ask Queen Catherine to become Regent, which she duly did. The King had already asked her to do so shortly before his death. A messenger was dispatched to tell the King of Poland he had succeeded to the throne. No one doubted that Henri III would hurry back with all speed.

Leaving the King's body at Vincennes, where monks kept vigil day and night, the Court returned to Paris in heavy mourning.

In Paris the Court was to return to the Louvre, where security could not be guaranteed as well as in the fortress of Vincennes. So the Regent had all the entrances to the palace walled up, with the exception of the main doorway, which was well guarded by constables and a company of Swiss guards. She feared conspirators still at liberty might try something else.

Victoire had been at Court for almost six months. She was tired of her duties and very much wanted to return to Montmaur to see her son. She had not so far dared to bring him to Paris, still fearing the journey would be dangerous for him. In the spring word was sent that several lambs had been born. Victoire was proud that her stock raising was beginning to be profitable, and was impatient to go and see for herself.

"I should so much like to show you all the changes I've made at Montmaur," she said to Guy one day. "I intend to ask the Queen to give me leave to spend the summer there. Why don't you come and spend some time with me?"

"I should love to," said Guy. "Unfortunately I must return to Venice with all speed. I have received a message this very morning telling me my presence is required there."

"So you'll be leaving soon?"

Victoire suddenly felt very disappointed. She had

already planned so many rides and walks they could take together, so many evening talks by the fireside.

"I am in despair having to leave you," said Guy. "I hope this is the last time I shall have to."

"I don't feel very happy you're going, either," said Victoire quite sincerely.

"I hardly dare hope that you will miss me from time to time."

Victoire smiled. "Surely you know how affectionately I feel toward you, dear Guy."

"In that case," he said in a voice that trembled slightly, "may I entertain some hope?"

She saw his keen eyes were full of anxiety. It was obvious he intended to propose, and she could see no way of putting him off.

"About what?"

"The only subject which touches my heart. When I return, will you agree to become my wife?"

Victoire was still not sure what she wanted, but she felt unwilling to commit herself irrevocably. She knew, however, that she would have to give him some reply.

"Give me a little more time to think," she begged.

Guy's face darkened. "You don't want to."

"I didn't say no."

Just then Anselme came into the small salon where they were talking and interrupted their conversation, much to Victoire's relief. "Guy has just told me he is leaving for Venice," she said.

"How I envy him!" said Anselme. "I should so much like to see Venice again before I die!"

"I should be very happy to offer you the hospitality of my house," said Guy Becavallo politely.

Then he had a sudden idea. "Why don't you both come with me?" he cried.

Tempted by this idea, which she had not even thought of, Victoire turned toward her uncle. "That would be marvelous!"

"That's true. But it's a long and tiring journey. I'm

too old now to travel so far," lamented the Comte de Montmaur.

"Come now!" said Victoire. "You're in perfect health."

"The idea deserves careful consideration," said Anselme thoughtfully.

When Guy had left he said to his niece, "I can see you're dying to see Venice."

Victoire smiled mischievously. "You must admit you're tempted, too!"

"Would it be reasonable to spend so much money?"

"We are making enough profits to do so," said Victoire proudly.

"You really do have an answer for everything. Perhaps it would be a good idea for you to get an idea of what kind of life you would lead if you married Guy."

"He proposed just now."

"And what decision have you reached, if I might be allowed to ask?"

"None."

All Victoire had to do now was to get the Queen's permission to leave the Court for several months. She had to decide whether to ask her directly, or through the Comte de Montmaur. Victoire had to admit the Queen Mother had always been kind to her and had seemed satisfied with her services. So she decided to approach her directly. She took advantage of a moment when Catherine was in a particularly good mood. The Queen had just returned from seeing Montgomery executed. He was the man who had involuntarily caused her husband's death, and was one of the most troublesome spirits in the whole kingdom.

"Well, so you want to go to Venice, Mademoiselle!"

"My uncle particularly wants to make this trip," she said, "while he still has strength to do so. He has so many happy memories of Venice!"

The Queen Mother remained deep in thought, and Victoire began to grow anxious. Perhaps Catherine would oppose the idea for some obscure reason which she would not even bother to explain. Victoire's fertile mind had already imagined a thousand delights, each more tempting than the last, which she might experience during her stay. Guy's own description, plus those which Sigismondo Cavalli had been only too eager to give, had provided more food for her daydreams.

"The King will stop at Venice on his return journey from Poland. The Ambassador has informed me that the Republic wants to welcome him and offer him a grand reception when he visits the city."

Victoire had no idea what connection there could be between the King's journey and her own. She gave the Queen a questioning look.

"You might be useful to me there. When you arrive you will contact our Ambassador, M. du Ferrier. I shall entrust you with a letter to him. Bring me a table, please."

Mademoiselle de Chabrière rushed forward with writing materials.

So the Queen was not opposed to her trip. Though Victoire felt very relieved, she could not stop herself from feeling a little anxious, too, wondering what services she could provide in Venice. She did at least speak the language—Anselme had taught her when she was still a child—but she would know no one there except Guy's family.

The Queen sanded her letter, then held it out to Mademoiselle d'Aillanges, who was heating the wax for the seal.

"You will mingle with the people around the King when he passes through Venice. M. du Ferrier will introduce you, and you will send me your observations through him."

"I shall try to give Your Majesty satisfaction."

In the depths of Catherine de Medici's dark eyes, Victoire detected a hint of melancholy. Was she thinking of her own country, which she had left at the age of fifteen and would never see again?

She wondered whether M. du Ferrier would be anything like his colleague in London. She found it quite amusing that, through a strange combination of circumstances, on this occasion, unlike when she visited London, her country's official representative would give her all the help she required.

Chapter XXXV

*V*ictoire had been in a state of almost permanent awe ever since she had arrived in Venice at the beginning of July. As she gradually got to know the city better, under Guy's guidance, she became entranced by its many charms. How would she ever manage to tear herself away from such a beautiful place? she wondered.

Venice had risen up out of the water and parts of it seemed only very shakily poised above the surface. They looked as though at any moment they might sink beneath the water once again. This was what fascinated Victoire about this strange city: it was constantly threatened by gradual decomposition. And yet what was still visible above the engulfing waters was more magnificent than anything she had ever seen before.

Guy's family—his mother, Donna Lucia, and his younger sister, Carlotta—lived in a huge palazzo looking onto the Grand Canal, alongside one of the most beautiful palaces in Venice, a wonderful example of elegant Gothic architecture. It was called the Ca d'Oro because of its glittering golden facade, which eclipsed all those around it in the first rays of the morning sun.

Donna Lucia had been born in France and had furnished her house with a mixture of the most beautiful objects from there and from her adopted country. Her husband had amassed an enormous fortune, to which her son constantly added, so she had been able to buy works of all the well-known artists. In comparison with her subtle, refined taste—and lack of funds to afford her self-indulgence—Victoire sometimes found the display of wealth she saw in other palaces ostentatious.

Though the Becavallos certainly did not belong to one of the oldest Venetian families, they occupied, Victoire realized, a very high position in Venetian society, since they had intermarried with many of the prominent families and, most importantly, that of the Doge Mocenigo.

Carlotta Becavallo, who was just sixteen, could expect to make a brilliant marriage, especially since she was exceptionally beautiful.

Donna Lucia was very pleased to have some fellow countrymen under her roof. She welcomed the Montmaurs very warmly and invited them to stay as long as they wished. In her magnificent apartment, with an army of footmen and maids to look after her every need, Victoire began to feel she could quite happily stay there for the rest of her life.

Guy would, she felt, make an admirable husband. His loving care enveloped her like a warm shawl.

He had presumably told his mother he wished to marry Victoire. Signora Becavallo made it quite clear by her whole attitude toward Victoire that she not only approved his choice, but that she already considered her as one of the family. But this, of course, made Victoire feel she had committed herself too soon. She felt she would shortly be forced to make a decision she would have preferred to postpone until later.

The Comte de Montmaur, to whom she confided her fears, reassured her. "It's true your reputation is compromised by your being constantly escorted by Guy, but only in Venice. Paris is a long way away. If you should wish to break off a relationship which would normally lead to marriage, you would, I feel sure, cause Guy terrible grief, but your own future would not really be affected."

"I'm still hesitating."

"You know I leave you completely free to make your own choice. I feel, however, that I must tell you that you could hardly make a better one."

Victoire sighed. "What about Emeric?"

"You'll have time to think about that when you've made up your mind. It will cause difficulties, there's no doubt of that."

Two days after they arrived in Venice, the Montmaurs and their hosts set off together one late afternoon in the grand blue gondola the Becavallos used on ceremonial occasions. From beneath the canopy which protected her from the setting sun, Victoire looked first one way, then another as Guy pointed out the palaces they went past on their way along the Grand Canal. The boats loaded with goods, whose sailors expertly avoided the richly ornamented private gondolas, were going, Guy explained, to unload their goods in the Fondaco dei Tedeschi storehouses which they passed, or in the Fondaco dei Turchi a little farther on.

"If it would interest you, I'll take you to visit the storehouses. A convoy is due to arrive shortly."

"Really, Guy!" exclaimed Donna Lucia, fanning herself vigorously to chase away the clouds of flies which at this time of day were buzzing above the fetid waters. "Is that a suitable amusement for a young lady?"

Guy smiled at Victoire. "I think it would interest Victoire to see them."

Victoire assented with a nod which only he could see. She had very quickly made up her mind about Guy's mother and sister. She found them charming, and delightful company, but was surprised by their frivolity. Both of them relied completely on Guy to look after the business, which they even claimed never to ask about at all. They spent money on their amusements without counting the cost, and lived in a style which many princesses would have envied.

Carlotta was very attached to her brother, who was ten years older than she. Since their father's death, Guy had done all he could to take his place. Carlotta had welcomed Victoire like a sister, and soon began to confide in her. She had told her, after first swearing her to secrecy, that she was in love with a young man who went past her windows every day at the same time and sang love songs to her in a beautiful voice.

Victoire was amazed she could fall in love with someone she had never even spoken to. But Carlotta had smiled, lost in her dream. "He'll find a way of sending me a letter. He must know who *I* am."

"But you never go out without an escort," Victoire had objected.

"He'll manage. He'll give one of my maids a purse of gold."

The gondola stopped in front of the Grimani Palace, which had been completed two years before. Two servants hurried to help the ladies get out without staining their dresses in the dirty water, which lapped against the green, slippery steps.

They went through an entrance hall paved with Istrian marble and already lit with a candelabra, its mirrors throwing back an infinite number of reflections of the warm, reddish light. They entered a huge, gold-ceilinged salon whose walls were hung with Flemish tapestries at least as beautiful as those in the Louvre. A group of people were chatting gaily together, drinking Cyprus and Samos wine from vermilion goblets, their base decorated with tourmaline.

The ladies who had been invited to the festivities had been ordered to appear in all their finery, and to display all their charms to honor their famous visitor, as living proof of the Republic's prosperity. The city's seamstresses had been at work day and night. On this special occasion, even the most avaricious husbands had agreed to open their purses so that their wives could appear suitably adorned.

The Montmaurs were introduced to the master of the house, Senator Grimani, and his wife, Donna Matilda.

"We are particularly pleased that you could come tonight since we are expecting the French Ambassador," said Donna Matilda graciously to Anselme. "We hope he will manage to slip away, though he must be very busy just now with your sovereign's arrival."

Since Victoire had arrived in Venice, the sole topic of conversation had, it seemed, been the visit of Henri III. Du Ferrier had a great reputation in the city, and this was at least partly the reason why the Doge and Council had decided to receive the King with great pomp and ceremony. They had come to believe it would be judicious to nurture their friendship with the French to counterbalance the influence of the Spaniards, whose ships were keen competitors of the Venetian fleet all over the Mediterranean.

The Republic intended to spare no expense to make the King's reception as brilliant and imposing as possible. Everyone in Venice knew about the celebrations to be held in honor of their royal visitor, the highlight of which was to be a banquet for three thousand guests in the Ducal Palace.

"Where will His Majesty stay?" inquired the Comte de Montmaur.

"At the Foscari Palace, which has been specially prepared for him," replied the Senator. "We very much hope the King will be happy there."

M. du Ferrier was announced. With the exception of the Papal Nuncio, he had managed to have precedence over everyone, including the Spanish Ambassador, to the latter's fury. Victoire watched an elderly man with a serious, kindly face enter the room. Everyone thronged around him, Victoire noticed, impressed, showing him every possible mark of respect.

The Ambassador bowed to Donna Matilda. "I dropped in to wish you good evening, Madame," he said in a gentle, steady voice. "But unfortunately I shall not be able to stay as long as I should have liked."

"I know that you must be overwhelmed with responsibility. Can you tell me what day His Majesty is due to arrive?"

"Doubtless July 18th."

"Goodness! So soon!" exclaimed one of the guests. "That only leaves us a fortnight to get ready!"

Just before du Ferrier left, Victoire went up to him. "Your Excellency," she said, "I have a letter for you from Her Majesty the Queen."

He stared at her in surprise.

"You have, Mademoiselle? But I received the post from France this very morning!" Then he added in an undertone, "It's true I'm convinced I'm not the first to read it."

"May I call upon you tomorrow morning?" Victoire asked respectfully.

"I shall be waiting for you, Mademoiselle."

Chapter XXXVI

*T*he Becavallos and their guests returned home after a pleasant evening at Senator Grimani's house, where several gentlemen had flirted assiduously with Victoire, to Guy's obvious displeasure. Alone in her room at last, Victoire leaned over the balcony and gazed at the stagnant black water beneath. She listened as the evening noises of the city gradually died down and its inhabitants prepared for sleep. In the palace on the opposite side of the canal, the candles were going out one by one, and the boatmen's cries had given way to a gentle splashing of water as the gondolas bobbed around their moorings.

The hot, humid July night enveloped the city, bringing sleep to many, but there were some who would experience fascinating adventures tonight, and yet others anguish. For it was during the hours of darkness that intrigues were plotted, when acts of revenge were committed, and all the world would know only the sight of a lifeless body drifting down a canal in the dawn light.

Victoire found even more disturbing the masked shadows tortured by envy, jealousy, and the desire for revenge which she imagined moving noiselessly along the alleys, disappearing into corners at the least noise, and breathing quickly when faced with the shining eyes of some other unknown murderer watching his prey.

She saw yet more shadows, clutching pieces of paper in their moist hands, hesitating for the last time before slipping their denunciation into the anonymous slot in the wall of the Ducal Palace. Then they left as quickly as they had come, but henceforth their peace of mind would be irrevocably destroyed.

Victoire hung over the balcony dreaming, quite forgetting to call the chambermaid to undress her. The door opened silently and two arms suddenly enfolded her and held her tight, making her heart beat quickly with fear.

"My love."

"You did frighten me," said Victoire, turning around. She smiled at Guy. "Haven't you seen enough of me for today?"

"And aren't you tired of looking at Venice?"

"No . . . and if I dared . . ."

"Tell me what you would do."

"I would tell you what I was wishing just then."

"I shall carry out your wish immediately if it is in my power to do so."

"I should like to go out very discreetly, with you alone," she said. "I long to make the most of this beautiful night."

"It shall be ours since you desire it."

Then Guy hesitated, looking at Victoire's brocade dress covered with pearls.

"You can't go out like that without a guard. By dawn the whole city would be gossiping about it."

Sadly Victoire had to admit that he was right. "So we can't do it?"

"There *is* one way."

"What's that?"

"You shall dress as my page, with a mask and a dark cloak. Then no one will guess who you are."

Victoire accepted joyfully, excited by the idea of disguising herself. A few moments later, when she had carefully hidden the white shirt and gray silk doublet Guy brought her, she called Antonella to undress her. She lay down on the bed and the maid drew the bed curtains and wished her good night.

She waited until the footsteps could no longer be heard in the gallery and then leaped out of bed. Rapidly she transformed herself into a young boy. She fastened on the mask and tucked her thick blonde hair beneath the hood of the cloak. Who would recognize Mademoiselle de Montmaur now, she thought, inspecting herself in the mirror.

Guy came to fetch her, also wearing a mask. Victoire noticed he had slipped a dagger into his belt and had taken off the long gold chain he usually wore.

The porter was half asleep; he opened a side door giving onto an alleyway just enough to let them slip out, and the motionless air, where the heat of the day still lingered, lapped around the young couple. At first they walked along in silence, guided by the smoky lamps which, here and there, at a crossroads or a square, made the shadows retreat.

This night expedition reminded Victoire of her panic-stricken race with Guillaume on Saint Bartholomew's Night, though this time she and her companion apparently had nothing to fear. Why was she so irresistibly reminded of the past? she wondered. Perhaps because it was so unusual for her to walk through a city at night, or perhaps because of the stifling hot air and the high walls which rose up on either side of them, hemming them in and almost meeting above their heads. It was strange that, in this city where she was so loved and where she had rediscovered, if not happiness, then at least a taste for life, she should be so strongly reminded of someone who was now dead. And this at a time when she was getting ready to marry Guy . . . or was she?

They walked across a square. Through a half-open shutter they saw a flickering light burning. They heard the noise of sword blows, and terrible groans.

Victoire stopped. "Someone's being murdered!" she whispered.

They shuddered to hear a heart-rending cry, quickly stifled.

"Shouldn't we do something?"

Guy held her firmly, and pulled her back beneath a porch. "Watch," he said.

Three gray silhouettes, which had until then been indistinguishable from the wall behind them, moved toward the house. Their slow, deliberate movements were both inexorable and agonizing.

An upstairs door was pushed sharply open and a body appeared. It seemed to hang in the air for a few seconds before hitting the ground with a dull thud.

One of the men lit a lamp and knelt down beside the corpse, whose bloodstained face could clearly be seen in the lamplight. He signaled to his henchmen to take hold of the head and the feet, and they all disappeared, following the man with the swinging lantern.

"Where are they going?" asked Victoire, her heart beating faster.

"It's better not to know."

A few minutes later they heard a splash as the body hit the water of a nearby canal. Then everything was still and silent once more.

The murder she had just witnessed quite by chance sharpened the parallel in Victoire's mind between the present night and that terrible night in the past, when Admiral Coligny had been assassinated. Though probably the world would hardly notice the disappearance of the man who was now floating in the murky waters of the canal.

"Do you want to go back?" asked Guy.

"No. Let's go on."

And yet, she thought, perhaps they should return to the safety of the palace. But, thinking back to that earlier night, they would not necessarily be safer indoors. The horror of that night had culminated within the Louvre itself with the discovery of her mother's bleeding body, and Father Izard's terrifying attempt to rape her.

As they came to the church of Santa Maria dei Miracoli, its doors opened and a young boy came out ringing a bell, though so quietly its sound was scarcely perceptible even in the still night. A priest in a surplice bearing the Saint Sacrament followed him.

"A Catholic is dying," murmured Victoire.

When the two reached the center of the square, the priest gestured to the child to stop and turned around, as though he was waiting for someone. Two figures, wearing vestments, closed the church door behind them and joined the procession, which set off again.

"They're going toward the Querini Stampalia Palace. They say the old Duke has been at death's door for the last two days. How you're trembling!" Guy went on, looking at Victoire. "Were you so upset at the sight?"

Victoire hugged Guy to her without replying, and the touch of his solid, comforting body reassured her. Once again he asked her, "Do you want to go back?"

"No," she said.

They went past a tavern from which lively talk and the laughter of drunken women could be heard.

"That's where the young men of Venice come to amuse themselves."

"Do you go there?"

"I have been," said Guy, smiling. "It's one of Alphonse d'Este's favorite places when he visits Venice. No doubt he will hurry here from Ferrara when he knows his cousin is coming."

"Which cousin?"

"Henri III, of course. Alphonse's mother was Renée of France, Louis XII's daughter. I imagine the Duke of Ferrara would be quite pleased to occupy the throne of Poland now that it is empty. He is probably counting on family solidarity to gain support for his plan from his French cousin."

"How do you know that?" asked Victoire curiously.

"Alphonse is one of my best friends. I'll introduce you to him."

When the bell tower struck three, Guy decided it was time they went home to rest.

"You've walked farther tonight than Carlotta does in a month," he remarked.

"I'm used to going riding almost every day. I need the exercise."

"That's enough for one night, however. We'll return by gondola."

"How can we?" asked Victoire, surprised.

"I asked Zuliano to wait for us at the Rio di Santa Luca. We're nearly there."

"I must admit I'm completely lost."

Guy smiled and pointed to a nearby palace. "Don't you recognize it?"

Victoire looked at the dark building. "No," she said.

"It's the other side of the Grimani Palace, where we were this evening."

But the house, which had seemed so lively and welcoming earlier, looked quite different now, with the pleasant dreams—or sleepless nights—of its inhabitants shut up close within it.

When they got to the canal bank, Guy whistled twice. A few moments later his personal gondolier, Zuliano, glided up to them from beneath a bridge.

Victoire was relieved to stretch herself out on the bearskins and soft cushions lining the boat. Whether she admitted it or not, her long walk over the paving-stones had tired her out. The gondola set off gently toward the Grand Canal.

Victoire laid her head on Guy's shoulder, and his arms tightened about her. "Are you just a little happy?" he asked.

"I think so."

"Would you like to live in this city?"

"Surely you can see I have already succumbed to its charms?"

"Venice is made for you," Guy said passionately. "You will be its Queen."

After all, why should she resist Guy's passionate embrace for which her whole body was longing? It was better to think of nothing, to forget the past and what might have been, and concentrate on the present.

But could she achieve with Guy the happiness she had glimpsed with Guillaume, and pursued in vain since? Would she achieve it here in the Doge's city, under the still-starlit sky that promised her so many more nights of love, like this one that was just beginning?

Chapter XXXVII

"*Well,* Mademoiselle, have you any idea what exactly Her Majesty is afraid of? Does she fear some attack on her son?"

Du Ferrier had just perused the Queen's letter. Perplexed by it, he was thinking out loud, staring at Victoire with his small, shortsighted eyes.

"After the events of the last few months, the Queen is surely quite justified in fearing a renewal of danger on every possible occasion," said Victoire, slightly embarrassed. "However, I do not know what danger a sovereign might risk in a city that is preparing a lavish welcome for him, and whose inhabitants are, or so I am told, kept under constant observation by a police force that is considered the best in Europe."

Du Ferrier smiled. "Goodness, you know that already? It's true that some things would be impossible in Venice. Others, on the other hand . . ."

He sank into his thoughts, which Victoire did not dare to interrupt. Was he trying to discover some hint between the lines of the letter that had so far escaped him?

"An attack," he murmured, as though trying out the various possibilities. "No, no one would gain from that. The King will be guarded all the time, not only by my own agents, which would make no difference, but by the Republic's agents, too. What else, then?"

Guy's remarks about Alphonse d'Este's ambitions came back to Victoire.

She suggested timidly, "During His Majesty's visit perhaps someone might try to obtain from him . . ."

She broke off, confused at having to express her thoughts before such a powerful person as the French Ambassador.

"Go on, I beg you."

"Promises, alliances, I don't know what else."

"The Doge doubtless hopes for a closer alliance with our powerful country. The Republic is now—a little late—regretting having given the Spanish ships a free hand; encouraging their supremacy by completely destroying the Turkish fleet at Lepanto. This attitude is what we expect, and is in keeping with our country's own interests. We are ourselves seeking allies to counterbalance Philip II's schemes. In any case, the Queen has already sent me instructions about that. You mentioned promises?"

Victoire hesitated. "A lot of people must have their eyes on the throne of Poland now," was all she said.

A spark of understanding flashed into du Ferrier's eyes. "Suppose an enemy of France occupied it?"

"Could that have serious results?" Victoire asked.

"Indeed," murmured the Ambassador, toying with a silver greyhound he used as a paperweight.

Victoire reproved herself for getting mixed up in all this. She knew nothing at all about Alphonse d'Este, except that he liked having a good time. She really did not know what had caused her immediate feeling of revulsion from him when Guy had said he was one of his best friends. She really was very illogical.

"Mademoiselle, the Queen assures me I can rely on you to carry out even the most delicate missions. And Her Majesty is not usually wrong about those she deigns to employ."

In the morning Guy usually went off to see about his business. Victoire often had to fall back on Carlotta's company, since her uncle went to Murano almost every day to see the glass blowers working. He was hoping to learn a few new techniques from them that would help him to perfect his art even further.

But unfortunately Carlotta was lazy. She rose late and then spent most of the morning putting off going out. She preferred long chats on the terrace, during which she ate sweetmeats until Victoire felt quite sick just watching her.

Carlotta's romantic imagination was just now in full flower since at last it had something to work on. As she had expected, the young man whose singing had so enchanted her had managed to send her a lengthy poem that celebrated her charms at great length.

Victoire was surprised she was contented with this fatuous correspondence, but she did not dare say anything to Carlotta, who was three years younger than herself. Guy's sister had never known the freedom of an adolescence spent galloping through the woods and meadows, had never in her life crossed the family threshold alone.

One day, to escape from yet another idle morning, Victoire begged Guy to take her to the storehouses as he had promised. He very readily agreed and they set off with Zuliano toward the Fondaco dei Tedeschi.

"Our trade and business, though it is still prosperous, does not bring in such huge profits as in the past," said Guy regretfully.

"Why is that? I thought the Republic was very rich."

"I didn't say it's poor. But competition is keener. And then there are the Turks. We have been at odds with them ever since the capture of Constantinople in 1453. The Ottoman Empire is always attacking our ships and coveting our possessions in the Mediterranean—in short, trying to ruin us."

"Haven't you fought them?"

"Only three years ago. We had to take revenge for our humiliations in Cyprus, and the terrible atrocities that followed, despite our heroic defense of the island. But alas! our victory could not bring us back the territories we had lost."

Guy was silent for a moment and then went on, "In addition to our defeats at sea, we have so often been at war, at first with France, then with most of our neighbors: Florence, Milan, and Genoa. As we have lost power, so Venice has declined. The riches no longer all come to us. In the past merchants from all over the world came to buy from us. Today most ships go through Lisbon."

"So you no longer receive taxes from them?" Victoire concluded.

Guy agreed, smiling. "Exactly. You understand the problem."

From the huge warehouses rose an extraordinary perfume that Victoire immediately knew she would never forget as long as she lived. The dock hands were neatly stacking sacks of spices; cinnamon, cloves, pepper, and ginger mingled their odors to produce a smell at once strong and heady.

"It's incredible!" she exclaimed.

Guy laughed at her enthusiasm. "I'll show you something more interesting than that."

They went through the main hall containing about twenty counters where employees were registering transactions, carrying out operations, and making evaluations. They entered another storehouse where the furs were kept.

"We have just received a consignment of sables," said Guy nonchalantly. "See if you like them."

Two men displayed the magnificent furs before Victoire. She began to think her own squirrel fur coat, which until then she had considered the height of elegance, would look shabby alongside them.

"Although it's not really the season, allow me to offer you a sable cloak, unless, of course, you would prefer marten or ermine," said Guy.

Even more beautiful furs appeared, and Victoire's head began to swim. "You choose for me," she murmured, dazed. "They're all so beautiful."

The whole city was feverishly getting ready to welcome Henri III, this twenty-three-year-old prince, the hero of the battles of Jarnac and Moncontour, who had just left a kingdom to whose throne he had only recently been elected. The reputation of his charm and good looks had preceded him, and all the ladies' hearts were already fluttering.

Palladio built a triumphal arch for the occasion, which Tintoretto decorated, and all the churches displayed their innumerable treasures.

Henri was arriving from Vienna, where he had been sumptuously received by the Emperor Maximillian, who was eager for Elisabeth of Austria to remarry with his brother-in-law. When he reached Pontalba he found waiting for him a carriage pulled by four horses: it was the Doge Alvise Mocenigo's generous present to welcome him. Wrapped in long black cloaks out of respect for their visitor's mourning, five hundred gentlemen were waiting, accompanied by the whole diplomatic corps, with M. du Ferrier at their head.

Then, at Meste, seventy senators dressed in crimson satin got out of their golden gondolas and prostrated themselves at his feet. Alphonse d'Este presented himself at Meste as well.

Alphonse had spent a few hours with the Becavallos before he hurried off to greet his cousin. He was a man of about forty; his face already showed signs of his indulgences, and his manners were too excessive to be sincere. Victoire found she didn't like him, and she particularly disliked his obvious influence over Guy.

She tried to hide her low opinion of him when Guy asked her what she thought of his friend.

"Don't you think Alphonse is charming?" he said. "And he's so intelligent."

"Do you really think he has designs on the throne of Poland?"

Guy smiled. "Why do you think he's in such a hurry to go to Meste? He wants to get to the King first."

"First?" asked Victoire.

"There will certainly be other candidates before

long. Another of the King's relatives, the Duke of Savoy, is also due to arrive."

"In your opinion there's a chance Alphonse d'Este might succeed?"

"I hope so," said Guy thoughtfully. "If he does, he's promised to make me Prime Minister. Then I should be able to offer you a much more exalted position . . . if you agree to marry me."

So Guy—reasonable Guy—was beginning to believe in what Victoire herself still considered to be a day-dream. She had no wish at all to go and live in Poland, a barbaric land with such a dreadful climate.

Chapter XXXVIII

The Doge Mocenigo went to welcome his royal guest at Murano. As the crowd shouted with joy, and the bells of all the many churches around the lagoon pealed out, Henri III embraced the Doge, refusing to allow him to kneel before him.

The King—together with the most important dignitaries, the Doge, and his cousin Alphonse, whose eagerness to see him he seemed to appreciate—went by galley to the Lido, where the Patriarch Trevisano and the Papal Nuncio were waiting for him. A solemn Te Deum mass was celebrated, after which came a long reception of welcome.

In the evening Henri III finally reached Venice, where an enormous crowd shouted its welcome as he drew near the city, a small figure standing in the prow of the *Bucentaure*. All the palaces glittered with a thousand lights, turning night into day. From the Becavallo family gondola tied up alongside the San Giogio island, Victoire and Anselme watched the fabulous display.

"I've never seen such a celebration."

"Not even for Madame Marguerite's wedding?" asked Carlotta. "There were fireworks over the Seine, I hear."

"It wasn't as beautiful as this."

When Henri III appeared on the balcony of the Foscari Palace, the crowd went wild with joy. A spontaneous ovation rose up from the people of Venice, who had been waiting all day to see him, and obviously liked what they saw. During the next few days quite a few women dreamed longingly of his subtly chiseled, somewhat triangular face, his blond beard, and his dark, piercing eyes which he inherited from his Italian mother.

The following morning Victoire received a message from du Ferrier asking her to find out all she could about what Alphonse d'Este was up to. She supposed the Ambassador must have found something out about Alphonse's underhanded schemings.

The night before, quite late, as Victoire was just getting ready for bed, she had heard a noise from beneath her open windows. Leaning over her balcony, she had caught sight of the Duke of Ferrara, dressed very simply. He went into the palace, leaving a large gondola driven by four sailors waiting for him at the bottom of the steps. A few minutes later he came out again with Guy. The gondola set off with them toward the Rialto bridge, where it disappeared around a corner.

Victoire immediately began to wonder why the two friends were going out together so late at night. The obvious conclusion was that they were off to have a good time together in one of the taverns Guy had pointed out to her.

And yet she felt sure there was some connection

between this late-night outing and the two men's joint ambitions. If she could find out what it was, she might be able to give du Ferrier some useful information. She was not at all sure that Guy would tell her the truth if she questioned him. If politics were by any chance involved, Alphonse would almost certainly have sworn him to secrecy. She would have to trick Guy into telling her, though she very much disliked the idea of doing so.

She knew quite well that she would not hesitate for a moment to betray Guy in order to help du Ferrier. She was quite convinced no good could come of Guy's friendship with this scheming fop. Moreover, like any other woman, she disliked seeing her lover under another—and stronger—influence than her own, which, worse still, she thought might well do him harm.

When she saw Guy the next morning, she was very cool toward him. He was immediately concerned.

"What's wrong? You look so distant."

Victoire turned her head away without replying.

"Tell me what's wrong, Victoire."

"I heard you come in . . . very early this morning."

Guy's face brightened. "Is that all?" he said, very obviously relieved.

"If you are already spending time with other women before we are even married, what happiness can I expect with you afterward?"

"Don't worry, my love. You have nothing to fear." He took her in his arms. "I can't tell you what it's about, because I've promised to say nothing, but I assure you I have not failed in my duty to you in any way."

Victoire looked unconvinced. "Why should I believe that?"

A struggle was clearly taking place in Guy's mind, which she was now sure she would win. \

He sighed. "All right, I'll tell you everything, but no one must know of it."

"Of course."

"The King is much honored by all the banquets he's being offered, and all the splendid receptions. But at the same time he wants to get to know Venice—which he loves—in complete freedom. In fact, he's doing very much as we did," said Guy, smiling. "He wants to be able to walk about Venice without a constant escort creating a barrier between him and the people. Alphonse and I are acting as guides on his nocturnal outings so that he can escape—however briefly—from protocol and ceremony. His Majesty must have been very bored in Cracow."

"What's happening tonight?" asked Victoire.

"We are to wait for the King at the Foscari Palace. If he can get away, we'll take him to see Veronica Franco."

"Who's she?"

"The most famous courtesan in Venice. His Majesty has said he'd like to visit her because her salon is said to be one of the most brilliant in the whole city. Has that reassured you?"

Victoire tried to smile. "I suppose the King will reward the Duke of Ferrara for his good offices."

"His Majesty is very pleased to be able to escape from the restrictions of his position for a few short hours," was all Guy would say.

As soon as Guy left for the Fondaco, Victoire hurried straight to Saint Mark's square, where she admired the basilica for a while before walking discreetly to the French Embassy. M. du Ferrier received her at once. He rose to his feet to greet her. "Already, Mademoiselle?" he said. "I didn't expect you to reply to my letter so promptly."

"I have been lucky enough to get hold of some information which I think will interest you."

"I'm listening."

"The Duke of Ferrara spent part of last night with the King."

"What?"

"And tonight he intends to take him to see Veronica Franco."

The Ambassador seemed overwhelmed by the news. "That's worse than I ever imagined! I won't ask you where you got your information. But are you sure of what you say?"

"You can easily check it. Have an agent posted outside the Foscari Palace this evening."

"There'll be more than one. I'm beginning to see why the King was so enthusiastic in his praise of his cousin this morning. He's very pleasant company, I must admit, but his reputation is not of the best. The Duke is currying favor with the King, finding entertainments for him and acting as a go-between. But what does he want from him?" asked du Ferrier thoughtfully. "Have you any idea?"

Could she trust du Ferrier? Victoire asked herself. Could she say more to him without compromising Guy?

"I know the Duke has the reputation of being always short of money. He spends money on his pleasures without ever counting the cost. But unfortunately, at the moment His Majesty is not much better off. If Queen Catherine hadn't sent him a hundred thousand pounds for the trip . . ."

"I'll try and find out what the Duke of Ferrara is after," she promised.

"We really must stop him from having such free access to the King."

"You need to provide a rival to him."

"Yes, but who?"

"Don't they say the Duke of Savoy is arriving soon?"

The Ambassador shook his head. "I don't think *he'll* entertain His Majesty very much. However, I'll send him a message telling him to hurry. He's a wise and cunning man. Let's hope his influence will counterbalance the Duke of Ferrara's."

Philibert Emmanuel of Savoy reached Venice two days after Victoire's talk with du Ferrier. He had galloped all the way after receiving the Ambassador's message. But by then the King had been constantly with his cousin for almost four days. Alphonse accompanied him to all the banquets and ceremonies he was obliged to attend. His obvious and growing favor with the King profoundly disturbed the cautious du Ferrier.

The Ambassador had thought it his duty to warn the sovereign about his nocturnal escapades and exorbitant expenditure, rumors of which had even reached the Doge, who of course had every reason to be delighted with it all. If Henri III was enjoying his stay in Venice, he would be more ready to be cooperative when the time came for serious talks.

The King's character had already been subtly changed by his experiences, as Victoire had seen when she had watched his behavior at a recent reception. He was no longer the quarrelsome Duc d'Anjou she had known at the Louvre, who was no different from all other Court gentlemen in his love of violent sports.

The young man had been profoundly affected by his discovery of the refined pleasures and the art of Venice, its almost Oriental ceremony and its subtle, perverse pleasures. Particularly since he had been beyond the reach of his mother's powerful influence for some months, an exile in a country that held no interest for him, where he had been counting the days before his return.

Du Ferrier was forced to watch, with a feeling approaching despair, this metamorphosis of his master. He knew he was quite powerless to struggle against the charm of a whole city.

For very different reasons, Victoire too was unhappy. Guy was following Alphonse d'Este about like a shadow, making plans which she was surprised to see such a normally sensible man let himself get involved in. By conspiring with the Duke of Ferrara, Guy was surely also exposing himself to danger.

On July 25 Victoire attended, with a marked lack

of enthusiasm, the sumptuous banquet given by the Doge Mocenigo in the Ducal Palace. Among the three thousand guests in the Great Council Chamber were the most beautiful women of Venetian society. They were dressed in white with jeweled collars and golden belts sparkling with diamonds, not to mention their necklaces, bracelets, and rings, and the pearl coils in their hair. Everyone marveled at this display of luxury, which Victoire was perhaps alone in finding somewhat excessive. There were so many jewels in the room that their individual beauty was lost in the crowd.

The ladies had the honor of performing a special dance for the King, who left his throne to join their revels. But all this display of pomp and beauty in his honor did not prevent the King, the following night, from slipping out with the Duke of Ferrara once again.

Chapter XXXIX

"We've been in Venice three weeks now," said Anselme de Montmaur to his niece. "Have you made your decision?"

Victoire sighed. "You must think I'm taking a long time to make up my mind. Before I met Alphonse d'Este I was almost resolved to marry Guy and live in this beautiful house. But now I find myself hesitating again, weighing the pros and cons."

"If I were you, I shouldn't worry about the Duke of Ferrara. When the King leaves, I'm sure we shan't see much of him again."

"But he's promised Guy that if he obtains the Polish throne he'll . . ."

"I can understand you're not very eager to go and live in Cracow. But you can be quite sure that when he leaves Italy, Henri III will forget all about his promises to his cousin. The likelihood of your friend becoming His Majesty Alphonse I's adviser is very remote, believe me."

"In that case . . ." She broke off. She was no longer sure exactly what she felt. She felt she loved Guy tenderly. He seemed to possess all the qualities necessary in a husband. She loved Venice and, in any case, she would often be able to visit France.

"I still haven't told him about Emeric."

"Think it over for a few more days. But this ambiguous situation can't go on forever, nor can this generous hospitality we are enjoying."

"It's terrible not to be able to decide!" exclaimed Victoire. "I've never been so unsure of myself in my life."

Despite the heavy humidity and heat the King managed to attend a session of the Senate, to visit the Arsenal where, in the space of a few hours, a galley was built in front of his eyes, to admire Titian's and Tintoretto's latest works, and to be very much entertained by a play by the Gelosi, a group of talented actors who had come from Milan to act before him.

Alphonse d'Este went everywhere with him, doing his utmost to amuse and make himself indispensable to his cousin. All the same, du Ferrier managed to have him excluded from the King's talks with Mocenigo. As a pledge of friendship between their two countries, the King gave the Doge a superb diamond. But to his great regret the Doge could not keep it: the customs of the Republic would not allow him to accept any gifts. The King bestowed ostentatious presents on all those around him: his host, Luigi Foscari, received a gold chain worth five hundred crowns. He bought pearls and diamonds. Meanwhile, du Ferrier had to beg for loans from all the city's bankers to pay for these expensive gifts. The hundred thousand pounds sent by Queen Catherine had not lasted very long.

But in the atmosphere of pleasure and delight characteristic of Venice, still dazzled by his discovery of a life so different from the French court—which was still dominated by hunting and sports—and despite all the Ambassador's solemn entreaties, Henri III seemed incapable of watching expenditures. Nor was he able to refuse the Duke and Duchess of Savoy—who had turned out to be more cunning than the Duke of Ferrara, despite appearances to the contrary—various strongholds in Piedmont, even though the citadels formed part of French territory. In despair at this display of frivolity, du Ferrier refused to be responsible for telling the Queen Regent the news.

The King finally tore himself away from Venice with great difficulty, promising never to forget his stay. He invited the forty young men who had made up his guard of honor to come with him to France as a gesture of thanks. His Majesty gazed sadly for the last time on the magnificent palaces, thinking no doubt of the gloomy, austere Louvre. For the last time he breathed the disturbing perfume of Venice, a mixture of jasmine, spices, sea air, and decomposition, and said farewell to the Doge, who had accompanied him by gondola as far as the first city on dry land.

Now all he could look forward to were the cares of government, an empty treasury, and a kingdom where anarchy reigned. If France's fortunes were to be restored and the warring factions stilled, if the Queen Regent's arduous and delicate work was to be fittingly continued, he would need to display exemplary firmness of character, tempered with tolerance.

After the whirlwind round of celebrations, the Becavallos and their guests were quite naturally tired, and ready for a more restful life. The magnificent dresses

The Priceless Passion

were hung up in the wardrobes and the jewels pu
away in their boxes until the next opportunity to show
them off.

A rich gentleman from one of Venice's oldest fam
ilies, Domenico Falier, had been so impressed by
Carlotta's beauty and youth, which had shone to per
fection at the Doge's reception, that he had asked fo
her hand. Both Signora Becavallo and Guy presse
her to accept such a brilliant match, which would
strengthen their position in Venetian society even fur
ther.

Carlotta was very flattered by his offer and did no
hesitate for long. Her future husband could hope to
occupy the most important offices in the Republic. Sh
herself would be in a very enviable position and migh
even one day find herself the wife of the Doge.

Once his sister was engaged, Guy began to urge Vic
toire to fix the date of their own marriage. He wante
the two ceremonies to take place on the same day:
they could hold a magnificent joint celebration.

Tormented by uncertainty, Victoire kept on postpon
ing giving him a definitive reply. She began to feel sh
needed to get away from Guy and Venice for a few
weeks. She felt too close to him to make a calm deci
sion about whether she really wanted to marry him
She realized quite well that the Becavallo family an
even her uncle found her attitude strange and irritating
After all, in Paris she had already promised that sh
would make her decision in Venice. And now that he
stay was coming to an end, she was asking for yet an
other postponement. She was anxious to leave for
France again, and above all to see Emeric.

She had considered at length how best to tell Guy
about her son. But as the days passed she found the
idea of telling him the truth face to face increasingly
difficult. Would he not feel—and justifiably so—that
she had shown a lack of confidence in him which he in
no way deserved? Ultimately she felt it would be easier
to reveal the *fait accompli* to her lover in a letter. Then

474

the choice would be up to him. Perhaps he would no longer even want to marry her.

They had just made love for the last time. The next day Victoire was to leave Venice. She rested her head on Guy's shoulder, their bodies still entwined. Once again, as after each time they made love, she was aware of a delicious, almost animal feeling of well-being. She told herself she must be mad to deprive herself of such pleasure voluntarily.

"I'm frightened of losing you," said Guy, holding her tightly to him. "I feel I shall never see you again if I let you go."

"How absurd!"

She leaned back on her elbow and examined her lover's finely sculpted face, just visible in the soft moonlight.

"Don't be sad. You know I'll come back soon."

"Perhaps."

She too was thinking "Perhaps." And yet she could not bear to make Guy suffer, after all they had shared and suffered together.

"Do you love me a little at least?" he questioned her anxiously.

She declared quite honestly, "There's no one I love as much as you." A shadow from beyond the tomb could not compete with a living person whose skin was soft to the touch and whose warm, tender lips were running over her body.

"Well, then," he asked, "why must you inflict the torture of this separation on me? I shall have to wait here alone for your return in a place where everything will remind me of you."

"I'm different from the Venetian women. They seem ready to accept their fate, but I want to choose mine. If my parents were alive, perhaps they too might have forced me into a marriage they thought advantageous for me."

"Do you think either my mother or I have forced

Carlotta in any way? You must realize this marriage fulfills all her dearest wishes."

Yet again she found it impossible to explain to Guy that Carlotta's aspirations were totally unlike her own.

"Since fate has made me free, I must not make a mistake," was all she said.

"So you think it would be a mistake to marry me?" exclaimed Guy so sadly that Victoire was overwhelmed.

"I couldn't imagine anyone who would make a better husband than you. But I want to be sure that *I* can make *you* happy. Three months will soon be over."

"They will seem like an eternity to me."

He began, with a mixture of fury and despair, deliberately to arouse Victoire's desire until she threw herself panting against him, impatient to be possessed.

Chapter XL

Victoire and her uncle crossed Venezia, Lombardy, and Piedmont and then began the steep climb up Mount Cenis. The weather was fine and they got through the pass without too much difficulty despite the steep, dizzily twisting roads. By the end of August they reached France.

The old man cast a last, melancholy look at the Alps, whose summits were haloed with the orange light of the setting sun. "I've crossed these mountains for the last time," he said sadly.

"Why do you say that?" Victoire protested sharply. "We shall be returning to Venice in three months."

The Comte de Montmaur looked skeptical. "That

would surprise me," he said. "I don't think you'll ever marry Guy. Otherwise you would have decided already."

"I *have* decided."

"Why couldn't you have told him, then? That was cruel of you."

"As soon as we get to Paris I'll write to him, and tell him about Emeric at the same time."

She had been missing Guy terribly since they had parted. When she remembered his attentiveness toward her and his unstinting tenderness, she wondered how she could ever have left him. She could no longer even understand herself why she had left the city where she had been so happy. Perhaps she was becoming difficult to please. She looked at the enormous sapphire ring she wore on her left hand that Guy had given to her as she was leaving.

"I shall give you the complete set when we are married," he had said, smiling. "The jeweler is mounting the stones for me."

As the Montmaurs were making their way toward Paris through countryside whose poverty and devastation caused them much sorrow, the new King was traveling to Lyon, where the Regent, the King and Queen of Navarre, and the Duc d'Alençon, who was now known as Monsieur, were awaiting him.

The King's accession had awakened a spark of hope in the French people, who were exhausted after twelve years of civil war. Would the new king have sufficient authority to maintain public order when even his own family was seriously divided?

When they arrived in Paris, Anselme and Victoire returned to stay with Alexandre d'Hautemart. Alexandre had left orders for them to be received, though he was not at home.

"Do you think I could have Emeric brought to Paris now?" she asked her uncle. "I haven't seen him for so long."

"I don't see anything against the idea. He is ten months old now, and quite able to stand the journey."

Victoire hastened to tell their steward to arrange for the child to be brought to Paris with his nurse and Godefroy. When she had sealed the letter, she remained seated at the writing desk, thinking how she should phrase her letter to Guy. She spent an hour trying out sentences in her head, but none of them sounded quite right, so she put it off until later.

One beautiful sunny September day, three days after she arrived in Paris, Victoire decided to spend the afternoon wandering about with Jacotte near the Saint Michel bridge, looking at the shops, and perhaps making a few purchases. She felt the need to renew her contact with Paris. She had finally fallen in love with the city despite the filth and the lack of open space to walk in.

The Comte de Montmaur disapproved strongly. He felt that Jacotte, who was only seventeen, was not sufficient escort for his niece. But he was incapable of refusing Victoire anything she really wanted, so he let her go, and then spent the time she was away anxiously waiting for her return.

The two girls walked along Rue Saint Jacques from Alexandre's house toward the Seine. They were constantly jostled by people and animals of every kind. Dogs, cats, chickens, and pigs were scavenging about in the street looking for food.

Victoire ordered some ivory-colored suede gloves, bought some iris water in a perfume shop, and then offered to buy Jacotte a lawn collar.

"Haven't you got a young man yet?" asked Victoire. She had taken a great liking to the young maid who had replaced Héloïse, and who was quite alone in the world.

Jacotte blushed. "That is to say . . . well, I'm very pleased that Godefroy is coming."

Victoire smiled. "You've chosen a fine boy there. I'll buy you your wedding dress."

"Oh, thank you, Mademoiselle."

Suddenly, among the crowd idling across the Petit Pont, Victoire caught sight of a man who looked amazingly like Guillaume! She only got a side-view of him as he bent over to look in a shop window, but his dark hair and profile looked the same. Feeling faint, she leaned against the wall for support. She trembled at the sight of this apparition from the dead, which had brutally shown her how important Guillaume's memory still was to her.

"What's wrong, Mademoiselle? You've gone all white. Do you feel ill?" inquired Jacotte anxiously. "Shall I run and fetch some salts from the apothecary? It's quite close."

"No. Don't bother."

She was panting with emotion. Gradually her breathing became regular and they resumed their walk.

"We'd better go back, Mademoiselle."

But Victoire wanted to see what the young man had been examining so attentively a moment ago. She looked in the shop window and saw a display of daggers. With a slight sense of shock, she noticed a dagger almost exactly the same as the one Guillaume had given her after the Saint Bartholomew Night massacre. The inlays of the handle were similar, though the blade was a little narrower. Hers must certainly have come from this shop. She almost went in to question the shopkeeper. But what good would that do?

Victoire did not mention this incident to her uncle. It would make him sad to no purpose to realize she could not forget Guillaume. He was constantly urging her to write to Guy and say when they would return to Venice. But she still couldn't make up her mind to do so.

Each day she went out with Jacotte and retraced their walk of that fatal day when she had thought she had seen a ghost. She hung about for hours near the arms dealer's shop, going back and forth in front of the gray-haired merchant, who finally became amazed at seeing her there so often.

One particularly warm afternoon Victoire came across the dealer as he was sunning himself on his doorstep. He watched her for a few minutes without speaking, then said gently, "Mademoiselle, you often come to look at my weapons . . . and you look so sad."

Almost despite herself, Victoire replied, "Someone once gave me a dagger which must, I think, have come from your shop. Here, it was almost the same as this one."

The old man picked up the dagger. "It's almost two years ago now," said Victoire with a sad smile. "How could you possibly remember who bought it?"

The old man shook his head. "I do remember," he said. "The gentleman has been back several times since then. He asked me to make a dagger for a young lady, so it had to be easy to handle. Was that for you, then?"

"Yes."

"I hope you were satisfied with it?"

"Indeed I was."

"He ordered another dagger like it shortly afterward."

"That was for me, too."

"Had you lost the first one?"

"No, I left it in the body of someone who attacked me."

"Well, I hope you still have the second one."

"I'm afraid not," Victoire admitted with a smile.

"Bless my soul! You're a dangerous lady! Well, then, your friend will have to give you a third dagger."

"He can't," Victoire murmured. "He's dead."

She felt on the verge of tears. The old man looked at her sympathetically, but also with surprise. "Oh, no, he isn't! Why, he came here only last week and ordered a particularly sharp dagger."

"Guillaume! It can't be true!"

"I don't know the gentleman's name. All I know is, I promised it for him by Saturday."

Victoire said to herself the dealer must have made a mistake and be thinking of some other customer. Yet she could not stop herself from foolishly hoping. She knew she would count the hours until Saturday came and on Saturday morning she would station herself opposite the shop and examine everyone who went in. Suppose one of them was Guillaume? She dared not think so.

Chapter XLI

*V*ictoire was so happy to see Emeric again. The crying baby she had left had grown into a handsome, laughing, lively little boy with Guillaume's bright blue eyes. For a few seconds Victoire quite forgot her conversation with the arms dealer.

But then, as the hours slowly went by and the fateful day approached, she began to feel feverishly impatient. She could neither sit still nor concentrate for more than a few seconds. Her mind kept racing ahead to her meeting with the unknown man. He might be Guillaume, or he might be a complete stranger who, like him, was a customer of this particular arms dealer who engraved the hilts of his weapons with such sure taste.

Reason told her she must not base her hopes on what would almost certainly prove to be a coincidence.

There must be dozens of gentlemen in Paris of about the same size and shape as Guillaume, with the same thick straight black hair. She hadn't even seen the man's face. On so many occasions she had—even in Venice or London, in spite of its being so improbable— thought she had glimpsed her lover turning the corner of a street, looking through a coach window, or seated in an inn. Yet she had never before been so struck by the resemblance: his image had never been so clear in her mind.

After supper on Friday evening the servants had retired and Anselme and his niece were sitting together in the small blue salon. For the first time in his life Anselme lost his temper with Victoire.

"Allow me to tell you that I find your conduct unthinkable," he said bitterly. "We've been here ten days already and, to the best of my knowledge, you haven't written to Venice."

"I've no excuse at all," Victoire admitted. "Guy would be right to feel angry toward me."

"What the devil are you waiting for?" exclaimed Anselme. "Until Emeric is ten? Now he would never know that Becavallo is not his real father. Think about your child a little if you're incapable of being reasonable about yourself."

Victoire sighed. "You're quite right."

"Added to that, I just don't understand you. During the journey you told me you had made up your mind, didn't you?"

"Yes."

"Well, then," said Anselme despairingly, "have you changed your mind again?"

"I promise you I'll write to Guy this evening. And I'll send the letter off tomorrow if . . ."

The Comte de Montmaur choked on a mouthful of brandy he was savoring and exploded.

"If what? What new excuse are you going to invent to delay your reply? That poor man . . ."

Victoire interrupted him. "I'd better tell you everything." And she told him about her walks to the Petit Pont and her foolish hopes.

Anselme softened immediately. "Poor child! It distresses me to see you at the mercy of such idle dreams . . . They're doing you harm. M. de Surgy told you he was with Guillaume just before he died. How can you be so mad as to believe a shopkeeper's idle chatter? He probably has ten customers who look like Guillaume."

"I know it's ridiculous of me to wait any longer," Victoire murmured, bowing her head to hide the tears in her eyes.

"Do you still love him as much as that?" asked Anselme, dismayed. "I thought you had forgotten him. In that case, you'd better not marry Guy. You'd only make him unhappy."

"Tomorrow evening I promise I'll give up all hope," said Victoire.

"You really would do better to admit the truth to yourself," said Anselme.

That night Victoire hardly slept at all. When she finally dozed off for a moment, she had a strange dream. She was in the vaults of the convent where she had once been imprisoned, searching desperately for Guy. Pursued by the Mother Superior and Gilone, she wandered interminably through a maze of corridors. She dared not call Guy's name for fear of revealing her whereabouts in the darkness. Finally she reached a kind of grotto which opened out onto a lake. On the other side of the black waters, quite out of reach, she saw Guillaume standing on a rock, dressed as he had been on Saint Bartholomew's Night.

She woke up with a start and soon afterward heard five o'clock strike. She waited impatiently until seven, but then she could bear it no longer and rang for Jacotte.

"You *are* awake early today, Mademoiselle."

"Help me dress, quickly. We're going out."

"So early!" cried Jacotte in surprise. "What are we going to do?"

"Walk to the Petit Pont, as usual."

"Again! Mademoiselle never seems to tire of that walk."

"This will be the last time. We may have to wait there for a long time."

She realized she had not asked the arms dealer what time Guillaume visited him. In any case, she was so afraid of missing him that she preferred to spend all day, if necessary, standing opposite the shop watching the passersby.

By nine she was pacing up and down the bridge with Jacotte, and her interminable wait began. Often during the morning she sent Jacotte to buy something for her; she desperately needed to be alone. She stared at every man who passed, and earned herself quite a few offensive remarks.

"Well, Mademoiselle, are we staying here all day? It's almost lunchtime."

"You go back if you like," said Victoire. "I'm staying here."

Jacotte realized Victoire would not budge from her observation post, so she bought them some fritters.

"The Comte won't be pleased," she said again.

"He knows where we are," was all Victoire said.

She bit hungrily into her fritter—she hadn't realized how ravenous she was—and for a few seconds her attention was diverted from the weapons shop. When she raised her eyes again, she saw Guillaume. He came out stealthily, as though he was afraid of something, then hastened away in the opposite direction from where she was standing.

Dropping her food, Victoire ran after him as best she could in her robe. In her haste she bumped into people hanging about in the street, knocked into a cart full of poultry, and then almost overturned a water carrier with his heavy buckets. By the time she finished apologizing, Guillaume had disappeared into the crowd.

She crossed the bridge and came to a halt in front of the Hôtel Dieu, not knowing which way he had gone, by the Notre Dame bridge or the Pont au Change. She searched all over the Ile de la Cité and was just about to give up in despair when she saw Guillaume emerge cautiously from a doorway near the Conciergerie.

She raced toward him, mad with joy. This time she wouldn't let him escape. He looked back toward her. She was only twenty yards behind him and the street was fairly quiet, so he could not possibly have avoided seeing her. She waited, out of breath, for him to turn back and greet her.

Instead he gave her, she thought, the ghost of a smile and then positively fled toward the Seine. He leaped into a boat, which set off immediately. Victoire had fallen in her haste. By the time she picked herself up and reached the water's edge, Guillaume was already at the other side. Out of reach, just as in her dream.

Dumbfounded, incredulous, Victoire stood stock-still, staring at without seeing it, the body of a ginger cat floating along in the muddy waters of the Seine. Why had Guillaume refused to recognize or speak to her? Why had he not let her go near him, as though he feared to come into contact with her? What was the meaning of his desperate flight, as though the Devil himself were at his heels?

She suddenly felt more miserable than she had felt at any time since she had learned of Guillaume's death. The only possible conclusion to be drawn from his strange behavior was that he no longer loved her—if he ever had—and no longer wanted to see her. But he might at least, out of politeness, have explained to her that his feelings had changed and he no longer wanted anything to do with her. Surely he knew Victoire well enough to be confident that she would have left him immediately, and he would never have set eyes on her again. This strange behavior was totally unlike what she knew of him. But the most extraordinary part of the whole fantastic incident was that he was truly alive. Why should M. de Surgy have lied to her?

Thoughtfully Victoire retraced her steps across the Île de la Cité, turning around on several occasions to look behind her. She had the impression that a small, sickly-looking, slightly bowlegged man was following her. She would never have noticed him at all—his appearance was perfectly ordinary—had she not realized he was trying to remain unnoticed.

She wanted to make sure, so she went into a herbalist's and bought some sage and lime blossom. She deliberately stayed there some time chatting to the shopkeeper. When she came out again the little man had gone. But five minutes later she caught sight of him again by the Petit Pont, partly hidden behind a street stall. He was obviously waiting for her. A little disconcerted, she stopped, and it was he who came up to her.

"Mademoiselle de Montmaur?"

"Yes."

How did he know her name? she wondered.

"You must not try to see M. de Louvencourt again. If you meet him by chance, ignore him. I am your humble servant, Mademoiselle."

Before she had had time to react, he had bowed to her and was swallowed up in the crowd.

Victoire thought she was going mad. She could not order her thoughts at all. For the moment, out of all the incomprehensible things that had happened that day, there was only one she would allow her mind to dwell on: Guillaume was alive. Despite his strange, upsetting behavior, she suddenly felt very, very happy.

On the bridge she met Jacotte, who was almost in tears. "Ah, Mademoiselle!" she lamented. "I tried to follow you, but you were going too quickly and I lost you. I didn't know what to do. But you've fallen! Your dress is all dirty!"

"It's nothing," said Victoire, who hadn't even noticed. "Come on, we'll go back now."

Jacotte remarked, "You look very happy."

It was almost two. Victoire had only swallowed two or three bites of food all morning, and she felt ravenously hungry. When they got back to the house, she asked the servant to bring her some food and wine immediately. She was just finishing some stuffed rabbit when Anselme came in. He was expecting his niece to be terribly disappointed, and had obviously been thinking how best to console her. But when he saw her radiant face, he cried, "So it *was* true? Guillaume's alive?"

"Yes."

"In that case, why didn't you bring him back here with you?"

"I didn't speak to him."

"Why not?"

"He ran away when he saw me."

The Comte de Montmaur stared at Victoire, wondering whether she was teasing him.

"I'll tell you the story. I expect it will seem as absurd to you as to me," said Victoire.

When she had finished explaining, Anselme shook his head. "I just can't understand all that at all."

"That's how I feel," Victoire agreed. "But I shan't write to Guy today."

"For once I agree with you," Anselme sighed. "We must wait until we learn more about all this."

Chapter XLII

*T*wo days later Victoire received a long letter from Guy Becavallo. He didn't seem as yet to be worried about not hearing from her. On the contrary, he described at some length all the preparations he was making for her return. He obviously considered she was engaged to him, and suggested they should get married at the beginning of February.

Dismayed by all this, Victoire read her uncle the letter.

"You can imagine how I feel. What shall I do in the circumstances?"

"I really think you shouldn't do anything at all until you have at least spoken to Guillaume."

"That seems the most difficult thing in the world to do," remarked Victoire sadly. "Of course, I shall return to the Ile de la Cité. I remember which house he came out of. Perhaps he'll go back there one of these days."

"Well, don't go out again with just Jacotte. Take Godefroy at least," Anselme begged her.

"If you wish," Victoire agreed.

There was a moment's silence. Somewhat embarrassed, the Comte de Montmaur cleared his throat before inquiring cautiously, "Well, if it *does* turn out that M. de Louvencourt is no longer interested in you, what would you do?"

"I haven't given it a thought."

"You'd better do so. I don't want to see you settled

down at any price. But you would be very unlikely to find such a good match as Guy again."

"Poor Guy," was all Victoire would say.

It was true, she really did pity Guy with all her heart for the terrible grief she would cause him—Guillaume would only have to say one word and she would follow him to the ends of the earth. Though he would have to contact her in some other way than through the little bowlegged man.

Followed by her two servants, she resumed her daily walks again. She paced up and down every street on the Ile de la Cité, though she concentrated particularly on the area around the Conciergerie. One day she thought she glimpsed Guillaume's messenger. This made her feel a little more hopeful, though she could not be absolutely sure it was him.

During the afternoon of the fourth day of her search, she suddenly glimpsed Guillaume's face for a second at a first-floor window. The head disappeared immediately, and a curtain was dropped back across the window. Victoire hesitated whether to go into the house and demand an explanation. While she was standing there indecisively, she made a careful note that the house was at an intersection. Glancing up once again to the window where she had seen Guillaume, she saw the little man, who was very clearly gesturing to her to go away as quickly as possible. More and more disturbed by all this, Victoire finally left the street, determined to return the next day.

Provided, of course, that Guillaume hadn't gone out of his mind, and that all this had some meaning, what could he possibly be doing in this very modest-looking house standing at an intersection near the Pont aux Meuniers?

At first there seemed to be only one possible explanation: he was running away from Victoire and hiding from her. But then she thought back to the moment when she had seen Guillaume come out from the arms dealer's shop. He had looked all around to make sure the way was clear before heading for the Seine. But at that time he had not even seen Victoire, so it couldn't possibly be *her* he was trying to avoid. They had met quite by chance, from his point of view at least.

She tried to form some coherent picture from the different information she had. Guillaume had ordered a particularly dangerous weapon to be made; he was hiding in Paris, and watching out from a window for something or someone that was certainly *not* Victoire. It was quite obvious he wasn't thinking about her at all.

Nevertheless, he had taken the trouble to send her a message that could be summed up as: "Keep out of my way!" He seemed annoyed for her to be anywhere near where he was.

Suddenly she found it strange she had not seen Boris; he normally never left his master's side. Had the sickly little man replaced him?

There was something mysterious going on, which Victoire swore to herself she would find out about. If someone had told Guillaume that Victoire had been staying in Venice and was engaged to Guy, he would have every reason to be bitter about her behavior. This would be one possible explanation of why he had refused to speak to her.

Utterly crushed by this thought, Victoire walked slowly back to the Hautemart house. She absolutely must let Guillaume know that she had thought he was dead, and that she had not forgotten him. But how could she speak to him when he wouldn't let her near him?

For a good part of the night Victoire turned the problem round and round in her mind. At some moments she felt almost brave enough to force her way into Guillaume's retreat on the island. If she managed to get in, should she tell him about Emeric? But she rejected this idea; she would not use blackmail to bring her lover back. She must try to reconquer his heart— if that were possible—some other way, and for that she would need to see him again.

The next morning it was raining hard, and Victoire had to wait until five in the afternoon to go out. To the usual filth cluttering the streets was added a layer of thick mud. The few pedestrians were liberally splashed every time a cart went past through the puddles.

"It's really not nice to be out in Paris in this weather," Jacotte complained, lifting her skirt almost up to her calves.

Victoire had mischievously told her that it wasn't absolutely necessary for her to come, as Godefroy was already accompanying her. But not for anything in the world would Jacotte have given up the opportunity to walk three paces behind Victoire alongside Godefroy.

As she went past the armorer's shop she met his eye and smiled good-day at him. He jumped up from his bench and she realized he wanted to speak to her.

Slightly surprised, she went into the shop, leaving her companions outside.

"It *was* him, wasn't it?" asked the shopkeeper excitedly.

"Yes."

"Don't go to the island, you know where. It may be for today."

"What?" asked Victoire, who hadn't understood this at all.

But two gentlemen had come into the shop to look at weapons, and she could get nothing else out of the man. So she walked on toward the Petit Pont, as she had been intending to. What was going to happen on the island, and why should she not go there? It was all becoming more and more mysterious.

The bridge was full of life. The shopkeepers were

uncovering their goods now that the rain had stopped, and their shrill cries began to ring out again.

"Try my fresh endives!"

"Two hares for eight sous! A bargain!"

"Who wants some eel pâté from Melun?"

"Ask for good Argenteuil wine!"

Glancing at the laden stalls without really seeing all the food and drink, indifferent to all the shopkeepers' cries, Victoire walked across the bridge at an even pace, without really knowing what she intended to do.

Godefroy came up to her and whispered, "Mademoiselle, I think we're being followed."

Victoire turned quickly around, expecting to see the man who had brought Guillaume's message. But he was nowhere to be seen.

"Which one?"

"I'm not quite sure, but I think the red-haired man with the curly mustache looking at the cockerels to the left of the canary bread seller."

"I see the one you mean."

"I'd already noticed him when you went into the armorer's. But perhaps he's just hanging about with nothing to do," said Godefroy, who was always cautious in what he said.

"We'll find out."

"I don't like these walks on the island," Jacotte sighed.

Instead of going to the left toward the Conciergerie, Victoire walked toward Notre Dame. On the square in front of the church a Dominican friar was preaching eloquently, exhorting Catholics to repent. Victoire made her way through the narrow alleys toward the Pont au Change.

"He's still fifty paces behind us."

Who *could* this man be? Was he yet another messenger from Guillaume who was taking his time to speak to her? Perhaps he wouldn't show himself until she came close to the house. The minutes went by and

Victoire grew more and more perplexed. It would soon be nightfall. She knew she really ought to turn back. But she refused to be kept away from whatever was going to happen today, according to the armorer, and which involved Guillaume.

For a few moments Victoire had been aware that Godefroy was feeling uneasy.

"Mademoiselle, don't go any further. It isn't a good idea to walk about in Paris after sunset."

Reluctantly Victoire conceded this was true.

"And then," the squire went on, looking constantly to right and left, "I have the impression we're being watched from every side."

"Oh, you're exaggerating!" said Victoire.

But she too could sense something unusual in the air. She kept glimpsing shadowy figures that melted away as they approached. Suddenly the narrow street seemed silent and deserted.

As they went past a door set back in the wall, an anonymous figure detached itself momentarily from the shadows and whispered, "In the name of God, flee! Soon it will be too late!"

By now it was too dark to make out anything clearly, and the man disappeared as soon as he had given his warning. Dusk was falling rapidly over the narrow streets. A hundred yards ahead was the house where Victoire had glimpsed Guillaume. "Mademoiselle! You heard that? Let's go!"

He took her hand decisively and pulled her in the opposite direction.

But he soon stopped. At the end of the street behind them a dozen or so fearsome-looking men had appeared, cutting off their retreat.

"Mon Dieu!" exclaimed Jacotte in complete panic. "We're lost!"

"Let's go in the other direction," said Godefroy. "Quick!"

"There's no point even in trying," replied Victoire calmly.

She had seen another group of men coming toward them from the opposite direction. It was too late; she at last realized that they were in mortal danger. Now at least she would find out what was happening.

Chapter XLIII

$\mathcal{V}$*ictoire* realized she was trapped. She had thrown herself into it voluntarily, ignoring warnings from all sides. It was entirely her own fault that she was now in danger, caught between two groups of armed men advancing slowly but inexorably toward her. She arrived breathlessly at the intersection, hoping desperately that the other two roads leading from it would be clear.

One of these ended in a blind alley, where they might possibly take refuge. A cart, which had doubtless been overturned deliberately, blocked the other. For want of a better way out, she was making her way toward the blind alley when the house door opened slightly.

"Quick, Mademoiselle Victoire!"

Without hesitation, followed by Jacotte and Godefroy, she plunged into a dark corridor and heard a heavy iron bar being replaced behind her. They were only just in time. The two groups of men must by now have met.

Suddenly she realized that the voice that had called her, and which she had had no choice but to obey, was a familiar one.

"Come."

This time her heart beat faster. "Boris!" she exclaimed.

"Yes. Follow me."

They climbed a spiral staircase to the first floor, where in the light of a few candles she saw a strange scene. In a huge corner room about fifteen men with pistols in their hands were grouped together, standing a bit back from the four windows that gave onto the street.

"I've brought you some reinforcements," said Boris.

Guillaume de Louvencourt turned around, his face pale and drawn. "How could you be so mad as to walk into this mess?"

"Guillaume!"

Her first impulse was to throw herself into his arms and kiss him. But she dared not move an inch in front of all these men, staring at her with a mocking curiosity.

"Are you a good shot?" Guillaume asked Godefroy.

"Indeed I am, Monsieur."

"Well, then, take a pistol and station yourself at this window. Don't shoot until I give the word."

"Who's attacking you?" Victoire inquired.

"Need you ask?" said Guillaume with a bitter smile. "My old enemy, who is, I believe, yours, too: Adrien d'Etivey."

"It can't be true!"

The nightmare was beginning again. For the third time she was facing this ruthless villain. But this time Guillaume was with her and she felt ready to die with him. Better that, she realized, than a life of luxury in a palace with anyone else.

"Don't worry. This time we'll finish the scoundrel off!" Guillaume led her over to the window. "Look!"

In the blind alley some twenty men were clustered around their leader. With a shudder, Victoire recognized the hawklike profile of her former captor, who was giving his final orders for the attack.

"What are you waiting for?" asked Victoire in surprise. "You would at least have the advantage of surprise."

She was worried to see that d'Etivey had more men than Guillaume. "Don't you have a dagger for me?" she asked.

Guillaume laughed. "You'll ruin me with your daggers! I've never met anyone who used them up so quickly! Anyway, I've ordered you a new one from the armorer. Don't worry, you won't need to defend yourself personally today."

Victoire let herself be won over by her lover's confidence. Outside it was now completely dark. As soon as they had seen the armed men, the people in the nearby houses had barricaded themselves in, bolting doors and shutters. From behind Victoire, in a corner of the room, came the voice of Jacotte reciting her prayers.

Guillaume leaned over the banisters and shouted down the staircase, "Are you ready?"

"You can start," replied Boris.

"What's he doing down there?" asked Victoire inquisitively.

"D'Etivey's men will attack the house," explained Guillaume. "I have taken care to make sure some false information reaches them about my men. They believe we are few and badly armed. We shall first of all kill as many of them as possible. Then we shall pretend to have run out of ammunition and let them get into the house. They will rush in blindly and fall through a trapdoor Boris has arranged for them just inside the front door. Naturally I have ordered Adrien d'Etivey to be spared. I need him alive."

"Do you want to know why your mother died?" asked Victoire gently.

"Yes."

"Suppose they set fire to the house?" she said suddenly. "We'll be caught like rats in a trap."

Guillaume smiled. "I've thought of that. This room communicates with the house next door. We should be able to get away."

He went over to the window. Their attackers were taking up their positions, hiding behind any shelter they could find.

"Fire!" shouted Guillaume.

For a quarter of an hour the shots rang out fiercely from both sides. Two of Guillaume's men were wounded. Victoire was glad she had not forgotten the first-aid techniques she had learned at La Rochelle. Unfortunately she only had spirits to clean their wounds.

"What's the position?" asked Guillaume.

"I think seven of them are wounded. But I can't see very well," said one of his men.

"Space your shots," Guillaume ordered.

M. d'Etivey's men were becoming harder to hit. In the beginning they had made an easy target. Two had even tried to climb the front of the house, and others had attempted to force the door. They had been easily shot down.

Thinking that Guillaume's men had run out of ammunition, three men now tried to ram the door with a beam. As the beam hit the door with a dull thud, the noise echoed around Victoire's mind ominously. If the trapdoor did not work, the bandits would be in the room within minutes.

Guillaume's mouth curved into a cruel smile as the door gave way with a horrible creaking noise. The attackers' shouts of triumph soon gave way to cries of pain.

"They've fallen into the cellar," announced Guillaume with satisfaction. "There'll be a few broken bones down there."

Soon the screams died down. All the watchers upstairs could hear were the groans of the wounded. "It's all over," shouted Boris from downstairs.

"What about Adrien d'Etivey?" asked Victoire, eager to savor their revenge.

"We'll go and get him. He'll be in a bad way."

One by one the wounded were brought out of the cellar. As a precaution they were tied up and then laid out in a room on the ground floor. While this was being done, Guillaume and Victoire were left alone upstairs. He looked down at her with all the warmth and tenderness she had dreamed of so often. "I'm so happy you're here!" he said.

"You didn't seem particularly eager to see me again!" she retorted.

Now that the danger was past and she had recovered her spirits, Victoire felt resentful toward Guillaume for his recent behavior.

"You must understand," he said with an apologetic gesture. "I was concentrating on d'Etivey and, above all, I didn't want to draw his attention to you. I wanted to spare you."

"I appreciate that. But, Guillaume, we have shared other dangers."

He didn't answer but instead said, "I've heard Adrien abducted you while you were with a banker from Venice."

"Guy Becavallo was escorting me to London. As I told you at La Chaudrée I had a message for the Queen of England. Because of my connection with you at that time, the poor man was also imprisoned."

Guillaume went on, "I was so afraid that M. d'Etivey might get his hands on you again. I've had time to find out . . ."

He broke off and looked at her. His dark-blue eyes

were suddenly very vulnerable, with a look in them Victoire had never seen.

"What?" asked Victoire.

"That you are important to me. Very important."

She did not intend to give way so easily, and when he tried to take her in his arms she moved back. But he advanced on her again, and she soon found herself with her back to the wall, alongside the door giving onto the house next door.

"Victoire, listen to me."

She turned the handle and retreated into the dark room. She tried to slam the door after her, but Guillaume already had his foot firmly in it.

"Don't be so stupid!"

All Victoire could feel for Guillaume now was hatred. He had not bothered to find out what was happening to her for months. He didn't even know he had a son.

She bumped into a piece of furniture and fell over backward onto a bed. He took advantage of her position to throw his full weight onto her, almost squashing her.

"Now you'll have to listen to me!"

She resisted furiously. And yet Guillaume was holding her tight in his arms and his lips were hot against hers. She had been dreaming of nothing else but this since she had seen him last. She had never once gone to sleep without thinking about him.

"Do you know what I shall give you as your wedding present? Adrien d'Etivey's skin. Come on."

Adrien d'Etivey had lost almost all his former confidence and arrogance. He had broken an arm and a leg in his fall to the stone floor of the cellar, and his face was stained with blood. He was obviously in great pain, though trying hard not to show it. From time to time a groan escaped through his clenched teeth.

"At last I've succeeded in capturing you," said Guillaume. "This time I won't make the mistake of proposing we duel. You deserve to be shot like the vicious creature you are."

"Kill me now," hissed the wounded man in a voice full of hatred. "Then I won't have to look at you for long."

"Don't worry. I'll carry out your wish very soon. But before I do, I want to know the truth about my mother's murder."

Adrien d'Etivey gave the ghost of a mocking smile. "That's a secret I'll take with me into my grave."

"You are going to talk," said Guillaume firmly. "Otherwise . . ."

"Otherwise what? Since I'm going to die, anyway."

"There are many different ways of dying. Some are very unpleasant and slow."

Guillaume unsheathed his dagger and advanced it toward his enemy's face. The dying man yielded. "Mme. de Louvencourt had discovered that my father . . ." He broke off, breathing hard.

"Go on," ordered Guillaume, leaning over so as not to miss a word of his explanation.

"That my father was illegitimate. My grandmother had had him by a groom while her husband, who was sterile, was away. My grandfather didn't want the line to die out, so he closed his eyes to what she had done. But my father finally learned about it. He could not bear that someone else—your mother—should know about it, too. So he waited for her one evening when she was out walking. He strangled her and then threw her body in the pond."

"At last you will be avenged, Mother," murmured Guillaume.

He was just about to plunge his dagger into the heart of the son of his mother's murderer when Victoire cried, "Wait! I want to know what happened to Gilone."

"That whore!" sneered d'Etivey. "I had her hanged

naked from the gibbet at Eglimont." He coughed, blood came spurting from his nose and mouth, and he died in a last convulsion.

Chapter XLIV

*T*he bells of Notre Dame rang eleven.

"Mon Dieu!" exclaimed Victoire, who had completely lost track of time. "Uncle Anselme will be worried to death. I said I'd be back by nightfall."

"I'll walk you home," said Guillaume.

"What will you do with your prisoners . . . and d'Etivey?"

"We shall throw his body into the Seine. He will be borne away by the waters, like my mother. My men will deal with the others."

Escorted by Boris, Godefroy, and Jacotte, they returned to the Hautemart house.

How unbelievably wonderful it was for Victoire, after so many ordeals, to be walking along through the night with Guillaume holding her hand tightly in his. She savored the greatest happiness she had ever known. The only sad thought in her mind was how desperately Guy would grieve to lose her.

"I was told you had died at the siege of La Rochelle," she said. "For months now I have thought you were dead."

"Oh, my darling."

"M. de Surgy described your last moments to me."

"He must have confused me with my brother, Gontran. He died at the siege from a crossbow."

"I'm sorry to hear that," said Victoire politely.

"I can't pretend to you a grief which I don't feel. My brother was not a good man. Before he died he was becoming more and more like d'Etivey." Guillaume shook his head. "Tell me, my beloved, when will you be ready to follow me to Lorraine?"

"To Lorraine!" exclaimed Victoire.

"I must introduce my future wife to my father."

"Will M. de Louvencourt be happy to have a Protestant daughter-in-law? I doubt it."

She could not really believe Guillaume was saying he loved her after so long a time without him, nor that she was really going to marry him after she had almost decided to accept Guy.

"Although he's from Lorraine, my father isn't as fanatic as the Guise family. I'm sure he will welcome you quite sincerely. You still haven't actually told me whether you will marry me, you know."

"You don't deserve it," she replied, laughing. "After all you've made me suffer!"

"I promise you that from now on we shall never part again."

All the lamps were lit in the courtyard when they arrived. A huge crowd of servants was gathered there getting ready to set off to look for Victoire. Léon caught sight of Victoire and her escort first.

"The Comte is in a terrible state! He thought Mademoiselle had been abducted. He had ordered us to go to the Ile de la Cité, where he thought you were."

"I was just a little delayed," said Victoire, who did not want to go into the details of her evening. "I shall tell the Marquis's stewart to give you all wine. You shall drink to my forthcoming marriage with M. de Louvencourt."

They clustered around Victoire to congratulate her.

Attracted by the noise, Anselme appeared in the main doorway. Victoire ran to him and threw herself into his arms.

"I've found Guillaume again, Uncle Anselme! Here he is, look!"

"You've given me such a turn again," grumbled the Comte de Montmaur. "I'm too old for all this emotion."

"It's the last time, I promise you. I'm going to marry Guillaume."

"Really?"

Guillaume came up. "Yes, Monsieur, with your permission."

To hide his emotion at seeing Victoire so happy with the man of her choice, Anselme embraced Guillaume affectionately.

"Come in, my children. You must be dying of hunger!"

"Indeed I am," Guillaume admitted.

The servants hastily began to lay out a substantial meal for the young couple. Victoire left the two men alone for a moment. She wanted to do her hair, wash her face, and—most important of all—fetch Emeric. Not knowing quite how to tell Guillaume about him, she had decided the best thing would be simply to show him the child. Emeric was asleep. She picked him up tenderly without waking him and carried him gently downstairs. When Guillaume saw the child, he leaped to his feet, his face pale.

"Say hello to your son."

"My son!" exclaimed Guillaume, astounded. "But how can that be?"

Victoire smiled. "He will be one year old in November."

"La Chaudrée," murmured Guillaume.

"Exactly. I named him Emeric in memory of my father. I hope you don't mind."

Just then the little boy opened his blue eyes and

met Guillaume's gaze, which was so like his own. He gave a gentle gurgle of pleasure and held out his arms, smiling.

"What a surprise!" said Guillaume, still quite amazed to discover he was a father.

Two days later Victoire was getting ready to leave Paris for Lorraine with her fiancé and Boris. Anselme was to return to Montmaur with Emeric, his nurse, Jacotte, and Godefroy.

"Of course," said Victoire, "we'll marry at Montmaur."

"When?" asked Anselme.

"As soon as possible. Perhaps on Emeric's birthday."

"If he was a year older he could hold your train," joked Anselme.

"Come, anyone would think you weren't pleased I'm marrying Guillaume."

"I'm pleased, of course, but the thought of poor Guy's disappointment breaks my heart."

"If you think *my* heart felt light when I told him I couldn't marry him, you're wrong," sighed Victoire. "But what can I do? I can't marry them both. I've sent him back his ring now that I'm wearing the one Guillaume has given me."

She held out her hand so that her uncle could admire the ring.

"What's this curious coat of arms?"

"A caprine. It's a fantastic animal. It seems the fortunes of the Louvencourt family are linked to it."

"Guillaume hasn't much money, has he?"

"No."

"You don't regret anything, I hope?"

"Oh, no," said Victoire. "And then, who knows, perhaps we'll find the hidden treasure of the Louvencourts."

"I shouldn't count on it."

"You know *I* prefer to count on my sheep and ducks."

Anselme smiled, then his face grew serious as he said, "I'm afraid you have been carried away by your happiness, and have neglected to consider the problem of your different religious beliefs. Are you going to convert?"

"Certainly not," Victoire declared. "In any case, Guillaume wouldn't think of asking me to."

"What about him?"

"He'll remain a Catholic. We shall follow the example of the King and Queen of Navarre."

"What about Emeric?"

"He will do as he wishes," said Victoire thoughtfully. "He'll be instructed in both faiths and he can choose when he is of age to do so."

"If everyone were as liberal-minded as you, we shouldn't have so many problems in France," said Anselme.

"You know," she said to Guillaume as they were traveling, "I never asked you if you were pleased to have a son."

"How could I not be when he's so like you?"

"He has your eyes."

"But he has your beauty, your gentleness, and your grace."

"I didn't realize you saw so many good qualities in me," remarked Victoire, smiling.

They had just passed through Toul, the last stop in their journey to Louvencourt.

"I shall find a lot more, too," he said, looking at her with a mixture of tenderness and desire. "I'll tell you what they are tonight."

At nightfall they reached Louvencourt. The château was about the same size as Montmaur but far more austere in style, in keeping with the rather stark Lorraine countryside.

"My father *will* be surprised," said Guillaume as they dismounted in the courtyard, which was uncared for, as the one at Montmaur had been in the past.

"Do you mean to say you haven't told him?" exclaimed Victoire.

"No."

"Aren't you afraid of his reaction?"

"We'll see soon enough," said Guillaume casually.

M. de Louvencourt was reading by a huge log fire when he was told his son had arrived with a young woman.

"Monsieur, I have the honor to ask you for your blessing."

"What for, my son?"

François de Louvencourt's gaze flickered from one to the other of them in surprise.

"If you agree, I intend to marry Mademoiselle de Montmaur."

"Well, I think all I have to do is to congratulate you, and to embrace you if you will allow me, my future daughter-in-law."

"I hope you aren't too angry," Victoire whispered in his ear.

"It's a long time since I've seen Guillaume looking so happy," said the old man.

In the huge bed where she lay waiting for her lover, Victoire relaxed pleasurably after the long and tiring journey. Being so used to difficulties, she was amazed at her future father-in-law's welcome. He couldn't have been kinder to her if he had chosen a wife for his son himself, she reflected.

Victoire had left the two men alone together so that Guillaume could tell his father about Adrien d'Etivey's death. Afterward he had explained to Victoire that for many years now his father's hold on the world of the living had been a tenuous one: all he could think of were his memories.

She was just dozing off, sleepily examining the frieze of caprines that decorated the mantelpiece, when Guillaume finally arrived. In a few seconds he had undressed and slipped naked into the bed alongside her.

"I told him there were already three of us in the family," he said, laughing.

"He can't have been very pleased."

"On the contrary," said Guillaume pensively. "Since my brother died, and I didn't seem in any hurry to get married, he has been afraid our line would die out."

"That's what has happened in my family. I am the last of the Montmaurs."

"When Emeric has a brother, we'll ask the King for permission to call your title out of abeyance."

"Anselme would be so pleased!"

"I do like your uncle," said Guillaume.

"I noticed that already. You must admit that that is part of the reason why you are marrying me!"

Their two eager bodies sought and rediscovered each other until the dawn came and found them exhausted. To Victoire's pleasure was added the secure knowledge that she was now loved in return. Guillaume's body and his tender, passionate caresses brought her a happiness that no other embrace had made her forget.

As she dropped off to sleep at dawn, when the birds were already singing, she had a strange dream, every detail of which remained engraved on her memory. Much later the dream came true.

She saw herself later—though she did not know how long afterward—returning to Louvencourt with Guillaume. Emeric was running along in front of them, and she was holding a younger child by the hand, though she wasn't sure whether it was a boy or a girl.

They had returned to Lorraine to be present at the lonely old man's deathbed. He was quite indifferent to the approach of death, being almost eager to rejoin at last the woman he had missed for so long.

Though his breath now came only in gasps, Monsieur de Louvencourt made a supreme effort and murmured in a scarcely audible voice, "Protected by fire, the caprine's treasure must be snatched from the unfaithful . . ."

"I don't understand," said Guillaume. "Father . . ."

But François de Louvencourt had slipped away and his son sadly closed his eyes.

Then Victoire saw herself in a strange room in the château, in front of a fireplace where no fire was burning. A frieze of caprines decorated the pediment. This fireplace was much the same as all the others in the house, which had been built at the time of the Crusades.

Suddenly Emeric, who was playing in the fireplace, bumped into one of the heavy bronze firedogs. It fell over, revealing a lighter place beneath it. Inquisitively Victoire came over with a candle. By its light she saw a crescent moon marked on the brick. She found another crescent underneath the other firedog.

A caprine was roughly engraved in the middle. When she stepped on the caprine's head to put the firedogs back in their place, Victoire saw the two bricks had swung back to reveal . . .

She woke up, murmuring, "The treasure . . ."

"*You* are the treasure, my love," said Guillaume, kissing her and drawing her closer. Never again would they be apart.